NEMESIS

NEMESIS

NEMESIS

PATRICIA WOLF

echo
PUBLISHING

echo PUBLISHING

Echo Publishing
An imprint of Bonnier Books UK
6/69 Carlton Crescent
Summer Hill NSW 2130
www.echopublishing.com.au

Bonnier Books UK
HYLO, 5th Floor,
103–105 Bunhill Row
London EC1Y 8LZ
www.bonnierbooks.co.uk

Copyright © Patricia Wolf 2025

All rights reserved. Echo thanks you for buying an authorised edition of this book. In doing so, you are supporting writers and enabling Echo to publish more books and foster new talent. Thank you for complying with copyright laws by not reproducing or transmitting any part of this book by any means, electronic or mechanical – including storing in a retrieval system, photocopying, recording, scanning or distributing – without our prior written permission.

Echo Publishing acknowledges the traditional custodians of Country throughout Australia. We recognise their continuing connection to land, sea and waters. We pay our respects to Elders past and present.

This is a work of fiction. Names, characters, businesses, places, events, locales and incidents are either the products of the author's imagination or used in a fictitious manner. Any resemblance to actual persons, living or dead, or actual events is purely coincidental.

First published in Great Britain in 2025 by Embla Books, an imprint of Bonnier Books UK

First published in Australia in 2025 by Echo Publishing, an imprint of Bonnier Books UK

Printed and bound in Australia by Opus Group

MIX
Paper | Supporting responsible forestry
FSC® C001695

Page design and typesetting: transformer.com.au
Cover design: Blacksheep
Cover images: © Depositphotos/Shutterstock

NATIONAL LIBRARY OF AUSTRALIA

A catalogue entry for this book is available from the National Library of Australia

ISBN: 9781786585745 (paperback)
ISBN: 9781471417917 (ebook)

echo_publishing

echopublishingaustralia

echopublishing

Also by Patricia Wolf

Outback

Paradise

Opal

About the Author

Patricia Wolf grew up in outback Australia, in the mining town of Mount Isa in far northwest Queensland, and now lives in Berlin. She likes whisky and strong coffee, busy cities, surf beaches and wild places. A journalist for almost twenty years, Patricia is a regular contributor to newspapers including the *Guardian*, the *Financial Times* and the *Daily Telegraph*. She was formerly a design columnist at the *Independent*, and the Lisbon correspondent for *Monocle* magazine.

IG: @patricia_wolf_crime

Prologue

Mildersee
Saturday, 7 p.m.

The little rowboat is rocking and swaying. The sun is warm on his face, the breeze coming off the water delivering only a fleeting breath of coolness to the humid heat of this late-summer evening. Mattias is half lying, half sitting where he's fallen on the deck, too weak to pull himself up, let alone row. The slight movement of the boat is adding to his nausea and confusion. He doesn't know what he's done with the oars – he's not even sure why he's in the boat. He can't remember where he was planning to go, what brought him here to the water.

His lips are dry and his heart is beating way too fast. A bitter taste fills his mouth. He lies down, hoping to ease the queasy feeling in his stomach, hoping to calm his heart, his mind. Tries to clear his head, to get a grip. Looks up. Time seems to be moving at an irregular speed: the world first spinning out of control then slowing so much that he can see every mote of dust, every leaf on the trees around the jetty quivering in the breeze. The sky, the vast blue depths of it, near enough to touch. He reaches up ... The boat pitches heavily and he swims back to reality. He's going to be sick. He hears a long low moan somewhere outside himself. Lies back down. Watches clouds gathering above him. They seem to mass slowly, forming to a horrifying size, turning from white to grey to a bilious green. A huge yawning gaping mouth of cloud reaching down towards him, coming for him. The moaning sound is louder now and he's taking fast shallow breaths. Can't get enough air, his heart hammering, hammering, hammering. He manages to pull himself up to sitting and the clouds recede, benign and pale again in the distance. His mouth is dry, so dry. He craves a drink, a bottle of ice-cold water, so badly he almost cries with desperation. He tries to slow his breathing, slow his heart, gather his thoughts. He remembers a text message, feels even more ill. It was a dick pic, someone else's dick, engorged and erect, on Nina's phone. They had a huge fight; she admitted to having an affair. Wouldn't tell him who with. But that doesn't make sense. They're about to get married. He hasn't asked her yet but that's the plan. He has his grandmother's ring, a band of sapphires and diamonds, in his pocket. He puts his hand down to feel for it, but the pocket is empty.

He's dreaming. He must be dreaming. Everything about this is like a nightmare. Nothing makes sense – he needs to wake up. He tries to remember what brought him here, but only strange, disjointed elements float back. Renate comforting him. Karin and Fran. He'd been sitting in their garden, drinking rosé with them. Upset. Raging and angry one minute, almost in tears the next. Then walking through the Mildersee colony. The thought is momentarily soothing. His favourite place, his little cabin by the lake, his retreat. Then walking past Leon Kaiser's cabin, thinking that Nina has always liked Leon; thinking that maybe Leon is the man she's having an affair with.

This dream is ridiculous. When he wakes up he'll tell Nina all about it, and they'll laugh together at his overwrought imagination.

Another picture forms in his mind: Willie Koch skulking around outside the cabin, stalking Nina. Frightening her. Willie's mouth grimacing into a devilish laugh, taunting Mattias for being the last to know about Nina sleeping around. He tries to wake himself up, shaking his head, anything to get himself away from this madness. Nina needs him. Nina loves him.

'Nina,' he tries to call, but his voice is nothing more than a croak, a groan. He's so thirsty right now he'd drink anything, even Nina's super-healthy breakfast juice, or that revolting green tea she made earlier. Minty, woody, tasting of pine needles. He hadn't liked it at all, but he'd drink another thermos of it now if he could. There's plenty of water in the lake, he only has to lean over the edge of the boat and scoop it up, but just the thought of it, murky and muddy, makes him gag. His stomach is cramping, nausea rising. He's going to be sick. He hears moaning again, a low terrible sound. The clouds are back, heavier again, hanging low, waiting for weakness, waiting to pounce.

He tries to catch his breath, clear his mind, wake himself. Hears footsteps thumping across the jetty, walking towards the boat. Fear crawls into his chest and throat. A dark shadow falls across him. He looks up, tries to focus on the shape looming over him.

'I don't feel good,' he says. 'Help me. Please. Help me . . .'

There's no help, only laughter. Mocking peals that echo across the water and reverberate around him. Something clatters at his feet. A moment later the deck tips wildly and the trees disappear as the boat floats away from the jetty and out into the lake. He can't see anything, only the endless sky above, tilting and shuddering as he drifts across the water. The movement makes everything worse. The clouds above, heavy, dark, rush down, and his nausea overtakes him; a retching heave spills out of his mouth, out of his nostrils. He loses control of his bowels, feels the warmth under his legs as they empty. He tries to call for help, but with the retching and cramping he can't breathe, can't make a sound, as the world goes dark around him.

Chapter 1

Canberra
Two days earlier: Thursday, 2 p.m.

DS Lucas Walker is forcing himself to sit still, to keep his frustration in check. He's in the small reception area outside his boss DCI Dan Rutherford's office waiting for a meeting that should have started ten – make that twelve – minutes ago. He watches the second hand of the clock on the wall tick slowly round, his knee bouncing, his fingers drumming on the arm of the chair, the sound earning him a quizzical glance from Rutherford's secretary. He gives her a half-smile in apology and stands, taking a few steps down the corridor, stretching his legs, rehearsing once again the words that he hopes might change Rutherford's mind about letting him transfer to the counterterrorism and special investigations unit.

It was supposed to be a sure thing. With Walker's identity compromised in the organised crime world, he's no longer able to take on undercover operations for the unit. He's been sitting it out on desk duty for over a year now, recovering from injuries, healing his mental trauma and, most importantly from Rutherford's point of view, using his considerable analytical skills and the intel he'd gathered on the ground to identify, track down and support the arrests of the Vandals motorbike gang leadership. The one man who continues to elude them is the club's former head honcho, Stefan Markovich, and Rutherford has been insisting that until Markovich is caught he needs Walker on his team.

Markovich had fled Australia, first to Ecuador, then Dubai and finally the Netherlands. Walker and the rest of the team had been working with Dutch federal police to bring him in, but it had been difficult to get the local team to prioritise the operation. Not surprising, given the situation there – a narco industry growing fast and running wild, assassinations of journalists and witnesses, and years-long court cases being compromised. They'd finally been getting close to putting together a joint op to pick him up when Markovich, with his innate instinct for trouble, disappeared again. Walker spent weeks following noise and rumours from local Vandals and from the club's international associates and is almost certain now that Markovich is in Berlin. The Berlin state force have indicated they'd be open to international cooperation if Markovich can be identified and found, and now Walker's been offered a chance to get over there himself and work with the Germans on pulling him in. And if he can get Markovich in custody, he'll be able to transfer to a new unit and get back to proper on-the-ground policing.

He's back on the uncomfortable chair, knee jiggling again, when, at 2.15 p.m., Rutherford's door opens and a bloke strides out. He's wearing jeans and a t-shirt, has long hair, a scraggly beard, and his arms are covered in tattoos. He looks more like a bikie than a cop. An undercover agent, thinks Walker, envy rising in his gut. This bloke is out on the streets, doing the kind of work Walker loves and knows he's good at, not stuck behind a desk. The bloke ignores Walker, gives a nod to the secretary and heads towards the bank of lifts at the far end of the corridor. The lift arrives with a ping and the bikie cop disappears, back to the streets, back to the freedom to do some real detective work, leaving Walker feeling more bereft and frustrated than ever.

'He's ready for you now, DS,' says Rutherford's secretary, and Walker stands, exhales and primes himself to fight for his future.

Rutherford is standing at the window, looking out across the treetops in the park over the road. He turns when Walker comes in. 'I only have a few minutes,' he says. 'I've got a meeting upstairs at two thirty. Can this wait until the team meeting next week?'

'No, sir,' says Walker firmly.

'Make it quick, then,' says Rutherford, still standing and not inviting Walker to sit either.

Walker gets straight to the point. 'The Germans are open to working with us to pull Markovich in, but it won't happen without one of us on the ground over there. It's the Dutch situation all over again. The Germans are caught up in their own priorities, they haven't been able to locate Markovich, and if we don't act fast we'll lose him again. The op we proposed for the Netherlands, where I go out there as the bait to lure Markovich out of whatever hole he's hiding in, is our only option.'

'I told you I don't have the budget for an international operation right now—'

'I might have a solution to that,' Walker interrupts, earning a hard look from Rutherford. 'There's a conference for cops involved in domestic extremism happening in The Hague later this month. Information exchange, best practice, building contacts, that kind of thing. Assistant Commissioner Hanson has asked me if I'd like to attend. He wants to send someone, and he thought it would be a good introduction for me, in advance of my joining his unit . . .'

Rutherford is scowling now. 'I told you that transfer can't happen either. Not now. This Vandals op is using more resources than I have.

I can't let you transfer to Hanson's unit, not this year.'

Walker presses on. 'The cost of travel to Berlin will come out of Hanson's budget and I have contacts in the city. I can spend a week or two over there, keep expenses low, liaise with the Germans, get Markovich pulled in. We have good intel on where he's based and who he's working with, and I can fine-tune the details when I'm in place. There'll be no budgetary cost to you. Afterwards I'll go to the conference for Hanson and then join his team when I get back.'

Rutherford is silent for a long moment. Walker knows how much all of them, Rutherford included, want Markovich in custody. And he also knows that Rutherford understands that, without some pressure, without AFP resources on the ground, picking Markovich up might never happen. Every police force has its own priorities, its own concerns. Markovich is a big player here but in Germany he's relatively small fry.

'Say you go and do this – then what? Does Hanson want you joining his unit immediately after you get back?'

Walker nods. 'More or less, yeah. The following month. You might talk him up to two months but no longer.'

'And this is what you want, is it? After all these years chasing down the big boys, the serious criminals, you've had enough, you want out?'

Walker breathes deep. This is it. Hanson has told him he won't fight Rutherford, won't pull rank. Unless he gets permission to leave organised crime, the new job he wants will go to someone else.

'Sir, I know how important the organised crime unit is – it's been my life for the past ten years. But sitting around in the office, chasing paper trails, is not my thing. I need to be back out there, on the street, and I can't do that in organised crime anymore.'

Rutherford runs his hand across his short hair, then glances at his watch, a big fat silver thing that hangs heavy on his wrist. 'I've got to go to this meeting,' he says.

Walker doesn't move. He needs an answer today. If he doesn't get the OK, he's decided he's leaving the AFP. He's going to apply to Queensland Police, get a detective job near home somewhere. He's not cut out for this office shit and he's been doing it for too long now. He's had enough.

Some of this feeling must transmit itself to Rutherford because he looks at Walker for a long time. 'You're one of my best cops,' he says eventually. 'I need you on the team. You're clever and you're committed and you're bloody good at what you do.'

'Thank you, sir,' says Walker, touched despite himself. Rutherford doesn't believe in compliments, abides more by the school of stick than carrot, so this is a real endorsement. But it doesn't change how he feels. 'It's been a privilege working with you, being part of the team, and I want to get Markovich into custody as much as anyone. I want to wrap this up. But I can't sit behind a desk any longer.' He realises he's edging close to resigning, that it might be happening right now, and his stomach lurches. He loves his job. He doesn't want to quit.

Rutherford looks at him long and hard. Walker meets his eye.

'Righto, then,' says Rutherford, his voice chilly. 'Go there, find Markovich and bring him in. Do that, and I'll let you go. But not one penny for this trip or this op comes out of my budget. Fucking Hanson can pay for the lot.'

• • •

Walker had thought he'd be punching the air with joy but now, back at his desk, his feelings are more mixed. He's confirmed to Hanson that Rutherford has agreed to his attending the conference, without mentioning his secondary mission. Rutherford likes to play his cards close to his chest and Walker's learnt not to share information unnecessarily. He reckons Hanson doesn't need to know how he's spending his last few weeks on Rutherford's team. He's received a brief message from Hanson himself – Welcome to the team, Stella will be in touch with the relevant info – followed by a much longer email from Stella, Hanson's secretary, with the conference agenda, a vast pile of background reading on the team's work, and the paperwork for his transfer.

Seeing it in black and white, the transfer date less than two months away, makes it properly real. He sits there looking at the team he's worked with for almost a decade: Sophie Bragg, Phil Lowe, the rest of them, heads down, immersed in their work, tireless in their search for Markovich and the other cases they're working on. Rather than euphoria, what he feels most is that he's committing an act of betrayal. He's leaving them short. He's abandoning them. There's only one way he'll ease his conscience and that's by pulling Markovich in, ensuring the big bikie faces justice at last.

Chapter 2

Kummerfeld, east of Berlin
Sunday, 9.30 a.m.

'Police have yet to make any arrests in connection with Wednesday's drive-by shooting in Berlin's Kreuzberg district. Two people were killed and four people seriously injured, including eight-year-old Mila Petrenko, who remains in a critical condition in hospital. The justice minister has said that she will allocate additional resources and that police—'

The report comes to a sudden stop as Maria Guerra switches off the kitchen radio with a loud 'Tsk!' 'Terrible! Just terrible,' she says. 'What is our country coming to? Drive-by shootings in Berlin? I can't listen to it.'

Barbara Guerra, who has her hands in a mountain of bubbles, riding high up the bright-pink rubber gloves that her mother insists she wears when washing up, decides against admitting that she fought hard to be part of the investigation into the shooting but was sidelined in favour of two of her male colleagues. The decision still stings, but she knows that her family don't fully understand her desire for policing in general and these kind of cases in particular, so she stays quiet. Her mother comes back to stand beside her, wielding a tea towel and gently drying the glassware and crockery that she deems too good for the dishwasher.

They work in companionable silence, the kitchen peaceful without the sound of the radio. 'It's been a good birthday for Rita, hasn't it?' says Maria. Something in the tone of her voice makes Barbara turn to look at her mother. Her eyes are glistening with tears.

'Of course, Mamá,' says Barbara, leaning over and giving her a kiss on the cheek. 'It's been perfect. She even drank a glass of champagne this morning.'

This weekend is her younger sister Rita's twenty-fifth birthday. The celebration has been low-key – the four of them for a family dinner last night, with all the Chilean dishes her mother makes for special days, and a celebratory birthday breakfast this morning – and exactly what Rita asked for.

Her mother lets out a long sigh. 'I'd hoped she'd want something more, maybe invite her friends around like she used to do. A family celebration made sense last year – even the doctors said she needed time to deal with everything she went through. But it's been almost two years now and she's still refusing to see anyone . . .'

'She'll get there, Mamá,' says Barbara, keeping her voice upbeat, though she has her own doubts and fears about Rita's recovery.

'Remember her twenty-first?' says Maria. 'Dios mío, what a chaos! They all came over here to get ready for the night out. There were clothes and make-up all over the house, the music was so loud, all of them laughing and singing . . .'

'I remember they ate about a ton of empanadas and we had to clean up all those empty wine glasses and were finding half-finished cans of beer for days afterwards,' says Barbara, laughing.

Rita always used to be full of life. Cheeky, flirtatious and fun, she was a centrifugal force that drew in a huge circle of friends. But since her abduction, the terror she survived in Australia, she's been holed up at their parents' home. A slight figure, shrouded in oversize tracksuits and pyjamas, she sleeps until the afternoon, then locks herself away in her bedroom watching movies or playing *The Legend of Zelda* until late into the night.

'Maybe next year she'll invite them all again,' says Maria.

'Absolutely,' agrees Barbara. 'I think Lola is already helping. She's spending less time in her room. She was in the garden with Papá yesterday, playing with Lola for hours.'

If Rita's birthday this year has been a success, at least by the Guerras' new definition of what constitutes success, most of that is down to Lola, a little Cavapoo puppy, a caramel ball of fluff that resembles a teddy bear on four legs, who has won the hearts of the whole family in the two days since Barbara brought her home as a surprise gift. The first night, her parents set up a dog bed for Lola in the laundry room, but Rita was indignant. 'We can't leave a little puppy alone in the dark all night!' she said. 'She'll be really scared on her own.'

Rita took the puppy to sleep with her and the two are fast becoming inseparable. The idea of getting a dog had come from Lucas Walker on one of their long, meandering telephone calls about work, life and almost everything else. Six months ago, when she'd been speaking to him about Rita, he'd said, 'Why don't you get her a dog?'

'A dog? Why would I do that?'

'Dogs are amazing, mate,' he'd said in his Aussie drawl, and even over the phone she could tell he was smiling. 'They give you unconditional love, they're there for you the whole time, never a cross look, just happy as hell to see you. And you need to take care of them. Take them for a walk, feed them, you know: get responsible. If Rita's sleeping the whole day or playing video games or whatever, a dog'll take her out of herself.'

She owes Lucas a thank-you for the suggestion. And she'll be able to thank him in person, since he's arriving in Berlin in just a couple of days for some kind of joint operation with German police. Her stomach gives a little flip at the thought. After all this time, she's really looking forward to seeing him again.

Her phone vibrates on the kitchen table, breaking into her thoughts. She glances over but can't see the caller ID. Probably Seb, wanting to arrange a drink for tonight. She hasn't seen him this weekend, Rita's birthday taking all her attention. Her hands are still in the pink gloves, so she leaves it and as it keeps ringing she tuts in frustration. Hang up already, she thinks, I'll call you back. As if the caller hears her mental admonishment, the phone stops, then, a second later, starts up again.

She steps away from the sink and walks over to the table, holding her hands in the air to stop the suds dripping on the floor. The caller ID reads Detective Senior Superintendent Uli Fischer. A work call, especially on this particular Sunday – when she's booked the weekend off because of Rita's birthday – means it must be urgent. She peels off one of the gloves and picks up. 'Good morning, sir.'

'Hello, Barbara. Are you still at your parents' place?'

'I am,' she says. 'But I can be back in Berlin within the hour if you need me.'

'No, no. You're not far from Mildersee, are you?'

'Mildersee? Yes, it's only a ten-minute drive,' she says, curious about where this is leading. Mildersee is one of more than three thousand lakes that surround Berlin. A teardrop-shaped body of water surrounded by forest, with plenty of little bays and small beaches for swimming. They had picnics there as a family when she and Rita were younger.

'OK, good,' says Fischer. 'I need you to go to the Mildersee colony. A body's been found there, and it's a suspicious death. With Vogel and the others working this drive-by, I'm short of manpower, so I'll need you to handle it. The local uniforms have secured the scene and called in the SOCOs. Check it out then report back to me and we can decide how we move it forward.'

'Yes, sir,' says Barbara, stung at the implication that she's his third choice for the investigation, that the only reason Fischer has asked her to head this up is because the men in the team are busy. He's been sidelining her recently. The drive-by her colleagues are working on is a massive multi-agency case. It seems likely the target was a senior member of a Balkan crime family who had been meeting associates in Kreuzberg. He survived, but one of his bodyguards and a man believed to be his second-in-command were killed. Two other men, also believed to be part of the clan, were seriously injured, and an eight-year-old girl, Mila Petrenko, was caught in the crossfire and is fighting for her life in hospital. The brazenness of the attack, the violence of it, has shocked the nation, and a major multi-force investigation has been launched. But, despite her record being one of the best in the department, Fischer didn't select her to be part of the operation.

As the only woman working for Fischer, she's beginning to feel that she's often given the raw end of the deal. At one level she understands it, particularly since she came back from Australia with some psychological struggles of her own. She's still not sleeping well, still has nightmares and some physical symptoms too: her sense of vulnerability to violence is much keener, and she occasionally finds herself almost stricken into inaction by residual fear. She's tried to hide it, push her way through, but perhaps some of it has leaked into her work and that's why Fischer has been allocating her the less important cases. As she takes in the details of the Mildersee assignment, she feels her nerves rising. A suspicious death, a possible murder, is an important case. This is her chance to prove to Fischer, and to herself, that she still has what it takes to do the job and do it well. She can't fail. She needs a result, now more than ever.

Chapter 3

Mildersee

10.30 a.m.

Less than half an hour later, Barbara is in her car, jolting along the lane that leads to the small colony of holiday cabins at Mildersee. The track to the colony winds first between fields of wheat, golden stalks moving in the breeze, then makes a left turn into the forest, the light dappled, the air a little fresher. She can see the deep blue of the lake through the trees as the first cabins appear, then the distinctive yellow of police incident tape ahead. She parks her car on the verge, breathes in and calms her nerves. 'I'm in charge here,' she says to herself. 'Make sure to project a good first impression.'

She walks up, ducks under the tape, ID in hand. Two uniform cops are standing chatting a few steps away, and the older, bigger one is immediately in her face. 'This is a crime scene—'

She holds up her badge. 'Detective Barbara Guerra. I've been asked to take the lead on this investigation.'

He looks her up and down. She's a few years younger than he is and she can feel his disdain. 'I can see they sent us their best man for the job,' he says, and his young colleague stifles a laugh.

She ignores him, pulls out her notebook. 'Your name?' she asks.

'Senior Officer Klein.'

'Tell me what's happened,' she says.

'One of the residents saw a friend's boat drifting on the lake early this morning and decided to swim out and row it back. When she pulled herself up into the boat, she found him in it . . . Well, his body, that is.'

Klein turns and points to two women standing on the other side of the track. In their fifties, one is wearing a bathing suit and shorts, while the other, in three-quarter trousers and a t-shirt, is comforting her, holding her close.

'The skinny one with the short hair,' says Klein. 'She's the one who found him. She called us, and we towed the boat and the body back.'

Barbara nods. 'Are the forensics team here yet?'

'They're on their way,' he says. 'Officer Schmidt, another one of our guys, is down by the boat waiting for them.' He gestures in the direction of a small sandy path, lined both sides by cabins and gardens and ending in a strand of trees, the lake directly behind.

'Thank you,' she says. 'I'll take it from here.'

She goes over and notes down the details of the witness, she'll talk with her shortly, but first she needs to check out the scene. Following the sandy path towards the water, she comes to more incident tape, blocking access to the walking track that runs beside the lake. Another uniform cop is standing on the other side of the tape. He turns at the sound of her approach, and she's momentarily taken aback by how good-looking he is. In his late twenties, tanned, with long blond hair tied up regulation-style, blue eyes, a square jaw and broad chest, he could pass for a male model.

'Detective Barbara Guerra,' she says. 'I'm heading up the investigation.'

'Officer Max Schmidt,' he says, extending his hand and smiling at her. He's not her type – she's not into the blond Teutonic god thing – but she finds herself grinning back until she catches herself, straightens her face.

'Talk me through what you know, please,' she says, using her most official tone.

'The body is in the boat,' says Schmidt, indicating a grey rowboat with a navy stripe that has been pulled alongside a jetty. 'We towed it in here because it was the most obvious spot, but a witness told us that it's usually moored three jetties down.' He points to their right. 'The deceased hasn't been formally identified but the woman who found the boat knows him. She says his name is Mattias Ritter and that he has a cabin here, the one on the corner. I've taped that off so the SOC team can check it too.'

Barbara nods. 'Let's start by looking at the body,' she says.

'You'll want to be quick,' says Schmidt. 'It's pretty confronting...'

Barbara nods. Schmidt is young and in a rural posting so he probably hasn't seen too many bodies. She hasn't seen so many that she's inured to them, but she is no longer shocked by violent death either and she doesn't plan on rushing. First impressions are important to her; she's often noticed things that have turned out to be useful later.

'You can wait here,' she says, and Schmidt is visibly relieved.

She walks onto the jetty and looks into the boat. Mattias Ritter is lying in the bottom, his head and shoulders propped against the plank that serves as a seat, his legs stretched out in front of him. His eyes are staring unseeing towards the sky, his mouth open in a terrible grimace. His face and lips are a dark bluish-purple and his chest is covered in pink-coloured vomit. There's more foul-smelling vomit and excrement across the deck. A haze of flies and other insects have been drawn to the body, their buzzing filling her ears. She understands why Schmidt found the scene challenging: just the smell alone is overpowering.

She pulls her phone out and takes a few photographs. The deceased man is wearing grey shorts and a lilac-coloured vest, his feet bare. The outfit is noteworthy because the morning is warm but not yet hot and the breeze from the lake is distinctly cool. Barbara is wearing trousers and a light cardigan. His clothes, together with the volume of insects and flies, could mean he's been out here all night. As she walks to the back of the boat, she notices that one oar is missing. She looks around for it, but it's not in the bottom of the boat, not lying on the jetty, and makes a note to ask Schmidt if it has been removed for some reason. If not, how was it lost? She looks hard at all the details, trying to ignore the stench. At the very front of the little boat she spots two bottles of beer lying on the deck at Ritter's feet. The bottles give her pause and she stands for a moment, thinking, until the smell of vomit and excrement comes close to making her gag. As she walks up the jetty towards Schmidt, she fishes a bottle of water out of her bag and takes a long gulp.

'Did you find anything?' he asks.

'The blue lips, the vomit and excrement – looks like he ingested something poisonous,' she says when she's cleared her mouth of the worst of the taste. 'I'll need a toxicology report to find out what he might have consumed and when. Did one of your team remove an oar from the boat when it was towed in?'

'No. We didn't move or take anything.'

'There's only one oar there,' she says. 'I wonder where the other one is and how it got loose. Did you notice the bottles of beer at the front of the boat?'

'Ah, no.' He looks a bit embarrassed. 'I didn't really look. They told me to keep people away and not touch anything.'

'Hmm. Well, as far as I can see there are no signs of physical violence to the body, but I don't think he was alone when he died, given the missing oar and the fact that there are two beer bottles by his feet.'

Schmidt has his notebook out, writing everything down. He's green but at least he seems keen to learn, thinks Barbara.

'You said he had a cabin nearby?' she asks.

Schmidt nods and leads Barbara a short distance back down the path. They're about to turn into one of the gardens when the SOC team, two female technicians, arrive. The older of the two is in her mid-fifties, with no-nonsense close-cropped grey hair and beefy arms. 'Marilyn Mather, senior forensic technician,' she says. She offers her hand and Barbara shakes it – Mather has a small hand but a very firm grip – as she points her towards the scene. 'I'll be back over when I've had a look at the deceased's cabin,' she says.

Schmidt pulls aside the incident tape that's been strung across Mattias Ritter's gate and they walk up a concrete path that meanders through a small garden to the cabin. It's Barbara's first time in one of the Mildersee cabins. She'd expected something rustic and simple but this one, although small, is stylishly decorated. The door opens directly into an open-plan L-shaped living-and-kitchen space, with a cane lounger heaped with white linen cushions along the wall beside the door and a daybed covered with a dark-green throw beneath the window on the left. The kitchen, in the shorter corner of the L, consists of two pale-green storage units, a gas stove and a table. There's another small room to the right of the front door, fully taken up by a double bed, which is made and hasn't been slept in.

'Have a look around the bedroom,' she says to Schmidt. 'Don't touch anything but shout if you see something that looks out of place.' She walks slowly around the living area, which is neat and tidy. There's no sign of any vomit or a struggle or anything otherwise untoward, so perhaps Ritter consumed whatever it was that killed him out on the boat. In the kitchen, there's a fruit bowl with two apples, half a baguette in a paper bag and a green cup with a red apple on it, which has dregs in it of something that might be tea. She sniffs it: peppermint, maybe. She makes a note to ensure the SOC team take it for analysis.

Schmidt emerges from the bedroom. 'There are no medicines, nothing obvious that could be poison,' he says. 'There's a small backpack open on the floor. Looks like it has a change of clothes and a mobile phone inside.'

'Bag it, and bag the phone separately,' says Barbara. 'We'll need to do a forensic analysis of the calls and messages.'

They go outside. There's a shed to the right of the garden and she sends Schmidt to check it while she walks slowly around the cabin. At the back, she finds a small outhouse with a drop toilet – nothing inside except toilet paper and a half-filled watering can. Outside, there's a rubbish bin and a separate one for compost, and an old-fashioned pump beneath a large oak tree. A bunch of flowers, hand-tied with a bright-red ribbon decorated with white hearts, has been stuffed into the top of the compost bin. It's a strange-looking bouquet, the flowers more like weeds than the kind of posy you'd gift. She's not sure what she'll learn from it, but she'll ask the SOCOs to bag that too.

The water pump is emerald green, and a bright-yellow washing-up bowl and a dish rack stacked with two plates, two coffee cups and a handful of cutlery stand beside it.

'The colony doesn't have mains water or electricity,' says Schmidt, coming up beside her. 'They can use the pump water for washing or for the garden but it's not drinkable.'

'The ground around the pump is dry, and the dishes too, so it hasn't been used this morning at least,' says Barbara. 'I think the death probably occurred sometime last night. And we could very well be looking at a murder. This bunch of flowers looks like a gift that's been tossed. And with the two beers in the boat, the two plates and two coffee cups on the rack, it seems as if Ritter had company at some point yesterday. Maybe, somewhere along the way, it all went horribly wrong between them.' They stand for a moment. 'Did you check the shed for chemicals or poisons?' she asks.

'Yes – nothing there aside from a crate of beer,' says Schmidt.

'What was the brand of beer on the boat?'

'Augustiner,' she says.

'The ones in the shed are Wulle. And there was no sign of the missing oar.'

Barbara's estimation of Schmidt is rising. He's answered her questions before she's asked them.

They walk back to the little rowboat. The technicians have pulled it onto shore at the end of the jetty and are working the scene in their white suits.

'Anything you can you tell me?' Barbara asks Marilyn Mather. 'Was he poisoned?'

Mather shrugs. 'It's a possibility, but I don't want to speculate. The cyanosis, the blue colour of the lips, is caused by a lack of oxygen, but you're right, it's also a symptom of specific toxins. You'll need a specialist to determine that. He's also ejected a foamy pink substance that looks like phlegm with blood in it, which probably means he has blood in his lungs. But you'll need the autopsy to confirm.'

Barbara nods. 'Do you have an indication of time of death?' she asks.

'I can't give you anything more than a rough estimate at this stage, but more than twelve hours ago, given the condition of the body, the lividity and degree of rigor mortis.' Mather turns the body slightly and points. 'Lividity is this bluish-purple discoloration of the skin. It happens when the heart stops pumping blood, and gravity pulls the blood to the lowest parts of the body.'

Barabara nods. This isn't her first postmortem, and she knows the terms, but her policy is that more information is always better than less, so she encourages Mather to go on.

'Lividity is sometimes a different colour if a victim has been poisoned. Cyanide poisoning can cause a pink colour, hydrogen sulphide poisoning is greener. But this darker colour is what I'd normally expect to see.'

'I didn't know that,' Barbara admits.

'The lividity here is fixed – it won't blanch under pressure – which means he's been dead at least eight to twelve hours,' says Mather. 'And the positioning of the lividity matches the way he's lying so I think he died here on the boat. He hasn't been moved.'

Barbara looks down at the two bottles of beer. 'You'll put these through forensics?' she confirms.

'Of course.' Mather looks mildly affronted at the question, so Barbara outlines her thinking. 'From our check of the cabin it seems likely he had company yesterday, so it's possible someone gave him something poisonous out on the boat and then waited for him to die,' she says. What she doesn't add is that, if this is the case, they're dealing with a particularly malevolent killer. Someone willing not only to administer poison but to sit and watch as another person dies in agony.

Chapter 4

Canberra
Sunday, 6 p.m.

Walker, Rutherford and DS Sophie Bragg are sitting in Sophie's living room. It's a decent-sized room in a nice house and it reflects her personality: neat, organised and stylish in a simple and understated way. Walker is beside Sophie on the sofa, and Rutherford on an armchair opposite. Sophie's laptop is open on the coffee table between them. The three of them, the only ones who know the full details of Walker's upcoming operation, are having a final run-through of the plans for his Berlin trip, looking for any details they've missed that might shoot down his tenuous cover story. The plan is last-minute by the team's standards, far from being as tightly managed and controlled as Rutherford favours. The overseas location, the language barrier and the significant time difference also complicate things. But Walker's OK with it. In his experience, you can't plan for every eventuality. Going undercover means being ready to think on your feet, to react to the situation as it plays out, which is rarely, if ever, the way you'd anticipated. And, unlike most of his undercover ops, standing out is the point of this one: the hope being that, as an Aussie far from home, his presence will grab the attention of Markovich quickly. Walker reckons he'll be fine. Well, as fine as you can ever be when you venture into the world of organised crime.

'I'll have to get off shortly,' he says.

'Let's go through it once more,' says Rutherford. 'Lucas?'

'I'm going in as Donnie Young,' says Walker. 'The story is that I'm just out of the bin, very skilled as a forger, offering top-quality counterfeit Aussie passports. We're hoping that, after a few years on the run, Markovich might be keen to get home and that he might see me as his ticket back. Wayne Hopkins is the bloke who has recommended I get in touch with Markovich.'

Wayne Hopkins is the cover name of one of Rutherford's undercover agents who has managed to infiltrate the Vandals at a very senior level and is still embedded with them, having avoided by the skin of his teeth being exposed during Walker's abduction last year. Walker has nothing but admiration for a man who has spent years putting his life on the line in the company of Markovich and his ilk, earning their trust and confidence.

Rutherford nods. 'I've briefed Wayne. If Markovich contacts him, he's going to recommend you as a forger he served time with, someone he reckons is good enough to fool the Border Force. And he'll let us know, obviously, if Markovich takes the bait.'

'I've had a briefing from the forgery specialists,' says Walker. 'Nothing super detailed but enough to sound convincing. The plan is to set up a meeting with Markovich, and then coordinate with Berlin state cops so they can pull him in.'

'It's not much,' says Rutherford. 'As a background story, we haven't had enough time to build it up the way that I'd like.'

'Germany is a long way away. There's no one there who knows me, no reason for them not to believe what I tell them.'

'That's what I'm counting on,' says Rutherford. 'But if Markovich digs into it, I'm not sure it'll hold. They have your ID. There's a chance he'll recognise you.'

'I look like a new bloke with this haircut,' Walker says with a grin, running his hand over his head. He's had most of his distinctive curls, which might get him recognised, chopped off. The barber left the top longer and shaved the sides. It's almost a mullet and a very different look to his usual mop. 'I'll keep it gelled back, put in a couple of earrings, lose the moleskins,' says Walker. 'Markovich has only met me once and that was years ago. I don't reckon he'll clock me. And if he does, well, the bloke hates me. The way he sees it, I'm the cause of all his problems – the Vandals going to shit and him having to leave the country. If he works out who I am, his emotions will override reason. I reckon he'll meet me, even if it's only to put a bullet between my eyes.'

'Not exactly a reassuring picture,' says Rutherford. 'You getting a bullet between the eyes is not the outcome I'm looking for.'

'No, me neither,' says Walker, laughing. 'But this time I know he's gunning for me. This time I have the advantage.'

Rutherford looks less than convinced. 'You have a contact point for this Balkan gang that Markovich seems to be part of?'

Walker nods. 'The Sofija. It's a bar that we think is operated by the Ulić group that Markovich runs with. The intel is that it's likely a money-laundering venue.'

'Sophie, you're handling the liaison with the German police?'

'Yes. I've arranged for Lucas to meet my contact at the LKA, the state police in Berlin. He'll be able to organise local support and provide intel on the ground. But you'll have to keep me tightly in the loop,' she says, looking at Walker. 'I'll need time to get the German operation authorised and implemented.'

Walker nods. 'Absolutely.'

There's a moment's pause, Rutherford and Sophie checking their notes. Walker feels a surge of energy. He's ready to go. His bag is packed. Ginger is with Annie, a cop friend of his who spoils the dog rotten and is Ginger's favourite alternative to being with Walker himself.

'Righto,' he says, pulling out his phone to order a cab. 'Reckon I'm good to go.'

Walker's fizz of excitement is overlaid with both a touch of nerves and a small sense of victory. It's finally happening. He's on his way to working another case, away from the desk job, back on the streets. Tomorrow he'll be in Berlin, starting his hunt for Markovich. This is what he's good at. He can help bring Markovich in, see the bloke doing a long stint in the bin, and move on to his new job. He'll be seeing Barbara again too, which, he admits to himself, is another reason he's buzzing. Even though he and Barbara speak to each other regularly, usually at least once a week, it's been years since they met in person and he's really looking forward to seeing her.

Rutherford walks him to the door. 'Good luck,' he says, shaking Walker's hand. 'And to reiterate: if it turns out the Germans can't get an operation together for whatever reason, you will walk away. Understood? You are in a different country, a different jurisdiction. You have no authority to arrest or detain Markovich. Going in alone could damage our long-term chances to bring the bloke to justice, not to mention endangering your life. Without a back-up team you are not to meet him. You're not even to enter the same building. I don't care if he walks away, I don't care how close you are. If you don't have local support, you are not going in. Am I clear?'

'Yes, sir,' says Walker, though mentally he's placing the order in the 'we'll see how it goes' bucket. If he gets a chance to meet with Markovich, he's going to be taking it. He'll be careful, he'll take precautions, he won't let himself be ambushed by the bikie again. But he's going to Europe for a reason and he's not planning to leave without Markovich in custody.

Chapter 5

Mildersee
Sunday, 12 p.m.

Barbara has sent Schmidt off to make a list of the residents who were in the colony yesterday and this morning. They'll need to interview them all, see if anyone saw Mattias Ritter in his boat yesterday, and if there was anyone with him. But her next step is to speak with Karin Weber, the woman who found the body this morning. She finds Karin sitting on the patio of her cabin, drinking a cup of coffee. Barbara notices her hands are shaking as she lifts it to her lips.

Still cradling the cup, Karin recounts her story for Barbara: waking early, deciding to have a swim, seeing the boat floating unmanned, swimming out, finding the body. Her face is pale and she looks shaken, but she's a clear and concise witness.

'You're sure the victim is Mattias Ritter?' asks Barbara.

'Yes, one hundred per cent,' says Karin, giving a slight shiver. 'We're very good friends. We often spend weekends out here together so I recognised him immediately.'

'When did you last see him alive?'

'Yesterday afternoon. He came to visit and we had a bottle of wine and a chat.'

'What time did he leave?'

'Um, I'm not sure. A bit before four p.m.?'

'Did you eat anything together?'

'Eat?' Karin Weber looks surprised by the question. 'No, not lunch or anything. We had some chips and olives with the wine. Some bread and dip too.'

Barbara makes a note. Karin Weber spent time with the victim yesterday afternoon and is well known to him. Despite the woman's obvious shock and distress, she can't discount the possibility that Karin Weber knew exactly what she would find when she went to fetch the little boat this morning. It could be quite a clever cover.

'Why did you swim over to the boat?' she asks.

'I thought it might float further away. He's had some trouble with it recently. People taking it out without permission, damaging it. He'd been angry about it, made a complaint. I thought maybe someone had retaliated by unmooring it.'

'Who are these people?'

'A young Berlin DJ called Leon Kaiser. He has a cabin near Mattias's place and he often invites friends up for the weekend. They party hard and some of them aren't well behaved.'

Barbara makes a note of Leon Kaiser's name. 'Who else at the colony is Mattias Ritter friends with?' Who else, thinks Barbara, might get into a boat with him and watch him die.

'Well, I mean, he knows ... knew ... a lot of people. He was the chairman of the residents' association for a couple of years. He was quite friendly with Renate Bauer – she's a local and she has a cabin up the lane from him. I don't think he was that close to the Krause couple or Herr Wagner, but they were on the committee with him so they knew each other.'

Barbara writes all these names in her notebook. 'Was there anyone at the colony who didn't like Mattias Ritter? Anyone he'd fallen out with, aside from Leon Kaiser?'

Karin Weber hesitates for a fraction of a second, then says, 'Willie Koch. He can be a bit intimidating. More than a bit. He's a creep, and Mattias thought he was stalking and harassing Nina Hartmann. She is, or was, Mattias's girlfriend. Willie's a hunter and he often carries a gun. You're not allowed to carry guns in the colony, but he just ignores the rule. His father is a local bigwig, so he gets away with it. Mattias confronted him a couple of times. About following Nina and about the gun too. Willie got quite aggressive.'

Barbara adds Willie Koch's name to her list. 'You said Nina "is or was" his girlfriend. Which is it?'

'Nina is his girlfriend. They were out here together this weekend. But when Mattias came round yesterday, he told us he'd found out that Nina was having an affair and that they'd had a massive fight and he'd ended the relationship.'

'He ended the relationship yesterday?'

'That's right,' says Karin.

• • •

Barbara stands in the shade of the pine trees on the sandy path outside Karin Weber's cabin, watching Officer Schmidt as he walks back towards her.

'There weren't many people who stayed overnight last night,' he says when he reaches her, 'and most of them are still here. My colleagues asked them to stay in case you had questions.'

'Good,' says Barbara. 'There are a few people I want to talk to. Karin Weber has given me the names of two residents who had bad blood with Ritter. One is a Berlin DJ called Leon Kaiser. Was he here yesterday?'

Schmidt looks at the list. 'His name is on the list – one of the residents said they'd seen him yesterday – but he's not here now so he didn't stay overnight.'

'OK. Can you get his contact details for me? The other person Ritter argued with is a local man called Willie Koch, who apparently lives nearby?'

Schmidt nods. 'I know him. He lives with his parents on a farm just outside the colony, by the edge of the forest. His name isn't on my list, but we didn't check non-residents, so I don't know if he was here yesterday.'

'What about the deceased's girlfriend?' asks Barbara. 'Her name is Nina Hartmann.'

Schmidt looks down at his list again. 'She was here yesterday but not this morning.'

'I wonder what time she left,' says Barbara, thoughtful. She's read somewhere that hate is the closest emotion to love and many murder cases seem to be evidence of that – the killer so often a person familiar to the victim. Perhaps it's no coincidence that Mattias Ritter breaks up with his girlfriend on the same day he is poisoned, possibly by someone angry enough to sit and watch him die.

Barbara decides her top priority right now has to be a conversation with Nina Hartmann, but when she dials her number there's no reply. Karin Weber has supplied a Berlin address for Ritter and Hartmann, so Barbara calls Berlin uniforms and asks them to pay the apartment a visit. She gives them details for Mattias Ritter's next of kin, a sister who also lives in Berlin, and asks for a team to notify her and arrange for a formal identification.

Then she calls her boss, DSS Fischer, with an update. He interrupts when she describes Ritter as a victim. 'Can we be one hundred per cent sure that this is a murder, rather than an overdose or suicide?' he asks.

'Not one hundred per cent, no. He could have taken something poisonous by accident or design. But with the missing oar, and the fact that the beers in the boat weren't from his cabin, my gut feel is that he wasn't alone and this isn't accidental.'

'Gut feel isn't enough, Guerra. I need facts.'

'Yes, sir. I'd like to request a toxicology report. I'll have the SOC information and the autopsy results tomorrow or Tuesday. Meanwhile I'm planning to interview the victim's – the deceased's – girlfriend, the residents here, and I'll need to put a call out for anyone who was around the lake yesterday afternoon and evening.' She hesitates for a moment, then bites the bullet. 'I'll need more manpower,' she says. 'I can't manage all the interviews on my own, not in a timely way.'

There's a short silence. 'Have you confirmed that this is our jurisdiction?' asks Fischer. 'Can we get away with saying that this is a Brandenburg problem?' Fischer wants rid of the case, thinks Barbara. But she needs it. She needs to prove to him that she's up to heading a murder investigation, needs to prove to herself that she's still got what it takes. 'The colony is on the Berlin side of the lake, sir,' she says. 'Kummerfeld is Brandenburg, but the lake is the border. Mildersee is in Berlin.'

'Scheisse. I don't have anyone I can give this to – this drive-by is eating up resources.'

'I can handle it, sir,' she says.

There's a pause. 'You're still working that shoplifting case, right?'

She has a few things in her inbox. She's managed to trace the organisers of a shoplifting gang, a professional group who use children to steal, but hasn't found enough evidence to prosecute them yet. There's also an ongoing investigation into a group who steal vehicles to order and a stalking and harassment case that Fischer wants her to drop but which she's keeping an eye on. But nothing like this. Nothing as serious as suspected murder. Fischer hasn't been passing those cases to her, not for a while.

'I can handle it,' she says again, keeping her voice firm, not pleading.

A longer pause. 'OK. Order the toxicology and carry on investigating but I don't have any extra manpower for this right now. If you need help, you can ask the local team. I spoke with the chief at Kummerfeld – he's volunteering assistance.'

'I'd rather use one of our guys...'

'This isn't a perfect world, Barbara.' Fischer's tone is brusque. 'Use the local team if you need them. I don't have any other options.'

As she pockets her phone, Barbara feels a rush of adrenaline. She's got the case, at least for the moment. Now she needs to solve it, and solve it fast, before Fischer reassigns it to Vogel or one of the others. She'll need assistance, though; it's too much to handle on her own. The local officer, Schmidt, has been helpful enough so far. Maybe she can use him for some of the interviews. She decides she'll talk to the most important suspects, Willie Koch and Leon Kaiser – the two residents Mattias Ritter had had arguments with – and his girlfriend, Nina Hartmann. Schmidt can take statements from the others.

As Barbara is planning her next steps, her phone rings – the uniform team calling to say that Nina Hartmann is back home after a night spent partying at a Berlin club. She's been given the news of Ritter's death and been told that Barbara needs to speak with her. Good.

She walks towards the cordon where Schmidt is talking to his colleagues and calls him over. 'I need you to talk to the residents who were here overnight. I want to know what they saw and heard, especially if they saw Ritter on his boat yesterday evening and if he had company. Find out what they think of Ritter, how well they know him, who he liked, who he didn't.' Schmidt scribbles furiously, writing down her instructions in his notebook. 'Keep an eye out for anyone who seems evasive, or anything that raises your suspicions. Call me immediately if anything urgent comes up. I'm going to talk to Nina Hartmann in Berlin. I'll call you when I'm done.'

With any luck, Barbara thinks as she drives her car out of the colony and turns towards the city, Nina Hartmann will prove to be the key to solving this case.

Chapter 6

Berlin
5 p.m.

Barbara parks her car on a wide tree-filled street in Schöneberg, a pretty part of the city, more gentrified than where she lives in Neukölln. No sirens, no homeless people, no drunks arguing on the benches in the park that surrounds the church. The street is lined by large apartment blocks painted in pastel colours with ornately decorated exteriors and generous balconies. Window boxes filled with flowers add further colour, and there's a noticeable absence of graffiti or bikes parked messily across the sidewalk. Tranquillity reigns, and Barbara feels a slight jolt of envy: to wake up each morning in this pretty, peaceful street must be nice.

She walks up to number 71, rings the bell marked with the couple's names. After a long wait, a crackly voice comes through the speaker: 'Yes?'

'Detective Barbara Guerra, Kriminalpolizei.'

'Third floor, left,' says the voice as the door buzzes open.

Barbara walks into a well-maintained foyer with polished floorboards, mint-green walls and a row of metal letterboxes, painted a contrasting shade of emerald green, on the wall to her left. A wide set of stairs curves up to her right, lit by a fancy skylight high above, and there's a lift on the left beyond the letterboxes. More functional than stylish, it's a new addition, she supposes, as she rides it the three floors to the couple's apartment. She exits, turns left and sees a beautiful woman of about thirty standing at the door. She's wearing a floral silk bathrobe that finishes high on her thighs. Her legs are long and tanned, her toenails painted shimmering blue, her hand on the doorframe sports matching fingernails and her long blonde hair, which looks slightly damp, falls in a heavy curtain to below her shoulders. A floral, fresh-out-of-the-shower scent emanates from her. Only her eyes, red and bloodshot, hint at anything less than perfection.

'Nina Hartmann?' asks Barbara.

'Yes. Are you here about Mattias?'

'That's right.' Barbara shows her ID. 'Can I come in?'

'Yes, of course. Sorry, I just got out of the shower so I need a minute.'

'I can wait here until you're ready,' says Barbara.

'No, it's alright, come in.' Nina Hartmann stands aside, letting Barbara into a high-ceilinged entrance hall.

'The living room is through there.' Nina points to her left. 'I'll just get dressed.'

Barbara decides to wait by the door, and it's only a couple of minutes before Nina is back, wearing a white t-shirt with pale-grey yoga trousers, her feet bare and brown, her damp hair casually pulled back. She's so beautiful that she even looks good in sportswear, thinks Barbara. Nina leads her into a large living space, with two caramel-coloured leather sofas facing each other across a coffee table on which stands a bright-yellow thermos with a large mug, also yellow, beside it. Two walls of the room are covered in shelves artfully filled with neatly arranged books and objects; a large palm tree, fronds touching the three-metre-high ceiling, stands beside French doors leading to a balcony, where Barbara can glimpse a variety of herbs and flowers growing in terracotta pots.

Nina walks over to the far sofa and sits heavily, leaning back, rubbing her hand across her eyes. 'I haven't slept and I'm in total shock,' she says. 'I can't believe this is happening. I was partying with friends all night. I was expecting Mattias to be here when I got back this afternoon, but the police were waiting. I just can't believe it. I can't believe Mattias won't be coming home...' Her voice trails off. Barbara notices Nina's hands are trembling, and she's shivering despite the warmth of the afternoon. Her shock seems real.

'Here,' says Barbara, leaning forward, pouring what smells like peppermint tea from the thermos into the cup and handing it to the woman opposite. Nina takes the cup, raises it to her lips, but then lowers it and holds it close to her body, both hands clasped tightly around it.

'Please,' she says. 'Please tell me what happened. When did he die? How? The police said they didn't have any information...'

'He was found this morning in his boat, in the middle of the lake,' says Barbara.

'In his boat!' Nina's eyes widen, and tears start rolling down her cheeks. 'Oh my god. This can't be happening. Did he have a heart attack or something? Mattias is so healthy – he takes such good care of himself.'

Barbara hesitates a moment. She's not convinced that Nina isn't somehow complicit in her boyfriend's death. Best, she decides, not to give too much away. Holding information back might come in useful during more detailed questioning if this turns into a full-blown murder inquiry and Hartmann becomes a formal suspect.

'The circumstances of his death aren't totally clear,' she says.

'That's why we're looking into it.'

'What do you mean?' Nina's voice is rising, her face getting paler, her hands trembling, the tea in the cup slopping with the movement. 'How can you not know?'

'I'm sorry,' says Barbara. 'I know how difficult this must be. It seems he might have consumed something poisonous but we're still waiting for the autopsy results. If you could answer a few questions, it would be helpful.'

'Poison? Oh god, this can't be happening.' Nina's hands are shaking so much that the front of her t-shirt is damp where tea has spilt onto it. Barbara resists the urge to take the cup from her and put it back on the table.

'When did you last see Mattias?' she asks instead.

'Yesterday morning – towards noon,' says Nina. 'We were at the lake cabin, we had a late breakfast, and then we... then he went to visit some friends of his and he hadn't come back when I left.'

'What time did you leave?'

'Just before eight p.m. I know because it's a twenty-minute cycle to the station and I caught the eight fifteen train. I was cycling extra-fast to try to catch it because the trains are an hour apart at that time of night.'

'And you didn't see Mattias before you left.'

'No.'

That's surprising information, thinks Barbara. According to Karin Weber, Mattias Ritter left her cabin at 4 p.m. Nina hasn't mentioned an argument, nor that she and Ritter were on the verge of breaking up or had actually done so. 'Is it normal that you would come back to Berlin without Mattias?' she asks. 'That you'd spend the weekend separately?'

'Sometimes, yes. We have different interests. I like to go dancing, Mattias isn't... wasn't that into it anymore.'

'You hadn't argued, hadn't broken up...?'

Nina's eyes narrow. 'Who told you that?' she says. 'Karin and Fran, right? They've never liked me. Us breaking up is wishful thinking on their part. Yes, Mattias and I had a disagreement yesterday morning, but it was nothing serious. I wanted to go dancing, he didn't, that's all there was to it. Like I said, we sometimes spend the weekend doing our own thing.'

This doesn't chime with what Karin Weber said, that there had been an affair, a bigger argument, the end of the relationship, but perhaps, as Nina claims, Karin read more into the argument than she should have.

'What did you do between noon and eight p.m. yesterday?'

'Um, not much. I slept in the hammock for a while, had a swim, went for a walk in the forest.'

'You didn't meet anyone? You don't have any friends out at the colony?'

Nina hesitates a moment. 'I know a guy called Leon Kaiser,' she says. 'He's a DJ. I've been to some of his parties. He has a cabin just up from ours.'

The DJ. The man who had damaged Mattias Ritter's boat, thinks Barbara.

'Did you see Herr Kaiser yesterday?'

Another hesitation, split-second, but it's there. 'Briefly,' says Nina. 'I stopped by and said hello, late afternoon, maybe sixish.'

Barbara makes a mental note, of both the friendship and the hesitations. She's certain that Nina Hartmann is withholding something.

'How was Mattias's mood generally?' she asks, changing tack. 'Was he depressed? Was he happy?'

'Depressed? No. He was ... normal. Busy with work, friends, the usual things.'

'Does he have financial issues that you're aware of?'

'Absolutely not. He's a journalist, he has a good job. And when his grandmother passed away a few years ago she left him some money and this apartment.'

Barbara's sure in her gut that this isn't a suicide, and Nina Hartmann's answers are confirming her intuition. There seems to be no reason for Ritter to have killed himself.

'Does Mattias use drugs?' she asks. Perhaps this is a case of an overdose rather than a poisoning.

Nina hesitates again. 'No,' she says. 'Not anymore. Back in the day, when he went clubbing maybe, but recently, no, he hasn't.'

'Was there anyone Mattias had antagonised? Do you know of any enemies he might have made?'

'No! He writes about music, mostly, and books and cinema and things like that. He's not political or anything.'

'What about at the colony? Had he upset anyone out there?'

'I don't know, I don't go out there all that often. You should ask Karin - she'll know better than me...'

'OK,' says Barbara. 'That's all for now. Thank you for your help, Frau Hartmann. I know this must be a really difficult time for you. Is there someone you can call to be with you?'

'My mother is coming down from Hamburg to stay with me. She'll be here in an hour or so.'

As Barbara is about to stand, a thought comes to her mind. 'Do you have a job, Frau Hartmann? What's your profession?'

'I'm a pharmacist, but I'm not working in the field at the moment. I run holistic well-being courses - you know, yoga and meditation, nutrition, mental health...'

Barbara's ears perk up at this. A pharmacist would know how to poison someone, what to use and in what doses. 'Thank you for your help, Frau Hartmann. This is my card. You can call me if you think of any other relevant information, and we might be back in touch as the case progresses.'

Nina shows Barbara to the door and is still standing there as the lift departs. She gives the impression of operating largely on autopilot, her mind seemingly miles away, a mix of exhaustion and shock, probably. But as Barbara takes the lift down, analysing the conversation, she realises it's raised as many questions as it's answered. Nina Hartmann's statement is quite different from Karin Weber's. She's denied she was breaking up with Mattias, and claims he didn't come back to their cabin on Saturday afternoon. Either of the two could be lying, but Hartmann also has knowledge of pharmaceuticals and has admitted to leaving the lake in a hurry on the night Mattias Ritter died. From where Barbara stands, Nina Hartmann is far from above suspicion in the death of her boyfriend.

• • •

Nina Hartmann stands at the door long after the lift doors have closed, her legs wobbly, her breathing shallow. She wonders how much the cop knows. Those cows, Karin and Fran – they've never liked her. They must have said something about the fight, maybe even about Leon. She wonders how much Mattias told them.

He would have told them about the argument, though perhaps not its details. It had been nasty, spiralling and growing, building into a storm, with things said that could never be unsaid, shaking the foundations of their five-year relationship. She's always believed in open relationships, and had thought he was on board with that. But this had been the cause of their argument, Mattias seeing a dick pic on her phone. He'd read all of Leon's messages too, and assumed, correctly, that Nina was having an affair. Luckily, he didn't know who'd sent them: she'd been sensible enough not to save Leon's details on her phone. But, cornered, she hit back, accused him of being old and boring, of not giving her enough sexual attention, of being selfish and crap in bed. At that last insult, Mattias shouted that he'd had enough of her lies and insults, that it was over, that she should leave as soon as possible, and leave the apartment too while she was at it. He stormed off, went to visit Karin and Fran, no doubt, and spill all their dirty laundry, and she went to see Leon. Partly out of spite and partly because she needed some reassurance, she spent the rest of the day with him. They got wasted, had sex, and she felt a bit better, though she was still angry with Mattias for the things he'd said and for being so lame, and that's why— She stops the thought, won't let herself go there.

She wonders if the cops will speak to Leon and what he might say. Closing the door, her legs feeling shaky again, she goes to find her phone. She needs to talk to him; they need to get their stories straight.

Chapter 7

Berlin

7 p.m.

It takes an age for Barbara to find a parking spot for her Peugeot 108, on a street that's at least four blocks from her apartment. She grabs her bag, locks the car and walks home. A group of young women are standing outside City Chicken, talking loudly, eating chicken and chips out of white polystyrene containers. The shisha bars on Sonnenallee are open, the warm evening enticing patrons to sit outside. Arabic music pumps out of one, and the crowd on the pavement, all male, are relaxed, smoking pipes, drinking coffee, chatting in small groups. Closer to home, the bars along Weserstrasse are busy too. People drinking beers at the tables outside the Späti, a group of women toasting a birthday with glasses of Sekt at the wine bar, young men spilling from Schillingbar accompanied by the sound of music and the scent of cigarette smoke and cologne. The balmy summer evening, the cheerful vitality – it's all a long way from the grim scene at Mildersee and Barbara is happy to be back.

She climbs the four flights of stairs to her apartment. The rooms are stuffy after the warm weekend, so she opens the windows and the door to the balcony, inhaling the scent of rosemary and thyme from the herb pot outside. She sits on the sofa, takes out her phone and calls Schmidt to see if he has anything to report.

'How did you get on?' she asks.

'I've spoken with the three other residents who were at the colony overnight,' he says. She hears him flipping through his notebook. 'Renate Bauer, Ralf Wagner and a married couple called Krause. They've all confirmed each other's alibis: they were seen in their respective gardens during the afternoon and evening. The only one of these who spoke to the deceased yesterday is Renate Bauer. She says she was good friends with him and that she saw him yesterday around lunchtime. He'd had a big fight with his girlfriend and was very upset because the girlfriend was cheating on him.'

Barbara is very interested to hear this. 'That tallies with what I heard from Karin Weber, but not with what his girlfriend said. What else did Renate Bauer tell you?'

'Not much; she was quite distressed by Ritter's death and I spent half the time comforting her,' says Schmidt. 'Ralf Wagner didn't see anything. He says he didn't know Ritter and was too busy working on his cabin to be watching what others were up to. But the Krause couple gave me some useful information.' Barbara can hear enthusiasm and triumph in Schmidt's voice. She knows how he feels: there's nothing better than finding an insight that could impact a case. 'They also heard an argument between the deceased and his girlfriend. They couldn't make out the details – I get the feeling they were disappointed about that – but they said that Ritter and his girlfriend were shouting at each other and that it went on for quite a while. They also saw Ritter, just before one p.m., speaking to Renate Bauer. But this is the interesting bit: they said they saw Ritter's girlfriend with another resident, a guy called Leon Kaiser, at around two p.m., and that the two of them were being intimate. I gather they were kissing.'

'Were they now...' says Barbara. Another point on which Nina Hartmann has seemingly lied or withheld information. 'That's good to know. Kaiser wasn't at the lake today, though—'

'According to Frau Krause, Leon Kaiser left Mildersee around nine p.m. yesterday evening,' Schmidt interrupts, keen to show he's on the case. 'She also told me that Mattias Ritter didn't like Kaiser much. Apparently he is always hosting noisy parties and his friends damaged Ritter's boat a few weeks ago, which confirms what your witness said earlier. I've got Leon Kaiser's contact details, so I'll send those through to you now.'

Schmidt is proving to be a good and thorough cop. 'This is really good work, Officer,' Barbara says. She's impressed both with his efforts and with his obvious enthusiasm. 'Anything else?'

'One thing. Frau Krause was swimming in the lake later in the afternoon, around five p.m., and says she heard Ritter having an argument with someone. She heard him say, "If it happens again, I'm calling the police." But she doesn't know who he was talking to. It might have been Kaiser but could have been anyone.'

This is probably the most pertinent evidence he's managed to collect and the information she'd have shared first. 'That's very helpful. Did she say anything more about who he was speaking with? Was it a man or a woman?'

'Umm, no, she didn't say...'

Barbara gets the sense that Schmidt hasn't dug too deeply, his inexperience showing. She needs to talk to Frau Krause herself. Still, he's done a good job. She thanks him for his help and he promises to send her a detailed report of his interviews, along with the contact details of all the lake's residents.

She puts the phone down and walks out onto the balcony. The sun's rays have disappeared behind the building opposite, and the sky is beginning to turn orange. She can see the plants in the window boxes that line the balcony's balustrade are dry and thirsty. She fills her neon-pink watering can and gives them a long drink, pouring until water is spilling out of the containers and cooling her bare feet. Then she takes a shower, standing longer than usual under the water, thinking about the Mildersee case. She feels like they're making some progress. It's still early but the picture is beginning to form. Like starting a puzzle, when small sections are the first to become visible, the outline of the case, its key players, is slowly coming into focus.

Afterwards, she makes a cup of evening tea – a blend of camomile, tilia and orange blossom that her mother swears helps you sleep – and sits on the balcony to drink it and to send a message to Rita: sorry I wasn't around today querida mia, I'll come and visit this week. besos grandes and a hug for Lola.

When she checks the rest of her messages, there's one from her best friend Monika earlier this afternoon: Hey! fancy meeting 4 a drink l8r? to which she sends a quick apology: sorry working today. let's chat 2mrw?

There's a hey! what r u up to? from Seb too. He's also police, in the elite SEK, a SWAT-style unit, and they're having . . . well, *something* together. He's not into heavy conversations or deep and meaningful anything; they go for dinner or a drink occasionally and the sex is good enough. A situationship, Monika calls it, and that's probably about right. She texts him quickly: sorry – work crazy today. see you this week maybe? then skips through group messages, various plans for nights out and pictures from a hike someone organised, and comes to a message from Lucas, sent earlier this afternoon. Hi Barbara. Here's my flight details: Qatar Airlines QR81, arrives BER 14.55 tomorrow. See you soon!

She puts her phone on the balcony table. It's hard to believe that Lucas will be here in less than twenty-four hours. Her heart lifts at the thought; a tingle starts in her belly. She can't wait to see him, although she hasn't had much time to plan for his visit. She's found him somewhere to stay – an apartment belonging to an artist friend of Monika's who is away in New York for a few weeks – but that's about it.

When he told her of his impending visit, just a few days ago, she was nothing but excited, looking forward to seeing him and showing him around Berlin. But now, as the moment of his arrival becomes real, she's starting to feel a bit more conflicted. She owes him so much. He was a huge help in the search for Rita when she went missing in Australia. A lifesaver, literally. And aside from his professional help, he was a friend too, took care of her, introduced her to his family. They only spent a couple of weeks together – though it felt like half a lifetime – but there was a strong connection between them, more than she normally feels for a colleague. She felt – still feels – as if she's known him forever, that she can count on him for help in any situation. As Monika has pointed out more than once, the fact that they've stayed in touch all this time demonstrates the strength of their friendship.

But now she's wondering if seeing Lucas might reawaken the traumatic memories of her time in Australia, memories she's fought hard to suppress and then only half successfully. A little worm of fear insinuates itself in her mind. She has this case now, a case she has to solve to prove herself. She can't have her anxiety firing up again. The tingle in her stomach turns queasy as her thoughts spiral: she wonders what Lucas is expecting from her, how much time he'll want to spend with her, how she'll balance that with work. She takes a sip of her tea and sighs. She's overthinking it, as Monika would say. Lucas is coming here to work, and despite her butterflies and fears it will be great to see him again.

• • •

The adrenaline rush that's been driving Stefan Markovich for the last couple of days is slowly starting to fade. The drive-by shooting he instigated was a massive success. He nailed a couple of blokes from a rival clan and delivered the message loud and clear that Vaso Ulić is serious about taking over in Berlin.

Vaso Ulić is the clan head honcho, above even the Banker back home, the boss of bosses, who can sit with the Mexican drug barons and be their equal. He's responsible for most of the gear that makes its way to Europe and Australia and has a shipping operation that would blow your mind. And, most importantly from Markovich's perspective, Vaso is his mum's uncle, or some kind of cousin – who the fuck knows with all these Montenegrin rellies. Whatever it is, they're related, and Uncle Vaso has taken to him. Got him out of Australia and into Ecuador when the shit hit the fan at home, and then, when the cops got wind of Ecuador, Vaso sent him to Europe. First to Rotterdam, where he did such a good job putting the frighteners on a group of young wannabes – didn't mess around, killed a couple of the so-called top blokes – that he's now in line to head up Berlin.

Germany has a lot of potential, apparently, but the Ulić clan isn't getting its share. The old bloke who's been in charge here forever, name of Popović but everyone calls him Popo, just isn't up to the job anymore. Fucken Popo, thinks Markovich. What a clown name. No wonder he's no fucken good.

Popo had tried to veto the drive-by. Had reckoned it would pull too much heat, that they should sit down with the other clans, figure out a way forward. 'Fuck that,' said Markovich, and Vaso agreed. After the drive-by, he'd been expecting thanks, if not congratulations, from Popo for a job well done. Instead, he was given a massive bollocking, and not in private either, in front of a handful of Popo's lieutenants, because some kid had got in the way. Stefan nearly popped Popo then and there but he doesn't have authority for that yet. He'll get it, though, probably sooner rather than later, so Popo better watch his back.

He got a small measure of revenge when Vaso Ulić called personally from Montenegro, to pass on his thanks and congratulations.

The call came in public, while Popo and the others were around, which was the perfect way to give them all the finger and to make it clear that Markovich is not to be messed with. He made the most of it – 'Yeah, no worries, anything for you, Uncle Vaso' and all that kind of shit. The looks on the others' faces were priceless. When he mentioned the kid who'd got in the way, Vaso shrugged it off. 'Drive-bys can be messy, that's just the way of it. We can tolerate a bit of hassle from the pigs, no problem.' Which was good news and meant that Popo had to wind his neck in and shut the fuck up.

The part of the conversation he kept to himself, though perhaps Popo already suspects, is that Vaso was extra-happy about the shooting because it proves Markovich is up to taking over from Popo. 'That's exactly why I want you there,' he said. 'We need someone like you – Popo is too fucking weak.'

After the call, everyone in the room could smell the shift in power coming and they were a lot fucken better behaved. Popo even shouted him a drink.

But Vaso had also instructed him to keep on the right side of Popo for the moment. 'I don't want him to know you're coming for him. It won't be long till you're in charge, but for now do what he says.'

What Popo said, after they'd finished one lousy drink, was: 'Go home and stay in your apartment for a few days until the heat dies down.'

Markovich wanted to go out with a mate, get wankered, find a woman, make the most of the buzz he was feeling. He'd have ignored Popo, but you don't ignore Vaso Ulić. He made one detour on his way home – the Sofija, a clan-run bar near his place – and bought a bottle of bourbon and a dozen beers. It wasn't the party he was after, but it would have to do for now. Things'll be different when he's in charge.

Chapter 8

Berlin
Monday, 9 a.m.

Barbara sits down at her desk with a coffee and opens her email, happy to find Schmidt's report already in her inbox. He must have worked late to get it to her so quickly. She reads it through, impressed with his thoroughness. Along with the statements of the people he's spoken with, he's included a map of the colony, with names marked against each cabin and the contact details of each resident.

She prints the map out, enlarges it on the copier and pins it to the wall behind her desk. It's a useful visual aid that helps her form a clearer mental image of Mildersee and what she's increasingly certain is a murder scene. The colony is crescent-shaped, curving to follow the shore of the lake. The water forms a natural boundary to the south, the forest borders the north, and there is farmland to the east and west. There's only one road, from east to west, across the top edge by the forest. That's the road she drove in on yesterday. Six small lanes run down from this road towards the lake, and are intersected by two that run east to west across the colony. Most of the cabins are arranged along the blocks formed by these lanes. Only one house has been marked outside these limits: the home of the Koch family, whose son Willie has had run-ins with the victim, Mattias Ritter, and who live a kilometre or so north of the colony, at the western edge of the forest.

There are around fifty cabins on-site but, including Ritter, there were only five owners in residence on the night of his death. Karin Weber and her girlfriend Fran, at their cabin near the entrance to the colony, a ten-minute walk from Ritter's lakefront place. Nearer to the scene of the crime, in the centre of the colony, a cluster of residents were on-site: Ralf Wagner, Birgit and Manfred Krause, Renate Bauer and Leon Kaiser, though Kaiser left around 9 p.m. The Koch family, a good fifteen-minute walk away through the forest, were also at home.

She pins the pictures she took at the scene to the map, then looks at it all for a long time, letting the details of what she knows of the day of Ritter's death run through her mind. Mattias Ritter and his girlfriend, Nina Hartmann, argue late morning, what about and to what severity is under debate, though Barbara thinks that, on balance, given other residents' statements, Nina Hartmann is probably lying and that the argument could have been a relationship-ending one about an affair. Possibly an affair with neighbouring resident Leon Kaiser.

Afterwards, Mattias Ritter talks with Renate Bauer, then spends a couple of hours with Karin Weber and her girlfriend. By 5 p.m. latest, he is back near his cabin, where he's heard by Frau Krause threatening to call the police on someone. Not long after this, Ritter is dead. She needs to talk to Leon Kaiser, see how his account compares with the others, but so far Nina Hartmann's story is the one that's posing the most questions. She claims to have spent the day in and around the cabin and not to have left Mildersee until almost 8 p.m., but not to have seen Mattias Ritter after their argument. If other witness statements are correct – and they seem to tally – Hartmann is lying and has real questions to answer.

Barbara sits back at her desk and makes a to-do list. A priority is to track down Leon Kaiser and arrange to interview him. She should also talk to Willie Koch, as much to confirm that she can rule him out as anything else. She needs to double-check Nina Hartmann's alibi and locate and interview any other witnesses who were at the lake on Saturday, who might have seen something unusual, or seen Ritter's boat at any point that evening. Mildersee is a popular swimming, paddling and sailing spot for local people as well as for colony residents. It may well be that someone who doesn't have a cabin saw Ritter in his boat on Saturday night. There are houses on the other side of the lake that also have access to the water and need to be door-knocked. It's too much to do alone, and Fischer is standing firm against her request for more manpower. Schmidt has done good work; she'll ask if he's available to help out.

She crafts a quick email to the chief of the Kummerfeld force, a Berthold Barsch, requesting Schmidt's assistance moving forward. She'll be judicious in what she asks of him, but it will be useful to have someone on the ground to call on. She also asks Barsch for assistance with locating and interviewing witnesses, and a door-to-door on houses that line the lakeshore opposite Mildersee.

Then she calls the numbers Nina Hartmann has sent through to confirm her alibi. Her friends' stories stack up. They'd met for drinks at around 10 p.m. on Saturday, then gone dancing at the Pony Club from 2 a.m. to mid-morning Sunday, after which they ate brunch together and finally made their way home around 2 p.m. She requests CCTV from the rail operator Deutsche Bahn, to confirm Nina left Mildersee on the 8.15 p.m. train as she claims. She calls Leon Kaiser several times to try to set up an interview, but he doesn't answer, so in the end she leaves a message asking him to contact her. She chases the autopsy and toxicology reports, more in hope than in expectation. Tomorrow morning at the earliest, comes the tetchy reply. Meanwhile, a response has come in from Chief Barsch in Kummerfeld, agreeing to handle the door-to-doors and to make Schmidt available for her investigation.

By the time she's done all that, it's almost 2 p.m. At a bit of a loose end until the autopsy and toxicology come in and Kaiser makes himself available for interview, she decides to revisit Mildersee. It will help to set the scene more firmly in her mind, and she wants to talk to Willie Koch and the Krause couple too. Perhaps there's more they can tell her about Ritter's final argument and who it might have been with. She won't be back in time to meet Lucas at the airport, so she texts Monika to ask if she could pick him up. Monika sends a thumbs-up and she forwards her a picture of Lucas and his flight details and writes: thanks schatz, where would I be without you? Then she sends a message to Lucas for him to read when he lands: Hey Lucas – my friend Monika will meet you at the airport. You can't miss her, look for the pink hair! Sorry I can't be there, work is busy. See you later for a beer?

•••

'Hey, pretty boy, come here a minute,' shouts Klein from across the room. Schmidt knows the call is meant for him, but he does his best to ignore it; it will be another of the bad jokes that Klein thinks are so funny.

They're in the small back room at Kummerfeld Police Station, Schmidt typing up a report on a break-and-enter he's investigated this morning. Money and some jewellery taken, most likely on Saturday when the old dear who owns the place spent the day with her son and grandkids. She only noticed it this morning. Whoever it was came in through a small bathroom window, so it was kids, most likely. He doesn't expect they'll find them, but he's gone through the motions and now he needs to get the paperwork off his desk.

He gets on alright with Klein. Lazy and unmotivated, Klein likes to stay at his desk, arrive late, leave early, but at least that means he offloads some of the more interesting jobs. But at thirty-seven, almost ten years older than he is, Klein is still only a senior officer, his career going nowhere fast. And when Schmidt looks at Klein's life and translates a bit of that future to his own, it's like a slick of ice descending on his hopes and dreams.

He joined the police after completing the policing degree, hoping to be fast-tracked into the detective programme. But he's already done two years in uniform, has applied for every post that's come available with no luck – recruitment freezes and strong competition slowing his ascent. He had ideas of chasing down bad guys, solving serious crime. Little did he know that most of his work would be admin and dealing with stressed people who are having a very bad day – property stolen or damaged, domestic disputes, arguments and assaults. The Mildersee inquiry is the closest he's come to actual policing, the kind of case he imagined he'd be working on, and he stayed up until after 2 a.m. to write a detailed report for the Berlin detective. She seemed happy with his work, but he hasn't heard anything from her, not even a thank-you, so it looks like he's back on the daily grind, and he's feeling more depressed than usual at the thought.

'Schmidt, get your arse over here, now!' Klein isn't giving up.

Schmidt raises a hand to say he's coming, finishes typing his sentence and pushes his chair back. 'What?' he says, walking over, trying not to sound frustrated.

'What happened with that Berlin detective? Did you get a piece of her? She had a nice body, especially for a Dago – they usually tend to be porky.'

'Nah,' says Schmidt. 'Nothing doing. I guess I wasn't her type.' Klein thinks Schmidt has women all over the place and he's usually happy to indulge the fantasy, but he's not in the mood today.

'Must be a dyke,' says Klein. 'Maybe she got it on with those lesbos...'

The door to the chief's office opens, breaking in on Klein's vivid imagination, and Barsch sticks his head out. 'Schmidt, get in here.'

When Schmidt goes in, he's not surprised to find Frank Koch sitting in the armchair to the left of Barsch's desk. Koch, the mayor, is one of Barsch's best mates and is in here most days. Elections for the district are coming up, and Koch's portrait and slogans – hard on crime a key message – are fixed to lamp-posts across town. Sometimes it seems like Barsch is managing his campaign from the station.

'I've had a message from Berlin,' says Barsch. 'They're asking for assistance with this case at Mildersee and they've requested your help.'

Schmidt's heart lifts. He's going to work on the Mildersee case. The detective must have liked his report.

'You can wipe that smile off your face,' says Barsch. 'I know women like your looks but that doesn't carry any weight in this office, and I don't approve of you using it to further your career.'

'But, sir—'

'Don't interrupt me. Despite my dislike of your methods, I've agreed you can assist on this case. Mildersee might technically be under Berlin jurisdiction but it's on our doorstep and I want someone involved who can keep us informed of what the investigators are thinking.'

'The man who died is a Berliner,' interjects Koch, 'and we all know they've brought nothing but trouble to the colony. This is something to do with them, mark my words, but knowing how they operate, they'll try to set up someone from round here. Find a stupid Ossi who'll take the heat...'

When the Berlin Wall fell in 1989, those who lived in the former East, like all of them here in Brandenburg, were nicknamed Ossis

– 'Easties'. Over time, as the states in the former East remained poorer, and with fewer opportunities, while those in the West seemed to profit on the back of reunification, the name became an insult.

Barsch puts up a hand to stop Koch's diatribe.

'You're part of this to be our eyes and ears,' he says to Schmidt. 'You're to report to the detective heading up the case from tomorrow. Make sure you keep us in the loop. I want daily updates. I want to know who's on their suspect list and why, and I want to know it as soon as they do.'

Chapter 9

Berlin
3 p.m.

Lucas Walker feels a buzz of anticipation as the plane touches down in Berlin. He's finally here. Back on the ground, back at work. In the same city as Barbara and, if their intel is right, his old enemy Markovich. But Markovich can wait. In just a few minutes he'll be seeing Barbara again and the thought brings a smile to his face.

The plane rolls to a halt, the seat belt lights ping off and all around him passengers move into action, standing, stretching, pulling luggage out of the overhead storage. He stands too, relieved after the long flight to be disembarking. The economy-class seat is a tight fit for his broad frame and long legs, and he's been sitting in the same cramped position for what feels like a lifetime: fourteen hours on the journey to Doha, and another seven to Germany. He stretches his shoulders and his leg, the old injury giving him gyp from the long stint in one spot.

He's only brought a carry-on bag and makes good time through the airport, striding out, happy to be moving. He signs into the airport WiFi while he's queuing for passport control and a message from Barbara arrives. She's caught up at work and a friend of hers is meeting him instead. Walker's conscious of a feeling of slight disappointment but shrugs it off. The job is the job, that's the way it goes, and he'll see her this evening. Maybe it's better – this way, he'll have a chance to freshen up a bit. He threw some water on his face, ran his fingers through his hair and changed his t-shirt before they landed but he doesn't think it's made much of an improvement. The time difference with Australia means his internal clock is all over the place; he's not sure if it's day or night back home but he feels pretty zonked. He needs a shower, a rest, a bit of fresh air.

Less than twenty minutes after touchdown, he's walking through the sliding doors that separate arrivals from the meeting hall. The space is airy and open and not busy, and he spots Barbara's friend Monika right off. Tall and striking, she's wearing black leather trousers, chunky boots and a black t-shirt, and her short hair is bright pink. She makes eye contact with him, he raises his hand in a wave, and she breaks into a smile, walks towards him, extends her hand. 'Monika Meyer,' she says. 'Barbara has told me a lot about you and she's very sorry she couldn't be here to meet you.'

Monika has a firm grip, her hand soft and cool, and her eyes, which hold eye contact with him, are a striking green. Her English is flawless, almost accentless, and he's relieved because his German doesn't extend much beyond 'Guten Tag' and 'Danke Schön'. She leads him to her car, a newish navy VW Golf, and drives, fast and confident, away from the airport and along a motorway. 'It should only take us thirty minutes or so to get to Kreuzberg,' she says. 'Some friends of mine are in New York and they were happy to offer you their apartment.'

'That's really nice of them,' says Walker. 'I told Barbara I could stay at a hotel . . .'

'No problem – we owe you big-time for what you did for Rita and Barbara. It's the least we could do.'

Monika takes an exit off the motorway and soon they're in the city proper, winding their way through tree-lined streets filled with historic-looking apartment blocks, cafés, bars and shops. It's mid-afternoon and the streets are buzzing but the traffic is much lighter than it is in Canberra. And unlike in Australia, where cars are king, here half the city seems to be on foot or under pedal power. Cyclists, male and female, young and old, not one wearing a helmet, vie with Monika's car for dominance of the road. They're mostly riding bikes with high handlebars and front or rear baskets: one filled with groceries; another holds a small dog, standing, paws on the edge of the basket; a third is a family affair, two children with school rucksacks sitting in a specially built compartment in front. The air is mild, the sun shining, a soft breeze blowing, the light softer and paler than he's used to. Walker finds he has a wide smile on his face. It's his first visit to Europe and the gentle sunshine and pretty streetscape are all living up to his expectations. The energy on the street, the sheer density of life here, lends Berlin a vibrancy he appreciates. His jet lag seems to disperse on the breeze as he absorbs the sounds and scents of the city around him.

A quarter of an hour or so later, Monika slows. 'Shout if you see a parking place,' she says, then hits the brakes and makes a tight turn for a spot on the other side of the street. 'We're in luck! The apartment is only a few minutes away.' As he grabs his bag from the back seat, she says, 'Is that all you have? Wow, I need more luggage than that for a weekend away with Babs.'

He laughs. 'Yeah, I try to travel light. But I might be going home with a few bags more if I bring my nieces the presents they've asked for.' Blair's daughters, Zoe and Ruby, have sent requests via Blair for something nice from overseas. When Lucas asked what they'd like, a long list had pinged in, followed by a message from Blair to say that he was only to bring one thing for each of them. He'll see. He loves the girls, and what's an uncle for if not to spoil them?

He shoulders his bag, follows Monika around a corner and finds himself in the middle of a street market. 'Turkish market day,' she says. 'It's not always this busy here.'

She turns right along a crowded footpath. Traders are calling and shouting their wares. He doesn't understand a word but it's the universal sing-song of the market, stallholders striving to outbid each other. An old guy with a long grey ponytail, wearing shorts, sandals and socks, is standing in front of a fruit and vegetable stall, buying eggplants, lemons and fragrant-scented fresh herbs. Another stall is selling cheese, olives and Turkish flatbread, whetting Walker's appetite after the hours of nondescript plane food, and a third is showcasing jewellery to a party of young women in Birkenstocks and short dresses. The scent of incense floats off a stall with an Indian theme, and a young couple are serving coffee, strong and dark, from a small cart. A man carrying a cat in a mesh carrier pushes past, followed by a young woman with neon-orange-rimmed glasses, walking a bike and talking on her phone.

Monika leads him across a bridge over a canal and turns left along a bike path that runs beside the water. They pass a boules tournament taking place on a sandy square to the right of the path, then climb a couple of steps, emerging on a cobbled street lined by four- and five-storey-high apartment blocks. Painted in pale yellow, cream and mint green, they have ornate plaster decoration on their facades and balconies protruding from each floor.

'This is where you'll be staying.' Monika stops in front of the mint-green building, fiddles with the keys and opens the door on to a black-and-white-tiled entrance hall. There's a lift. Monika presses the button, they wait, but it seems to be stuck on the top floor.

'I don't mind walking up,' he says. To be honest, he fancies the exercise, some movement after all those hours on the plane. They walk up three flights of stairs with two apartments per floor and decorative stained-glass windows illuminating each landing. In the apartment he'll be staying in, there's a long, high-ceilinged, light-filled hallway. To the left is a bathroom and then a kitchen with a square wooden table in the corner beside a window.

'The bedroom is through here,' says Monika, turning the other way into a double-aspect room. The first half is a living space with a black-and-white rug on the pale wooden floor, an L-shaped white sofa facing big windows, and striking artworks on the walls. French doors open to the second half of the room, the bedroom, where a big bed with large pillows and a soft duvet looks very inviting. A glass door opens from the bedroom to a sunny balcony that is a riot of plants and flowers. He steps outside; the balcony overlooks the trees and the canal and he can see the colourful awnings of the market stalls on the other side of the water. There are birds chirping in the trees and the sound of the market drifts across the water.

'Wow, nice place,' he says, for it is. It's very different from the modern homes he's lived in, both in Australia and in Boston, and he likes the feel of it, taking in the decorative plasterwork, the floorboards, the wooden doors with brass handles, and the contrast with the clean modern decor and contemporary art. It's not huge, just these few rooms, but the ceilings, perhaps three metres high, and the big windows, give it a sense of spaciousness and charm.

'Do you want a coffee?' asks Monika.

'That'd be beaut,' he says. He needs one. His eyes are scratchy with tiredness and his brain foggy.

She pulls down a beaten-up stovetop espresso maker from a shelf in the kitchen, fills it with water and coffee and sets it on the stove, then opens the fridge and points inside. 'I got a few bits and pieces for you. Milk, cheese, ham, eggs, gherkins. There's fresh bread in the bread bin too.'

'Thanks so much,' he says. 'You've gone out of your way here.

I really appreciate it.'

The coffee, when it comes, is strong and fortifying and helps him to stay awake and chat to Monika, but he's relieved when, after downing hers, she pushes her chair back and says, 'OK, I have to get back to the gallery. Babs says she'll text you and make plans for later.'

'Righto,' he says. 'Thanks again for everything.'

After she leaves, he grabs his wash bag and stands under the shower. It's a vintage model, over the bath, but the pressure is good and the water is hot and relaxing. Then he pulls the curtains to darken the bedroom and sets his alarm for 7 p.m. A couple of hours' kip will do him good and Barbara probably won't be finished much before that.

• • •

Monika has forced herself to leave; she could have stayed chatting to the sexy Aussie but he looked tired and she wants him to be on good form when Babs finally gets her arse away from work and pays him a visit. If it were her, and some hot guy had travelled halfway round the world to see her, you wouldn't find her hanging around at work, let alone at a crime scene or something gruesome like that, which is probably where Babs is right now. She sighs, pulls out her phone and sends Babs a text:

> All good, I've left him at the apartment. And he is hot! Fire girl! You need to get over here asap and give him a proper welcome.

Chapter 10

Mildersee

4 p.m.

The lake colony is deserted and still. It's a sunny afternoon and Barbara had expected there would be people around, but the local police have kept the entire place cordoned off, a baby-faced rookie, sitting in his car at the turn-off, blocking access. He let her through and she drove to the edge of the colony and left her car in the small parking lot. As she's about to set off on the ten-minute walk to the lakeside and Ritter's cabin, a message from Monika pings in: Lucas is safely here. Her stomach gives a little leap of anticipation. She can't quite believe she'll be seeing him later. She's putting her phone back in her bag when it rings, the noise startling in the silence of the empty colony.

'Johannes Reimann – I'm the technician that's working on the Mildersee forensics,' says the voice in her ear when she answers it. 'I thought you'd like to know that we found quite a lot of DNA traces on the beer bottles from the boat. That's not unusual – from the brewery to transportation to the store, they'll have been handled by any number of people. But what is interesting is that we found no trace of the deceased's DNA or fingerprints on them. He never touched either of them.'

Barbara thanks him and, as she puts the phone away, she thinks that this is confirmation of what she's believed all along – Ritter wasn't alone in the boat when he died – and that this is very much a murder inquiry. She strides out along the path towards the scene but she's barely walked a few minutes before the silence and emptiness of the place presses in and she feels a slight sense of unease creep up on her. The same residual fear that she seems to carry with her since Australia, of spaces too quiet, too empty, devoid of people. The forest to her left is dark, a cluster of spruce trees sucking up light, dense shade beneath and between them. On her right, pine trees, their branches high above her, shudder in the wind and throw their dry needles onto the sandy ground at her feet. The clouds are scudding across the sun, the light brightening and fading in quick succession. She's wearing a thin t-shirt with her trousers. It was warm and muggy in Berlin, but out here, by the water and with the threat of rain in the air, she can feel goosebumps rising on her arms.

Even as children, she and Rita never felt fully at ease in Mildersee. Something about its shaded lanes, the mix of half-abandoned plots – with gardens dry and dying, cabins mildewed and forlorn – and the high hedges that fence in the hard faces of the residents who remain, has always given it an unsettling, slightly eerie feel that's at odds with the tranquillity of the natural surrounds.

In the past, when this region was part of communist East Germany, Mildersee had been a perk for members of the Party, the Stasi secret police and other loyalists. By the time she and Rita were children, those days were over, but something of the energy remained. A toxic mix of faded exclusivity and secrets long held. In the last five to ten years, Berliners – young families and others like Mattias

Ritter – have been reclaiming some of the cabins, and she's heard her parents talk about the bad feeling the incoming gentrification has caused among some long-term local residents.

She turns down one of the lanes that run towards the lake, using her mental image of the map Schmidt sent her to navigate, walking briskly now, disconcerted by the stillness. She can hear her footsteps scrunching along the sandy track, the rustle of tiny birds in the brush and a woodpecker somewhere in the distance, its distinctive tat-tat-tat echoing in the silence. It's rained out here recently; the top layer of the sandy path is dark grey and as she walks she leaves pale footprints in her wake. Slugs, every shade of brown from russet to mahogany, some tiny, others as long and fat as a man's little finger, are congregating on the damp track beside fallen pinecones. The grass to either side is up to her thighs, damp hairy fronds brushing against her legs as she passes. The breeze is picking up, the sky darkening. She stops to take a cardigan out of her bag, the silence heavy in her ears. Even the birdsong seems to have stopped.

She's about to set off again when she thinks she hears footsteps. The back of her neck prickles. She slows her breathing, listens again, but the sound is gone. Or perhaps it was never there. You're such a city girl, she tells herself, unnerved by the absence of noise.

She starts walking, paying more attention this time, and a moment later she's certain. There are footsteps, following hers. She spins around but, by the sound of it, they're off to her left, a parallel lane, a couple of blocks over. She can hear the soft, slow steps of someone creeping along. If it weren't for the unnatural stillness of the colony, she wouldn't have noticed. She spies a lane ahead intersecting the one she's walking on. If she turns there, she'll be able to cross over and confront whoever is tracking her. She steps onto the thick grass that grows in the middle of the lane and breaks into a measured run, using the lush foliage to muffle the sound of her footsteps, making quick work of the two short blocks that separate her from the next lane. Just before she reaches it, she slows, pulls her service revolver from its holster, cocks it and stands, her gun pointed towards the intersection.

A moment later a man in his early twenties, wearing khaki trousers and a camouflage-patterned t-shirt, carrying a hunting rifle under one arm and the corpse of a small animal in the other hand, comes into view. He's creeping along. As she watches, he stops, head to one side, listening: he's lost the sound of her footsteps. His rifle isn't cocked: she has the advantage. She steps out into the lane, her gun pointed at him.

'Police! Drop the gun and put your hands up.'

She sees shock flit across his face, then his features harden into contempt. 'I've got a hunting permit – I can carry,' he says.

'Not here, you can't. This is a crime scene, it's cordoned off. You're not allowed to be here. Drop the gun.'

He thinks about it for a moment. She feels a tremor in her hand; she's in a dangerous position here. Eventually he steps to one side, hangs the dead animal – a rabbit, she notes – across the fence and lays the gun down on the grass. 'Happy?' he says.

With the immediate sense of threat diminished, Barbara looks more closely at him. He's tall and heavy-set with a thick neck. His hair is shorn close to his head, and he has a close-cropped beard and small light-blue eyes. A knife in a holster is strapped to his thigh and he's carrying a hip pack, khaki-coloured, that's stuffed with plants. Barbara can see that his right bicep sports a crossed-hammer-and-sword tattoo that has neo-Nazi connotations, and a skull that could be the SS Totenkopf is inked onto the side of his neck. As she looks at him she has the sense he's assessing her too, noting her immigrant background, judging her, dismissing her.

'You don't look like a cop,' he says, confirming her perception. 'Show me some ID before I take that little pistol from you . . .'

She reaches her free hand into her pocket, flicks open her ID.

'Detective Barbara Guerra, Berlin Kriminalpolizei. Who are you and what are you doing here?'

'I live here. It's a free country. You can't stop me from walking here.'

'What's your name?' she asks.

'Koch. Willie Koch.'

This is the man who Mattias Ritter thought was stalking his girlfriend. Ritter had grounds to be anxious, Barbara thinks: the man in front of her exudes aggression.

'The colony is closed to the public after this weekend's death,' she says. 'And you're not a resident. What are you doing here?'

'We've got a fucking cabin – I've got every right to be here. More right than you.'

No one has mentioned the Kochs having a cabin at the lake and Willie Koch obviously knows about Ritter's death, notes Barbara. He isn't surprised at the news, hasn't asked any questions.

'Were you in the colony on Saturday?' she asks.

'What is this, some kind of interrogation? Fuck you. I'm not answering any more questions.'

'You were following me,' she says.

He looks contemptuous. 'You? You wish. You're not my type. I heard something. I thought maybe it was a deer.'

She ignores the insult and the belittling tone but doesn't believe him. She's almost certain he was tracking her; with what intent, who knows. 'You'd be pretty unlikely to find deer in the middle of the colony,' she says.

'That shows how little you know. They come through here when it's quiet, to drink at the lake.'

Before she can ask anything further, he says: 'Can you stop pointing that pistol at me. I don't trust a cop not to put a bullet in me when there's no one around to witness it. Especially a girl cop who's got the shakes.'

Barbara looks down at her weapon, half surprised to find herself still holding it. She clicks the safety back on and holsters it. She might be overreacting here, the silence and the unfamiliar territory making her jittery. She acknowledges, angry with herself, that she hasn't got a proper handle on her nerves since Australia and all that happened there. Maybe Fischer is right: maybe she's not fit for policing anymore.

'You can go,' she says. 'But stay out of the colony. We'll let you know when you're allowed to return. And I need to ask you some questions about the weekend. I'll have Officer Schmidt call to arrange a time with you.'

She wants to clarify his whereabouts over the weekend and his relationship with Ritter, but she suspects that, right now, she won't get any cooperation from him. A fact that's confirmed when he clears his throat and spits a phlegmy glob in the direction of her feet.

'Fuck you. You can't tell me where I can and can't walk on my own land,' he says as he picks up his gun and his kill and pushes past her towards the lake.

Chapter 11

Berlin

7 p.m.

Barbara is almost back at home, the residual fear from her encounter with Willie Koch taking time to dissipate. She's annoyed with herself for giving in to anxiety, for overreacting, but there's something about him – the buzz of underlying aggression, the weapons he carries, the blatant misogyny. He's threatening. She wouldn't be surprised to find a record of violent behaviour, assaults and the like. She's making a mental note to look into his criminal background – if Mattias Ritter was murdered, their history of run-ins, added to any past convictions, would clearly make Koch a potential suspect – when her phone buzzes on the passenger seat beside her. She looks down. A message from Lucas.

> Hey! I made it, just had a bit of a snooze, feeling pretty good. U up for grabbing something to eat?

Her heart skips a quick beat. With her focus on the case at hand, she put Lucas to the back of her mind after receiving Monika's text.

Now he's here. Around the corner.

At the next red light, she picks up her phone and replies, typing fast.

Yes! Finishing work, can come by and pick you up in an hour?

That will give her time to get home, have a speedy shower and walk to where he's staying. She feels her heart lift. Lucas is here and they're having dinner together. It seems surreal, though in a very nice way.

But by the time she rings his bell forty-five minutes later, she's feeling slightly panicky with nerves again. All the emotion and horror of her visit to Australia has been building inside her during her shower and on the short walk to Lucas's apartment. The endless heat, the dust, the isolation, the daily fear of Rita missing, maybe dead. She remembers it viscerally, feels it as strongly as if she were still in Caloodie, alone and far from home. As she stands by the front door, she can feel her heart beating fast. This isn't a good idea. Why did she say yes to a visit from Walker? He'd been the only light in a dark time and place, but he's so indelibly associated with that moment that his being here is bringing everything she's pushed far down back to the surface.

The front door buzzes open and she goes inside and stands, momentarily undecided, before stepping into the elevator. She's put on her favourite red blouse and her fire-engine-red lipstick, but the mirrored walls of the lift reflect a pale and anxious face. She turns away, faces the door, as the numbers inch upwards – *1, 2, 3*. The doors slide open and there he is.

His hair is shorter, almost shaved at the sides, but the top is as curly as she remembers, his eyes are warm, and he's smiling broadly. He's wearing a t-shirt that accentuates his broad shoulders and tanned arms, and a pair of jeans. And in the instant of seeing him, her fear and anxiety recede, and she finds she's smiling too.

There's a millisecond of awkwardness as they look at each other. They've talked so often, been friends for over two years now, but it's the first time they've seen each other in person since she left Australia, a few days after they'd found Rita. Then he laughs and says, 'Bloody hell, it's beaut to see you, Barbara!' and she instinctively steps forward and hugs him.

His hug back is warm and comforting. When they move apart, they look at each other for a long moment, big smiles on both their faces. Walker looks well. He's obviously recovered from his various injuries; he's fit and tanned and seems happier than the last time she saw him, when his grandmother was dying and he was grieving.

'How was the flight? Do you like the place?' she asks.

'Yeah, it's great. Come in,' he says. 'I need to put my boots on and then we can go eat. I'm bloody starving – I could eat a horse and chase the rider!'

She laughs. Walker's Aussie-isms are impenetrable to her, but she likes the sound of his voice and she usually gets the gist of his meaning.

'I know a place that serves very big portions,' she says.

'That's exactly what we need,' he says, and leads her into the apartment, which to her relief is large, bright and stylish and obviously doesn't belong to one of Monika's more anarchist friends. It's bigger than her own and nicely fitted out, and she's happy that Monika found such a welcoming place for Walker to stay. It's no less than he deserves. He saved her life and Rita's, and she'll be forever in his debt.

• • •

When the lift doors open and Barbara is standing there, Walker feels a surge of warmth and protectiveness. She's exactly as he remembers, petite and striking, with the upright posture, the core of determination and strength that he so admires. When she steps forward and hugs him and he smells the newly washed scent of her hair and skin, a shiver of recognition runs through him. It's been too long since they've seen each other.

He leads her inside, puts on his boots and they walk down the stairs rather than wait for the lift, chatting in that rapid, disjointed way that you do when you haven't seen someone for a long time and there are a hundred things you want to tell them and ask them all at once.

The restaurant she's chosen offers German cuisine, and is fifteen minutes' walk from his place. It's casual and pleasant, with windows on three sides, wooden tables flanked by benches, vases filled with wildflowers and candles in mismatched vintage candleholders. The place is buzzing and the low rays of the evening sun spill through the west-facing windows. The smell of food gets him salivating. It's probably breakfast time at home but he's got an appetite for a big meal, no matter what time his body clock thinks it is.

'If you're hungry you should order the schnitzel,' she says.

He does and it's a good decision: the piece of crumbed veal, so big it hangs over the edge of the large plate, is served with a potato salad that is tangy and rich and flavourful. 'I must be hungry,' he says, laughing. 'Even the salad tastes bloody amazing!'

He finds himself more relaxed than he's felt for a long time. As they chat, thoughts of Markovich, of organised crime, of his future career, all disappear. The food is warming and delicious, the beers are cold and refreshing, Barbara is sitting opposite him, and life is good.

As the evening darkens, a server comes by and lights the candles, creating a softer, more intimate mood. Their conversation gets easier, the friendship finding its feet again. He tells her about Blair and his family and Grace's progress at law school. 'How about you? How are things with you?' he asks.

There's a brief pause and then she exhales a small sigh and tells him that she's struggling a bit at work. 'Walking to meet you earlier brought it all back. The isolation, the fear. I thought I was having a panic attack. And this afternoon, on a case, I overreacted. I was more scared than I needed to be. I wonder if that's why my boss is sidelining me. I think he has the feeling that I'm not ready for tough cases yet. Maybe he's right . . .'

Walker hears the doubt in her voice, so unlike the strong woman he knows her to be. 'Look, I suffer from it too,' he says, thinking of Markovich, of the feelings that flood through him when he hears the big bikie's name; even when he sees a Vandal or simply hears mention of the club. 'I'd bet my bottom dollar all the cops you work with have times when they feel like this. Don't beat yourself up. You're a great cop and your boss is an idiot if he can't see that.'

She makes a face, a half-grimace, but then a smile breaks through. 'I'm very happy you're here, Lucas,' she says. 'It's so good to see you and to have someone to talk to who really understands.'

He smiles back. 'Me too,' he says, knowing it's true. No matter what the next week brings, going back into the lion's den that surrounds Markovich, it will be worth it because it's given him the chance to finally spend more time with Barbara.

Chapter 12

Berlin

Tuesday, 6 a.m.

Walker wakes to soft morning light filtering through the gauzy white curtains of the bedroom. Nothing about the room is familiar and it takes him a second to figure out where he is. Berlin – he's in Berlin, about to start his hunt for Markovich. His stomach tightens at the thought, and he rolls over, picks up his phone from the bedside table: 6 a.m. He's had less than six hours' sleep but he's wide awake and ravenously hungry, the jet lag, the time difference, still messing with his internal clock.

He goes out to the balcony, wearing only his boxers, the morning air cool on his bare chest. The sky is pale blue, streaked with a hint of white cloud. Below him, the city is quiet. A lone jogger runs along the path beside the canal, where the water gleams in the early sunshine. He stands for a moment, savouring the foreignness of it all. The nineteenth-century apartment blocks, the cobbled street, all so different from modern Canberra, and even more so the tiny outback town of Caloodie that he calls home. He takes a picture of the view with his phone to send to his sister, Grace.

When he opens his WhatsApp messages, he can see that she's online. She's up late – it's gone midnight in Boston. He pulls up the photo and writes in Berlin, pretty cool, and sends it.

It's only seconds before she answers him. Nice!! Then: what are you doing in Germany?

Here for work and to visit my friend Barbara, he replies.

The box at the top tells him she's typing. Finally!!!! comes the reply. Did you two get together yet?

Hahaha, he answers. What's up with you? How's law school?

Grace is at Harvard Law School, at the start of her journey to become a defence attorney. She came to visit him in Australia last year and though the holiday didn't go exactly as planned, they grew closer through the experience. He's proud of her decision to study law, and all the hard work she's putting into it. They spend fifteen minutes texting back and forth and the chat leaves him, as ever, with a warm feeling in his heart for his little sister.

Despite the large meal he ate last night with Barbara, his stomach is rumbling. He pulls on a t-shirt and walks into the kitchen, where he finds a loaf of bread, crusty and fresh, part of the haul that Barbara's friend Monika brought with her yesterday, in a bread bin on the countertop. The fridge has eggs, butter, milk, cheese, ham and a punnet of fresh tomatoes, and he finds coffee and jam in a cupboard. He ponders his options and decides on a ham, cheese and tomato omelette. It takes him a while in the unfamiliar kitchen but the result – four eggs, generous grating of cheese, plenty of ham and tomatoes and three slices of fresh bread and butter – soothes his hunger. The coffee maker is a tiny black espresso pot that looks like it's been in the family for generations and he has to google how to use it, filling the base with water, the small metal stopper with coffee, boiling it on the stovetop. It may be old-fashioned but the coffee it produces, strong and flavourful, meets with his approval. He drinks it, sated and relaxed, on the balcony and plans his day.

First on the list is a meeting with Sophie's German police contact at the LKA, the Berlin State Criminal Police, a division that handles supra-regional and very serious crimes. He's due to meet the head of the team that specialises in the Balkan mafias in Berlin. He's hoping they can begin to work out the details on how they'll find Markovich and bring him to justice.

When Walker checks the location of the LKA on his phone, he discovers it's not a long walk, less than an hour. He puts on his most respectable outfit – ironed shirt and his only pair of non-denim trousers – and heads off with plenty of time to spare. Google Maps directs him along the canal. He walks along the towpath, past a café with an outdoor terrace strung with fairy lights and a handful of tables with people sitting in the sun drinking their first coffee of the day, then turns right across a little bridge, walking through a pleasant and leafy residential zone. He notices again how quiet the streets are, as many bikes as cars bumping along the cobbles, and there's a relaxed vibe, even now coming up to 9 a.m., what is likely the start of the working day. No one seems to be in a hurry, or even heading to work. He passes several more cafés, most with outdoor terraces filled with people enjoying the sunny morning. The look here is very different from Canberra or Sydney. There's a punk edge to the crowd, lots of Doc Marten boots, even in this summer weather, black t-shirts and black jeans or black dresses. But the atmosphere is peaceful, and he decides he has time for one more coffee before his meeting. He finds a table at the next café and orders a flat white from a bored young woman who, to his relief, speaks to him in English. He sits, absorbing the unfamiliar but pretty streetscape of this very European capital. The coffee is invigorating and the buzz of being far from home, and back at work, runs through him.

When he walks on, his route takes him across a busy road and into a large park. Mature trees line the pedestrian path and he passes a young couple practising walking a tightrope they have strung between two of the trees. Only a handful of dog walkers, the occasional jogger and cyclist, pass him during the fifteen minutes it takes him to walk across the park, but as he approaches the exit it starts to feel a bit seedy. A handful of people sitting on benches, their clothes threadbare and dirty. One guy is arguing with himself, shouting profanities into the air; a woman, stick thin, her hair straggly, approaches him, hand out, looking for money, he presumes. He shakes his head and she mutters something as he walks away. At the park's exit, a small group of men loitering near the gate check him out, their eyes making calculations. One steps forward. 'You want weed ... marijuana?' he asks. Walker shakes his head again and keeps going, slightly surprised at the brazenness of the offer.

He emerges onto another busy road and walks for ten minutes alongside an old airfield. He's at the top of a slight hill that offers views across the city, and a striking building with a bulbous top and tall spike above it catches his eye. It's giving off distinct space-age vibes, standing proud against the blue sky. Intrigued, he googles it and discovers it's a former TV tower, now city icon, Berlin's equivalent of the Eiffel Tower. The airfield, too, is impressive, with a terminal building that curves in a crescent shape, facing the former runways. The sense of history in this city is palpable, he thinks, as he turns left into a largely residential street lined with shops and apartments, and finds the five-storey police HQ he's been aiming for. He goes into reception, negotiates the security process, and is told to wait. It's a good few minutes before a slim man wearing a dark suit and a white shirt with a striped tie approaches him.

'DS Walker?' he asks.

Walker straightens up. 'That's right,' he says.

'Welcome. I'm Detective Director Günther Schneider. I work with Senior Detective Director Graf on organised crime. His wife had a baby at the weekend, and he is on leave, so he asked me to meet with you.'

Günther Schneider doesn't look much like a cop; he could go undercover as an accountant, or maybe a banker, thinks Walker. He's slim, shorter than Walker, with conservatively cut blond hair and a beaky nose propping up a pair of wire-rimmed glasses. He seems distinctly unlikely to head up a division of organised crime and couldn't be more different from Walker's boss, Dan Rutherford, who is bulky, burly and more like a boxer than a banker.

Schneider leads Walker up a couple of flights of stairs. He pauses at the top. 'Would you like a coffee?' he asks. Walker, who generally doesn't rate the quality of police station coffee, declines, and Schneider directs him into a large meeting room, where they sit opposite each other at a conference table that could comfortably seat twelve.

'So how can I help you?' asks Schneider. 'I understand you're here on a case pertaining to a Balkan cartel . . .'

Walker nods. 'That's right,' he says, giving Schneider the run-down on Markovich and how the team's search has led them to Berlin. 'We obviously want to bring him in and I'm sure there'd be big wins for you in it too. He's a fairly big deal.'

Schneider raises an eyebrow. 'Your intelligence is incorrect: I doubt he's a big player,' he says. 'While the Balkan cartels certainly cooperate with biker gangs like the Hells Angels or your Vandals, it is extremely unlikely that your man would be influential or working at a very high level. These Balkan groups are very much family-based. Membership is usually limited to blood relations, and they only use non-family for smaller jobs. That's a problem for us, of course – it's hard to get brothers and cousins to inform on each other. But it means your man is likely on the outside, even if he is Serbian. Markovich is a Serbian name?'

'Yes, his dad was Serb, but his mother's family are from

Montenegro, and we've discovered he has a close family connection to Vaso Ulić.'

Schneider nods, exhibiting interest in the conversation for the first time. 'Ahh, then that's a different story.'

'You know Ulić?' asks Walker.

'Of course,' says Schneider. 'Europe is the world's number-one cocaine market these days and most of that is down to Balkan traffickers like Ulić. The Balkan cartels dominate the logistics of moving coke from Andean production labs to European streets.'

'And Australian ones,' says Walker. 'Look, Markovich is close to Ulić. If I can find him and we put together an operation to pull him in, you might get some intel that leads to a big bust.'

'The clans have very strong traditions of honour and revenge and a law of silence that prohibits cooperation with the police under the threat of death,' says Schneider. 'If he is here, and if you find him, I doubt very much your man will talk.' Walker tries to keep his face neutral but perhaps some of his frustration bleeds out into his expression because Schneider adds: 'I checked with my team before I met you and they don't believe this Markovich is in the city. He's quite distinctive in appearance so it's not as though he would be easy to miss. I will pass the information on to the Hamburg team. If your man is dealing with imports and exports, he is more likely working a port city.'

It's true that Markovich has been in two port cities, first Guayaquil in Ecuador, then Rotterdam, but Walker's certain that his intel is right. Markovich is in Berlin.

'I'm certain he's here . . .'

'I'd like to help you, DS,' says Schneider, sounding anything but inspired to assist, 'but, as I'm sure you understand, there are many bigger problems that my team are dealing with. Last week a thirty-four-year-old man and a forty-nine-year-old man were killed outside a bar in a drive-by shooting that has Balkan links. Imagine – dozens of gunshots, sprayed indiscriminately from a passing vehicle. An eight-year-old girl was shot and is fighting for her life in hospital. The Balkan cartels have access to firearms and are inured to violence after decades of war and criminal activity. They are involved in long-running feuds, brazen in their criminality and largely indifferent to law enforcement. One man may be important to you, but we have bigger issues to deal with.'

Walker breathes deep. This German cop is patronising him. Markovich may only be one man, and he's the first to admit that he has personal reasons to want to see him behind bars, but Markovich also holds the key to significantly reducing drug imports into Australia – and, Walker would bet good money, into Europe and Germany too. Bringing him in will strike a significant blow to Ulić's organisation. He breathes once more. Antagonising the local cops won't help bring Markovich to justice.

'If the drive-by has Balkan links, maybe my bloke is involved?'

Schneider thinks it through. 'I don't think Ulić is involved. Although his clan are big players in the Netherlands, Spain and the Baltics, they're still relatively minor here in Germany. But I'll pass the information on to my investigating team. If they need more, they'll be in touch.'

As a final ploy, Walker tries pulling rank with Sophie's original contact. 'Senior Detective Director Graf promised my boss that you would have resources to help us with this operation,' he says.

'That's not correct,' says Schneider, not sugarcoating the rejection. 'The director told me he'd arranged to meet you, that is all. We will keep this Markovich on file and I will pass the information to our teams. But as it stands, with last week's shooting, we do not have the resources to assist you further.'

Walker is at a loss. He'd been expecting to talk to someone who had been briefed by Sophie and who was behind this operation – if not enthusiastic, at least willing to help. Schneider is the exact opposite. 'Fair enough,' he says eventually. 'If I can find Markovich, if I can direct you to him, would you be willing to run an operation to bring him in? That's obviously outside my jurisdiction here.'

'I will not make any promises,' says Schneider. 'Find him first and let us see where that takes us.'

Chapter 13

Kummerfeld

8.30 a.m.

Barbara is eating breakfast at the kitchen table at her parents' house. She drove out early this morning, planning to go back to Mildersee with the autopsy report in hand, and dropped in to see Rita and Lola and earn back some brownie points with her mother after her early departure on Sunday. But Rita's still in bed, there's no sign of the autopsy report and she's just heard from Leon Kaiser's lawyer that he'll be available to give a statement in Berlin this afternoon, so it might have been a wasted trip. She picks up her phone, refreshes her email. Still nothing.

Rita appears, Lola in her arms, both of them looking sleepy. 'Hello, you two,' says Barbara with a smile, standing to hug her sister and give the puppy a pat. 'I see Lola's still sleeping with you . . .'

She hears her mother's half-hearted 'Tsk' behind her.

'She doesn't like sleeping alone,' says Rita. Maria, who is standing at the stove making the scrambled eggs that Barbara said she didn't need, tsks again, but there's no heat in it. Lola has won everyone's hearts.

Maria comes over and points at the bread, jam, cheese and ham on the table. 'You both need to eat,' she says, hands on hips. As Barbara, dutiful as ever, sits down and reaches for another slice of bread, the doorbell rings.

'Can you get that, Rita?' says Maria. 'It's probably the Lauter boy for the paper money. My purse is on the hallway table.'

Rita looks at Barbara, who shakes her head. 'I'm eating,' she says. 'You get it.' Rita's therapist has told them that she needs to start engaging with the world again, that they can't let her keep on avoiding people, avoiding life, so her parents have been asking Rita to run errands, go to Aldi for bread and milk, answer the door, little things like that.

The bell rings again, echoing down the hallway. 'Rita, get that now, please...' Maria's voice is firm, but Barbara can hear the tremble beneath it. After all this time, Rita doesn't even want to open the door to the paperboy.

'*Alright!*' Rita sounds like a petulant teenager. She picks up Lola, holding her tight against her chest like a shield, and stomps down the hallway. Barbara can see her mother's shoulders shaking. She goes over to the stove, gives her a big hug.

'It's going to be OK, Mamá,' she says.

Her mother wipes a hand over her eyes. 'Rita, our little adventurer, the one who always talked to everyone, tried anything...'

'She'll get there, Mamá, I know she will.'

As Barbara hugs her mother tighter, she hears a voice that sounds like the local officer, Schmidt. What the hell is he doing here? She walks into the hallway – Schmidt and Rita are standing at the door. Schmidt has his smile on full beam and Rita is saying something to him. Barbara stands for a moment, unobserved. These small things – Rita talking to someone she doesn't know, and a man at that – can feel like monumental steps. She senses her mother's tearfulness creeping up on her and steps briskly forward.

'What's happened, Officer? Is there some news on the case?' she asks, walking down the hallway towards him.

He looks at her, and Rita takes the chance to slide away. 'Nice to meet you!' calls Schmidt to her disappearing back, but Rita doesn't respond. Barbara notices that he watches for a second longer, before pulling his eyes back to her, smile undimmed.

'No news, Detective,' he says. 'I'm reporting for duty.'

'Here?' She is incredulous. 'How did you know where my parents live?'

'Well . . .' He looks momentarily embarrassed. 'I'm police, right? And I saw your car out front. Chief Barsch told me to report to you and I thought it would be easier to catch you here. Sorry, I should have called—'

'Yes, you should have,' she says. 'I'm not sure if I'll need you today or not. I'm waiting for the autopsy and toxicology reports and then I'll make a decision.'

'OK, right. So . . . I'll head into the station and wait to hear from you?'

'Right,' she says. As he turns and walks down the path, something about his body language, a dejected slope of his shoulders, makes Barbara feel guilty. He's just being helpful, keen if a bit over-enthusiastic.

'Schmidt,' she calls. He turns immediately. 'Sorry, you took me by surprise. Come in for a coffee. I'll chase the autopsy results, and we can make a plan for the rest of the day.'

•••

Schmidt's smile should be registered as a public service, thinks Barbara. He sat at the breakfast table, drinking a coffee, smiling at her mother for the twenty minutes it took her to chase the coroner's office, receive the autopsy report, finish her breakfast and get them out of the house. Rita had disappeared, but her mother was clearly smitten. She offered Schmidt breakfast and then a packed lunch for the two of them and only Barbara's firm hand and sideways glare had prevented her from pressing the issue.

Barbara tosses her keys to Schmidt on their way out. 'You can drive,' she says. 'I'm going to chase for the toxicology report.'

She pulls her seat belt on, looks over at Schmidt and says, 'I ran into Willie Koch at the lake yesterday, and he told me he had a cabin at Mildersee. But when I checked the map you sent me, he's not listed as a resident.'

'Ah, yeah, sorry. The Kochs do have access to a cabin. It's not theirs – it's a cabin for whoever is the mayor of the town. The council keeps it maintained. Because they live so near, I don't think they ever use it.'

'OK. We'll have a look at it when we get out there,' says Barbara, pulling out her phone to call toxicology. As she's looking for the number, an email alert pops up. The report she's waiting for has landed in her inbox. Miracles will never cease – this day is looking better already. She reads quickly through both the autopsy and the toxicology, does a bit of research on her phone to help her understand the findings.

• • •

When the Berlin detective puts her phone away, Schmidt says, 'Your mother is very nice. I don't think my parents would be so kind to a stranger at the breakfast table.'

'Don't get used to it,' she says. 'I don't want you becoming a morning fixture.'

He laughs. 'Noted. Was that your sister who answered the door?'

'Yeah,' she says. 'Rita, my younger sister.'

Schmidt hasn't stopped thinking of the striking woman who

opened the door to him, similar in looks to the detective sitting beside him but more delicate, and with eyes that were wounded and fearful. He'd had an urge to tell her everything would be alright, that he would make sure of it, without even knowing what it was that had hurt her so badly.

'I think I frightened her somehow,' he says. 'When she opened the door and saw me, she looked really scared. I thought she was going to shut it in my face until I told her I was a colleague of yours.'

Barbara lets out a long sigh. Schmidt looks over at her. 'Rita went through a very traumatic experience a couple of years ago,' she says. 'And she hasn't really recovered. It's horrible, for her and for all of us.'

Chapter 14

Mildersee
10 a.m.

'Male, forty-eight years old, cause of death pulmonary edema, that's fluid in the lungs, caused by congestive heart failure. Time of death between eight p.m. and midnight on Saturday.' Barbara is standing with Schmidt outside Mattias Ritter's cabin at the Mildersee colony, reading from the autopsy report.

'I thought he was poisoned?' Schmidt is confused.

'Yes, I'm coming to that. Analysis of the upper gastrointestinal tract, mouth and pharynx proved inconclusive, however evidence of a toxic substance, *Taxus baccata*, was found in the lower GIT. Given this, and the ancillary evidence found at the scene, along with the symptoms preceding death, it's possible to conclude the deceased ingested a fatal dose of *Taxus baccata*.'

'What's *Taxus baccata*?' asks Schmidt.

'Yew needles,' says Barbara, pulling up the toxicology report. 'Food from all locations we tested were clear,' she reads. 'However, when we tested liquid found in a cup at the deceased's cabin, we found it to be tea made from a combination of mashed yew needles, *Taxus baccata* and mint, *Mentha spicata*.'

'Yew? As in the tree?' asks Schmidt.

'Right,' says Barbara. She keeps reading. 'Yew needles contain taxine B and are toxic in very small doses. Signs of yew poisoning are non-specific, including nausea, vomiting, impaired vision, abdominal pain or muscle spasms, followed by . . .' She flicks on. '. . . various medical things including heart arrhythmia and then heart failure. When the heart is not able to pump efficiently, blood can back up into the veins that take blood through the lungs. Symptoms include coughing up phlegm that looks pink or has blood in it—'

'That fits with what we saw at the scene,' says Schmidt.

Barbara nods. She goes back to the toxicology report. 'According to this, tea made from yew is a clear, light-green liquid that is hard to differentiate from other types of tea, and the mint would have largely masked the odour and flavour of the yew. And a fatal dose can be contained in one glass. Wow, you really don't need to drink much of it.'

'Someone added mint to the tea so that he didn't know he was drinking poison?'

'Right. There's some background information in the toxicology that's quite interesting,' says Barbara. She looks down, keeps reading. 'There is no known antidote to ingesting yew, but inducing vomiting within one hour and the recovery of plant matter from the stomach, which can be performed up to several hours after ingestion, can save a life. OK, that means if someone had found him early enough, he might have lived. Maybe that's why the murderer put Ritter on the boat . . . So that no one would find him in time.'

The two of them stand in silence, digesting what they've read. The morning sun is warm on their shoulders, the colony quiet. The water is shimmering blue, the breeze gentle. It's a lovely summer day by the lake, a similar day to Saturday, when, it seems likely, someone rowed out onto the water with Ritter, drank a beer and watched him slowly and horribly die.

Barbara dismisses the vision and goes back to the report, orders the facts in her mind. 'The time from ingesting a lethal dose to death is usually two to five hours, with symptoms occurring from thirty minutes to an hour following ingestion,' she says. 'Given the time of death and the last time he was known to be alive – when he was arguing with someone over at the lake around five p.m. – that means Ritter drank the tea sometime between six p.m. and ten p.m.,' she says, thinking out loud. 'We need to narrow down what he was doing during that time and who he was with.'

Schmidt nods, writing the information into his notebook.

'And the other questions are why and who,' says Barbara. 'Who here has a motive to murder Ritter? Nina Hartmann, perhaps – her relationship with Ritter was ending. It seems that Leon Kaiser might be involved with Hartmann in some way, and lust and betrayal are often behind a death like this. We also know that Ritter argued with someone shortly before he died, and we need to pinpoint who that was.'

'I think his girlfriend fits the bill,' says Schmidt. 'They'd had an argument that day, and they were about to break up. You say she was a pharmacist, so she'd know what she was doing with regard to poison.'

Barbara thinks back. 'She was drinking peppermint tea when I spoke with her. And she says that she didn't leave here until just before eight p.m. on Friday, so she's not in the clear for the time of death either. She's a suspect,' she agrees. 'But we can't jump to conclusions. We need to consider Willie Koch too. He has a bad history with Ritter and I found him very aggressive yesterday.' Another thought comes to her. 'And he was carrying foraged plants.'

'Not Willie,' says Schmidt. 'There's no way Ritter would go out on a boat with him.'

It's a fair point; the men disliked each other. 'We don't know exactly what happened on Saturday,' says Barbara. 'Maybe Ritter was already unconscious, and Willie rowed him out to prevent him being found.'

Schmidt shrugs, looking doubtful.

'Let's have a look at the Koch cabin anyway,' says Barbara.

Schmidt pulls out a map of the colony and consults it. 'It's not far,' he says. They walk along the lakefront track for a few minutes, Schmidt counting off the cabins as he goes. 'This one,' he says, stopping in front of a cabin which, like Ritter's, has a lakeside view. The garden is neat and functional – the grass is mown and watered, a stand of three pine trees in the front right-hand corner of the block, but there are no flowers and no garden furniture. There's a shed, locked, in the back right-hand corner of the block and an outhouse, also locked, in the far left. Barbara walks up and peers in the window of the cabin. The room is simply furnished: a table with four chairs, a small kitchen beyond. No personal effects are visible.

'Like I said, I don't think they use it much,' says Schmidt from over her shoulder, and by the looks of it he's right. The cabin is clean and tidy but doesn't feel occupied.

They walk back onto the lakeside path and Barbara stands for a moment. 'We need to find out if Willie was here on the weekend anyway, even if just to rule him out,' she says. 'And we need to find the missing oar from the victim's boat. That might give us a DNA trace to match to those on the beers—' She stops talking as she hears footsteps on the path. She and Schmidt turn to look and a moment later a woman in her mid-sixties comes into view. Her silver-grey hair is pulled back into a tight bun and she's wearing grey trousers and a long-sleeved pale-blue blouse buttoned almost to the very top. She's pushing a bike and carrying a small backpack. Her eyes flit over Barbara but she seems to recognise

Schmidt and directs a small smile at him.

'Officer,' she says, coming towards them, 'I hope you've come back to keep us safe.'

Schmidt employs his high-watt smile, though Barbara feels it lacks a little of its previous conviction. 'This is Frau Renate Bauer,' he says, turning to Barbara. 'She lives here and she knew Mattias Ritter.'

'Have you found out more about what happened to Mattias?' asks Renate, keeping her focus on Schmidt. 'Is it true he was murdered? That's what everyone is saying. If someone killed Mattias . . . Mein Gott, it's too horrible to think about. He was such a lovely man.'

It's Barbara who answers. 'We don't know exactly what happened yet but we're making good progress with our investigation.'

Renate turns to look at Barbara, who can see that the older woman's eyes are glistening with tears. 'You really need to find out the truth. He deserves that. I'm going to miss him so much.'

'You were good friends?' asks Barbara.

'Yes. He often came to have a coffee and helped me with things around the cabin. I saw him on Saturday, you know. I can't believe it was the last time I'll ever speak with him . . .' Her voice catches.

'What time did you see him on Saturday?' asks Barbara. Schmidt has already asked Renate these questions, but it doesn't hurt to double-check.

'It was just after lunch. He was quite upset. He told me things weren't going well with his girlfriend. They'd had a big fight that morning, she was screaming and shouting at him – the whole colony heard her!' Renate Bauer shakes her head, her mouth in a disapproving line. 'She's not a good woman. She's having an affair with that Leon Kaiser. Betraying Mattias in full public view.' She shakes her head again. 'Poor Mattias. I know how awful that feels. He deserved better.'

'Did you see anything else on Saturday – anything out of the ordinary?' asks Barbara.

'No. I saw Nina go over to Kaiser's cabin not long after I spoke to Mattias, but that's hardly out of the ordinary.'

This information tallies with what the Krause couple told Schmidt and is further confirmation of Nina Hartmann's involvement with Kaiser, thinks Barbara. She needs to reinterview Hartmann, perhaps formally with a prosecutor, challenge the young woman's lies.

'Did you see Mattias Ritter later on Saturday? Perhaps talking to someone else?' Barbara is hoping Renate might have seen who Ritter was arguing with.

'No . . . I didn't see him again. But have you spoken to Willie Koch? He was waiting outside Mattias's cabin on Saturday afternoon. He wanted to talk to Mattias's girlfriend. He might have heard or seen something . . .'

Schmidt and Barbara exchange a glance. This is new information. 'What time did you see Willie?' asks Barbara.

'Oh, goodness – I don't keep track of time, not out here. It was not long after I saw Mattias's girlfriend go to visit Kaiser. Around three p.m., something like that . . .' Her voice trails off as she sees Schmidt and Barbara exchange another look. 'Oh no! You don't think Willie could have hurt Mattias, do you?' she says, doubt and shock in her voice.

Chapter 15

Mildersee
12 p.m.

'She's convinced it's a murder and she thinks Willie might be involved.' Schmidt is on the phone to the chief, keeping his voice low, trying to be discreet, his back turned to the Berlin detective, who is in her car checking something on the police database. 'The victim was poisoned, and she saw Willie in the colony yesterday carrying a bag of forest plants. And now a witness claims they saw Willie hanging around by the victim's cabin on the day of the murder. She's going to talk to Willie and confiscate his foraging bag for analysis.'

'Shit,' says Barsch. 'How the hell did you let this happen? I told you to keep her focus on the Berliners. I should have given her Klein to work with - at least he can follow orders—'

'The victim's girlfriend is a suspect too, and some Berlin DJ called Leon Kaiser,' says Schmidt, interjecting hastily. 'The two of them are supposedly having an affair, which might give them a motive. The detective also wants to find the missing oar from the boat; she thinks it might give us some DNA traces.'

'You said the victim was poisoned?'

'Yes, with leaves from a yew tree mixed with peppermint tea—'

'Yew leaves and peppermint tea! For fuck's sake. Willie'd be more likely to stab a knife in your throat. Tell her that - get her investigating these Berliners.'

Schmidt pauses. He's not totally sure that Barsch is reading Willie right. He knows Willie socially, from parties he's gone to with Klein, and Willie's always talking about how much he knows about forest animals and plants. He's heard Willie talk of how city folk have no idea, can't look after themselves, wouldn't last a day without a supermarket or a restaurant but that he could live off the land with the knowledge he's learnt from his grandmother and his mother, both locally born and bred. In the end he says, 'I tried, sir, but she won't listen—'

'For god's sake, you're useless,' says Barsch. 'Right, take her the long way round - I need to call Koch and give him a heads-up. And get her focused on someone else. I don't care how. Do what you need to do and find a way to get her interested in the Berliners instead.'

'Yes, sir,' says Schmidt, speaking into a void. Barsch has already hung up. He pockets the phone and walks back towards the car. The Berlin detective is intense and serious and good at her job. He's already learnt a few things from her, and he doesn't feel good about deceiving her. But he has to keep Barsch on side; he needs his approval, and a good reference, if he's ever going to get a promotion to detective. He'll have to do what he's told, or he'll end up stuck in this dead-end job for good.

• • •

Barbara has been checking INPOL, the police database, to see if Willie Koch is on the system. She can't find him, which means he doesn't have a criminal record and there are no outstanding warrants. She's surprised: by the look of him yesterday, the simmering aggression, she'd have bet he had a misdemeanour or assault against his name. Still, he had run-ins with Ritter in the past, was seen near Ritter's garden on Saturday, and the little bag he was carrying yesterday was full of plants. She needs to interview him and have his bag analysed for traces of yew too.

She gets out of the car and says, 'OK, let's go,' to Schmidt, who is pocketing his phone and looking more serious than usual, the big smile absent for once. They set off towards the Koch house, Schmidt leading the way. It's a fifteen-minute walk along a forest path that runs behind the colony. The path is wildly overgrown. Branches hang low, blocking the sunlight, and shrubs and bushes, lush and green, are colonising the track, their twigs and leaves grabbing and catching on Barbara's hair and clothes. It's quiet, even the bird calls are stilled, and despite the sunny day the forest is gloomy. The path is clearly not well used and she wonders how Schmidt seems to know the way without thinking about it.

'Are you friends with Willie Koch?' she asks as she follows behind him, the narrow path necessitating single file. She needs to know. This could mean there's a conflict of interest.

'No, I'm not,' says Schmidt. 'But everyone locally knows the family because his father, Herr Koch, is the mayor.' Barbara hasn't lived in Kummerfeld for quite a while but she remembers her father complaining about the Koch administration, allegations of corruption or something. Before she can ask Schmidt more about it, he says, 'I know Willie's a bit of a thug but I don't think he would kill someone. Especially not someone like Ritter, whom he barely knows. What would be his motive?'

'Karin Weber told me that Ritter thought Willie was harassing and stalking his girlfriend,' says Barbara.

Schmidt turns back towards her and makes a doubtful face. 'Willie likes girls – he's that kind of guy. Him flirting with someone's girlfriend doesn't sound like much of a motive to me.'

'Stalking isn't flirting,' says Barbara firmly, but her mind is elsewhere. She's had another thought. 'I wonder if the argument that was overheard by Frau Krause, when Ritter said he'd call the police, was with Willie Koch,' she says. 'Maybe Willie was there when Ritter came back. Poisoning is premeditated, it's not a spur-of-the-moment thing, and we suspect that the poisoner also watched Mattias Ritter die. That fits with Willie sticking around, waiting for Ritter to come back, so that he could watch.'

'Just a heads-up,' says Schmidt. 'You need to tread carefully where the Kochs are concerned. They won't take being investigated very well – they'll fight back.'

'I don't care how important they think they are. No one is immune from prosecution if they've committed a crime.'

They walk in silence for a few minutes before emerging from the forest at the edge of a small meadow with a two-storey A-frame house on the other side. There are red geraniums in pots on the balcony and the windows have lace curtains hanging in them. A high flagpole topped with a German flag, drooping in the still air, stands in the front yard. They walk over and, as Schmidt pushes open the garden gate, a dog at the back of the house starts barking. By the sound of it, it's not a small dog either. Schmidt doesn't seem nervous; he walks across the grass and leads her around the corner of the house to a side door. She's certain he's been here before – he knows his way around the place. Maybe he and Willie are better friends than he's letting on. As they approach the side entrance, the barking reaches a crescendo and she can see a German shepherd with a heavy leather collar pushing its nose up against the broad panels of a wooden fence at the rear of the property, growling and barking and scrabbling against the barrier.

The door opens and a man in his mid-fifties emerges, shouting at the dog to be quiet. He turns to face them, his broad arms crossed over his chest, his legs slightly apart. This must be Frank Koch. He doesn't introduce himself but the resemblance to his son is striking. His hair is also shorn and, as with his goatee beard, is going grey. He's wearing a shirt, so she can't see if he has any tattoos, but he's also tall and well built and Barbara, at least a head shorter than him and standing a step lower, feels the disparity in their sizes. She straightens her shoulders, refusing to be intimidated.

'We're looking for Willie Koch,' she says. 'Can we speak to him, please?'

Before Frank Koch can say anything, Willie appears at the door and steps out, imitating his father's stance. 'Yeah?' he says.

'We're investigating a suspicious death at the Mildersee colony and I want to ask you a few questions about your whereabouts on Saturday afternoon,' says Barbara.

'The Berliners at the lake sent you to us, did they?' says Frank Koch, taking front and centre in the conversation again. 'They've made nothing but trouble since they started coming here. Acting like they own the place, trying to get rid of us, kick us off our own land.'

'We're talking to everyone who was here at the weekend,' says Barbara.

'We had friends over on Saturday night. Lots of people who can vouch for us,' says Frank Koch. 'You can rule us out of your investigation.'

'Just a few questions to clarify everyone's movements,' says Barbara, her eyes on Willie.

'We had a party, my son was here all afternoon, that's it. The commandant of the police was here – he'll confirm it.'

'Your son was seen in the vicinity of the victim's cabin on Saturday—'

'I'm not listening to this. I won't have you investigating my son. He's got nothing to do with it. This is harassment and I won't have it...' Frank Koch's face is puce.

Barbara ignores him and looks at Willie. 'We have a witness who says you were outside Mattias Ritter's garden on Saturday,' she says.

A half-grin comes onto Willie's face. 'Maybe. I'm always in the colony. I saw you there yesterday, remember.' He makes a pistol gesture with his thumb and forefinger, then lets his hand tremble a little. 'Gave you a proper fright,' he says, the nasty grin fully out now.

'What is your relationship with Nina Hartmann?' says Barbara, pushing down her feelings of distaste for Koch.

'Who?' Frank Koch is butting in again.

'Nina Hartmann, Herr Ritter's girlfriend.'

'We don't know her.' Frank Koch's voice is loud and domineering.

'A witness told us you were waiting to talk with Nina Hartmann on Saturday afternoon,' Barbara interrupts, looking directly at Willie.

'What are you talking about?' Frank Koch is obviously not going to let his son speak.

'Herr Koch, I need to talk to Willie. If you wouldn't mind staying out of this . . .'

Frank Koch stares at her. 'Tell them, Willie,' he says, turning to his son.

'She keeps picking cherries from the orchard,' says Willie. 'I told her once that she could have some and now she treats it like her personal property and she always takes too many.'

'Cherries? Are they still in season?' says Schmidt. It's a perceptive question, thinks Barbara, pleasantly surprised.

'For fuck's sake, why are we talking about cherries?' says Frank Koch. 'What's all this got to do with what happened at the weekend?'

'Your son was seen waiting by Herr Ritter's cabin on Saturday afternoon, shortly before Herr Ritter's death,' says Barbara. 'He told a witness that he was there to talk to Nina Hartmann.'

Frank Koch stares at his son, whose face and beefy neck turn red.

'Like I said, I wanted to tell her to stay out of our orchard,' says Willie.

'How well do you know Nina Hartmann?' asks Barbara.

'I've met her at a couple of parties, that's all.' Willie's face is back to its insolent stare. But something about Nina Hartmann has touched a nerve.

'Did you speak with Nina on Saturday?' she asks.

'Nah, she wasn't there. She was off fucking that DJ, Leon Kaiser.'

'Was your interest in Nina Hartmann the cause of your argument with Herr Ritter on Saturday afternoon?' Barbara takes a punt. She wants to test her hunch that it was Willie who Ritter was heard arguing with.

'I just told him a few facts and he couldn't handle it. Ritter was such a loser. Everyone else knew months ago that his bitch of a girlfriend was cheating on him. When he finally worked out that she was fucking someone else, he lost it, started saying that I was stalking her, that he would call the police on me. I told him: go ahead, loser.' Willie laughs. 'He couldn't cope with being a cuckold...'

Barbara's heart thumps in her chest. Willie Koch has admitted to arguing with Ritter on the day of his death. She glances over at Schmidt, but his face is expressionless.

'Thank you,' she says. 'That's all the questions I have for now, but I need to impound the foraging bag you were carrying yesterday as evidence.'

Willie Koch's upper lip curls disdainfully. 'You got a warrant for that?'

'I do,' says Barbara, taking out her phone and pulling up the document.

'You need a magistrate's permission for this.' Frank Koch steps forward, off the step, right into her personal space. 'I'm the mayor of this town – you don't want to mess with me or my family, and you don't want to break the law around me.'

He's much taller than she is, much bigger, but she stands firm. 'I'm not breaking any law. If there is danger in delay and the matter is urgent, the law permits us to issue a warrant.'

Willie Koch barely glances at the document and ignores his father's interruption. 'Yeah, well, I can't give it to you. I don't know where it is – I must have lost it.'

'You had it yesterday,' says Barbara.

He shrugs. 'I dunno where it is,' he says again.

'I can get a warrant to search your entire property,' she says. 'We will fingertip-search every inch of your home to help you find it. Is that what you want? Who knows what else we might uncover.'

'I don't know why you have it in for my son. He hasn't got anything to do with this. You're looking for a scapegoat. Don't think you're going to find it here!' Frank Koch is fuming.

'I'm only doing my job, Herr Koch. I can apply for a warrant to search your home but if I do that, as you said, I'll need to hand the case over to a prosecutor to begin a formal investigation. You can be present during the search, and you can also have your defence lawyer present. If a judge or prosecutor isn't available to attend the search, we can call two local government officials, unless of course you prefer to dispense with that? Or you can simply find the bag your son was using yesterday and hand it to us. We'll submit it for forensic tests and then return it to you. If your son is innocent, as you say, this is the simplest way to prove that, and we don't need to make a formal accusation at this time.'

Frank Koch glares at her, then grabs his son by the elbow, marches him inside and slams the door behind them. Barbara breathes deeply, calming herself after the confrontation.

'It takes a lot to stand up to Herr Koch – not many people manage it,' says Schmidt, breaking his silence for the first time. She thinks she detects a hint of admiration in his voice.

'We're just doing our job,' she says, but she feels a sense of achievement. She's stood up to a bully, she's pushing this case forward, she's not a total failure at her job.

As they wait, she can hear raised voices inside, but she can't make out the details of the argument through the closed door. After a few minutes, the door opens again and Frank Koch comes out, holding Willie's bag in his hands. 'Here,' he says, thrusting it at her. 'Take it. Do your tests. But my son had nothing to do with this. I tell you who you should be talking to: that Berlin DJ who has the parties all the time. Him and Mattias Ritter hated each other. He was fucking Ritter's girlfriend on the side. He's the one you should be investigating.'

Chapter 16

Berlin

2 p.m.

Walker's meeting with Schneider has left him feeling both frustrated and vindicated. Schneider has made it discouragingly clear that he'll get little assistance from the local team, their priorities focused elsewhere, but it proves the point he made to Rutherford that, without him on the ground here, Markovich is unlikely to be picked up anytime soon.

He's come back to the apartment, sent an email to Sophie, explaining that her contact is on paternity leave and asking if she has any other suggestions or can find someone to pull rank on Schneider and encourage a bit more cooperation. The time difference, which slows all communications, means it's unlikely he'll hear back from her until later this evening, and she won't be able to talk to the German police until tomorrow. It'll be at least twenty-four if not forty-eight hours before they make progress. Meanwhile, he might as well get moving on locating Markovich. He changes into his undercover look – slicking his hair back, putting in an earring, losing the shirt and trousers in favour of a t-shirt and black jeans – then pulls out his phone and looks up the address of the Sofija, the bar that Rutherford's undercover guy has supplied as a possible starting point. Their intel says that Markovich occasionally picks up messages there.

He walks to the nearest station, his route taking him through a less salubrious neighbourhood, the buildings a little more decrepit, litter blowing along the streets, until he hits a busier road with a train track running above four lanes of traffic. He crosses to the centre of the street and climbs the stairs to the station. A few minutes later, a bright-yellow train rattles in. He has to duck to enter the low-ceilinged, old-fashioned carriage, and takes a seat between a guy drinking a beer and a woman holding a small black pug with a fluorescent-pink collar. A couple of young blokes with attitude – tight jeans, box-fresh red trainers, fancy haircuts – are leaning against the doors. They exit at the same station he does and he follows them down graffiti-covered stairs and onto a busy street. They head confidently over a crossing and turn left. He follows them for no particular reason – a hunch, a scent of some low-key criminality. But after a couple of blocks the young blokes disappear into an ordinary-looking shopping centre. Maybe he's misjudged them. With everything so foreign, he can't read the cues here as easily as he does at home.

He walks on, waits at an intersection for the lights to change. The street is wide and busy, with two lanes of traffic in each direction, divided by a centre meridian where a few thirsty-looking trees offer shade to a host of cars parked up on the island. As he glances around, he notices a place on the opposite corner that gets his radar twitching. He crosses the street and walks up to it. There's a name painted above the door and with a jolt he realises he's found the Sofija, the bar connected to Markovich. The door is closed and one of the two tables outside is occupied by a couple of intimidating-looking blokes, not as big as Markovich but well built all the same, with small cups of dark coffee in front of them. Walker ignores them, pushes the door open, goes in as if he owns the place. It's a gloomy little space. A TV high in the far corner, a soccer match playing with the sound off, a scattering of wilted-looking plants sitting on the windowsill, a couple of gaming machines to the left, and on the right a bar, unmanned. There are a handful of tables but only one is taken, by three older guys. He steps towards the bar. The brown patterned carpet must rarely be cleaned – it's sticky underfoot.

'Ja, hallo?' It's one of the blokes from outside, coming up behind him. Walker turns. The man is standing close and is bigger than he looked sitting down. His hair is short, and he's wearing a leather jacket, tight t-shirt and fitted jeans. Goon uniform in any language, thinks Walker. Taller and wider than Walker by a good couple of inches in every direction, he has a distinctly unwelcoming look on his face.

'Ah, sorry, man – do you speak English?'

'Can I help you, brother?' says the bloke, his English accented from somewhere Walker can't place. Could be Montenegrin. Could be anything.

'I'm looking for a coffee and something to eat,' says Walker. He wants to get the lie of the land before he starts throwing Markovich's name about.

'No coffee here. The machine is kaput.' Walker looks back over his shoulder. Two of the three older blokes are drinking coffee, the third has what looks like a Coke in a glass with ice. They're deliberately avoiding eye contact, ignoring what's happening at the bar. The bouncer puts his arm behind Walker, directing him back to the door, shepherding him out. 'Over there,' he says, pointing across the road at a kebab place. 'They have food, coffee.'

Walker's hungry enough and curious enough about what's happening here to take the goon's advice. 'Thanks, mate,' he says, keeping it friendly. The bloke only nods at him and Walker feels eyes on his back as he waits again at the light to cross the street.

The kebab store has a fragrant hunk of meat rotating on a spit, and there's a small queue ahead of him. By the time he orders, he's properly hungry, and the doner, which he takes to eat at a white plastic table out front, is delicious. The flatbread is fresh and warm and stuffed with flavourful lamb, salad and a strong garlic sauce. He sits eating it, watching the Sofija opposite. The two big blokes are still sitting outside, though they've seemingly lost interest in him. He's almost finished his kebab when one of them gets up and pokes his head into the bar, then backs out and makes a call on a mobile. A few minutes later, two black Mercedes arrive, one after the other, double-parking, disrupting traffic, until two of the older blokes emerge and climb into separate vehicles. If he was at home, he'd have this place under surveillance, he thinks. It's so obviously dodgy but brazen at the same time. He has the distinct sense that these old blokes run these streets, that they're not intimidated by the law or trying to hide their activities. Before long a third black Mercedes arrives and the last of the men, probably the host of the meeting, climbs inside, the two goons joining him. Walker takes out his phone and snaps a couple of shots of the car, zooming in on the licence plate. Maybe Sophie can trace it for him or give it to the Germans as part of her intel package.

He begins to appreciate what Schneider told him about the arrogance, confidence and power of clan members; their closed networks, their omertà of silence, the relative powerlessness of authorities to shut them down. He picks up the greasy remnants of the kebab and his empty can of Coke and drops them in a bright-orange bin on the street corner. If Markovich has found a way into this clan culture, if he's found a way to gain their protection, to hide behind their silence and opacity, it will be more difficult than ever to find him and bring him to justice.

Only one way to find out, he thinks to himself, crossing the street in a break in the traffic and ducking back inside the bar, which is empty and silent. At the sound of his entry a man steps out from behind a curtain made of strips of colourful plastic, which divides the bar from a room at the back. He's young, early twenties, slim and slight, almost elfin-looking with wavy auburn hair to his shoulders and grey-blue eyes. He has tattoos above his eyebrows, words in a cursive script that Walker can't read, curving to follow the shape of his brows, and the numbers *2020* and *2022* tattooed in the slight hollows beneath his eyes. Another tattoo, which looks like it's mapping the capillaries and veins under his skin, runs from his ear down his neck, and when he puts his hands on the bar Walker can see that the skeleton of his left hand has been perfectly tattooed on the skin above it. He watches Walker approach but doesn't say anything; despite his youth and slight build, he emits a menacing aura.

'Alright, mate,' says Walker, searching for bonhomie in his tone. 'You speak English?'

The youth nods.

'I'm looking for a bloke called Stefan Markovich. A friend of mine said I might find him here.'

The bloke sends his eyes around the empty bar and shrugs. The silent type, thinks Walker.

'Yeah, well, I can see he's not here now,' Walker says, 'but I wonder if you know him? Maybe you could give him a message?'

The young bloke shakes his head.

'Could be he's not using the name Markovich. Sometimes he goes by Milan Pejovic. He's a big bloke, an Aussie like me but built like a brick shithouse.' Walker uses his hands to indicate Markovich's size and width. The bloke shakes his head again. 'Well, a mutual mate of ours, a bloke called Wayne Hopkins, said this is the place to leave a message for him. So if you do see Stefan, tell him that

Donnie Young is looking for him and that Wayne Hopkins sent me. I've got a proposition he might be interested in. I'll come back later in the week. Tell Stefan to leave a message if he wants to meet me.'

The bloke behind the bar still hasn't spoken a word. He doesn't nod or shake his head or shrug his shoulders. He just stands there, looking at Walker, his eyes icy.

• • •

Vuk Nikolić goes to the door and watches the Australian walk away down the street, disappearing into the crowd on Müllerstrasse. He turns the foreign names over in his head a couple of times, Donnie Young and Wayne Hopkins, debating how to move forward with the information. The bloke didn't look like a cop, and he sounded Australian. Vuk's uncle Dragan, who moved to Australia years back, sounds the same these days, lost his real accent to the same lazy drawl. The guy didn't look like trouble, at least nothing that he or Stefan couldn't handle. But the timing is dubious after the shooting last week. He might be with the Kavački clan, out to get vengeance.

Vuk doesn't know if the Kavački have Australian contacts but, if they do, word must have got out fast that Stefan was responsible for the shooting. Could they have found out that Stefan was the shooter, then flown someone over here and pinpointed where Stefan is based, all in a few days? Unlikely. But you never know. Better safe than sorry. He pushes back through the plastic curtain, picks up his phone, dials a number.

'An Australian called Donnie Young came in here asking for our new friend,' he says. 'Said he knew our friend through someone called Wayne Hopkins and that he had some kind of deal he wants to discuss. Said he'd be back later this week.'

Chapter 17

Berlin
3.30 p.m.

In the interest of speed, Barbara decides to deliver Willie Koch's bag to forensics personally. She's pushed back her interview with Leon Kaiser to 4 p.m. so she has time, on her way, to visit the lab first.

When she explains what she needs from Willie's bag, the receptionist directs her to a botanical specialist called Amina Khan. In her early thirties, with big brown eyes and thinly plucked, highly arched eyebrows that give her face a look of wide-eyed surprise, Khan is excited to help. 'I'm a palynologist – I'm into pollen,' she says. 'This is right up my street.'

'I didn't know your job existed,' Barbara admits, a little embarrassed.

'Don't worry,' says Khan, 'a lot of investigators don't. Then they're amazed when the whole case ends up hanging on a tiny speck of plant matter that's turned up somewhere it doesn't naturally belong. That's where I come in.'

Barbara is impressed. She's not sure how she can use the expertise, but she files it away for future reference.

•••

The interview with Leon Kaiser gets Barbara's hackles up. Tall, slim, wearing black Birkenstocks, slouchy black trousers, a grey t-shirt with a black logo she doesn't recognise, and with a piercing in his upper lip, he exudes the kind of Berlin cool that she sees in Monika's friends: arty, a bit punk. She's happy he's turned up, even with his lawyer in tow. His name has come up regularly in her investigation and she wants to get a measure of the man who might very well be more than simply a bystander to the murder of Mattias Ritter.

'We wanted to chat with you because one of your neighbours at the Mildersee colony, Mattias Ritter, has died in suspicious circumstances,' she says.

'Yeah, so I heard . . .' Kaiser seems unaffected.

'Who told you?' asks Barbara.

The question gives him pause. 'Nina Hartmann,' he says after a moment. 'Mattias's girlfriend.'

'You're friends with Nina Hartmann?'

'Yeah,' he says. 'She likes to dance and have a good time. She comes to my parties sometimes.'

'Nothing more than that? If I ask around, am I going to find out that you and she are in a relationship?'

There's another pause. 'No,' says Kaiser eventually. 'We've slept together a couple of times, but it isn't anything serious. She's into Ritter, though I don't know why. He was a miserable old git.'

It's confirmation of an affair that seems to be general knowledge among those at the colony but which Nina Hartmann has denied. Whether Kaiser is downplaying the extent of it remains to be seen.

'Did you see her on Saturday?'

'Yeah. She stopped by my cabin at Mildersee for a while in the afternoon.'

'How long is a while?'

'I don't know. From sixish to around seven thirty p.m., something like that. She had a train to catch at eight.' The details match Nina Hartmann's account, but contradict what both Renate Bauer and the Krause couple said, that they'd seen Nina with Kaiser mid-afternoon.

'What was your relationship with Mattias Ritter?'

'I didn't have a relationship with him. I prefer women . . .'

Barbara decides she doesn't like Kaiser. Too cocky and self-confident by half. Whether he's feigning lack of interest or is genuinely unbothered by the death of a neighbour, she can't tell. Either way, it's odd behaviour.

'Did you see Herr Ritter on Saturday too?'

'Nope.'

'I understand Herr Ritter made several complaints about noise and your parties . . .'

'Those old Ossis tell you that?'

Barbara doesn't answer.

'Tell me you're not talking to me because I might have killed Ritter following a noise complaint?' Kaiser lets out a snort of laughter. 'Fuck's sake, love – if I knocked off everyone who complained about my noise, I'd be the world's biggest serial killer. I'm a DJ, I host parties every week. There's always someone bitching and cops turning up and shutting us down. I don't give a shit. If you don't like to party, you shouldn't live in Berlin.'

Her dislike of Kaiser goes up a notch. 'What makes you think Mattias Ritter was murdered?' she asks.

Kaiser rolls his eyes. 'Cops are so fucking predictable,' he says. 'Why else would you want to talk to me?'

Barbara presses on. 'I heard you had an argument with Ritter about his boat.'

'You *have* been talking to those miserable Ossis. Yes, we had a disagreement a couple of weeks ago. Some friends of mine were wasted, they took Ritter's boat out and banged it up a bit. He was pissed off. Fair enough. I told him I would pay for the repairs, and he said he'd send me the bill. That was all there was to it. If you want to talk to someone who has a grudge against Ritter, you'd be better off talking to that Nazi who lives out back of the forest.'

'Willie Koch?'

'That's him. He pretends he hates us, but he hangs around all the time. He's even come to a couple of my parties. He had the hots for Nina, but she told him to leave her alone and he got a bit nasty after that, following her around. I stopped inviting him and I know Ritter had words with him too.'

'Did you see Willie Koch on Saturday afternoon?' she asks.

Kaiser shakes his head. 'Nah, other than Nina, I didn't see anyone else.'

'Not even Mattias Ritter? You didn't have any conversation with him?'

'I think my client has already answered that,' says his lawyer, a trim woman of about forty, whose bobbed blonde hair is as solid and shiny as a helmet. 'If there's nothing else?'

• • •

Back at her desk, Barbara reviews her progress. Someone other than Mattias Ritter was in the boat with him, drinking beer. Willie Koch is one potential suspect; Nina Hartmann and Leon Kaiser are two others. She's convinced that Kaiser isn't being entirely truthful. He's too blithe, too relaxed, and although most of his account ties up with what Nina Hartmann has told her, it contradicts what other witnesses saw. She's almost certain the two have spoken and agreed their stories. Nina Hartmann has lied about her relationship with Kaiser, so there's no reason to believe the pair of them are telling the truth now. She needs to speak with Hartmann again and dig deeper; keep poking at the holes in her story until she finds out the truth. With a bit of luck, she might even extract a confession.

Chapter 18

Canberra
Midnight

The burner phone on DCI Dan Rutherford's bedside table gives a couple of urgent squawks, waking him from a restless sleep. He picks it up fast. The phone is his last-resort connection to his Vandals undercover cop, Wayne Hopkins, and Wayne doesn't use it unless it's urgent.

'One second,' he says, walking in the dark towards the bedroom door, not turning on the light to avoid waking his wife, Leanne. He flicks on the hall light and goes into the spare bedroom, which doubles as a study, drops onto the sofa bed. 'Tell me,' he says.

'I've just had a Vandal come to see me. He was on holiday in Adelaide and he reckons he saw Nick Mitchell's wife in a shopping centre. He followed her. He lost her towards the end but he says he thinks they're hiding in Hewett—'

'For fuck's sake,' says Rutherford. This is very bad news. Nick Mitchell is in witness protection. He's spent the last eighteen months giving up insider secrets on the Vandals' drug-making and drug-running business, information that has helped convict a number of senior members of the club. He's been placed in a safe house in Hewett, a suburb about forty clicks north of Adelaide. He doesn't know why the fuck Mitchell's wife was out shopping, but now that their location is blown they'll need to be moved. And a move to a new location will be fucking expensive. He doesn't have budget enough for more cops on his team, let alone to find a new place for an arsehole like Mitchell. 'This Vandal tell anyone else?' he asks.

'Not yet. He came to me first because I'm leading the search for Mitchell. But I'll have to act on it. I have to share it upwards. It's gold information. There's a massive reward out for anyone who can find him.'

'Understood. I'll get Mitchell moved asap.' Rutherford thinks for a moment: he doesn't want Mitchell's relocation to throw suspicion on Wayne. 'Will that cause you problems at your end?'

'Yeah, nah. I reckon I've got a way round that. I haven't heard from Stefan. He's probably pissed that I gave your other bloke the name of that Berlin bar and I need something to get him back on side. I was thinking I'd tell him that we've found where Mitchell is. I can say I wanted him to be the first to know. Wanted his input before we move forward. He'll like that. And that keeps me in the clear if Mitchell is moved – not like I was trying to hide it or nothing, just a coincidence that you lot moved him again. It might be a way to slow things down too. I'll leave an urgent message for Stefan to get in touch but it always takes a while before he gets back to me.'

'Good idea, especially if it gives us a few more days to make arrangements for Mitchell,' says Rutherford. 'We'll have to move him either way, so it's not intel Markovich can act on. Do it.'

After he ends the call, Rutherford dials the protection team in Adelaide. It takes a good minute before a voice answers. 'Yes, sir?'

'You lot asleep down there or what? There's supposed to be

someone on the job twenty-four-seven.'

'Yes, sir. I'm on duty. I was doing a quick perimeter check and I didn't want to take your call outside.'

'Alright,' says Rutherford, only slightly mollified. 'We've got a problem. Someone saw Mitchell's missus at a shopping centre in Adelaide and followed her back to Hewett.' He leaves out the information that it was a Vandal who'd spotted her. 'Who the fuck let her go shopping?' he asks. 'This is a major cock-up.'

'Sir, I wasn't here but I know the duty officer tried to stop her, tried to talk to her. She wouldn't have it. Wouldn't even put a wig on or wear a big pair of sunnies or something to make herself less recognisable. We've been having problems with both of them. They don't want us in the house, say it upsets the daughter, that it's stopping them from living a normal life. We've been pushing back but we lost this round. I'm sorry, sir – I'll take responsibility.'

'What a pair of idiots,' says Rutherford in disgust. 'Costing the taxpayer an arm and a leg and acting like fucking toddlers. We should cut them loose, see how long they last. Maybe the fact that someone recognised her will wake them up a bit.'

'Who was it who saw her, sir?'

'One of my undercover blokes,' says Rutherford, stretching the truth. 'But if he can spot her and tail her, so can a Vandal. I'll speak to command in the morning. They've been in Hewett long enough – it's time for a move. Meanwhile, you'd better drum some sense into them. We need Mitchell. We're still putting together a case for the top bloke in this gang and Mitchell's testimony could make or break the conviction. Him and his missus can't go wandering around ignoring protocol. As a safeguard, I'll sign off on some additional resources for your team, just until we move them.'

'We'll be extra-vigilant, but I think they'll push back on any demands we make, sir. And I don't think they'll accept the extra manpower either. They've already evicted us from the house – we're taking turns sitting outside in the car.'

'Fuck's sake, what is wrong with them? We're doing them a favour!' Rutherford can't believe what he's hearing. 'Tell them the news, tell them we're moving them, tell them to grow the fuck up.'

He ends the call, opens his laptop, signs in to his email and sends a message to the witness protection team, requesting a precautionary move, necessary because of the high value of the witness, blah blah. He goes back to bed, Leanne fast asleep beside him, her breathing measured and relaxed. But Rutherford finds sleep eludes him. He lies there, staring at the ceiling in the dark. They need to find a new address for the Mitchells and fast, though Wayne's idea of involving Markovich has at least bought them a bit more time.

• • •

Nick Mitchell is sitting in the kitchen in the dark, looking out at the back garden. It's the middle of the night but the cops have installed a motion sensor light and it goes on the whole bloody time, not least when the stupid pricks walk around the garden every hour. They think they're in some sort of action movie. 'Perimeter checks', one of them called it. Fucksake. The little brick bungalow that witness protection has put them in sits bang in the middle of a crowded suburb. Neighbours on all sides. Neighbours with neatly mowed lawns, two-point-five kids, barbecues and trampolines in the back yard, 4x4 SUVs that have never seen an off-road in their lives sitting on the driveways. Nothing dangerous within a hundred miles.

This morning, Shell called time on their pig bullshit, told them they weren't wanted, they could sit in the car or piss off if they'd rather. He has to admit it was a good decision. He's sick to the back teeth of pigs. The last eighteen months, first in the bin, then here with Shell and Megan, there's been cops hanging around 24/7 like a bad smell. He's spent the best part of every day being interrogated by them, telling them everything he knows, almost, about the Vandals business. He's avoided jail but he's a marked man. And now him, Shell and Megan are stuck here, in a shitty little house in a part of the country where they've got no family or friends. It's not much better than being inside. Nat, their eldest, who's working in Melbourne, can't even visit them or call them. It's worse than being fucken inside.

Half an hour ago, one of the pigs came in and said Shell had been spotted and recognised by some cop this afternoon and that there were concerns a Vandal might find them. They want to move them again. Nick went to the bedroom and told Shell and she said, 'No fucken way!' Then: 'Get rid of him. We need to talk.'

'They finally gone?' As if she can hear his thoughts, Shell now comes into the kitchen, drops a package wrapped in an old towel on the table, then walks over, puts the kettle on, pulls two mugs from the cupboard and plops a teabag in each. The kitchen light is still off, the bright garden lights making it unnecessary.

'Yeah,' he says. 'I told them to fuck off.'

'I'm not moving, Nick. I'm not doing it. I don't believe a word these pigs tell us. It's bullshit, a power play to keep us scared and dependent on them. Moving us every few months. Megan is finally settled and I'm not doing it again.'

'If we've been spotted—'

'Bullshit we've been spotted! I was in some shitty shopping centre in the middle of nowhere, getting my hair done, surrounded by women. They're lying.'

'Maybe. But you know Stefan won't let this go. He'll want me dead.'

'Stefan's not even in Australia. And the rest of them are in the bin—'

'Thanks to me!'

'Whatever. They're not getting out anytime soon. We're safe here for a bit longer. Just until Megan finishes grade twelve. It's only four months. When she's done, she can go to Nat in Melbourne, we can get our money, and you and me can disappear to WA like we wanted.'

Thank god for Shell. Long before the whole shebang fell apart, she'd always put money aside in an account in her maiden name. The pigs never found it, so they've got a stash to keep them going. She fills the two mugs with boiling water, adds milk and brings them over to the table. The light outside finally clicks off and they're left in the dark. It takes a few seconds for Nick's eyes to adjust. He looks across to where she's sitting opposite him.

'We probably need the pigs to stick around until Megan's done. Just in case,' he says.

'No we don't,' she says, and by the sound of her voice she's got a big smile on her face. She pushes the package she brought to the table across at him. 'Have a look at that.'

As he pulls it towards him, the weight and shape feel familiar. 'What the fuck?' he says. 'Is this my handgun?' He's unwrapping the fabric around it as quick as he can, pulling the Glock out, holding it in his hands, the smooth heavy weight of it as reassuring as a blanket on a cold night.

She laughs. 'It sure as hell is.'

She's managed to bring him his weapon. Fucken ace. He's finally armed again and with his favourite piece. 'How did you get that past the pigs?'

She laughs again. 'You know me,' she says.

'You're a fucken legend, Shell.' He's laughing too. He's missed having a weapon, being able to take care of himself and of Shell and the girls. Having to depend on others for safety, especially pigs, goes totally against the grain. He can't imagine how she got it past them but Shell is no one's fool.

'Send the pigs on their way,' she says. 'Let's get our lives back. No one's coming after us, and even if they do you've got the Glock. You'll see them off – you'll take care of us.'

Chapter 19

Kummerfeld Police Station
Wednesday, 8 a.m.

Frank Koch won't stop pacing around Barsch's office – taking three steps and turning, taking three steps, turning again, like a caged big cat, prowling and restless. His anxiety is making Barsch twitchy too.

'We don't fucking need this, Berthold,' Koch says, turning to Barsch, who is sitting behind his desk. 'We're less than a week away from the election and I've made "hard on crime" a key plank of my campaign. Now some fucking Berliner gets himself killed at Mildersee and they're trying to fit Willie up for it. The minute the media gets hold of this, it's all they'll talk about and they'll find a way to turn this against us—'

'Are you one hundred per cent sure Willie is in the clear for this?' Barsch interrupts the tirade. 'Because if not, I can't save him this time. It's a murder and that detective won't turn a blind eye or do you any favours.'

'You were there on Saturday. You know it's nothing to do with Willie.'

Barsch thinks back to the party at the Kochs' place on Saturday. He doesn't remember seeing Willie that afternoon. Not that he'd been looking for him. He doesn't like the kid – never has. Willie's got none of his dad's smarts, buzzes with aggression, takes a ton of illegal drugs. He even got himself inked with a fucking Nazi tattoo. Not somewhere discreet either: on his fucking neck where everyone can see it. And he's got form. They've always kept it out of the courts, kept it unofficial so he doesn't have a record, but Willie's been reported for stalking and has been in the frame for a sexual assault too. Frank swore blind that Willie wasn't involved that time as well, but Barsch talked to the girl and believed her. She'd been drinking with Willie and his friends, but had left when the party got too rowdy for her taste. Willie followed her out. He grabbed her and assaulted her on a quiet side street, just yards from her family's home. It might even have ended up as rape if she hadn't managed to scream her head off and if a late dog walker, attracted by the noise, hadn't scared Willie away. The witness wasn't able to identify Willie, though, and Barsch convinced the girl not to press charges: she'd been drinking, she'd been flirting with him at the party – who was going to believe she hadn't invited him to walk home with her and then had a change of heart? If the victim at Mildersee this weekend had been a woman, well . . . Barsch wouldn't have put it past Willie to have done something stupid. He doesn't say any of this to Frank. He's a good man, but he's got a blind spot for his idiot of a son.

'I don't remember seeing Willie at the weekend,' is all he says.

Frank scowls at him. 'Willie had nothing to do with this. He barely knew the bloke.'

There's a knock on the door and Klein sticks his head round. 'Schmidt's arrived . . .' he says.

'Send him in,' says Barsch. When Schmidt appears a moment

later, his good looks do nothing to soothe Barsch's nerves. He's never liked the lad – he's too handsome, the type who never has to work to get the things he wants in life. He doesn't invite him to sit. 'Tell me . . .' he says.

Schmidt looks at Koch, hesitates.

'It's fine,' says Barsch. 'Frank is here in an official capacity.'

'She's sent Willie's foraging bag for forensic testing.'

'Willie didn't fucking do it. This Berlin detective doesn't want to investigate, she wants an Ossi dupe . . .' Koch is fuming, his face red with anger.

'She's a local, actually,' says Schmidt. 'She grew up in Kummerfeld – her family still live here.'

Barsch is happy to see that Koch looks like he wants to punch Schmidt hard on his perfect face. A part of him is willing Koch to do it, the other part of him is thinking and plotting.

'We can use that,' he says after a moment. 'Get to know her family, get cosy with them, fuck her if you have to. Find any dirt you can – dig deep, dig around her whole family. There'll be something. There always is. I want her as compromised as possible.'

There's a long pause. Schmidt glances at Koch as if expecting assistance from that corner but there's none forthcoming. 'I don't think that will work, sir,' says Schmidt. 'She's not interested in me.'

'Then get her interested, you idiot. Use your looks, the one thing you've got going for you, and find some dirt on them.' Schmidt opens his mouth to argue, and Barsch narrows his eyes. 'Am I understood?' he roars.

'Yes, sir.'

'Anything else?'

'She wants to find the missing oar. She's asked if we have any spare manpower to do a search to see if it's drifted ashore somewhere. I think she's going to email you the request.'

'No. I've got half the fucking team door-knocking and taking witness statements already, and nothing to show for it all either. Was that everything?'

'Yes, sir.'

'OK, that's all, you can go.' Barsch waves the officer away.

When the door shuts behind him, Koch starts pacing again. 'She's got it in for Willie, I told you. You need to get on top of this. Find out who really did it.'

'Yes, alright, I'll sort it,' says Barsch. Like I always do, he thinks to himself. Still, if Koch wins the vote, keeps charge of the budget for another four years, they'll all profit. They've done well out of the last four; the next four should be equally lucrative. It's worth the effort he's putting in now.

When Koch has gone, Barsch takes his hip flask from the top drawer, pours a generous shot of schnapps into his coffee and props his feet up on his desk. He's wondering if Schmidt will be able to dig up any dirt on this Berlin cop. He doubts the kid will be up to the job. But he can ask a few of his better-connected friends to investigate the family history; there's bound to be something there somewhere. And they may not even need it. If the detective finds the missing oar it might still be OK. As long as it's not in Koch's fucking shed and covered in Willie's DNA.

Chapter 20

Berlin
12 p.m.

Walker is sitting outside the kebab place opposite the Sofija, a lukewarm Coke on the table in front of him. He spent until late last night doing a full reconnaissance of the neighbourhood. He drank a couple of beers at the Sofija, the young barman seemingly not recognising him. Then he walked the streets, finding plenty of similar places, bars and cafés with the scent of low-key dodgy around them and a clientele that fit the bill. The kind of places Markovich might hang out. He had beers in a few bars, and drank enough coffees to keep him buzzing in an equal number of cafés, but it was a largely wasted night. He asked everywhere about Markovich, but they all shook their heads or didn't understand. He can't even eavesdrop on conversations here, doesn't speak a word of German or Serbian. He didn't notice anyone paying particular attention to him or following him – he's just another foreigner in a big city. Normally that would be a good thing, but in this instance he wants to be conspicuous, wants Markovich to get the message that there's an Aussie in town, wants to flush the big bikie out.

He's come back this morning but the blinds at the Sofija are still down, the place closed. He really needs help from the local cops if he's going to get Markovich in custody. He can't just walk around hoping to bump into him; he needs a more focused search. He needs someone who knows the Balkan gangs, knows where they hang out, knows who the players are. Someone who can give him names, give him an introduction. That way he can get himself in front of the right crowd, stir the water a bit, maybe bring Markovich to the surface. He's got virtually no chance of finding Markovich without help, and if he doesn't get it soon he'll struggle to locate the bikie in the time he's got left. He checks his phone: 10 p.m. at home. Not too late. He dials Sophie's number.

'Sorry, mate,' he says when she picks up, her voice sleepy. 'Did I wake you?'

'Not at all,' she says. 'I'm watching a series on Netflix. How are you – have you made any progress?'

'Nah, nothing doing. I can't find him on my own, not over here. I don't reckon we'll get Markovich if we can't get the local blokes interested. Did you have any luck with your contact?'

'Not yet but I'm on it. They've got some big case they're working on and they say they're short of resources. I've pushed it up the chain. I'll let you know as soon as I hear something. Have you spoken to Rutherford?'

'Nah,' says Walker. 'Why?'

'I think he wants a word. There's been a development. Give him a call.'

'Righto – thanks, Sophie. And let me know what they say about the local manpower, yeah?'

'Will do. Take care of yourself . . .'

Walker dials Rutherford's number, wondering what might be

going on. He wouldn't usually call this late at night but he trusts Sophie's judgement.

'Walker,' says Rutherford, answering almost immediately.

'Boss. I just spoke to Sophie and she said I should give you a call.'

'I had an update from one of my undercover blokes last night,' says Rutherford, his voice grim. 'The Vandals have found out where we're holding Nick Mitchell and his family. There's a big bounty on Mitchell's head, upwards of a hundred K, so they're going to be onto this like a shot.'

'Shit. How did that leak?' asks Walker. He's never been comfortable with the deal that was made with the former Vandals number two – one of the men who tried to kill him – allowing him to turn state witness in exchange for limited jail time and then enter witness protection with his wife and daughters. But it wasn't Walker's call and Mitchell has given them plenty of intel that's led to the arrest and conviction of a few big criminals. They'll need Mitchell if Markovich comes to trial, too. With Mitchell as state witness, the big biker's conviction is a shoo-in.

'Mitchell and his missus aren't playing the game, the fucking idiots,' says Rutherford. 'But it puts an extra urgency on this Markovich op. We can't let the Vandals find Mitchell before we get Markovich in custody.'

'I was just telling Sophie that I can't do this without some local assistance on the ground here. I need help.'

'Yeah, she knows – she's escalating it. But don't undersell yourself. You know how the bloke thinks, the kind of places he might hang around. Once you have Markovich in your sights, the Germans will find the resources to bring him in.'

'Yes, sir,' says Walker, but as he hangs up he's thinking: easier said than done. He doesn't have the kind of intel for Berlin that he has back home, and even his nose for what's dodgy and what isn't is blunted by the foreignness of it all.

∙ ∙ ∙

Walker is happy to find the train out of the city is sleek and quiet, with air-conditioned carriages that are clean, comfortable and have none of the shake and rattle of the old-style underground trains he's been riding in town. He's on his way to meet Barbara, who called him an hour or so ago. 'How do you feel about a trip out to Mildersee?' she asked. 'They've reopened the colony and the lake, so you could have a swim. I think you will like the lake. And it's only twenty minutes or so on the train – I can send you the directions. Afterwards we can visit my parents. They want to meet you, thank you, and then I'll drive us back to Berlin.'

He jumped at the chance to see Barbara and have a swim. There's nothing doing here and a swim will help clear his mind. He might come up with some ideas for finding Markovich, but if not, it will slough off some of the jet lag at least.

For the first ten minutes, the train passes through the centre of the city. He glimpses the country's parliament, the Reichstag, then a host of grand buildings – big, impressive, classical architecture – beside the city's river, water gleaming in the sun, tourist boats gliding along it. The TV tower appears – he's almost at its base, can only see the bulbous top by craning his neck, the huge concrete tower stretching high above him. The train leaves the river and city behind, the passengers changing from youthful hipsters to an older crowd, men and women from a variety of cultures, wearing the weary faces and tired eyes of hard work, as it rattles through the suburbs. Slowly the carriage empties, leaving only a group of three teenagers talking loudly at the far end and an older couple with expensive-looking bikes standing silently by the doors.

He looks out the window. Bales of hay, bound in circular form, dot a harvested field. A platoon of wind turbines, the great blades turning slowly in the summer breeze, march in a line along the horizon. He's noticing how different Germany is to home. The colours especially.

So much green, in every shade from lime to emerald. The scale of it too, the towns and villages blurring into each other, not hours of empty horizon. The tiny train, the picturesque little villages – it all feels a bit like he's travelling in a toy world, a miniature tableau.

A disembodied voice begins burbling from the speaker, giving information in German. Walker's been watching the progress on his phone and he's pretty sure the upcoming station is the one he needs. As the train slides to a halt, he spots the sign for Mildersee and sees Barbara standing on the platform. She's the only person waiting and he's the only person who gets off. The doors close behind him with a loud beep and the train departs with a soft swoosh of air as he walks towards her. He can see the rooftops of a couple of houses and a church spire in the distance. He's struck again by how foreign this is – even the bird calls are different.

'Hey.' Barbara is smiling. 'You made it.'

'No worries,' he says. 'It was easy as. How's your day been?'

She makes a face. 'Progress . . . of sorts. I have a couple of leads but nothing concrete. I'm suspicious of the victim's girlfriend – she's lying to me and I don't know why. And there's a local guy who's got the capacity for violence and who was seen hanging around the victim's cabin and argued with him on the day of his death.'

'Sounds like you're narrowing it down,' says Walker.

'Let's see. The evidence is all a bit circumstantial. It would be useful to get your perspective. The officer I'm working with is keen, but he's young and inexperienced and all the detectives in my team are on another investigation. After your swim, before we go to my parents', maybe we could walk around the colony. I could use a sounding board, and a fresh set of eyes on the scene might be helpful.'

'No worries, happy to help if I can,' he says. And it's true. He likes working with Barbara – they play off each other well and his own case is stalled right now anyway.

Barbara points her keys at a small hatchback, a Peugeot, sky blue;

the lights flicker and the doors click open. Walker automatically heads to the wrong side, the Aussie passenger side, the German driver's side, and has to walk round the bonnet. Once inside, it's a bit of a squash; even with the seat pushed right back his legs aren't at full stretch and his head is almost touching the roof.

Barbara laughs. 'Sorry, it's not built for someone your size. We call it the roller skate, but it suits Mamá and Rita and me. Anyway, we haven't got far to go – we're not in the outback now.'

It had blown her mind, he remembers, the hours-long drives between towns, the vast empty plains, the long straight roads, not a curve in sight, nor a vehicle most times either. He understands better now how different their two countries are.

The road she takes curves past a development of small houses with neat gardens, two windows at the front, and each topped by a triangular roof. They remind Walker of the kind of houses kids draw. The road straightens as they leave the village and carves through a pine forest, sun-dappled and peaceful, then opens up to small and neatly demarcated fields of grain, wheat perhaps, and within minutes another village, another church, more small houses and tidy gardens. She turns right at a crossroads and he glimpses snatches of blue behind the houses on their left; their gardens seem to run directly to the water. A minute later she turns left onto a smaller track and the lake becomes clearly visible, sunshine reflecting off the water, shimmering blue. She pulls into a small car park overlooking a strip of sandy beach and the water. There's no one else around.

'This is it,' Barbara says. 'Mildersee. This is the public beach, and over there – can you see those jetties?' She's pointing to his right, where he sees a series of small pontoons and jetties jutting into the lake like so many fingers. 'That's the holiday colony. There's fifty or so cabins there. That's where my case is.'

They walk down to the edge of the lake. The water is clear and clean. Walker can see a sandy lakebed and a few tiny fish darting in and out of the tall reeds that line the side of the swimming area. The sun is warm, and the water looks inviting.

'Do you want to swim?' she asks. 'I need to talk to my boss and maybe afterwards I can make use of your detective skills? I really need a breakthrough in this case.'

Chapter 21

Mildersee

4 p.m.

The lake is balmy, cool but not cold, and soft, almost velvety, against Walker's skin. He takes it easy, not pushing himself, just enjoying the immersion in the silky water, which feels quite different to swimming in the ocean or a pool - different to the minerally artesian billabongs of the outback too. As always, being in the water revives him, clears his mind. He dries himself off, then - towel around his shoulders - walks up to where Barbara is standing by the car, looking a bit dejected.

'I spoke with my boss,' she tells him. 'He says I haven't got enough yet to move this into a formal investigation on either of my suspects. It's true. There's nothing concrete tying either of them to the murder.'

'I reckon he must be pretty stoked that you've got it narrowed down to two suspects, no?'

She shrugs. 'He's not the kind of guy who acknowledges progress. He'd rather point out what's still missing. At least with me, anyway.

I get the feeling that he's not convinced I'm up to the job and he's never happy unless I'm actually bringing someone in and locking them away.'

'Well, I reckon he's mad. You're one of the best cops I know. What do we need to do next to get someone locked up?'

'Find more evidence,' she says, laughing. 'Why don't I show you the colony, and I'll tell you about it while we walk . . .'

He gets dressed, leaves his damp towel and boardies in the car, and Barbara leads him along a sandy track lined with pine and birch trees, giving him a rundown of the case.

'I was doing some research into plant-based poisoning this morning,' she says. 'The forests and fields around Mildersee have more poisonous plants than I'd realised. Wolfsbane, belladonna, hemlock – all deadly – and European yew, which is the plant that killed the victim, Mattias Ritter. But poisoning someone isn't easy. You need to know where to find the plant, what parts of the plants are poisonous. Sometimes it's the fruit, or seeds, or roots, or – as with yew – the leaves or needles. And the severity of toxicity depends on how it's presented: crushed plants apparently release more toxic agents. You really need to know your stuff and the person who ticks all those boxes is the victim's girlfriend. She's a pharmacist, she knows about plants, and she'd have been able to give the victim tea without suspicion.'

Walker is intrigued. He's never worked a poisoning case himself, and the use of natural poisons, local plants, is unusual. If he was in Australia, he'd ask his cousin Blair for advice. Blair knows all about Aussie plants and their medicinal uses, though probably even he would be at a loss over here – the natural world is so completely different.

The lake is visible on their left as they walk along, and the fields on their right give way to a forest, which gets thicker and darker with every step, the trees high and tall. After a few minutes, the track divides, one path turning left along the lakefront, another leading straight ahead, deeper into the forest. 'The local suspect, Willie Koch, he lives down there,' says Barbara, pointing towards the forest as they turn the other way, following the path along the lake edge.

She takes him on a meandering route through a network of lanes into the colony proper. Set on small plots, the cabins look to be almost identical – small rectangular buildings with a porch out front and private gardens, separated from their neighbours by head-height dense green hedges. The cabins aren't all that much bigger than caravans, and the gardens, too, are compact, maybe fifteen by twenty metres, no more. There are pine trees and oak trees and plenty of birds around, but to Walker the colony feels strangely suburban. So many neighbours, the tiny plots, the neat grid-like layout: it reminds him of a budget holiday village, the cabins you sometimes find attached to caravan parks back home. But without the energy and noise, the people and music, the scent of meat on the barbecue, the sound of kids playing and shouting. Something about the place is unappealing; he can't put his finger on what it is. The silence, perhaps, or the fact that at least half the cabins look to be uninhabited, or maybe he's simply absorbed the malice behind the murder that Barbara has just told him about.

The colony seems empty. It's only when they are already deep into the place that he spots an older man, late sixties perhaps, pushing a hand lawnmower, its compact barrel rolling silently across what is already a tidy lawn in front of a freshly painted cabin, gleaming white with blue trim, and the number 11 painted in the same blue on the gate.

'Number eleven, I think that's Ralf Wagner – he was here on the night of the murder . . .' says Barbara. Her voice trails off and she comes to a stop, looking down the lane towards a young woman who has come out of a garden fifty metres or so ahead of them. She's wearing denim shorts and a pale-green vest and is carrying a linen tote across one shoulder, the leaves of some kind of plant poking out the top. She's followed by a young bloke, topless, barefoot, wearing loose black trousers.

'That's Nina Hartmann,' says Barbara softly. 'The victim's girlfriend. And the guy she's with is Leon Kaiser.'

As they watch, Kaiser grabs Nina Hartmann by the arm and she spins back towards him, an angry look on her face. He says something to her in a low voice. Walker can't make out the words, couldn't understand even if he did hear them. But he sees Nina Hartmann's face twist in contempt and she shrugs his hand off her arm. Walker can hear her voice clearly and though he still doesn't understand what she's saying he gets the gist: she's angry as hell. She turns and walks away and this time the bloke lets her go, watching as she strides off down the path.

Walker turns to Barbara, who is watching the scene intently. 'She was pissed off,' he says.

'Yes,' says Barbara, a gleam in her eye. 'She said: "I can't believe you'd be so fucking stupid. You're lucky I'm not going straight to the police."'

• • •

Barbara feels a buzz of excitement as she and Lucas walk down towards Kaiser, who is still standing on the path, a buzzing jittery restlessness to him, his hands jiggling in the pockets of his shorts.

'Herr Kaiser . . .' she calls out.

A look of shock passes across his face as he turns towards her.

'What's going on?' she says. 'Why does Nina Hartmann want to call us?'

She can see he's working hard to control his face, recover his equilibrium.

'No fucking comment,' he replies, then turns into his garden, striding quickly away from her.

'We can get a warrant. Why don't you talk to me now? It'll be easier, quicker.'

'Call my lawyer,' he shouts, not bothering to turn around.

'What happened? What did he say?' asks Lucas as Kaiser goes into his cabin, slamming the door behind him.

'He was no-commenting,' she says. 'But I need to talk to Nina Hartmann. I think she has something to tell us.'

They walk down to Ritter's place but Nina Hartmann has vanished. Barbara goes up to the cabin and knocks on the door. Receiving no answer, she squints in through the window. It's empty. She tries the door. Locked.

'She's not here,' she says. 'I wonder where she's disappeared to. Maybe she got straight on her bike to the station.'

As she turns, she spots Hartmann's bright-yellow thermos on the table in the garden and the linen bag stuffed with plants on the bench beside it. She goes over and looks at the bag. It's just so many green leaves to her but she snaps a couple of pictures on her phone. Maybe Amina Khan can identify the plants for her.

'I don't think she's gone far,' she says to Walker. 'Let's wait and see if she comes back.'

Chapter 22

Kummerfeld

5 p.m.

Rita is in the living room playing *Zelda*, Lola lying beside her, snoring and snuffling, when the doorbell rings. Lola wakes and gives a startled squeak of a bark. 'It's alright, babe,' Rita says, reaching down, patting the soft fur. 'It's nothing to be scared of.'

'Can you get that, please, Rita?' her mother shouts from upstairs. 'I'm cleaning the bathroom.'

Rita pauses the game but doesn't move. With a bit of luck, whoever it is might go away. She sits for a long minute, is about to press Play again when the bell rings once more.

'Rita!'

'Alright, alright.' She stands and walks to the door, Lola following her, tail wagging with pleasure at this small excursion. Through the frosted glass pane she can see the shape of someone standing a metre or so away, off the step. Good. She doesn't like it when people stand too close; her heart starts hammering and her hands get sweaty, and she struggles for breath. She opens the door a few centimetres, the chain engaged, ready to slam it shut if she doesn't like the look of whoever's out there.

It's the policeman, Barbara's colleague, the handsome one, with his big smile and broad chest and long blond hair. His hair is tied back and the thought runs through her mind that she'd like to see how it looks when he lets it down.

His smile gets even wider when he sees her. 'Hello,' he says. 'I don't know if you remember me – I'm Max Schmidt, I work with Barbara.'

'Barbara's not here,' she says, playing with the chain but staying at the door.

'Actually, it's you I want to see. I came to give you these,' he says. He holds out his hand. He's holding a small posy of flowers, a mix of colours and sizes, wildflowers by the looks, not something he's bought from a shop. 'I've got a garden and these are flowering now. I was thinking who might like them and I thought of you. Barbara says you're going through a tough time . . .'

She looks at the flowers, at him, then back at the flowers. She can feel her face flush and her hands start shaking. She doesn't know what to do, doesn't know how to respond, so she does the first thing that comes to mind – slams the door and then runs upstairs to her bedroom, slams that door too, and sits on the floor by her bed, curling her arms around her knees, breathing deep.

The door opens and her mother is there, worry etched across her face. 'Rita, darling, what happened? Are you OK? Who was it?'

'Nothing. I don't know. It was Barbara's colleague, the policeman from yesterday. He brought me flowers . . .'

Maria looks perplexed. 'He brought you flowers?' She looks around the room. 'Where are they?'

Rita shakes her head. 'I didn't know what to do,' she says, and out of nowhere tears are running down her face, she's crying and sobbing, and her mother comes over and sits beside her, pulling her close, holding her tight, letting the tears flow and flow and flow.

It's a long time before Rita stops crying. Wet tissues are scattered on the floor around her, her eyes are puffy, her nose red and running. Lola is sitting beside them, licking Rita's hand, looking concerned. Maria loosens her arms from around her daughter, leans forward and strokes the hair off Rita's damp face. 'I'm going to get you a glass of water,' she says.

Rita nods, sniffing, and Maria gets up, knees creaking from having sat in the one position for so long, and goes downstairs to the kitchen. Her hand is shaking as she takes the bottle of water from the fridge and fills a glass. She stands for a moment, fighting back tears of her own. She feels like they've made a breakthrough. It's the first time since her ordeal that Rita has cried, the first time she's properly let herself feel something. She stands for a moment and offers up a prayer of hope that her daughter is beginning to recover, that she is on the slow road back towards living again.

Before she goes back up with the water, she walks down the hall and opens the front door. On the front step is a small posy of flowers – lilac, asters, cornflowers and a white one that she doesn't recognise – the stems wrapped in damp newspaper. She considers it for a moment then bends down, picks it up and brings it inside.

Chapter 23

Mildersee
6 p.m.

Barbara and Walker have spent the best part of half an hour waiting for Nina Hartmann, leaning against the fence, speculating about what might have caused the argument between her and Kaiser, what she had been threatening to tell the police.

'Maybe the two of them were in on it together,' says Lucas. 'That happened in a case I was working on.'

Barbara nods. 'Maybe,' she says. 'Or maybe Kaiser took an executive decision that Nina isn't happy with.'

Eventually, the sun sinking lower, Barbara decides to call it a day. 'Seems like we missed her. Probably she's already gone back to Berlin,' she says. 'I'm going to call my boss and see if he can get the prosecutors to interview Nina Hartmann and Leon Kaiser formally, tomorrow. Nina forages for plants and she's a tea drinker – I saw that thermos at her home too. She knows about plants and probably poison through her pharmaceutical training. She has motive too:

they'd had a fight, their relationship was ending. And that argument with Kaiser – I think he knows something. He was so unaffected by Ritter's death when I spoke with him. It was odd.'

They walk back to the car and Barbara calls Fischer with an update while Lucas stands at the water's edge, watching the late-afternoon sunshine play across the water.

'I'll talk to the prosecutor,' says Fischer when she finishes outlining her case. 'Let's leave this Kaiser for the moment but we can pull the girlfriend in for formal questioning.'

The good buzz that the conversation gives her lasts approximately thirty seconds after she hangs up the call, when a message from her mother dampens her mood.

We need to postpone tonight amor. Rita can't manage it today.

She calls her mother, gets no answer, so she texts Rita. Hola guapa. R U ok? Call me! Love you xxx

As she's typing, another message pings in, from Seb this time. hey sexy! what you doing tonight? want to hang out?

She hasn't seen Seb for a while . . . She thinks through her options, impulsively sends a quick message: Want to meet me and my Australian friend for dinner at Al Yacoub?

Al Yacoub is a Middle Eastern restaurant they sometimes go to. The food is good, not expensive, and Lucas will like the grilled meat, she thinks.

Seb replies with a thumbs-up.

• • •

Barbara drives, not saying much, negotiating a series of country roads and then onto a motorway signposted *Berlin*. Walker can see she's still distracted, whether with the case or her sister, he isn't sure.

'Rita's still struggling, is she?' he asks.

Barbara looks in her mirrors, pulls into the middle lane and then nods. 'Yes,' she says. 'She's never really recovered. She's locked herself away, she barely leaves the house, she's lost contact with all her friends... She used to be so happy-go-lucky, so easy-going, and now she's...' Barbara's voice trails off. After a moment she says, 'She's so frightened of everything. She won't talk about it with anyone, not with me, not with a specialist. I think she blames herself for what happened out there, for Berndt's death. I don't know. But she's not getting better.'

'It was pretty rough alright,' he says. 'It'll take some time for her to recover.'

'I'm worried she's never going to get over it,' says Barbara. 'And it's my fault – I didn't find her quickly enough...'

Walker knows that Barbara did everything she could to find Rita, that Rita owes her life to her sister. He tells her this but she only shrugs. He can see tension in her face, fear too, and realises that Rita isn't the only one still struggling.

'How are *you* feeling?' he asks. 'Are you still having the nightmares? Trouble sleeping?'

She looks over at him. 'I'm fine,' she says, and he can hear the irritation in her voice.

'You don't have to be fine,' he counters. 'You went through it too.'

There's a long silence, Barbara watching the road, focused on driving. They're doing a reasonable 110 kilometres per hour. In Australia they'd be at top speed, but here they're back in the slow lane. Cars in the other lanes pass them easily, probably driving at 130. Occasionally some idiot in the fast lane, usually in some kind of sports roadster, roars past at closer to 200. Walker had heard there were no speed limits on parts of the motorway here but, seeing it in action, he reckons it's madness.

He looks at Barbara's profile, feeling a surge of warmth for her. She's protective, and worrying about her sister like she always has. He hopes someone is taking care of her too. She must feel his eyes on her, for she turns slightly and glances at him. When she looks back at the road, she sighs and then says, 'Yes, I still have problems sleeping and bad dreams also. And I worry this has made me too nervous for the job. I get tense, on edge, so fast. The other day I pulled a gun on a guy – it wasn't necessary, I shouldn't have done it.'

It's the second time she's mentioned this incident to him; it's obviously playing on her mind. 'You should talk to someone...' he says.

'I can't! They're already sidelining me. Work hasn't been good since I got back from Australia and had to go on leave. Everyone is cautious around me, and my boss, Fischer, is giving me the safe and easy and boring jobs and cutting me out of the challenging cases. If I ask for more counselling, it'll be the end of my career. And I need to work – I love the job.'

'This case doesn't seem too safe or boring,' he says, but she just humphs and, a moment later, changes the subject.

'What do you think of Berlin so far, then?'

He looks over at her, decides to revisit the subject of counselling another time, over a drink maybe. It's concerning that she feels under pressure at work, that she feels she can't get the help she needs.

'I love how old everything is. Even the apartment blocks would be listed buildings at home,' he says. 'But compared to home, and to Boston even, it's... well, it's a bit cramped, I guess. That's not exactly the right word but you know what I mean? Coming out here on the train, every bit of land fenced off, there's towns every few minutes. I guess I'm used to more space. And everyone lives in apartments, right on top of each other. At home we mostly all have our own yard, a house, even in big cities like Sydney or Canberra. In Boston too, unless you're right in the centre, there's more space.'

'I forgot you lived in Boston,' she says.

'Yeah, high school and college,' he says, remembering his fish-out-of-water feeling in the city, a feeling that didn't go away even after Grace was born and he had his little sister to love and care for.

'Why did you leave? Your parents and your sister still live there, don't they?'

'Yeah, my mum and her husband Richard, and Grace, my sister. But I never really connected with the place. I always felt like an outsider and I missed home. I missed Grandma and Blair, I missed the outback. I remember one freezing January day in Boston, when I was in college, everything grey and icy and dark, and I was thinking: it's summer in Oz now . . . Thinking of Caloodie and the light and the sky and knowing that's where I wanted to be. That was the moment when it wasn't a question anymore. I knew I had to go back, that I wanted to be home.'

She's quiet for a moment. 'I know that feeling of being an outsider. That's some of the reason why I became police. Me and Rita, we were bullied a bit at school. We were outsiders too. And I thought joining the police would, I don't know, prove I was a real German somehow.' She sighs. 'It hasn't quite turned out that way.'

'What do you mean, "real German"?' Walker is perplexed. 'You were born here, you're a German – a German cop no less. How much more real can you get?'

She sighs. 'My hair, my skin – I don't look German. My parents are Chilean immigrants. It doesn't matter that I was born here – to some people it doesn't count. I'm not "biodeutsch".'

'What's "biodeutsch" when it's at home?' asks Walker.

'It means Germans who don't have an immigrant background – you know, real Germans.' He can hear the frustration in her voice.

'Are you being bullied at work because of your background?' Walker is shocked.

'No, not bullied. But I'm the only woman in the team and I had to take time off after Australia and, well . . . sometimes it's hard to fit in.'

There's a pause as Walker digests what she's told him.

'What are you working on here anyway?' she asks. 'You're keeping unusually quiet about your case.' She's changed the subject again, he notices, and wonders what's really going on for her at work, what she's not telling him. He debates with himself for the slightest moment about how much to push it, decides again to park it for another time. They have more days together – maybe she'll open up after a beer.

He ponders briefly whether to involve her in his case and decides it can't do any harm. She's worked in Berlin for years: she's likely to have some insights. He gives her a quick rundown of the Markovich situation. 'I'm one hundred per cent certain he's here in Berlin, working with some Balkan mob. But I'm struggling to find a way in.'

Barbara's been listening intently. 'The Balkan clans ... That's interesting,' she says. 'There seems to be some kind of Balkan gang war going on. There was a drive-by shooting last week. One of the top guys in the Kavački gang was shot and there's a big investigation taking place right now. I wonder if your man has something to do with that.'

This is the case that the Fed spoke of, thinks Walker. 'Yeah, I heard about that. I also wondered if Markovich's arrival might have caused a shake-up. A drive-by sounds like his kind of thing. Do you know anyone working on the case? I really need some local assistance. I don't think I'll make progress without it.'

'Maybe. Two of the guys in my team have been seconded to the investigation – perhaps they can help you or give you a contact. I'll put in a call for you,' she says. 'But first, let's eat. Are you hungry? I know this great Middle Eastern place I think you'll like.'

Chapter 24

Mildersee
7 p.m.

Nina Hartmann is sitting at the table in the garden. After her argument with Leon, still furious with him, she came back to Mattias's cabin, poured herself a cup of tea from the thermos she'd forgotten to take on her walk. Her thirst had been building through the hot afternoon and she drank the first cup in big gulps. It was still warm but a bit stewed, the flavour stronger than usual. Still, it was wet and refreshing and she'd been desperate for hydration. She went to use the toilet behind the cabin just before the cops arrived. When they knocked and called her name, she stayed in the outhouse, didn't answer. She can't speak with them yet. She only came out here to meet Leon, to find out how his interview with the cops went - never expected the police would be here too, asking more questions. She needs time to consider her next move, decide how to play this. She can't believe Leon would be such an idiot and, by extension, involve her in his idiocy too. He's even told the cops they're having an affair. He can't keep his mouth shut about anything, always boasting about how much the ladies like him. For god's sake. And now this. If the cops find out, it's not just Leon - they'll both be in trouble. It took an age for the cops to leave and she sat in that horrible outhouse, the smell of the drop toilet making her feel nauseous, for the whole time they were hanging around, cursing them under her breath. They finally gave up and she came back to the table, poured another tea, trying to decide what to do next.

She knows how it looks. Mattias wanted to break up with her, she was having an affair, and now her lover has gone and incriminated them. Maybe her best bet is to stay quiet. To pretend she knows nothing about it. But there's no telling how much the cops know, or what Leon will say, especially if he's high or drunk like he often is. He has the kind of ego to think he can get away with anything.

Nina licks her lips. Her mouth is horribly dry and her lips are too. She's unbelievably thirsty - she obviously hasn't taken in enough fluid this afternoon. She takes another gulp of the tea. It really does taste weird. She should make another batch but she can't be bothered.

She thinks back to her walk in the forest, that creep Willie coming out of nowhere, in his camo gear as usual. He'd been stalking her again, gave her a proper fright. Then he had the nerve to ask her if she'd seen the flowers he'd left for her at the weekend. She had seen them on Saturday evening, lying on the table in the garden, wrapped with a cheesy ribbon covered in hearts, already wilted and dying, insects crawling out when she picked them up. Eeeuugh. She'd thrown them straight into the compost. What kind of freak leaves a weed as a gift?

She made a face at him, asking how he could think she'd be interested in him, with his Nazi tattoos and weird plants. He looked so angry she thought for a minute he was going to hit her, but then he spat at her feet and turned away, fading into the forest. She was angry enough to yell after him to stop following her and just leave her alone.

She twists the ring on her finger, watching the sapphires and diamonds glint in the low evening sun. Two uniform cops turned up at the apartment with it yesterday. Investigators had found it in Mattias's backpack and, 'given its value', returned it to her. She took it from them, hiding her confusion. She'd only seen the ring once before. It had belonged to his grandmother, and she'd commented on how beautiful it was. It has a lovely vintage setting, and though the stones aren't huge there are a lot of them and they're well cut. Mattias must have been planning to give it to her; there's no other reason he would have been carrying it around. Maybe he'd even been planning to propose. They'd talked about it a few times, but she hadn't taken him seriously, hadn't thought herself ready for marriage. But seeing the ring, thinking that he might have been about to ask her, sent a sharp pain of regret and sorrow to her heart. She's been an idiot. She let a loser like Leon drive a wedge between her and Mattias and now Mattias is dead and she'll never be able to apologise to him or make things right.

She wipes the tears that are leaking from her eyes off her cheeks. She hates this place. She didn't like it much when Mattias was alive, and now he's died out here and the whole place is redolent with his death and with the mistakes she's made. She's never coming back, she decides.

She checks the time, then her Deutsche Bahn train app. Fuck – nine minutes until the next train. She won't make it – it's at least a fifteen-minute ride, more like twenty given how crap she feels right now. The train after that one is in fifty-five minutes. She'll aim for that. The sun is almost down, evening coming in. She picks up her cup, empties it in one long gulp. Ick. The flavour is getting worse as it gets cooler. She picks up the thermos, inhales the scent of it. All wrong – maybe the rosehips were mouldy or something. She tightens the lid on the thermos, then loosens it again. Her mouth is dry and burning. Maybe there is something wrong with the tea, maybe she's having some kind of allergic reaction to it. But that would be weird. It's just rosehip; she made it herself this morning and she's drunk it lots of times without problems.

She walks back to the cabin, feeling weirdly unsteady on her feet, and rootles around in her bag for an antihistamine. Finds the blister pack empty. Fuck. She walks across to the crate that holds the water bottles. They're all empty too. She feels a tremor of anxiety. She needs more liquid. Her face is warm. Actually, her whole body is hot, a flush of heat running from her heart up her throat, down her torso. Perhaps it's not an allergy; more likely she has heatstroke from the warm weather, from not drinking enough. She considers taking off her top, feeling the breeze on her skin, or maybe jumping into the lake to get wet. That's the best for heatstroke, right? Cool down? Her mind is fuzzy; she can't think clearly.

She goes back to the table, sits down. The last of the day's light is spilling across the trees and water in a rainbow of colours. For a moment she thinks she sees Leon, dancing on the jetty in front of the house, and then it's Mattias dancing like he used to when they first met, lit by the setting sun, hands in the air, moving his feet. This heatstroke is worse than she thought – now she's seeing things. The idea that maybe she's having some kind of allergic reaction to the tea floats back into her mind, but she can't hold on to it. She's feeling anxious but can't grab onto why. She sits there, watching Leon, or is it Mattias, she can't decide. As she watches, his dance slows and distorts, his movements become jumpy, and dark nightmarish shadows flow across the jetty beside him. She stands to call out to him, warn him, and sees someone opening the gate, coming down the path towards her. She feels a rush of fear, then she recognises the face. She thinks, god, I don't need this right now, as she sits back down.

● ● ●

I'm standing, screened by the trees, watching her drink the tea. The cops have gone. The colony is empty. Earlier today I saw my chance and took it. She left that stupid yellow thermos she always carries, as if she's a baby who can't be away from her mother's teat for a second, sitting on the table in the garden. I walked over and opened it. Full, freshly made, steam rising. Some kind of floral tea by the smell of it. I thought about my options. Yew is too easy to detect – the taste isn't floral enough. Hemlock, perhaps? No, that's hard to mask too. When it came to me, it was perfect. *Atropa belladonna*: deadly nightshade. Perfect for someone who thinks so much of herself, thinks she's so beautiful, thinks *she's* a bella donna.

Because I know the forest, I know where there's an *Atropa* in a lightly shaded clearing, quite deep in, where the municipal workers can't be bothered to go. You can recognise *Atropa* by its finely haired stem: Belladonna is a lady who doesn't bother to depilate. And though she looks pretty enough, she's a vicious bitch. Her smooth, pointed leaves look innocent but they're noxious. In early summer she flaunts purple bell-shaped flowers, but it's in late summer and through autumn that she really bares her teeth. Her shiny black berries – the devil's cherries, they call them – are lethal. Usually I don't pick them, but I had a sense last week that I might need some, and I collected a couple of handfuls.

Today, I knew why. I picked up the thermos and took it with me. Back at mine, I crushed the berries to make a juice. You only need ten or twelve but I used more than two dozen. I'm sure she's the devil's type, she'll be welcome in hell, but you can never be too certain so I gave her a push. I put the thermos back on her garden table. She was off whoring with Kaiser as usual, so it was easy. And then I waited, patiently, concealed by the trees.

Now I can see the tea is working. When she went to the cabin she looked unsteady on her feet. Time to enjoy my handiwork close up. I walk over, open the gate and go across to her. She looks at me, eyes unfocused, face flushed. I smile at her.

'Can I have a drink?' I ask.

She shakes her head. 'I'm not in the mood to talk to you,' she says.

Rude bitch. But I keep smiling – I want to stay to watch this, I don't want her to make a fuss, send me away.

'Don't sit down,' she says. 'I'm about to leave.'

I ignore her and sit opposite her. She giggles, a little hysterical, licks her lips. I can see she's thirsty. She twists the cap on the thermos, tips it up for the last drops of liquid. That's it, girl. Drink it all down.

She stands, takes her top off. 'It's so hot,' she says. She's wearing a pale-green bra. Shameless slut. She looks at something over my shoulder, staggers towards the gate. 'Mattias?' she calls. 'Is that you, Mattias . . .'

Good. The hallucinations have started. She walks out of the garden, towards the jetty. I follow her but turn the other way. I can hear her talking and shouting, the words indistinct, as I leave. She needs time, an hour or two, no more.

When I come back, it's dark. I've brought a torch in case I need to search for her. I look around the garden and shine the light inside the cabin, but she's not there. She's not on the jetty either. Perhaps she jumped into the water, drowned. That would be a pity. I'd like to watch the devil claim her.

I shine the light down the path that runs beside the lake. Perhaps she set off for the train. I walk along, the pale beam of my torch the only light in the dark night. Clouds have come in, covering the stars and the third-quarter moon.

I'm barely outside the colony when I see her. Well, *smell* her is more accurate. The smell of vomit and excrement. The smell of a body puking and shitting in a vain attempt to lose the poison that's killing it. She's lying off the path, under a bush, naked, curled on her side. As I watch, she gives a faint mewl, shudders and trembles. I turn the beam of light towards her, shine it in her eyes. She makes a sound. She might say 'Help', or maybe it's an exhale. I can barely hear it. I don't answer, keep the light on her face, waiting for her to surrender to the devil. It doesn't take long – less than five minutes. She stops moving, stops mewling. I think she's stopped breathing. To confirm it, I push forward until the leaves and twigs catch at my clothes, and listen. After a minute I'm certain she's gone. I stay a while longer, feeling less than I expected. Feeling nothing.

She deserved this. She was an ungrateful bitch. She thought her pretty face was enough, that her life would always run smoothly, that she could behave as she wanted. That she could treat people like dirt, and everyone would still take care of her. No. Welcome to the real world. Where no one could save you from me.

Chapter 25

Berlin
9 p.m.

For once in his life, Walker's appetite has deserted him. The restaurant Barbara has chosen is simple and low-key. A counter at the front where you place your order and a back room crammed with tables, Turkish music playing on the speakers. They'd been standing in a short queue waiting to order their food, the scent of barbecuing meat and rich spices hanging in the air, whetting his appetite, when she'd said, casually, 'By the way, Seb is joining us too.'

'Oh yeah?' Walker hadn't paid much attention, too busy taking in the menu and then following Barbara to a table for four at the rear of the place, sitting with his back against the wall, scanning the clientele out of force of habit. Groups of youngsters, couples and large families, all relaxed, nothing out of order. When a muscular blond bloke came in and looked around, Walker instantly assumed that he must be Barbara's friend. His hair was cut short at the back and sides, his shoulders and arms emphasised in a tight t-shirt, and his thighs straining at the seams of his jeans. With his bulky frame, the way he was dressed, he looked every inch a cop, and very much the outsider among the crowd here. Sure enough, he caught sight of Barbara and weaved his way through the crowded space, plenty of eyes following him, the sounds of conversation subduing momentarily as he approached their table.

'I think your friend is here,' Walker said.

Barbara turned; he couldn't see her face, but he could see the bloke smile. 'Hallo, Schatz,' he said, bending down and kissing Barbara full on the lips, lingering and saying something in German. Walker noticed Barbara blush, and in a moment of crushing awareness he realised that Seb was more than a friend. Barbara has never mentioned a boyfriend, but why should she? He's never asked, and their friendship, even at a distance, is mostly work-based. Even so, he felt a tide of embarrassment rising inside him, aware that at some level he hadn't expected her to be in a relationship.

Barbara, turning back to him, her face slightly pink, introduced them: 'Lucas, this is Seb Huber; Seb, this is my friend from Australia, Lucas Walker.'

The big man plonked himself down on the chair next to Barbara, spreading his legs wide and taking up so much space that she had to shift a little to her right. He reached a hand over the table, saying 'Nice to meet you' in a thick accent. He was smiling but when Walker shook his hand, Seb's steely grip took him by surprise. He decided he didn't much like the bloke and got the sense, from the way Seb was looking at him, that the feeling was reciprocated.

When his and Barbara's food arrived, it tasted as good as it smelt – the meat juicy and perfectly barbecued, served with a piquant tomato-based sauce and a salad flavoured with spices he can't quite place. He started eating but watching Seb, one arm strung along the back of Barbara's chair, helping himself proprietarily to food from her plate while he waited for his own meal to arrive, hasn't done anything for his mood or appetite.

'So,' says Seb eventually, 'what are you doing in Berlin?' He pronounces his 'w' like 'v' and sounds like a war-movie villain, thinks Walker.

'Working on a case and taking the chance to spend some time with Barbara,' says Walker, smiling at her. He's aware he's slightly shit-stirring but he's taken against the bloke.

'Will you be staying long?'

'I'm not sure,' he says. 'It depends a bit on work.'

'Walker is with the federal police in Australia,' says Barbara. 'He's working a case here and afterwards he's going to the Netherlands to take part in an international conference on domestic extremism.'

Seb nods, looking unimpressed, picking at more of Barbara's meal but saying nothing.

'You're police too?' Walker feels he should make an effort.

'Ja, that's right. SEK Berlin.'

Walker hasn't heard of the acronym. 'What does SEK stand for?' he asks.

'Spezialeinsatzkommando. We are the special forces, what you call the SWAT,' says Seb.

'They're an elite unit,' says Barbara. 'They handle high-risk situations, hostages, kidnappings, security, stuff like that.'

'We are the very best. If you need to fix a problem, you call SEK.'

Seb's food arrives and they continue making awkward conversation while he eats, Seb mostly speaking German to Barbara, Barbara translating and involving Walker in the conversation as much as she can.

Walker's appetite has fully deserted him. He pushes the plate away, half uneaten.

'You didn't like it?' asks Barbara.

'No, no, it's great. Really good. I think it's the jet lag. I'm all over the place and it's messing with my appetite.'

She laughs. 'The jet lag must be bad if it means you cannot eat.' She turns to Seb. 'Lucas has the best appetite of anyone I know. He could be an honorary Chilean.'

Seb says something in German and Barbara shakes her head. 'It's not a competition,' she says in English. Seb shrugs and Walker feels the mood around the table grow colder. He should leave them to their night, give them space.

'I might head off. I'm beat. I think I need to get some sleep,' he says.

Barbara looks at him. He has the feeling she's disappointed, but he doesn't think a night out with her bloke will be fun for any of them. After a second, she nods. 'Sure,' she says. 'We'll go too.'

They make their way out and walk a short distance together.

'I live down here,' she says, pointing to her left. 'Do you want to come for a drink?'

Walker sees Seb's face fall and for a moment considers saying yes just to annoy the bloke, but then thinks of Barbara and shakes his head. 'I need some sleep,' he says. 'Maybe tomorrow?'

'OK,' she says. She points directly ahead. 'Keep walking until you hit the canal, it's less than ten minutes, then cross over the bridge, turn left, and your place is on the next corner.'

'Good one,' he says. 'See you tomorrow?'

'Absolutely, yes, I'll call you. We'll make a plan and visit my family.'

'Righto, goodnight,' he says, smiling at Barbara. He manages a 'Nice to meet ya' to Seb and sets off. As he heads home, he's in no mood to appreciate the Berlin nightlife – the bustling bars, the groups of people drinking beers on the bridge across the canal, a busker playing a piano that he's rolled out onto the street, soft notes drifting over the petrol-blue water. Walker doesn't see or hear any of it; he's too busy chiding himself for his disappointment and his expectations.

• • •

'You've never taken me home to meet your family,' says Seb.

'What?' Barbara is only half listening. Watching Walker disappearing down the street towards the canal, she's conscious of a sense of regret. She would have liked to sit with him a bit longer, drink a couple of beers, talk about life and work. She wants to find out more about his Berlin case and his upcoming new role. Monday, their first face-to-face encounter since Caloodie, had got off to an awkward start, with too much to say, and residual memories of her Australian trip dampening her mood. But they'd quickly fallen back into their easy friendship. And she enjoyed this afternoon; the two of them work together well, they're able to bounce ideas off each other, find clarity. She can talk to Lucas, too, about her fears and her failings. Seb is a decent person, but he's not interested in policing in the way she is. He's more at the barge-in-and-use-brute-force end of things. And if she shares her trauma with him, she's worried he'll say she's not tough enough, that she should find another job, and think less of her for it. Though perhaps she's not being fair to Seb; she's never really tried to talk about these things with him.

'Why haven't I met your family?' says Seb again.

She looks up at him. 'Well, I mean . . .' She's surprised, searching for the right words. She and Seb don't really have that kind of relationship. It's casual, low-key, not meet-the-parents level. 'Do you want to meet them?' she asks.

He shrugs. 'You're taking that Aussie to meet them.'

'That's different. He saved Rita's life. My life. My parents want to meet him, to thank him. Rita too.'

'Well, even so. You've never invited me.'

'It's not a great time at the moment,' she says. 'Rita is struggling. They don't have a lot of guests.'

They walk in a silence that's not entirely companionable back to her place, but once they arrive his mood lifts. The door has barely closed behind them when he pulls her into his arms, kissing her, running his hands to her waist, lifting her as easily as if she were a child and carrying her into the bedroom. She's not totally in the mood, half a mind still on Lucas, feeling weirdly guilty and thinking it was a misjudgement to have invited Seb tonight, but Seb doesn't seem to notice.

Afterwards, she lies beside him, his arm heavy on her waist as he falls into a half-sleep. One of the things that attracted her to Seb was his bulk, his physical presence. It made her feel safe and she's needed that. But tonight she's thinking that she's ready for more. Lucas makes her feel seen and heard in a way that Seb just doesn't.

As if he reads her mind, he stirs beside her, rolls onto his back and says: 'How's your case going, that murder you're looking into?'

'Mmm, making progress,' she says.

'Do you have a suspect?'

She rolls to face him. He doesn't usually ask questions about her cases. Detective work doesn't interest him – he likes the crash, bang, thump of policing.

'You know the way to a girl's heart, with this romantic post-sex chat,' she says, smiling.

'I thought you liked talking about your cases.' He looks hurt, and she moves closer, kisses him.

'I do. But, well, I sleep better if I don't think about them last thing at night.'

He still looks a bit put out, so she says: 'We have a couple of suspects. Literally. Might have been two of them involved. That would explain the two beer bottles . . .'

She starts explaining the relationship between Leon Kaiser and Nina Hartmann but after a minute or two she can see he's bored of the details, and drops it. They lie there for a while longer, not speaking, then he stretches his arm and moves her gently aside, sitting up and swinging his legs to the floor. 'I have to go,' he says. 'I'm on an early shift tomorrow morning.'

She nods. Seb rarely stays the night and that's fine with her. And tonight, if she's honest, she's relieved that he's going. She's feeling something complicated and not entirely fair to him – that he fails somehow in comparison with Lucas.

She gets out of bed to see him to the door, wrapping herself in her summer dressing gown, soft pale-green cotton with a delicate floral pattern, a gift from Rita, sent from India in the early days of her backpacking trip, before Australia and all that happened there. Seb kisses her goodbye, sliding his hand inside the dressing gown, caressing her. She steps back out of reach, and the put-out look comes back into his eyes.

She smiles at him to soften the rejection. 'Not if you're going home,' she says. 'That's not fair.'

That brings an answering smile to his face. 'I can stay . . .' he offers.

'No, go on. You need a good night's sleep. I'll see you soon.'

After he leaves, sleep eludes her. She picks up her phone, relieved to find a message from Rita. It's not much, just dulces sueños under a picture of Lola fast asleep on Rita's pillow. But Rita must be OK – she doesn't text or call or respond at all when she's in her really low place.

The case is still running through Barbara's mind and she considers calling Lucas for a chat. But he was tired and the evening had been a bit of a disaster. She'll talk to him tomorrow instead. She lies there, thinking about Nina Hartmann and her relationship with Leon Kaiser. About Hartmann's foraging, and her penchant for tea. Thinks, too, about Leon Kaiser and how unaffected he seems by Ritter's death. The two of them are the most likely suspects. But Willie Koch has lied to her too; he obviously has a knowledge of forest plants and he was seen around Ritter's cabin on the day of his death. She sighs, turns over, pulls on her eye mask. Any of them might have murdered Mattias Ritter, and truth be told she's still no closer to pinpointing who it was.

Chapter 26

Berlin
Thursday, 8 a.m.

'I might have someone who can give you an insight into this gang shooting case,' says Barbara. She's in the office, on the phone to her colleague Karl Vogel, who has been seconded to work on the drive-by shooting investigation.

'Why are you working on that?' says Karl. 'You're not part of the operation.'

'I'm not working on it. My friend is an Australian federal cop and he's here in Berlin looking for an Australian bikie—'

'I don't see how that's useful,' Karl interrupts. Barbara sighs. Karl has never liked her much. He was friendly enough when she first joined the team, but since she's proved that she's as good a detective as he is, maybe better, he's been chipping away at her ideas and contributions, jostling for favour in Fischer's eyes.

'Let me finish. This biker's name is Markovich and he's closely connected to the Ulić clan leadership. He was working for the clan in Ecuador and the Netherlands, and Lucas, my contact, says the intel is that he's now in Berlin, and it's plausible he could have been involved in the shooting.'

There's a long pause; she can almost hear Karl's brain winding into gear. 'They briefed us this morning that Ulić might be involved,' he says eventually. 'He's apparently vying for a bigger share of the German market. What is this biker's name?'

She spells it out and gives him Lucas's details too.

'I'll pass it on to the cop who briefed us, a detective superintendent called Martin Hammer,' says Karl, making it sound as though he's doing her a favour rather than the other way around. Whatever, she thinks as she hangs up. She's helping Lucas, not Karl.

She gets up from her desk to make herself a coffee. She's already spoken with Fischer this morning and he confirmed that the prosecutor has agreed to investigate Nina Hartmann. 'Good job, Barbara,' Fischer said, and she felt a flush of pleasure. Hopefully she's reminded him that he can trust her with these kinds of cases, and has earned a bit more of his respect.

She needs to get Hartmann in for an interview as soon as possible. She's already called her a couple of times but the phone is going directly to voicemail. She's left a message but so far no reply. Barbara is walking back to her desk, wondering if she needs to pay another visit to the Schöneberg apartment, when she hears her phone ringing on her desk. That'll be Hartmann now. The phone stops and then a second later starts up again, shrill and insistent. She walks over, grabs at it, doesn't recognise the number.

'Detective Guerra,' she answers.

'Detective, it's Officer Schmidt. We've found another body at Mildersee . . .'

• • •

Schmidt meets Barbara at the station and drives her to the lake, following the same route she took with Lucas yesterday. He parks by the public beach and leads her on the short walk through the forest, the sandy track covered in pine needles soft and cushiony under their feet. The same burly uniform cop, Klein, is guarding a scene that's been taped off, and an older couple are standing beside bikes a few metres away, their faces grey with shock.

'They were on a morning ride,' says Schmidt, nodding towards the couple. 'They could smell something bad, so they stopped, looked a bit more closely, and that's when they saw her and called us.'

The young woman's body is virtually hidden by the undergrowth. Covered in thick foliage, only one foot, wearing a pale-green Birkenstock sandal, is visible. The sandal is vaguely familiar and, as Barbara crouches down to peer through the leafy twigs and branches, she's rocked by a moment of shocked recognition. The dead woman is Nina Hartmann, curled into a foetal position, naked except for the pale-green Birkenstock sandals she was wearing yesterday afternoon.

Barbara edges slightly forward, trying to see more details without leaving an impact on the scene. Even from where she's crouching, some metres away, she can see that Hartmann's hair and face are encrusted with vomit and her lower body and the ground around it are covered in excrement. Hartmann's skin has a blue tinge to it and her legs and arms look slightly swollen. Barbara thinks back. Ritter had blue lips but not such blue-tinged skin. Hartmann is naked too, another difference. The thought crosses her mind that Hartmann might have been sexually assaulted before she died. She rocks back and gets slowly to her feet, chilled from the shock of seeing the young woman's body.

'This path isn't used much, mostly by people going to and from the colony to the train station, so she was probably coming from or going to Mildersee,' says Schmidt.

Barbara realises Schmidt has never met Hartmann. 'It's Nina Hartmann, Mattias Ritter's girlfriend,' she says. 'I saw her at Mildersee yesterday afternoon.'

Schmidt looks shocked. 'His girlfriend dead too. That can't be a coincidence.'

'No,' she agrees. 'And given the vomit, it looks like she might also have died from ingesting poison.'

The bushes around Nina Hartmann's body are dense and dark. Barbara is looking at them, wondering why Hartmann crawled underneath. Perhaps someone was chasing her and she was trying to hide from them. Another thought occurs to her. She pulls out her phone and calls Amina Khan, the forensics expert she gave Willie's foraging bag to. This might be the kind of scene where Khan's expertise could come in helpful.

'Frau Doktor Khan? This is Detective Barbara Guerra – I brought a bag in to you on Tuesday?'

'Hello, Detective,' says Khan. 'The bag is next on my list. I'll have something for you by this afternoon.'

'Thank you, but it's not that. I have another crime scene, a murder, where I think you could be helpful. Do you have time now? It's in Brandenburg, about thirty minutes' drive from your office.'

'Absolutely,' says Khan. 'Send me the details. I'll be there as soon as I can. Try not to disturb the scene. If you can leave it as pristine as possible, that will help me.'

Barbara's not sure she has the budget to involve an expert like Khan, but she'll deal with that later. If Khan can help solve the case, Fischer will sign it off for sure.

She and Schmidt go over to the couple who found the body. 'Did either of you push aside the bushes around this woman, get close to her at all?' she asks.

They shake their heads. 'No,' says the woman. 'We haven't left the path. We stopped and saw her foot and I was so scared that I wanted to ride away. But my husband insisted we call the police. We haven't touched anything.'

Barbara leaves Schmidt taking their statements and contact

details and walks back to Hartmann's body, casting her mind back to what she was wearing yesterday. Denim shorts, a pale-green top. She walks up the path a little, looking in the bushes on either side. There's no sign of any of the clothes, but a glint of yellow catches her eye, under one of the shrubs not far from Nina Hartmann's body. It's the thermos, the one she and Walker saw on the table in the garden yesterday afternoon. The tea could have been poisoned again, thinks Barbara. But knowing how Ritter died, surely Nina Hartmann would have been cautious about her tea? Then it dawns on her that she hadn't shared Ritter's exact cause of death with his girlfriend. They didn't yet know the details when she spoke with her on Sunday, and because she considered Hartmann a possible suspect she subsequently kept them to herself, wanting to use the information during questioning. Barbara feels a sharp rush of guilt. If she'd shared the information fully, maybe Nina Hartmann would have been more careful, maybe she'd still be alive.

She hears bicycles moving, turns to watch the older couple cycling away, Schmidt walking back to join her.

'I think we're looking for a person who has now killed twice,' she says when he reaches her.

'What makes you say that?'

'Nina Hartmann's thermos is in the bushes over there. It might be she was poisoned by her tea, the same as Ritter.'

There's a pause as Schmidt digests the information. 'But who would want both Nina Hartmann and Mattias Ritter dead?' he asks. 'That means it can't be someone from the colony. By all accounts Nina wasn't even at Mildersee all that often.'

'First, we need to talk to Leon Kaiser. I saw him arguing with Nina at Mildersee yesterday afternoon, shortly before she died,' says Barbara. Schmidt writes the name in his notebook.

'Then we should talk to Willie Koch. We know he has a history of harassing her and that he argued with Ritter.'

Schmidt opens his mouth as if he's about to say something. She looks at him but after a moment he says, 'OK', and adds Koch to the list.

'We also need to talk to anyone else who was at Mildersee yesterday. I saw Ralf Wagner when I was there in the afternoon. Check if Renate Bauer or the Krause couple were around yesterday at all. Someone might have seen something suspicious. I want to interview anyone who was out here.'

'I'll get it organised,' says Schmidt.

'It needs to happen this morning,' she says. Someone connected to the colony has now killed twice and there's no reason to think they won't do it again.

Chapter 27

Mildersee

10.30 a.m.

Amina Khan is the first of the forensics team to arrive. She suits up and starts looking at the scene, beginning close to the body, working slowly, her movements tiny. Every branch, every twig, every leaf gets a look, the ground around the body subject to the same detailed inspection. A little later the SOC technician Marilyn Mather and her partner turn up, Mather looking decidedly grumpy, her face even less impressed when she's asked to wait until Khan has finished. The minutes tick by as Khan widens her search, metre by metre, working in concentric circles, her attention to detail unwavering. Occasionally she stops to take a photograph; once, she picks up something and places it in an evidence bag.

Barbara walks over, excited. 'You found something?' she asks.

'If you can give me a bit more time, please. I need to survey the whole scene. I'll let you know as soon as I'm done.' Khan's voice is firm, and she doesn't raise her eyes.

She works on, and Barbara can feel the SOCOs beside her becoming restless. She takes Mather the short distance and points out the thermos in the bushes; they'll need to bag and examine it as evidence. Finally Khan straightens, smiles and says, 'It's all yours,' to Mather, who nods brusquely.

When Khan walks over to where she is waiting, Barbara asks, 'Did you find anything useful?'

'Well, I can tell you that the victim crawled under there herself,' Khan says. 'Her hair is covered in the same leaves and twigs and her arms and body are scratched in the places you'd expect. She's also broken twigs and crushed leaves beneath her as she moved. So she wasn't placed there – it's not that someone hid her body there, she crawled in.'

'Good to know,' says Barbara, wondering again if Nina Hartmann was trying to hide from someone.

'You say you didn't move any of the branches? No one else has looked at the scene?'

'That's right. The two people who found her didn't leave the bike path. Local police taped it off and waited for me. I crouched down where I showed you, but I didn't touch the foliage.'

Khan nods. 'OK, then someone else has been here. I can't say specifically when, it's all very fresh, but someone came close, pushed branches aside, probably to look at the victim. It's very subtle, but you can see the impressions in the leaves on the ground and there are some broken and damaged twigs too. I've taken some photos for you and I can send them over but I would say they were crouched down, looking at her . . .'

'Watching her die, perhaps?' says Barbara, thinking of Ritter's companion in the boat.

'Perhaps,' says Khan, her face grim at the thought.

'Anything else?' asks Barbara.

'I only found one other thing that might be useful,' says Khan, pulling out an evidence bag with a pinkish-red seed head inside.

'What's that?'

'It's part of the capsule of a castor bean plant,' says Khan. 'It's already seeded – that's why there's only a part of it here. The seeds are very handsome, brown and speckled; they look a bit like a beetle. They're the source of castor oil but they're also very poisonous. They contain ricin, one of the most toxic substances known to man. If you chew the seeds, they can be lethal.'

'Is it possible that's what killed the victim?'

'Perhaps. If ricin is ingested, initial symptoms include nausea, vomiting and abdominal pain. But from what I recall, the symptoms of ricin poisoning aren't fast, they progress over twelve to twenty-four hours – and you exhibit severe dehydration, as well as kidney and liver problems. You'll have to ask the pathologist or toxicologist, but somehow I think these symptoms are different. The victim seems to have been vomiting not long before she died.'

'I'll order a full toxicology,' says Barbara. 'Could ricin be mixed with tea? This is the second death out here in a few days and the previous victim was poisoned using yew mixed into peppermint tea. I found a thermos belonging to the victim in the brush near her. It's possible she was poisoned by the tea inside.'

'Yew . . . That's interesting.' Khan's voice is thoughtful. 'Someone who knows how to use plant-based poisons would know about ricin too. I'm not sure about ricin in tea – you'll need a specialist to confirm. But this capsule could be important for other reasons, especially if ricin wasn't the poison the victim ingested. Castor bean plants aren't native to this region. They're widespread in the tropics but they're frost-intolerant, so they're only grown here for decorative purposes, usually as an annual. And because they're toxic, most gardeners avoid them.'

'Right . . .' says Barbara, not sure where this gardening lesson is leading.

'You see the spikes?' Khan directs Barbara's eyes back to the evidence bag. The red capsule is covered in small spikes. 'They're quite sticky – they'll attach to clothing or to animal fur. I think, based on where I found it, that this could have come in with the person who was observing the victim.'

Khan watches the relevance of the information dawn on Barbara. 'Find that plant and I might find who was here watching Nina Hartmann die,' says Barbara.

Khan nods. 'That's right.'

Chapter 28

Berlin

1 p.m.

Stefan Markovic is bored and pissed off. He's been sitting in this shitty apartment for days, following instructions not to the leave the place until he gets the all-clear. Popo is taking his time about it, happy to have him off the scene, no doubt. And, as the days pass, he's started wondering if he even wants this Berlin job anymore.

The longer he sits here, the less the idea appeals. From what he's seen of it, Berlin is dirty and grey. The apartment they've got him in is tiny – the whole thing would fit into the bloody kitchen of his Surfers place. The sofa is hard and uncomfortable, the bed too small, the shower piss-weak. The decor looks like something out of the eighties, chintzy fucken curtains and lace tablecloths. There's no soundproofing, he can hear the family next door, kids screaming all hours, the parents arguing and shouting at each other, the bloke upstairs listening to TV and stomping around like he's wearing hobnail boots, which given it's Germany he probably fucken is. Someone, somewhere, is playing techno music at full volume, the kind of music he hates, the kind of music that makes him want to bash the shit out of someone.

He's been stuck here, drinking JD on his own, getting drunk and moody, but now he's out of booze. He ordered a pizza a few hours ago and it tasted like shit too. He fancies a kebab from the place opposite the Sofija; he fancies sitting in the bar talking to a few other blokes, getting some respect, having a laugh. Not that most of them speak fucken English, and he doesn't speak much Serbian, not enough to understand the Montenegrin dialect they all rattle on in. He wishes to fuck he was back in Queensland, at the coast, drinking a coldie by the pool, taking the bike for a ride in the hills, meeting some mates at a pub, maybe even having a rumble somewhere for the fun of it. Not bored shitless in a crappy country in a shitty apartment that looks like it belongs to a Serbian granny.

He picks up his phone. A message from Wayne came through earlier. He reads it again – *got some big news 4 ya* is all it says. He thinks about replying, reluctantly decides against it. Wayne is one of the last blokes standing from the whole Surfers debacle, and he's always been reliable, but Markovich can't be sure that Wayne's phone isn't being monitored or tracked. He'll wait until he's about to change his number – he does it regularly, at least every couple of weeks – and get back to him then. Keep things tight and safe.

Bored, he flicks through the pictures on his phone and finds some from the last summer he was at the Gold Coast. Him, Aaron, Wayne and Nick, the fucken traitor, sitting by the pool at his place, beers in hand. Him and some chick whose name he can't remember at a bar in Surfers. His place in the hills, the view falling away to the coast in the distance, the light bright and harsh. He can almost hear the kookaburras, smell the gum trees, feel the sun burning his bare skin, taste the coldies.

He's been gone a couple of years now and it's not getting easier.

The opposite, in fact. At the beginning, in Ecuador, he'd gotten a buzz from being somewhere different, from being closer to the real power, close to the real deal. Proper hardcore gangsters everywhere, Mexican narcos, their eyes so cold even he'd felt a shiver of apprehension. His connection to Vaso Ulić, his proximity to the power behind the whole clan, gave him prestige, and he lapped it up. The country's a shithole, not developed at all, but the crims are in charge, you can do what you fucken like, make a shit-ton of cash, stay untouchable. Cops are bought off, the women hot and willing, the houses big and comfortable, swimming pools and Jacuzzis, maids and cooks. The weather is decent too. A bit muggy but better than this European shit, where it rains all the fucken time, there's no good beaches, no decent place to live, no space to breathe.

Fuck this, he can't stand it another second. If he doesn't get outta here he's gonna lose it, punch that fucker down the hall's lights out and throw his sound system out the fucken window. He pulls on his boots and his jacket, slams the door behind him and takes the stairs two at a time. Opens the heavy front door, steps onto the footpath, the feeling of freedom close to that of coming out of the bin after a few years of hard time. He walks down the side alley and then turns left onto the main street. Noisy, smelly, ugly, but at least he's not sat staring at his four fucken walls or some foreign bullshit TV. He ambles across the road, ignoring the traffic, giving the taxi that honks its horn at him a hard stare and the finger. Walks up to the kebab place, breathing in the smell of meat and chillies. Orders himself a kebab with the lot, takes a Coke from the fridge to the outside table and exhales. Fuck the police.

The bloke behind the counter brings his kebab out. They must know who he is, or who he's connected with, because they won't take his money – 'Family discount,' says the waiter. And whether it's a family special or just the way they make them, the kebabs are bloody good. It's the one saving grace of this shithole. He eats the lot – even the salad is tasty – wipes his greasy fingers on the napkin and burps with satisfaction. Time for a beer.

The Sofija is empty. No one sitting at the tables, only the kid standing behind the bar. Vuk or some weird name like that. Vuk doesn't look like much, slim and not even that tall, but he's got the same cold dead eyes that he saw on the narcos in Ecuador. He reckons Vuk's done some shit, probably got plenty more to do too. He wouldn't trust the bloke not to put a blade in his neck if he thought it would help him get a bigger job either. When he takes over, if he hangs around, he needs to promote Vuk, keep him close.

Markovich nods at him, finds a table facing the door. 'I'll have a beer,' he says.

The kid brings over a bottle of beer – the bar doesn't have any on tap. Another fucken minus point for the place. There's a phone at the back ringing, and the kid moves quickly, light on his feet. Talks in Montenegrin; Markovich, not really listening, only picks up a couple of words: his name, 'Australia'. Telling Popo that he's here, probably. Well, fucken whatever, he thinks. I'm my own boss and it's staying that way. The kid pockets the phone and comes over. Markovich gives him a look, daring him to say something.

'You talk with the boss today?' the kid asks.

Markovich shakes his head.

'A guy's been in here a couple of times looking for you,' says Vuk. 'Australian.'

Markovich sits up straighter. That's not good news. Hardly anyone knows he's here. No one who'd be visiting, that's for sure. 'Who was it? What did he look like?'

'Said his name was Donnie Young. Said Wayne Hopkins sent him.'

He doesn't recognise the name, but he relaxes. If Wayne sent him, it's probably alright. Wayne shouldn't be giving out the name of the bar, but he must have his reasons. Probably that's why he texted earlier.

'He's been going bar to bar asking for you,' says Vuk. 'Popo says he wants to check him out, wants to make sure this isn't connected to the drive-by. He thinks it might not be a coincidence that there's someone looking for you the same week this shit goes down. Popo says it's better you stay low, stay at home, just till we know who he is. Says you're not to meet him until we've checked him over. Next time he comes round, we're gonna tail him.'

Chapter 29

Berlin

1 p.m.

Walker is waiting in reception at the LKA HQ once more. A couple of hours ago he had a call out of the blue, from a detective called Hammer.

'I hear you have a connection into the Ulić clan,' Hammer said after introducing himself. 'I am investigating them and I'd like to talk to you. Maybe we can help each other . . .'

Walker wondered if Sophie had applied pressure from Canberra or if the skinny detective from the other day had finally worked out that Markovich might have relevance, but he didn't bother clarifying – the main thing is that someone is interested in helping him.

He's finishing off a pretzel he bought at a bakery just down the road. He'd passed by, the scent of freshly made bread and pastries luring him inside, where a wooden stand hung with large salty pretzels had caught his eye. He'd decided to try one and is finding it chewy and salty and delicious.

He's still chewing his last bite when a man comes out of the lift and looks around. He spies Walker and comes over, taking quick, punchy steps. A bit younger than Walker, mid-thirties perhaps. He's not tall but he's bulky all over, one of those big men who are somewhere between muscle and fat, with a broad chest, thick neck and round cheeks. His shirt is crumpled, his trousers have seen better days, he has big heavy bags under his eyes and his short hair is standing in messy tufts, but he exudes a sense of urgency and energy.

'Detective Superintendent Martin Hammer,' he says, offering his hand.

Walker thinks Hammer is an apt name for the bloke, who looks like he could stand up for himself against most opposition. 'Nice to meet you,' he says. 'DS Lucas Walker.'

They shake hands and Walker notices Hammer give him a quick once-over. Walker, who is planning to go back to Markovich's neighbourhood after this meeting, is wearing a black t-shirt and jeans, hair brushed off his forehead and slicked back with gel, the small fake-diamond stud in his ear. A quick smile, there and gone again, crosses Hammer's face. 'I can see why Schneider didn't like you,' he says. 'Australian police uniform is very different.'

Walker laughs. 'It's my undercover look,' he says. 'I scrubbed up a bit better than this for Schneider but I guess it wasn't enough.'

Hammer leads Walker to a smaller room than Schneider chose on Tuesday, a round table for four, with a window overlooking the brick wall of a neighbouring wing. Another cop joins them. Hammer introduces them. 'This is Detective Karl Vogel. We are on a task force for a drive-by shooting that I believe is connected to the Ulić clan. I've been investigating them for some time. I believe they are growing their German operation. It could be that this shooting is part of a war for control of the German market.'

Vogel shakes Walker's hand but doesn't offer a matching smile. As they sit and Walker lays out a file of documents relating to Markovich, a background report that the team had translated into German, Vogel says something to Hammer. It sounds like a question. When Walker looks up, Vogel is giving him a hard look.

He starts by passing over a photograph: a full-body shot of Markovich wearing black jeans, a black t-shirt and a leather vest with the Vandals insignia visible above the left breast pocket. He's holding an almost empty pint of beer, his muscular arms visible, his distinctive tattoos too, and he's standing next to an ex-girlfriend. Walker had asked the team to blur the woman's face, but he's left her in the picture to give a better sense of Markovich's size. He towers over his girlfriend, almost a foot taller and twice the breadth, if not more.

The German cops scrutinise it closely. Walker is relieved to see them taking a genuine interest. They discuss something for a moment in German and Hammer turns towards him.

'We do not know this man,' he says. 'But we would like to take this picture to show a witness. We have found one person who could tell us something about the shooting. A German, of course.' Walker assumes he means that the surviving Montenegrin victims wouldn't discuss the shooting. 'This witness saw the car come past very fast but noticed the passenger, the shooter. When we showed him all our known criminals, he could not identify the man. But he said the man was large, too big for the seat of the car, so perhaps . . .'

'Sure, that's your copy, feel free,' says Walker, nodding.

Vogel leaves the room, taking the picture with him. Walker gives Hammer an update on Markovich and his family connection to Ulić, then hands over the translated briefing. 'The German might be a bit rudimentary,' he says, 'but I hope it makes sense.'

'Thank you for all this information,' says Hammer. 'Even if this Markovich is not part of the shooting, it is good to know that such a man is now in Berlin and working with Ulić. It is probable that he will make trouble somewhere.'

'He will,' says Walker. 'That's for sure.'

Hammer pushes back his chair, and Walker realises the meeting is over.

He puts up a hand. 'Hang on a second,' he says. 'I want some information from you too.' He pulls out his phone and brings up a picture of the Sofija bar. 'Do you know this place?' he asks.

Hammer looks at the picture and shakes his head. But when Walker tells him the address, he twists his mouth into a grimace. 'This street, this area, it is the heart of the Balkan criminal community in Berlin.'

That's good to know, thinks Walker. The intel from home is clearly not totally wrong. If Markovich is staying close to his people, this bar could well be a meeting point.

'I've heard that it's the best place to contact Markovich, so I'm starting my investigation there. What will be your next steps?'

Hammer hesitates for a second, then says, 'Our investigation has reached something like a wall. We are interviewing witnesses but they are saying nothing and the known members of the Ulić clan have not been visible this week.'

'It makes sense that they'd keep a low profile after a shooting,' says Walker. 'Look, I'm in a good position here. They don't know I'm a cop, they think I know Markovich from home, they believe that I have criminal connections—'

Hammer laughs. 'My colleague said the same. He said you do not look like police. He was a bit suspicious.'

'Seems like the look is working, then,' says Walker with a smile. 'But that means I can hang out in this bar, in this neighbourhood, and keep an eye out for Markovich or others you're looking for without raising their suspicions. Show me their mug shots – I'm good with faces. Use me, and we can both end up with what we want.'

'We also have undercover police,' says Hammer.

'Are you using them?'

Hammer shakes his head. 'No. I am not leading this operation. Schneider and the officers in charge are taking a different direction.' He pauses for longer this time, evidently considering whether to share more, before he continues. 'They believe this is a transnational problem. There was a shooting in Barcelona, a dispute over stolen cocaine, and they believe this is tit for tat. They do not want to know my ideas . . .'

'I get it,' says Walker. He met Schneider – not a friendly, inclusive sort of bloke.

'But I've worked these clans for many years and I am sure that Ulić is making a bid for more power. There have been other signs,' says Hammer. 'And if this Markovich is close to Ulić, then he could be here to help with this.'

'He could have been brought in as an enforcer, for sure,' says Walker. 'Given his family relationship to Ulić, he might even be heading it up. He's a bit of a big deal in Australia – I don't reckon he'd be happy with a back-seat role here.'

Hammer nods slowly. 'I have heard that there is some competition among the leadership, that something is shifting. So perhaps it is your man.'

'Look,' says Walker, 'let's work together. We'll both win. I don't care about jurisdiction or who should be doing what, I just want Markovich under arrest and I'm happy to do my bit to lure him out. That's why I'm here.'

Hammer pauses for a long moment, then he says, 'There are a few other places you could try, cafés that the Ulić clan runs. Perhaps your friend is there.' He reels off a series of names and Walker adds them to the notes on his phone. 'The boss of the clan here in Berlin is called Popović, he's an older man—'

'I might have seen him outside the Sofija,' says Walker, describing the meet he witnessed. He digs out the number plate he wrote down and passes it over, along with the photo he took.

'That's Popović,' says Hammer, nodding. 'I am sure the drive-by shooting is not his work, it's not his style. He's clever and cautious. We have never been able to arrest him.'

'I'd bet any money it was Markovich,' says Walker. 'It's right up his alley. Look, thanks for all the intel. I'm going back over there this afternoon. If I see anything, I'll let you know. I'd appreciate it if you'd return the favour.'

Chapter 30

Kummerfeld

1 p.m.

'Herr Wagner and Frau Bauer were both at the lake yesterday and have agreed to come in to speak with us, but Willie Koch is refusing.' Schmidt seems nervous, embarrassed maybe, as he shares the news with Barbara. 'His father is saying that we have to press formal charges and involve a prosecutor, or we can go to hell.'

'Unfortunately, that's his right,' says Barbara, resigned. 'Let's talk to the others first and see what that brings up. Then I'll make a call on whether we need to press for a formal accusation or not.' Schmidt looks relieved and she wonders again what his relationship is with Koch, but parks it for the moment. If they interview Koch formally, Schmidt won't be involved anyway.

The first of the other interviewees to arrive at the station is Ralf Wagner. It's the first time Barbara has met him. He's in his late sixties, fit and lean, wearing navy-blue working trousers and a pale-blue t-shirt. His hair is short and he has a lined and bitter-looking face.

A man who doesn't smile too often, thinks Barbara. She introduces herself and cuts to the chase.

'You were at Mildersee yesterday afternoon,' she says.

Wagner nods.

'Did you see Nina Hartmann at all?'

'Who is she? I don't know a Nina Hartmann . . .'

She slides a picture of Nina across the table at him. He looks at it, nods. 'Yes, I did see her yesterday. In the afternoon, maybe three thirty p.m., something like that. She was walking back from the forest, down the lane towards the lake. I didn't talk to her.'

She and Walker saw Hartmann arguing with Kaiser around 5 p.m., so it's possible the pair spent an hour or more together before that. Plenty of time for Kaiser to poison Hartmann.

'How long were you at the lake yesterday?' she asks Wagner.

'I arrived just after lunch, around one p.m. I was mowing the lawn, doing some work on the cabin, and then I left around five thirty. I was home for dinner at six. Why are you asking all this?'

'There's been another death at Mildersee,' says Barbara. Wagner doesn't exhibit any obvious shock or surprise, beyond compressing his lips into an even tighter line. 'This young woman's body was found just outside the colony this morning.'

Wagner shakes his head. 'It's nothing to do with me,' he says. 'I don't know anything about it. I don't know her.'

'You're not under suspicion,' says Barbara, though she's noted his lack of reaction. 'We're hoping you might have seen something that could help our investigation. Did you see anyone else at Mildersee while you were there yesterday afternoon?'

Wagner thinks for a moment. 'Renate was there. She came and went a few times – she likes to go walking in the forest. I'm not sure if she was still there when I left. I saw Willie too. He walked past mid-afternoon. And then I saw you and your companion not long before I left.'

Probably not a coincidence that Willie Koch was there, thinks Barbara. She needs to chase Khan for the forensics on his pouch. As she writes it all down, she notes how accurate Wagner's statement is. 'You have a very good memory for details,' she says.

He looks at her for a moment, then says: 'I worked with the security services before the wall came down.' It takes her a second to decode: Wagner is ex-Stasi, the East German secret police force. The news isn't all that surprising. The Stasi were endemic in the country; with close to 100,000 employees and well over 150,000 informants, they led one of the greatest surveillances by a country of its own people in history. She doubts Wagner's past is pertinent to her case, but she makes a note of it.

Renate Bauer arrives shortly after Wagner departs. She's wearing a rather prim-looking summer dress – pale-pink floral with long sleeves and a crisp white button-up collar. As before, her hair is tied up tightly in a bun, but this time she looks tired and her eyes and nose are red and swollen, as if she's been crying.

'Why did you ask me to come in? Do you have some news about Mattias?' she says as she settles herself into a chair, placing her handbag on her lap, her hands twisting the strap. 'I don't have much time – my son is leaving for America this afternoon, I have to go to the airport shortly.' Barbara thinks she can detect a crack in Renate Bauer's voice, a suspicion that's confirmed when she digs out a damp-looking handkerchief and dabs at her eyes.

'This won't take long, Frau Bauer,' says Barbara. 'We're talking to everyone who was at Mildersee yesterday . . . I understand you were out there yesterday?'

Renate Bauer nods. 'Yes. I was there most of the day. I go whenever I have a bad day. Being out there makes me feel better. My husband died a few years ago and the cabin saved me. The cabin and Max – my son. He's the only family I have left. But he found a job at the new Tesla factory and he met a woman there, an American. Now they're moving to America. He's leaving me ...'

To Barbara's surprise and Schmidt's obvious discomfort, Renate Bauer dissolves into tears. Barbara turns to Schmidt. 'Can you get Frau Bauer a glass of water?' she asks. He's up from his chair and out the door at speed. Barbara sits and waits as Renate wipes her eyes and blows her nose.

'I'm sorry,' she says. 'Max is all I have and it's very hard to see him go so far away.' When Schmidt returns with a plastic cup of water from the cooler, Renate has mostly composed herself. She takes the cup, gives Schmidt a tremulous smile of thanks and swallows a sip. 'I'm sorry,' she says again. 'What did you want to know?'

'Yesterday at Mildersee – did you see anyone else out there?'

'Herr Wagner was there. I didn't speak to him but I heard his lawnmower. I saw that Leon Kaiser. And Willie. I saw him too, later in the afternoon.'

Willie Koch again, thinks Barbara, underlining his name in her book with extra force.

'Where was Willie when you saw him?' she asks.

'He was walking past my cabin, heading to the lake, I suppose.'

'What about Leon Kaiser?'

'I saw him sitting in his garden, at the table, talking on the phone.'

'Herr Wagner says you came and went a few times during the afternoon. What were you doing?'

'I didn't know Herr Wagner paid me any attention.' Renate Bauer perks up, looking girlish despite her tears.

'Where did you go?' Barbara presses.

'Nowhere really. I went for a walk in the forest in the morning and I sat by the lake in the afternoon for a while. That's when I saw Leon Kaiser.'

'What time did you leave Mildersee?'

Renate hesitates a moment. 'I'm not good with time; I don't really keep an eye on it. I know I was home by eight p.m.... I watched

Jenseits der Spree and it starts at eight fifteen.'

Barbara thinks back. She'd noticed Wagner's vehicle in the little car park yesterday but no others. Then she remembers that Renate Bauer was pushing a bike when they saw her. 'Did you cycle to the lake yesterday?' she asks.

'Yes, that's right. I usually ride my bike. My home is just the other side of Mildersee.'

'You have one of the houses by the water?'

'Oh no, no. They're too expensive. I have a smaller place, on the road from Kummerfeld, but it's not far.'

'What about Nina Hartmann? Did you see her yesterday at all?'

'Mattias's girlfriend? No. She doesn't come to the lake very often. Mattias mostly came on his own.'

'Nina Hartmann has died,' says Barbara, watching for Renate Bauer's reaction.

'What? Mein Gott! Poor girl. What happened? Was she at Mildersee . . . ?' Renate brings her hand to her mouth. Barbara notes the contrast to Wagner's composed response.

'We're still looking into it, but yes, she died at Mildersee, so that's why anything you can tell us is very helpful.'

'Mein Gott,' says Renate again. 'I can't believe it.' She takes a sip of water. When she puts the cup down, she says: 'Nina was always with Leon Kaiser. Have you spoken to him?'

'We're speaking to everyone,' says Barbara. Before she ends the interview, she asks, 'What's your profession, Frau Bauer?'

'Oh, I don't work anymore. But before the wall came down I worked at Intershop – a department store, very exclusive. It was a prestigious job.'

Barbara has heard of the chain, which sold Western-brand consumer goods in formerly communist East Germany. Because the stores only accepted foreign currency, only members of the elite had regular access, and the shops helped create a visibly upmarket social class. Another fact comes to her mind: Intershop stores were closely monitored by the Stasi, with relatives of Stasi employees or officials often working as cashiers. As Schmidt shows Renate Bauer to the door, Barbara thinks that maybe she hasn't dug deep enough into the histories of the residents at the colony. Perhaps that's a mistake. Ralf Wagner and most likely Renate Bauer both have Stasi connections. There might be something more going on here than she's seeing.

• • •

'We should dig into the backgrounds of the residents of the colony,' says Barbara, running her hands through her hair. She is sitting with Schmidt, debriefing from the two interviews. 'Maybe there's something in the past that will give us a clue.'

'OK. Although both victims are from Berlin, they don't have any connections out here. And Nina Hartmann wasn't even alive during the GDR times . . .'

'That's true,' says Barbara. 'Did you notice Willie Koch's name come up in both witness accounts?'

'I really don't think Willie is involved in this,' says Schmidt. 'What motive would he have? He didn't really know these Berliners.'

'Yes he did. He was interested in Nina Hartmann and Mattias Ritter was heard arguing with him and threatening to call the police on him,' says Barbara. 'If Nina rejected Willie, that could give a guy like him motive. He strikes me as aggressive – I was surprised to find he didn't have any previous.'

Schmidt looks away, doesn't meet her eyes. 'I could ask around,' he says eventually. 'See if he ever talked about Nina. My colleague, Officer Klein, knows him quite well.'

'Do that. I'm going to chase the forensics results on his pouch and, depending on what that shows, I'll speak to the prosecutor about a formal accusation. But first we need to talk with Leon Kaiser. He still has the clearest motive. He and Nina were arguing yesterday; there was obviously something going on between them. I've arranged for us to speak with him at his Mildersee cabin' – she looks at her watch – 'in thirty minutes. We've got authorisation to search it too. The prosecutor signed off on it, given his proximity to Nina Hartmann and the argument I overheard yesterday.'

Before they drive to Mildersee, she puts a call in to Marilyn Mather. 'Did you find anything useful at the scene?' she asks.

Mather sighs. 'I can't give you certainties without the autopsy, but it looks like she's consumed something poisonous, though perhaps not the same as the previous Mildersee victim. There was no blood visible in her vomit, and her lips are less obviously blue. I'd put her time of death roughly within the last fourteen to eighteen hours...'

That would mean Nina Hartmann died last night. 'I saw her alive at around five thirty p.m. yesterday,' says Barbara.

'OK,' says Mather. 'Was she exhibiting any signs of distress?'

Barbara thinks back. 'No, I don't think so.'

'So that narrows the time of death down a little. Say between seven and ten p.m. last night.'

'Were there any signs of sexual assault?' asks Barbara.

'You'll have to wait on the autopsy for that.'

'When do you think that might happen?' she asks. 'This is quite urgent...'

'We are going as fast as possible. Yours aren't the only cases we work on, you know. We can't do everything. Do you want us to work all day and all night?'

Yes, thinks Barbara, I do, but she murmurs an apology and hangs up.

Chapter 31

Mildersee
3 p.m.

Barbara and Schmidt are standing outside Kaiser's cabin at Mildersee, watching Kaiser and his lawyer walking down the lane towards them. Kaiser is in his trademark loose trousers and t-shirt and has added a bucket hat to the ensemble today. His lawyer, wearing a skirt suit and carrying a capacious and expensive-looking handbag made of tan leather, is walking slightly off balance as the heels of her sandals sink into the sandy track. The lawyer nods at them as they reach the gate; Kaiser ignores them. Barbara and Schmidt follow the pair to an outdoor table in the shade of a large oak, festooned with a disco ball and various charms made of feathers and twigs bound with ribbons.

Barbara sits on one side of the table, facing Kaiser and his lawyer, Schmidt takes a seat at the far end. Kaiser's fingers are drumming the table, his right leg bouncing up and down. Nerves, maybe, thinks Barbara. She looks at him, not saying anything, and when he finally meets her eye she notices his pupils are dilated. Perhaps he's been using cocaine or another stimulant.

'Let's do this – I haven't got all day,' he says.

'Nina Hartmann is dead,' says Barbara.

Kaiser freezes, all movement stilled. 'What? No. She can't be. I saw her yesterday afternoon. She was fine.'

'She died last night,' says Barbara.

Kaiser shakes his head. 'Fuck,' he says, drawing the word out. 'How? What happened?'

'We're not sure yet.'

Kaiser shakes his head, runs his tongue over his lips. 'I need a drink of water or something. This is fucking mad.'

His lawyer leans down and pulls a small bottle of water out of her bag and hands it to him. Kaiser's hands are shaking as he twists off the top. Barbara waits while he drinks. It's more of a reaction than he showed to Ritter's death at least. When he puts the bottle back on the table, she says: 'As you know, I saw you with Nina Hartmann here yesterday afternoon. Why was she here?'

'She came back because of Mattias . . . I don't know, she wanted to say goodbye or something. She saw I was here and stopped by for a chat. We were friends and she needed some comfort.'

'What were you doing here?'

'I come out here when the weather is nice. Have a swim, have a rest. That's why I've got this place.'

'When I overheard you arguing with Nina Hartmann, she said she was thinking of going to the police.'

'Nah,' says Kaiser, shaking his head, face impassive. 'You must have misheard.'

Barbara decides not to press this. 'What time did you leave here yesterday?'

'Around six p.m.'

'How did you get home?'

'I drove.'

'Anyone who can confirm where you were last night?'

'I met a friend around ten p.m. for a drink. You can talk to her.'

'What were you doing between six and ten p.m.?'

'I don't know. Drove home, had a shower, made something to eat, had a smoke on the balcony . . .'

'There's no one who can confirm where you were during those hours?'

'Maybe a neighbour in Berlin,' he says, shrugging. He's trying for nonchalant, but his leg is jiggling again. Barbara feels a pulse of excitement. His shock at Nina's death seemed genuine but he's lied about the argument she overheard and he doesn't have an alibi for the time Nina died.

'We're going to conduct a search of your cabin and garden,' she says. Kaiser stiffens slightly, a fraction of a second, but she spots it. He looks across at his lawyer.

'I presume you have a warrant for that?' says his lawyer.

Barbara hands the warrant to her. The lawyer takes it, reads it quickly, nods at Kaiser.

'Why do you want to search my place?' he asks. 'Who've you been talking to? Whatever they've told you, it's bullshit . . .'

'You were one of the last people to see Nina Hartmann alive,' says Barbara. 'It's standard procedure.'

As Barbara and Schmidt walk up to Kaiser's cabin, trailed by the lawyer, Kaiser climbs into a faded hammock hanging in the shade of the tree, pulls his hat over his eyes and seems to go to sleep. Barbara watches him for a moment. Nina Hartmann was a friend, a lover, and aside from the initial shock he's exhibiting few signs of stress, no sadness, not even much curiosity. It's not normal. Perhaps the drugs he uses have numbed his reactions. Or maybe he's a psychopath, she thinks. The kind of person who has no empathy or care for anyone, who thinks they're smarter than everyone else. The type of person who is perfectly capable of murder.

The lawyer fumbles with the key to the cabin but eventually pushes open the door. The layout is similar to Mattias Ritter's – an L-shaped open-plan living space and kitchen and a bedroom to the right. But, unlike Ritter's place, it's a huge mess. In the living area, a turntable by the window, incongruously high-tech in the small space, has a bright-orange electrical cable leading from it out the window to a generator somewhere nearby, presumably. A tall pile of records beside it has toppled to the side, vinyls and album covers scattered across the floor. Two Scandinavian-style armchairs face a coffee table that is covered with half-empty glasses, an overflowing ashtray and a red candle that has burnt three-quarters down, its wax spread in a puddle around the base. The merest trace of a line of white powder runs along the tabletop. Barbara notices it – cocaine, no doubt. It's an insignificant amount but Kaiser is probably a regular user. She takes some pictures of the table and leaves it at that for the moment. There's not enough there to warrant a charge.

In the bedroom, black trousers and men's underwear lie on the floor beside the bed, which is covered in rumpled and stained bedding. Schmidt moves the clothes to one side with his foot, exposing the spine of a large book. Barbara glances at it and then crouches down for a closer look. '*Psychoactive Plants: All You Need for a Natural High,*' she reads out loud. 'Looks like he doesn't just rely on chemical highs,' she says to Schmidt.

She bags the book as evidence, then stands and goes through to the filthy kitchen – dirty dishes and wine and beer bottles sit on the countertop beside a fallen packet of potato chips, its contents spread across the floor, a line of ants marching to and from the litter towards the wall. There's a cool box with a bottle of sparkling wine, two beers and a vacuum pack of pork sausages, the latter looking decidedly sweaty. The shelves are stacked with plates and glasses but no food. There's no sign of any herbs, dried or fresh. No sign of any teas either.

She and Schmidt walk out and around the back of the cabin. There's an outhouse with a drop toilet, a bucket of brackish water and a giant pack of toilet paper with a few rolls missing. In the corner, three crates of beer are stacked one above the other, beside a crate filled with water bottles.

Schmidt points to the beer bottles. 'Augustiner. The same brand as we found in the boat.'

'Well spotted,' says Barbara. The brand is popular so it's not evidence of much, but still useful.

Behind the outhouse is a rubbish area. Three disposable barbecues, grimy with grease and meat remnants, sit on the ground next to a large bin overflowing with empty bottles – beer, Sekt, vodka, wine – flies and wasps buzzing around the sweet alcoholic detritus.

There's one final building, a small storage shed in the far corner of the block. One door, off its hinges, is leaning against the frame of the shed, the other is swinging open. She can see inside – a disorganised storage space with a broken deckchair, an inflatable unicorn, saggy and flat, a bag of cement mix leaking onto the ground, and behind all that a mass of firewood and spiderwebs and god knows what; she can't make it out in the dark. Schmidt takes his phone and uses it as a torch to shine a light into the gloom. Nothing much to see: a few garden tools, rusty and unused, the stack of cut wood. Barbara spots a gleam of something as Schmidt says, 'Nothing here.'

'Hang on a second,' she says. 'Shine the light towards the back again.'

He steps forward, sending the beam of light further back, and she hears him inhale. A second later she spots it too, the distinctive shape of an oar painted with a fat horizontal navy stripe, which has been thrown on top of the woodpile.

She goes back to Kaiser, out of the hammock now and back at the table eating a sandwich. His lawyer, on the phone, hangs up as she approaches.

'Do you have a boat, Herr Kaiser?' asks Barbara.

'Nope.'

'Then can you tell us why there's an oar in your shed? An oar that looks very much like the one that is missing from Mattias Ritter's boat.'

Chapter 32

Berlin

6.30 p.m.

Walker hasn't made any concrete progress but he has a better feeling about today. Meeting Hammer has been useful: he finally has an ally on the ground here. He's also visited the list of cafés that Hammer gave him, and he dropped the Popović name too. It didn't elicit any strong reactions but he's sure there were glimmers of recognition in a few eyes and that his persistence is being noted. If Markovich is in town, he'll likely hear that someone is looking for him. With a bit of luck he'll be tempted to contact Wayne Hopkins, their undercover guy in Australia, or, better yet, get a message to Walker.

He leaves the last café on his list and looks at his phone. Just gone 6.30 p.m. He and Barbara are having dinner at her place tonight. He's hoping Seb won't be there. He'll claim jet lag if he is, have a quick beer, leave them to it. He checks directions: a twenty-five-minute ride on the U-Bahn and a short walk at the other end. This U-Bahn station is underground, the walls tiled in pink and lime green, the platforms crowded and stuffy. The train rolls in, the little yellow carriages packed with people. Commuters, he supposes, not that anyone looks like they've been in an office. No suits, no laptops – plenty of jeans, backpacks, tattoos, piercings, black the colour of choice, everyone with headphones on, zoning out. As the train rattles and shakes its noisy way forward, he catches sight of his reflection in the window opposite, stifles a grin. His undercover look barely merits a glance here, in fact seems positively tame. He stands, pressed in among the crowd for a couple of stops, then finds a seat, closes his eyes, lets the hum of the train lull him.

Hermannplatz, his destination, is a big station. Yellow tiles cover the walls, and high ceilings give the impression it was once a grand space, that its designers had visions of something airy, light and impressive. No longer. Today it's packed and grubby, everyone swarming towards the stairs, heading for fresh air, away from the sweaty, humid subway. He goes with the flow and emerges in the middle of a large square. Market traders are packing up their stalls, a busker is strumming a guitar, a paltry haul of coppers in the case by his feet. Two lanes of busy traffic surround the square on all sides. Walker pulls out his phone, checks the directions, orients himself. It's only a five-minute walk to Barbara's. He cuts diagonally across the square, heading to his right, and joins a mass of people waiting to cross. When the pedestrian light goes to green, it's not the standard Aussie-style green man – instead there's a jaunty little bloke wearing a hat and striding out.

Walker follows the throng over the crossing, up a main street and into a different world. He hears the poetic rhythm of Arabic, Turkish and other languages he doesn't recognise. It feels as though he's left Berlin and been transported to Damascus, Beirut or Istanbul. He slows, absorbs it all – a bakery with trays of sweets piled high in the window: puff pastry, honey, bright-green pistachio and mounds of piped cream. The tables outside the coffee shops are filled with men, sitting in groups of three and four, drinking coffee and vividly coloured soft drinks. There are bridal shops, the dresses long, lacy and embellished, a furniture store shimmering with white and gold furniture and glittering chandeliers, and plenty of the globally ubiquitous mobile phone stores. He's winding in and out of crowds of people, huddles of men standing in conversation while their wives buy fruit and vegetables or sweet pastries from stores with names in Arabic lettering. It's only when he crosses the road and turns left onto a side street that the crowds dissipate.

A few blocks further on, he turns right again and passes one of the corner stores that sell booze. A bit like a bottle-o at home but smaller-scale, a combination of corner store and bottle shop. Walker goes in and stares at the beers in the fridge. A huge variety of brands, none of which he recognises. A young woman comes in, chooses a couple of one brand, and he follows her lead and picks up four. Thinks of Seb, sighs and grabs another four.

The streets around Barbara's place are lively. Early diners sitting outside a Vietnamese place slurping noodles; two older women drinking a bottle of wine outside a bar smile at him. He smiles back. Berlin is OK. It's grungy and a bit grubby but there's an energy too, a good vibe. He turns left again, onto a quieter side street, and finds Barbara's place, number 42. He looks up at it, a four-storey building painted pale grey, balconies on each floor, a double-width front door painted black and covered in graffiti. There's a big brass rectangle to the left of the door, with a host of names and buzzers beside them. It takes him a while to find *Guerra*, on the top, the far right.

'Hallo,' she says through the intercom, the big front door buzzing open. 'Fourth floor, all the way up . . .'

As he pushes the door open, a well-built bloke wearing jeans and a t-shirt follows him in, nods and walks past him and out through a door at the back of the entrance hall. Walker can see it leads into a back yard – gravel and concrete, a few trees, bikes chained to a stand, an area for bins. Something about the bloke gives him pause.

He hesitates for a beat, thinking maybe he should follow him, make sure he isn't stealing something, but then the front door buzzes open again and a young woman wheeling a bike comes in, talking on her phone, barely registering his presence, and walks through to the garden as well. It's a big block and there are lots of residents – he's being suspicious about nothing.

He starts up the stairs to Barbara's. He's climbing steadily, almost at the top, when he hears footsteps behind him, a couple of floors below. Stops for a moment, listening, wondering if someone is following him. The steps keep coming, casual and relaxed, so he keeps climbing too. There's nothing to worry about; he's just not used to these big blocks, with people coming and going all the time.

...

'I think we might have him,' says Barbara. 'Leon Kaiser, the guy we saw arguing with Nina Hartmann yesterday. He had run-ins with Ritter, the first victim, and we found the oar to Ritter's boat in his shed. He's claiming he didn't put it there, that he's never seen it before, but the prosecutor agrees it's enough to start a formal investigation. They've sent the oar to forensics and he'll be interviewed after that. We should have the autopsy back from Nina Hartmann tomorrow, so we'll know more about how she died too. It could be that Kaiser killed Ritter and then killed Nina when she figured it out . . .'

'That's great work, mate,' says Walker. 'Your boss must be happy.'

She and Lucas are standing on her balcony with their first beers. She's happy with the progress she's made today but is feeling slightly distracted by his presence, the fact that having him here is simultaneously a bit odd yet also natural and easy. He's slicked back his hair and is wearing a black t-shirt that shows off his arms and chest, and tightly fitted black jeans. He looks more Berlin, less outback Aussie, and for a moment she can imagine him living here, coming over regularly for dinner, someone she can talk to, someone who gets her. She realises she's never had Seb here for dinner or breakfast. The thought crosses her mind that it would be nice to wake up with Lucas, sit on the balcony with him, have a coffee, chat about the day to come. Lucas says something, but she's lost in her thoughts.

He looks quizzically at her. 'Penny for them?' he says.

'Sorry?' she asks, not understanding.

'You were miles away. What were you thinking about?'

'Oh, nothing, just thinking about the case,' she says, turning away to hide the fact that her cheeks are heating up. 'I still have some other questions. There's a local, Willie Koch – I can't rule him out. And then there are a group of older residents who seem to have connections with the Stasi. I wonder if there's anything in that.'

'Stasi? Weren't they secret police?'

'That's right. They were pervasive in East Germany. In places like Mildersee, cabins were a reward for members of the Party elite, including the Stasi, so it's probably just a coincidence.' She smiles at him. 'I'm doing that thing of complicating things that don't need to be complicated! I'm happy we've got Kaiser under formal investigation. Are you hungry? Shall we eat?'

They go inside and she heats up the big tortilla her mother gave her – despite Barbara being almost thirty-five, Maria insists on sending her home with food whenever she visits – and brings out the green salad she's made and the fresh bread and cheese she picked up on the way home. Lucas offers to set the table; he even finds a tablecloth her mother gave her years ago that she barely uses. It looks nice and feels homely. She puts the tortilla on a big plate between the salad and bread, and as she gets them both another beer she realises she's happier than she's been for a long time. It's great having Lucas around. There's no one else she feels this relaxed with, who she can share her thoughts with so freely. Seb is a steamroller – he hasn't got the patience for details or batting around ideas; her other colleagues are tied up in their own cases and she can't share her work with friends like Monika.

She picks up her beer. 'Prost!' she says. 'It's great having you here.'

• • •

'Yeah, boss, I followed him . . . Nah, he didn't clock me. He wasn't looking and it was busy enough, plenty of cover. I got a couple of pictures of him, I'll send 'em through . . . Just off Weserstrasse, in Neukölln. Name on the bell is Guerra. I got inside no problem, followed him right to the front door. I've been watching the building like you said. When he first got there, they came out onto the balcony, him and a woman. Since then, nothing happening. I'd say he's here for the night. You want me to wait? . . . OK, yeah, I'll be there in thirty minutes.'

Chapter 33

Berlin
Friday, 10 a.m.

Stefan Markovich pulls up the photos Popo sent him last night, taking a fresh look with more sober eyes. He's been up all night, most of it anyway; can't sleep anymore, fed up to the back teeth of being stuck in this shithole. He drank another bottle of JD, fell asleep as the sun was coming up, woke a few hours later, cramped, uncomfortable, the thin curtains letting in light, his head thumping, mouth dry, feeling crap.

The hangover is making him paranoid. He's wondering if maybe Wayne has turned traitor too. Is sending someone to get him. Wayne shouldn't have told this Donnie Young character about the Sofija - it's a need-to-know thing only. Maybe Wayne wants to be the boss now, reckons Markovich can be got rid of now that he's a long way away. I'll fucken kill the bastard, is his first thought. But could be he's overreacting, probably there's a reason Wayne's sent this bloke to see him. Maybe there's news of Nick Mitchell. The thought of Nick fills him with a rage as strong as he's ever felt. He's gonna find Nick, sooner than later, and Nick's gonna pay hard for ratting on them. He sits there for a while, playing through scenarios where Nick gets to watch as Michelle, his stupid bint of a woman, and his daughters, his pride and joy, take a bullet. Or worse.

That starts him thinking about the rest of it: being out on the bike, a group of Vandals beside him, wading into a fight, fists swinging, drinking too much, partying and getting wasted. Once these thoughts arrive he can't stop them building up, and no matter which way he cuts it, the life he's living now is shit in comparison. He can't imagine spending years here in the cold and grey, watching his back as Popo or his loyal lieutenants try to bring him down. Fuck that.

He picks up his phone, looks again at the pictures of Donnie Young. They're crap, can't see fuck-all of the bloke. Popo is fucken useless. He must have sent some blind cunt with the shakes and shit for brains to take them. The first couple, on a train by the looks, the bloke is sitting down. But you can't make out his face – the focus is fuzzy and he's mostly obscured by the people standing around him. A third, taken from behind, he's walking down a street. All you can see are black jeans, black t-shirt and brown hair, shoulder-length. He's quite tall by the looks but he doesn't have the bulk of a bouncer or a heavyweight muscle. Could be any one of a million blokes. The last picture, taken in front of a doorway, is a profile shot, the bloke with his head half turned away. Markovich can see he's got a couple of earrings, hair gelled back, his arm more muscular-looking in this shot. Something about him looks vaguely familiar but from these shit-quality photos he'd barely be able to pick out his best mate.

He messages Popo, *no clue never seen him before*, then sits for a minute thinking. The Banker, the big cheese back home, the only other one with a direct line to Vaso Ulić, has told him on no account to contact anyone in Australia. Literally fucken no one. The Banker is taking care of Vandals business, the money is still coming in. He's done as he's been told, hasn't even spoken to his mum for almost two years.

But these last few months, since he left Ecuador and Rotterdam, the long dull days in Berlin, feeling like shit the whole time, his resolve has wavered and he's sent a few messages to Wayne and a couple of other blokes that aren't in the bin. He hasn't told them anything, just asked after what's happening, following up Vandals business, chasing down Nick. It's his right. The club is his. Nick is his. He needs to remind them, can't let them forget who's the boss. And he wants revenge on Nick more than he's ever wanted anything. He wants to be the one who pays him back for his betrayal, for all these years spent in exile, far from home.

His head is pounding from too much booze. He needs to go out for a coffee but even the coffee here is shit. Europe is the pits. It's the middle of summer but the cool breeze coming through the window makes it feel like a winter day in Surfers. He can hear the neighbours starting up again, shouting at each other, their baby screaming. There's no space, no fucken room to breathe. His frustration mounts. He switches his speaker on, pulls up a playlist on his phone, 'Aussie Bangers'. It's on shuffle and as the first chords kick in he recognises the unmistakable intro to 'Highway to Hell'. It feels like a sign, feels fucken prophetic. He cranks the volume up, lets the sound crash and thump around the living room.

He roars the words, blood pumping in his veins. The tune rolls on, the guitars kicking in. He joins in with the chorus, shouting it loud, letting the music wash over him, cleanse him. He's back on the road, he's back on the bike, riding the winding track out to his place, the ocean off to his left, Aaron and Wayne beside him, the rest of the club following. The sun is burning his arms, he can feel the wind on his face, the bike thrumming beneath his thighs, hear the roar of the engines behind him. The song climaxes to a finish, the screaming guitar solo, the drums, and he hits Repeat and then Repeat again, turning up the volume until there's nothing but noise around him, and the fucken neighbours are thumping on the walls and he's roaring back at them, lifting his fist, punching a fucken hole in the shitty plasterboard wall. The music, his rage, both give him the lift he needs. He feels like getting on a plane and flying back to sunny Queensland right fucken now.

Then his phone rings and the blare of the ringtone cuts off the music. He looks down. *Popo*. That's all he fucken needs. 'Yeah,' he answers.

'Arrange to meet this bloke. We need to find out who he is, what he wants, how he found you.'

Markovich pauses. He's not taking orders from fucken Popo. And he's not meeting this bloke until he knows who he is. But no point arguing about it with Popo.

'Righto,' he says.

Popo doesn't answer him – the fucker just hangs up, the tune blaring back out of the speakers. But he's lost his mojo, turns the volume down, sits on the sofa. Fuck, he wants out of here. Wants to go home.

'Highway to Hell' finishes again and the next song starts up. Moody intro, synths. 'Great Southern Land'. Not a song he likes. But today, the first words about standing at the edge of the ocean light a flame of nostalgia in him so big he can barely contain it. A fire of homesickness rages inside him. He wants to be back on that prisoner island – he wants to be home. He'll fucken do time. He doesn't even care, he'd almost rather be in the bin with Aaron and the others than at someone else's beck and call in this fucken shithole. Ecuador was alright. Hot, loud, and some crazy shit going down. He was given respect, the women were sexy, the local dudes were a fucken laugh even if they were mental as hell. But this lot. Moody fucking Serbs that remind him of his dad and his uncle: hard, cold. There's no fun, just business all day, every day. Fuck it. He picks up his phone, looks up Wayne's number. Hesitates for the briefest second, then presses Call.

• • •

Walker has slept late, jet lag still playing games with his body clock. He was restless most of the night, the noise of the city intruding into his sleep. Cars accelerating as they come off the bridge and rattle across the cobbles outside, a garbage truck that stood beneath his window for what seemed like half an hour before dawn. The bins of the entire neighbourhood clattering and banging and crashing into the back, the engine roaring and choking, the noise and stink reverberating off the water into his bedroom. Then the sound of someone upstairs slamming doors, thumping around, clattering down the stairs. He finally fell asleep as first light was coming through the curtains and has only woken now, gone 10 a.m., his head heavy and groggy.

He gets up, makes himself a coffee and goes out to the balcony. The breeze from the canal is fresh, the bird calls loud and cheerful above the cyclists riding along the canal path. A couple of homeless men are sitting on a bench under one of the trees that line the path, drinking and arguing, their voices raised. Seems the whole city is awake and buzzing. He sighs, feeling momentarily a long way from home. Markovich is still out of reach and he's at a bit of a loss as to what to do next. Thinks of Barbara and feels his mood lift, a smile edging onto his face. Last night was great. They stayed up talking about their cases, catching up on life, setting the world to rights, until almost 2 a.m. And there was no sign of Seb, for which Walker was grateful.

He finishes his coffee and wanders inside, picks up his phone. A message from his sister, Grace, has arrived overnight. She'd been curious to find out more about Barbara, who he so often talks about, so he sent her a selfie last night of the two of them standing on Barbara's balcony, holding beers, Barbara laughing at his failed attempts to take a decent shot, him smiling too. It's a good picture, the only one he has of the two of them together.

He opens Grace's message. You guys are cute together, she's written, with a heart emoji. He shakes his head, laughing. A second message below: Even mom says so! She sends love by the way.

Walker wonders if Grace has spoken with their mother or is simply trying to mend a rift. He messages his sister and his stepdad, Richard, quite regularly but his relationship with his mum, never that close, has been decidedly frosty since Grace's visit to Australia. His mum is delighted that the trip inspired Grace's desire for a law career, but that has only slightly tempered her anger at the danger he unwittingly put his sister in. He understands – he hasn't forgiven himself for that either.

He's sitting on the edge of the bed, wondering what the best use of his day might be, when his phone rings. *Dan Rutherford.*

'G'day, sir,' Walker answers, doing a rough calculation of the time difference: 8 p.m. over there, middle of winter, dark already, working day over.

'Success,' says Rutherford, and there's an edge of excitement to his voice that Walker hasn't often heard. 'Markovich has bitten.'

'What's happened?' Walker's buzz is back, Rutherford's energy contagious.

'He called Wayne back,' says Rutherford. 'Good news about Nick Mitchell too: we've bought ourselves some time. Markovich told Wayne to hold off, he wants to handle it himself. And he asked about you too. He wanted to know who you were and why you were out there. Wayne told him he was in the bin with you a while back, like we agreed. He told him you're a genius at forgery, that you're in Europe selling fake Aussie passports. Markovich didn't say much but Wayne reckons he took the bait. Said Markovich is fed up and, like we thought, wants to come home. Wayne reckons he'll meet you.'

'Good one,' says Walker. 'Bloody hell, tell Wayne I owe him several beers.'

'How's it going with the local cops? Can you get a team lined up to manage the arrest and so forth? Sophie says her contact still isn't much interested . . . ?'

'I've found a detective that's keen. Markovich might have been behind a drive-by shooting here last week. Couple of gangsters died, young kid badly injured. This detective is working the case and he reckons the mob Markovich runs with are behind the shooting. If I can promise him Markovich, I reckon he'll cooperate.'

'Good,' says Rutherford. 'If Markovich serves some time in Germany, we can extradite to our end afterwards. Any luck, we'll have him locked up for the foreseeable. We've got his phone number now too. Stupid cocky bastard didn't hide it from Wayne. I'll send it through – the local cops will be able to trace it.'

'Most likely it's a burner. Don't reckon he'll hold on to it for long,' says Walker.

'Well, do it smartish, then, before he dumps it.'

'Righto,' says Walker, thinking that he's not really in a position to start ordering German cops around.

'Keep me in the loop. I want to know every detail of any op you set up.'

'Will do,' says Walker. After he ends the call, he feels like punching the air. Markovich has crawled out of his hole. The possibility of apprehending him has suddenly become real.

Chapter 34

Berlin
11 a.m.

Nina Hartmann's autopsy has come back frustratingly inconclusive. Barbara reads through the report one more time. No sexual assault and no other signs of violence to the body. Samples of Hartmann's body fluids have been sent for analysis for toxic compounds and the request has been marked as urgent, but toxicology takes time and it's likely she'll have to wait at least another day for the report.

They found her clothes – denim shorts, pale-green top, along with her bra and pants – on the jetty in front of Mattias Ritter's cabin. Perhaps Hartmann went swimming before she died, but Barbara still can't understand why she didn't get dressed afterwards, why she walked, or ran, naked, away from the colony. She drinks the last of her coffee, thinking of Nina Hartmann drinking whatever was in the thermos – tea, most likely – that poisoned her. The symptoms building, the fear, the confusion. As a pharmacist she would have known that she was having some reaction, perhaps even known what she'd ingested. Maybe that's why she wasn't dressed – she was running for her life. Barbara feels a shiver of empathy for the young woman and the fear she must have felt. It renews her determination and she pulls out her phone and calls the toxicologist.

'I can't magic up these results; these tests take time,' says the man at the other end of the phone.

'Is there anything you can tell me, anything at all? We're desperate.'

There's a long sigh down the line. 'Look, I can't confirm this but I've read the pathology report, and the symptoms – the blue tinge and swelling of her body – it's possible she ingested *Atropa belladonna*, deadly nightshade.'

'That's a plant, right?' says Barbara, double-checking. 'I mean, not a manufactured drug?'

'That's right. It grows wild in woodland, along the edges of paths and fences, but farmers usually remove it if they find it. The forest authorities too. It has small black fruits that sometimes tempt kids because they look a bit like cherries. But fatalities are comparatively rare. Most victims recover unless an extremely high dose has been ingested.'

'How high a dose?' asks Barbara. 'If she drank a thermos of tea laced with it, would it kill her?'

'It depends how much was used and what part of the plant.'

'Can you test for it? Is there a way of being sure?'

'Yes, I've already requested analysis for atropine, scopolamine and hyoscyamine in her body fluids. They'd be present if deadly nightshade is the cause of death.'

'Can you test the liquid we sent through in the thermos too?'

'Yes, that's gone for the same analysis and we'll test for other toxins in that too.'

'If she was poisoned by this plant, what would the symptoms be?'

'Not very nice,' he says. 'Atropine initially affects the parasympathetic nervous system. That's the part of the nervous system that regulates the heartbeat, manages digestive juices, and so on. Atropine is pretty fast-acting, within fifteen minutes to half an hour you'd have some concerning symptoms, like a very dry mouth and a fast or irregular heartbeat. As the poison progresses through the system, you can experience hallucinations, paralysis, unresponsiveness and, occasionally, death.'

'If she had a dry mouth and was feeling her heart beating fast, she might have kept drinking the tea, to quench the thirst, to calm herself down . . .' Barbara is thinking out loud.

'Some people also exhibit hyperthermia, that's abnormally high body temperatures, which might have caused her to drink more too,' says the toxicologist.

'Our victim was naked when we found her. Maybe she was feeling so hot that she took her clothes off.'

'Could be. There was a case of a monk in Bavaria who was found wandering around naked and very confused. He'd taken his clothes off because he was feeling overheated after eating deadly nightshade fruit. He was taken to hospital and survived. As I say, fatalities are rare.'

'Why do people eat it if it's so poisonous?'

'The fruit is hallucinogenic. Some people take it for the high, although I don't think it would give a good buzz. The symptoms are more disorientation and confusion.'

A hallucinogen, thinks Barbara. The kind of plant that gives you a high; the kind of plant that Kaiser has books on.

'This is super helpful,' she says. 'It fits with the way Nina Hartmann died and how and where we found her. The thirst, the overheating, the confusion, the disorientation—'

'Look, I'm glad you think it's been useful,' he interrupts. 'But I have to point out that it's conjecture at this stage. I won't have confirmation until I get the results. I'm hoping it will be tomorrow sometime.'

It all fits, though, thinks Barbara after she hangs up. The symptoms match the way Nina Hartmann died, and the kind of poison – not yew, but still plant-based – means her death can be linked to Mattias Ritter's murder too. She googles deadly nightshade to find out more. As the toxicologist said, it grows in woodland and fields and is common enough in the Berlin region if not managed. It's a plant that can probably be found in or around Mildersee.

She decides to go down to the evidence room to look at the book they confiscated from Leon Kaiser. She wants to see if yew, deadly nightshade or the castor oil plant are mentioned in it. If Kaiser could have found the information he needed to poison Mattias Ritter and Nina Hartmann by reading the book. She's heading for the lifts when her phone buzzes in her pocket.

'Hello, Detective, this is Amina Khan. I've got the results back from the bag you asked me to analyse. I didn't find any trace of yew leaves in it . . .'

'OK,' says Barbara. 'It was a long shot anyway.'

'No, but I have found something you might be interested in. The bag had a lot of traces, bits of flowers, stems and leaves of *Solidago canadensis* – Canadian goldenrod.'

Her voice is excited and Barbara forces herself not to sigh. Specialists so often assume that something that excites them will also be understood by a cop. 'How is that useful in this case?' she asks.

'I was reading through the original crime scene report, just as background, and there was a bunch of Canadian goldenrod found in the victim's rubbish, wrapped with a ribbon. I thought it was strange when I read the report. Goldenrod isn't really a plant you'd gift. It's an invasive species – I mean it's good for bees and butterflies and I think deer eat it, but it's not a decorative flower, really—'

'So it's possible that the owner of this bag left the flowers at

Ritter's cabin?' asks Barbara, interrupting the biology lesson, her interest fully engaged now.

'Yes. I took samples from the original bunch found at the scene and when I compared it to the traces in the bag, there is a close match. There's a very good chance that the owner of this bag supplied them.'

This means Willie Koch was at Ritter's cabin on the day Mattias Ritter died. Leaving flowers for Nina. He was interested in her, but she obviously didn't reciprocate. If Willie saw Nina throwing his gift into the rubbish, rejecting his advances, that could well have enraged him. Kaiser is still the more likely suspect, given the argument he had with Nina and the presence of Ritter's oar in his shed, but Khan's findings confirm that her gut feel about Willie was right. He's lying. He's more involved with Ritter and Hartmann than he's owned up to. Good to know she hasn't totally lost her policing instinct.

'Thank you,' she says to Amina Khan. 'We have a suspect that we're questioning but this is very useful background information.'

'I hope it helps,' says Khan. 'I can't stop thinking about the girl from yesterday. It was such a distressing scene. Do you have any more information on how she died?'

'Not yet,' says Barbara. 'I'm still waiting for the toxicology report, but the working theory is that she maybe ate or drank something containing deadly nightshade. The colour of her skin and the swelling are symptomatic, apparently, and some of her behaviour suggests she might have taken something hallucinogenic.'

'Oh, *Atropa belladonna*,' says Khan. She pauses. 'Your first victim was poisoned with yew and both yew and *Atropa* are local plants. Plants you could find growing wild if you knew what you were looking for.'

'That's what I thought too,' says Barbara. 'Would it take a lot of knowledge to identify and use these plants?'

'No, not really. Some basic research on toxic plants would probably bring up these species. You'd need to know a little bit more about how to prepare them, but I'm sure an internet search would turn something up.'

'Good to know,' says Barbara, thinking that while Kaiser is no forest expert his taste in books suggests he's done at least a modicum of research.

'Would you like me to look into this a bit more for you?' asks Khan. 'I could come out to Mildersee again. I could try to find the yew and deadly nightshade plants, and *Ricinus communis*, the castor bean plant too . . .'

'I'd love your help, but I don't have the budget for it, unfortunately. And as we have a suspect we're investigating, I can't justify asking for more resources right now.'

'Of course,' says Khan. 'I understand. I wouldn't usually ask, but this case has hit me quite hard. Thanks for updating me – I appreciate it.'

When the cop in charge of the evidence room brings Kaiser's book over, Barbara sits at a nearby desk to flick through it. She's astounded, as she turns the pages, by the number of plants that have psychedelic properties. Hundreds of different plants, from all around the world. She figures the author, if he tried them all himself, must have properly fried his brain. Of the plants she's looking for, yew isn't included but – bingo – deadly nightshade gets a mention.

'*Atropa belladonna*: beautiful, psychoactive and dangerous,' she reads. '"Atropa" refers to Atropos, one of the Three Fates in Greek mythology, who snipped the string of a person's life and decided their death. Found in scrub and woodland, the deadly nightshade lives up to its name. Though highly poisonous, it has medicinal properties and has been used in the past to treat abdominal pain and motion sickness. Psychoactive ingredients present in the plant's leaves can cause euphoria and hallucinations or, if too much is taken, disorientation and memory loss.'

None of it sounds particularly pleasant to Barbara, but Kaiser has admitted to regularly taking drugs and maybe it offers a different kind of high. She signs the book out of evidence and takes it upstairs with her. She'll bring it up during questioning. It's evidence of his knowledge of the poisonous properties of the plant, if nothing else.

When she gets back to her desk, she finds that the forensics report on the oar they found in Kaiser's shed has arrived. As she reads it through, a smile comes to her face. They've got him. Leon Kaiser has some real questions to answer now.

Chapter 35

Berlin

12 p.m.

Markovich has been sitting and thinking since he hung up on his call with Wayne. It was a call worth making, that's for fucken sure. The lead Wayne's given him on Nick's whereabouts is gold. He'll find Nick now, no worries. He's told Wayne to leave it with him because finishing off Nick and his missus is a job that Markovich is very much saving for himself. He puts in one call, though, to a cold little bastard they call Brains. Asks Brains to find exactly where Mitchell is hiding in Hewett. Brains is expensive but he's the best. And he's not a Vandal, so there's no danger he'll get sentimental about Nick and maybe decide to give him a heads-up, a chance to run. No. Brains'll find Nick and, once he does, Markovich will get his revenge – and he's gonna enjoy every fucken minute of it.

The fact that this Donnie Young bloke who's over here looking for him is into dodgy passports is good news too. The timing couldn't be better. He'd got a new ID in Ecuador, a Serbian passport, name of Pejovic. But then a mole in the local cops had told them the AFP had traced him on that name. He left the country sharpish with another ID. They stuck with Serbian, easier to get hold of, apparently: welcome, Dragan Antić.

A dodgy Aussie ID, though – that would be the thing. That would make it a lot easier to get home. They don't check citizens the way they do foreigners. He'll have to do something, cut his hair, grow a beard, get some surgery maybe, who knows – maybe this Donnie Young will have some ideas. But this might be a way out of this shithole, a way back home.

He'll have to play his cards close to his chest, though. Vaso and, equally importantly, the Banker in Sydney don't want him going back yet so he'll have to do it on the quiet. But once he turns up out there, there's not much they'll be able to do about it. He can take his revenge on Nick, which'll be good news for everyone, then find himself a place under the radar somewhere. Australia's so bloody big there's plenty of room to disappear.

He could go out bush again. At least the weather's good and there's plenty of space, and he can always spend weekends down the coast. Or, better yet, he could go to WA, a long way from everyone who knows him. Yeah, that'd be the thing. Go to WA, get himself set up over there. He lies back on the sofa, daydreaming about getting drunk in Perth, riding his bike up the coast all the way to Broome. The freedom of it. Nowhere to be, no one to please. And when he gets bored of all that, there'll be plenty of trouble to be getting into out west for sure. He laughs, cheered at the thought.

First things first, he needs to meet with this Donnie Young, find out what the score is. Wayne reckons he's pretty good, but he's never tried one of his passports for real so who knows. That shit isn't easy. He needs to see what the bloke can do. If he's the real deal, maybe the rest of the Ulić clan will have use for him too. Not only Aussie passports but dodgy IDs generally.

He picks up his phone, looks at the shitty pictures Popo sent one more time. He's certain that he doesn't know the bloke but still, caution rears its head. Don't go rushing in, he thinks. The thought of nights out in Perth washes through him again but he pushes it down. Slow and steady, slow and cautious.

He pages through his contacts until he finds Vuk's number, calls him.

'Yeah?' says Vuk, as monosyllabic as ever.

'Listen, that Aussie bloke that was looking for me. Has he been in again?'

'Yeah, couple of nights ago. I didn't talk to him.'

'If he comes in again, get his number, tell him I'll meet him.'

'Alright.'

'Popo wants me to go to Hamburg tonight. I'll be there a couple of days. So, say Sunday sometime.'

'OK.'

After Markovich finishes the call, he takes out the SIM card and crushes it; gets a new one from the kitchen drawer. Can't be too careful. Could be the fucken Feds at home are listening to Wayne's phone, you never fucken know.

• • •

Walker is sitting with Hammer, on the fourth floor this time, in a very small office that gives no hint as to who might usually use it, not a piece of paper or any personal effects on display. He updates the German cop on his conversation with Rutherford, Hammer listening intently.

'I will ask someone to look at that phone number immediately. We can only hope he's too stupid to get rid of it,' Hammer says. 'Wait one minute, please.' He goes to the door, speaks in rapid German to someone outside of Walker's eyeshot. When he comes back, he says: 'I'm taking this seriously because I am very interested in this man. We showed his picture, the one you gave us, to our witness and they recognised him. They are certain he was the gunman on the drive-by.'

The news doesn't shock Walker. Trouble follows Markovich wherever he goes. 'OK,' he says. 'So we need to plan how we'll handle this. If he contacts me or if I can arrange to meet him, how are we going to pick him up?'

Hammer hesitates. 'I would rather you were not involved,' he says after a moment. 'You do not have jurisdiction here. This is something my team can manage.'

'Fair enough,' says Walker. 'I don't want to be part of the arrest, but I'm the bait... You'll struggle to make contact with him without me.'

Hammer nods slowly. 'Maybe,' he concedes.

'I'm going back to the Sofija and the other bars today, see if anyone has a message for me. If not, I'll try calling this number myself. I'll say Wayne passed it on.'

As he's speaking, there's a knock on the door. A young cop, very neat and correct, the kind of bloke who irons his jeans, comes in and stands stiffly by the door and says something in German. Hammer interrupts him with a question, another burst of German, and the young cop turns and goes, closing the door quietly behind him.

'The number you gave us is no longer working,' says Hammer.

'He's changed numbers,' says Walker, disappointed but not entirely surprised. 'He's pretty clued up. He hasn't got this far by being careless.'

Chapter 36

Berlin

3 p.m.

'We sent the oar we found in your shed for forensic analysis,' says the prosecutor.

Barbara is sitting beside him on one side of the table, Kaiser and his lawyer facing them on the other, Kaiser looking pale under the blue-white light of the interview room.

'There were significant DNA traces on the oar and a good number of these traces match the DNA sample you provided. According to our specialists, it's beyond doubt that this oar was handled by you.' The prosecutor lets this information sink in and then he asks: 'How do you account for that, Herr Kaiser? In your preliminary interview you told us that you had no idea how the oar came to be in your shed. Do you want to tell us the truth this time?'

Kaiser shakes his head. 'I don't know how it got to be there,' he says, but to Barbara his voice lacks conviction.

'Then how do you explain the fact that your DNA is all over it?' asks the prosecutor.

Kaiser shrugs. 'It was in my shed, so, I don't know, maybe it got contaminated...'

The prosecutor pulls out a diagram. It shows the oar in sketch. Marked across the middle section of the oar is a thick red line. He shows the diagram to Kaiser and his lawyer. 'One of the most surprising areas in which DNA was found is across the middle of the oar. Hair and skin – your hair and skin, Herr Kaiser – in a position that is consistent with someone carrying the oar across his shoulders. It's not a few random cells picked up through contamination. It's a large section of the oar, almost forty-five centimetres in length, covered in your DNA.'

Kaiser doesn't say anything.

'We also found something on the blade of the oar, but this was not consistent with your DNA—'

'There you go, then,' says Kaiser. 'The thing is covered in DNA, not just mine.'

'The DNA on the blade of the oar matches the DNA of our second victim, Nina Hartmann.'

'Nina was in that boat all the time,' says Kaiser. 'It belonged to her boyfriend.'

'That's true,' says the prosecutor. 'But this was a strand of long blonde hair found on the blade of the oar. This is quite unusual. Oars are dipped in and out of water, any hair would be washed away quite quickly, so this hair obviously came from a time after the boat was last used...'

'So maybe Nina put the oar in my shed.'

'Maybe. But the forensics team also ran some checks on evidence that was found in Herr Ritter's boat on the day of his murder and your fingerprints and DNA came up on those too...'

'What evidence?' asks Kaiser's lawyer.

'Two beers that were found in the bottom of the victim's boat clearly have your client's fingerprints and traces of DNA on them.'

'No comment,' says Kaiser, but his eyes are darting nervously between the prosecutor and his lawyer.

'What do you know about deadly nightshade, sometimes known as belladonna?' asks the prosecutor, changing direction.

'Umm ... Nothing,' says Kaiser, looking confused. 'What is it? Some kind of pill?'

The prosecutor pulls out a picture of a leafy green plant with shiny black berries and slides it across the table to Kaiser.

He looks at it and shrugs. 'What's this?' he asks.

'It's a plant called deadly nightshade,' says the prosecutor.

'I know nothing about plants,' says Kaiser.

The prosecutor looks at Barbara and she leans over and puts the book they took from Kaiser's cabin on the table in front of him.

'Do you recognise this book, Herr Kaiser? We found it in your cabin.'

'Yeah ... but it's not mine, it's Nina's. She was into that natural shit. She was always picking stuff in the forest and making teas or putting things in vodka to preserve it. She wanted to find out if she could get high on any of it but that's not my gig at all. That's what dealers are for.'

The prosecutor looks at Barbara. 'Your fingerprints and DNA are all over this book, Herr Kaiser,' she says.

'It was in my cabin. I must have moved it or something—'

'I believe we have enough evidence to charge you with the murder of both Herr Ritter and Frau Hartmann,' interjects the prosecutor. 'Your DNA is on the oar to Herr Ritter's boat and on two beers found in the boat with his body. You have a history of disagreements with him. You were seen arguing with Frau Hartmann the afternoon before her death and you have a book in your possession that details the plants used in her death. We will be arresting you and you will be remanded in custody until a preliminary hearing.'

'I didn't kill Ritter or Nina - this is fucking crazy!' Kaiser's voice is raised.

'Well, do you have any explanation for how this oar came to be in your shed? How it came to be covered in your DNA and Frau Hartmann's hair? What you and Frau Hartmann argued about?'

There's a long pause. Kaiser looks at his lawyer and she turns back to them. 'I'd like to consult with my client for a moment,' she says.

Barbara leans over, pauses the tape, then she and the prosecutor leave the room and wait in the corridor outside. The prosecutor is a lithe, slim guy of about her age, with rectangular steel-rimmed glasses and short dark hair. As they wait, he bends from side to side, stretching his arms above his head, then leans over and touches his toes, exhaling noisily. Barbara raises her eyebrows, but rearranges her face to neutral as he straightens up again. 'It's very important to stretch your glutes after you've been sitting for any period of time,' he says.

Barbara nods. 'Right,' she says, but then he looks at her as if he's waiting for her to start bending and stretching too. She spies a vending machine at the end of the corridor. 'Coffee?' she asks, walking towards it.

'No thanks,' he says. 'I never drink caffeine after eleven a.m.'

Barbara, who can't imagine getting through a day without half a dozen coffees, gets herself one, in defiance of the prosecutor's health regime more than any great need. She's halfway through a very bad cup when the door behind them opens again and Kaiser's lawyer sticks out her head.

'My client has a statement he'd like to make,' she says.

Chapter 37

Mildersee
3 p.m.

Amina Khan parks her car in the small parking area at the Mildersee colony. The forest is on her left, the cabins running down towards the lake on her right. She gets out of the car, breathes in the pine-scented air. As she looks around, the sun warm on her arms, the blue sky dotted with a few small white clouds, the trees of the forest casting light shade across the car, she thinks how peaceful and pleasant it is here. It's hard to believe there have been two murders in less than a week, and that the colony likely harbours a killer.

    She finished work at 2 p.m. today, extra hours worked over the last few weeks meaning she can take part of this afternoon off. Rather than go home, she's decided to pay Mildersee another visit. She can't stop thinking about the young woman who died out here. The awful reality of her death, her naked swollen body, the terrible violence of it. She's decided she'll have a look around for an hour or two, see if she can find anything that might help the detective working on the case. She loves looking at plants, and exploring this area where forest meets lake will be a pleasant way to spend a sunny afternoon. If she can find some plants that offer clues as to how that poor girl died, that will be a bonus.

Despite the warm day, the colony is quiet. There are no other cars and there doesn't seem to be anyone around – the trees whispering in the breeze, the coo of a pigeon the only sounds. Perhaps people are anxious, the two deaths naturally casting a long shadow. Still, for her purposes, it's better this way. The empty colony gives her space to have a good look around without being interrupted.

She starts by walking into the forest – it's far more likely she'll find European yew and *Atropa belladonna* among the trees than in the gardens of the colony. She's soon lost to the plant life around her, her mind absorbed in this favourite and familiar task. When she next looks at her watch, well over an hour has passed and it's 4.25 p.m. She's quite deep in the forest now and hasn't spotted either yew or deadly nightshade, but it hasn't been a wasted afternoon. She's found quite a few interesting species, including some wild sorrel growing in a sunny glade that she picked. It will make a delicious soup for dinner – a green borscht, with potatoes, onion, egg. She pulls out her phone and checks her position on the map. It seems that, if she walks a little further, she'll come out of the woods and onto a path that runs back down to the colony. She walks purposefully, no longer examining each plant that catches her eye, her mind drifting between the recipe for sorrel soup and monitoring Google Maps.

The forest is already beginning to thin when she spies a soft green needle-like foliage out of the corner of her eye. She stops, walks closer – it's a yew. A youngish tree, not tall, the greenery dotted with bright-red berries. She switches into work mode, looking at the ground around the tree for any obvious marks, tracks or traces. Nothing. The roots and base of the tree are healthy. She switches her thinking mind off, lets her eyes roam across the foliage, and that's when she spots it. The natural shape of the tree is ever so slightly distorted, a small branch missing. She moves closer, phone out, taking pictures. She can see where someone has cut the branch, a clean mechanical cut, not a natural break. This could be the tree, she thinks. This could be where the yew for the first murder was harvested. She takes a few more pictures, then drops a pin in the map so she can find it again.

She stands for a moment, wondering if she should call the detective right now, get her to come out this afternoon. But the detective is busy and Amina's not sure how much it will mean to the investigation to have found the tree that was likely used in the first murder. It proves, perhaps, that the murderer knows their way around the forest, not much else. She looks around the spot, committing it to memory, then walks on, coming to a slim path that runs alongside the forest edge and which, according to her phone, will lead her back to Mildersee.

The path meanders along, the trees dark and gloomy on one side, fields of wheat almost ready for harvest gold in the sunlight on the other. The fields curve away as a house appears ahead on her right, white curtains in the windows, red geraniums growing on the balcony. As she approaches, admiring it, thinking how typically German it looks, a huge dog bounds towards the fence, barking ferociously. She jumps in fright – she's never really liked dogs and this one looks dangerous. She slows down, keeping her eye on the dog, which has its paws on the gate and is growling low and deep. A young man appears, hair cut short, wearing a vest, tattoos on his neck and shoulders. He grabs the dog by its wide leather collar, watching her, taking in her headscarf, eyes contemptuous. Neither man nor dog makes her feel safe and she turns away, avoiding eye contact. The path curves just ahead: she'll be out of sight in a few steps. She's walking faster, focused on putting distance between them, when she hears him shout: 'Germany for Germans. Fuck off back where you came from.'

She feels the familiar flush of shame and anger, wants to turn and shout, 'I *am* German', but stays silent, keeps walking, around the corner and out of sight.

The ugly taste of the encounter is still with her when she reaches her car. She puts the bag with the sorrel on the passenger seat and thinks again about calling the detective. But she's not in the mood. Not in the mood to be helpful, not in the mood to deal with police, even one as approachable as the female detective. She curses the man who's stolen the pleasantness from her afternoon. Then tells herself: no, I own my own mood. I will not let him take this productive afternoon from me.

She looks at her phone: *4.55*. She still has time to explore the colony, but the confrontation with the angry local has shaken her and drained her enthusiasm. Still, she doesn't want to go home feeling like this either. She decides she'll walk down to the lake, sit by the water, relax and reclaim her good mood before she drives home. She locks the car, leaves her bag inside, hoping the sorrel won't wilt too badly, and walks down into the colony proper, her natural curiosity returning as she passes the gardens. Some are barely cared for, dry and thirsty in the summer heat, others are tended in a way that's not exactly to her taste – very neat and tidy, vivid-green lawns and colourful flower beds that feel somehow unnatural in the sandy pine forest. But one or two are in the style she'd have herself: meadow-like lawns, hardy plants such as lilac bushes, herbs in containers. Not surprisingly, she sees no sign of deadly nightshade; she's certain it wouldn't be allowed in a holiday colony like this. No sign of another yew either, or the castor bean plant she found at the scene of the young woman's death.

She wanders aimlessly, twisting and turning through the little lanes in a meandering direction towards the water. The stillness brings back her sense of calm and peace. No people to hassle her, just plants and trees and birds. She can just see the lake glinting in the sunshine ahead when she glances through an open gate and glimpses a plant dotted with pinkish-red buds. She stops, feeling a tingle of excitement. She needs to get closer to confirm, but she's almost certain that it's *Ricinus communis*, the castor bean. She puts her hand on the gate, then hesitates. This is someone's private garden.

'Hello?' she calls. 'Hello? Is anyone home?'

Her voice reverberates in the silence. She calls again. Still no answer. There's no one here, no one anywhere in the colony. She hesitates for a fraction longer, then steps past the open gate and walks quickly across the unfamiliar garden. She's not doing any harm, she tells herself. She only wants to get a closer look at the plant.

It's growing in a large terracotta pot on the far side of the garden. The leaves are right: glossy, alternate and palmate with five deep lobes and coarsely toothed segments. But it's the spiny pinkish-red capsules that convince her. Definitely *Ricinus*. She looks closely at the capsules. The colour is very similar – it could be the very same plant that she found at the scene of Nina Hartmann's murder. She'd like to compare it properly with the specimen back in the lab and give a sample to the detective, but she needs a proper cutting for that. There's a small shed in the far-right corner of the garden – perhaps there'll be scissors or shears there.

Caught up in her work, her mind busy with thoughts of *Ricinus*, no longer concerned about trespassing, she walks over to the shed. The door is unlocked and it's neat and clean, a long wooden table in the centre, a pile of firewood stacked at the rear. She hears the rustle of a rodent in the woodpile and shudders. She doesn't like mice or rats but she wants this cutting, so she steps over to the table. The woody scent of linseed oil emanates from the tabletop – it's only recently been oiled and cleaned. Two cutting boards, homemade by the look of them and also oiled and clean, are stacked at the far end, beside a mortar and pestle. No tools, though.

Beneath the table are a series of wooden boxes, and she bends down and pulls one out. It's filled with glass jars, all empty save a trace of leaves in one. She opens it and sniffs: herby but indistinct. The second box has more glass jars, not empty this time but filled with herbs, leaves, roots, berries and more. They're neatly stacked and labelled, some with common names, others with the full scientific name. Whoever this cabin belongs to is very knowledgeable about plants, perhaps even a botanist, she thinks.

She looks through the collection, curious as to what's been preserved, when one of the labels catches her eye. She stops, feels her heart beat a little faster. The pale-green needles are familiar and the label on the front confirms it: *Taxus baccata*, European yew. She rifles through the box more quickly now, and her hand shakes a little when she comes to a jar that holds a handful of shiny black berries. She doesn't have to read the label to recognise them: *Atropa belladonna*, deadly nightshade.

She's certain now that she's found the person who killed both Nina Hartmann and the first victim. She should have brought her bag – she could have taken a picture on her phone to show the detective. Lost in her thoughts, she doesn't hear footsteps crossing the garden and coming to a stop at the door of the shed.

'Who are you and what are you doing here?'

The voice behind her takes Amina by such surprise that she screams and drops the jar she's holding in shock. It clatters onto the floor as she turns and leaps to her feet, her hand to her throat, feeling her pulse racing beneath her skin.

Chapter 38

Berlin

5 p.m.

'I didn't kill Ritter, and I didn't kill Nina either,' says Leon Kaiser. He's slumped in his chair, deflated, completely altered from the cocky and confident man Barbara first spoke with earlier this week.

'That's your statement?' says the prosecutor, sounding frustrated.

Kaiser looks over at his lawyer, licks his lips and says: 'I didn't kill them, but I saw Ritter on the afternoon he died. Me and Nina saw him.'

'And . . . ?' The prosecutor sounds more interested.

'Mattias had lots of money and he knew some cool people because he was a journalist. He got invites to gigs and backstage passes and shit like that. I never liked him, he was a poser, but Nina was into him. He took her to expensive restaurants and on nice holidays and then he asked her to move in with him. After that, it all went to shit. He was super old and dull and Nina was bored out of her mind. She was hardcore, she liked dancing and partying, and she came to my gigs a lot. She wasn't really into having a monogamous relationship and we started having a thing together. It was nothing serious, a bit of fun when we were in the mood. Last weekend, I sent her a dick pic and Ritter found it. Ritter hated me because I reminded him of who he used to be and he was jealous as fuck . . .'

Kaiser pauses, takes a sip of water.

'On the day of his death . . .' the prosecutor prompts.

'Yeah, so Ritter saw the picture, that day out at the lake. He was using her phone for some reason and there it was, larger than life.' Kaiser gives a barking laugh, and Barbara is reminded of why she doesn't like him. 'Yeah, anyway, they had a big argument, and he told Nina it was over. She came to see me afterwards. She was angry at him, said he totally overreacted, and she was pissed at me for sending the pic too. I told her it was her own fault for not being straight with Ritter. She was mad as hell – she didn't have anywhere else to live and she'd gotten used to the lifestyle with Ritter, so she had a lot to lose. She wanted to get wasted, forget about the fight. We smoked a spliff and then we did some coke and some other stuff. I can't remember exactly what, but we were mixing it up. Later, like early evening, Nina and I went down to my jetty to have a beer. We were sitting there and we saw Ritter, coming from his place, walking across to his jetty. He was totally fucked up, off his head. I don't know what he'd been taking but he was carrying the oars to his boat and he was all over the place, couldn't have walked a straight line to save his licence. We watched him for a while. It was funny. He could barely untie the boat and then he fell inside and dropped the oars. One of them was in the boat, the other one was still lying on the jetty. We thought he'd just tripped but when he didn't get up Nina got a bit concerned and went over to check on him. Ritter was lying in the boat. He was so spaced out he couldn't sit up and he wasn't making much sense, saying he was thirsty, saying his heart was beating too fast. She said maybe we should do something but I figured he was just wasted, that he'd taken too much of something, maybe he'd needed a pick-me-up too after the big fight they'd had. We didn't have any water, but Nina made me put the beers we had with us in his boat, so that he had something to drink, and then I used the oar he left on the jetty to push the boat out. He was just lying there, spaced out. I told her he'd be fine. I figured he'd trip for a bit then come out of it. You gotta remember we were wasted too. I never liked him much and Nina was still pissed at him. For some reason, I took his oar back to my cabin. I don't know why. Like I say, I was wasted, I wasn't thinking things through. I threw it in the shed and forgot about it.'

Barbara and the prosecutor exchange a glance. There's a ring of truth to the story, she thinks.

'What time did you see Mattias Ritter that day?' she asks.

'I don't know. Nina left around seven thirty, so maybe sevenish...'

'Neither of you checked on Ritter again?'

'Nah. Well, I didn't. I had a gig that night and after Nina left I started planning my set and forgot about him. I mean, I didn't think there was anything wrong with him, just that he was a bit wasted. I left Mildersee not that long after Nina did, around nine. I only heard he'd died when Nina called me the next day.'

'She told you how he died?'

'She said he died in his boat, that's all. I thought it must have been an overdose, that shit happens. I couldn't work out why the cops were so interested. She said she hadn't told you that we saw him getting in the boat, she thought it would look bad, and she asked me not to say anything either.'

'What about the day Nina Hartmann died? The two of you were arguing...'

'She came to see me after I spoke with you.' He nods at Barbara. 'She wanted to make sure we were telling the same story. She asked me what I did with the oar and that's the first time I remembered it was there. She got crazy. Said I should have ditched it, that having it made us look like we'd done something to Ritter. I told her to chill but she wouldn't have it. She said she was gonna tell you that I had the oar. Whatever. I let her go. Best thing when women are moody is to let them cool down. I knew she wouldn't talk to you – I figured she'd calm down quick enough.'

'And that night . . . ?'

'I came back to Berlin, right after I saw you.' He nods at Barbara again. 'Like I already told you, I met this other chick for a drink. I can't believe Nina's dead. I liked her. And I didn't do anything to her.'

Chapter 39

Berlin
6 p.m.

It's taken him most of the afternoon, but Walker has finally hit pay dirt, back at the Sofija, the very first bar he visited. At all the other cafés and bars, Markovich's name met with the same shaken heads, hard faces. He bought a coffee in one and sat there for a while, the focus of stares and simmering tension. He tried to order a beer in another, but the bloke who was serving put his hands up, shook his head, refused to serve him. After that he gave up trying to make a connection, simply asked for Markovich, watched for the reaction. He thought he saw a glimmer of recognition in one place, made a note of the name of the café. Most of the others don't want to know him, a foreigner in a closed world.

The Sofija isn't empty this afternoon, a group of three young blokes sitting at a table outside, legs outstretched, empty cups of coffee and small plastic bottles of water dotting the table in front of them. One of them gives him a side-eye glance as he goes in, but the others ignore him. The same young bloke with the dead grey eyes and tattooed face is standing behind the bar. Walker orders a beer, and the bloke fishes a bottle out of the fridge behind him, opens it. Walker pays, takes a long drink still standing at the counter, and then says, 'You remember me? I'm looking for a mate, a bloke called Markovich – Stefan Markovich. He been around at all since I was here last?'

The bloke assesses him. Walker feels the same chill he felt the first time he was in here. This young man, not much older than his sister Grace, has a coldness, a palpable sense of cruelty. He's capable of violence, has delivered it more than once, Walker would bet on it.

'He wants to meet you. Leave your number,' says the bartender.

Walker, who'd been expecting silence or rejection, is momentarily taken aback by the answer. But once it sinks in, he has to work to keep his face expressionless.

'Righto,' says Walker. 'You got a pen?'

The bloke slides over an ordering pad and a black Bic. Walker writes down his number and hesitates for the slightest millisecond before writing *Donnie Young* underneath. He'd been about to write *Lucas Walker*, about to give his real name. He looks up; the young bloke is watching him, eyes as emotionless as a bird of prey's. He's noticed the hesitation, thinks Walker, berating himself internally. He hasn't inhabited Donnie Young this time, hasn't lost himself in the alter ego like he does when he's properly undercover. He's almost blown it, just as Markovich is hovering into view.

'Here,' he says, pushing the piece of paper over. 'When does he want to meet? I'm only in town for a few more days . . .'

'He'll call you.'

'Yeah, alright, but tell him I won't be around much longer. I'm leaving town after this weekend.'

'Wait till Sunday,' says the bloke.

'OK,' says Walker, picking up the bottle of beer, aiming for nonchalance, going outside and choosing a table at the far end, away from the group with their coffees. Takes his time drinking his beer, doesn't want to give the impression he's in a rush, that he's worried or excited. The traffic rumbles by – a yellow bus, plenty of white vans, the smell of diesel heavy on the warm air of the afternoon. A group of teenagers, laughing and shoving each other, pass him on the footpath, followed by an old woman wheeling a shopping trolley and a young bloke on his phone arguing with someone. Walker looks without seeing. He's still angry with himself for his near miss with his name but he's excited too. Markovich has taken the bait. Markovich is going to meet him and there's a chance they'll be able to bring him in.

He drains the last of the beer, walks off towards the U-Bahn. The train is packed, people standing, jostling, no seats available. He stands by the door, scanning the crowd around him to see if they've got someone tailing him. No one stands out but he opts for caution. Rides two stops, waits until the doors are about to close then steps out. If there was anyone on the train, he's lost them. He goes up to street level, catches a taxi back to the apartment and calls Hammer.

'Sunday,' he says. 'I reckon he'll meet me Sunday. But we'll have to be flexible – they haven't given me a time or place, and Markovich will probably only call shortly before he wants to meet. We'll need a team ready to work with whatever he gives us.'

'OK,' says Hammer. 'It's not ideal but we can try. We will meet tomorrow morning. In case they are following you, it's best you don't come here. There's an office we sometimes use in a hotel not far from where you're staying. I'll text you the address. We can meet at nine a.m. and put together the plan.'

Walker checks the time: 2 a.m. in Australia. He sends an email to Rutherford, then jumps under the shower. He's having dinner with Barbara's family tonight. He'll put work out of his mind until tomorrow morning. There's nothing more he can do until then anyway.

• • •

Vuk watches the Australian through the window of the bar. As he finishes his beer and stands, Vuk gives Danilo, sitting outside with a coffee, the nod. Danilo rises slowly to his feet and follows the Australian down the street. Vuk picks up the phone and calls the boss. 'That Australian who is looking for Stefan was here again. I told him Sunday, like Stefan said. But there's something about him that isn't right. He's lying about something.'

There's a pause. 'Stefan said Sunday?' says Popo.

'Yeah,' says Vuk. 'He said he wanted to meet him on Sunday.'

There's a longer pause. 'Alright. But when this man arrives on Sunday, call Boris too. Whatever he's lying about, Boris will get to the bottom of it.'

After Vuk hangs up, he feels a momentary pang of disappointment. He'd like to be the one the boss turns to for jobs like this. He can do anything Boris can do. Patience, he counsels himself; the time will come. Maybe he can get himself involved in the action someway. That will liven up a slow Sunday.

Chapter 40

Mildersee

6 p.m.

Amina's hand is shaking as she closes the garden gate behind her with a clang. That was close, too close, but she got away with it, thanks to some quick thinking.

'You scared me half to death,' she'd said, backed up against the table in the shed, no option but to go on the attack. 'What are you doing sneaking up behind me like that? You could have given me a heart attack. I knocked, I called, I looked around, but there was no one here and I didn't think anyone would mind. I'm a botanist and I saw the *Ricinus* in the garden - it's a beautiful specimen so I wanted to take a cutting. I was looking for shears, but then I saw this amazing collection of herbs . . .'

The story, close to the truth, was a good one, she thought. It had bought her no sympathy but some time.

'You don't belong here. You've got no right going into private gardens uninvited, helping yourself to other people's things. I don't know how it works in your country but that's not how we do things in Germany. I don't care what you need or who you are – get out, now!'

She put her head up as high as she could, bluffing anger. 'There's no need to be so rude and aggressive. I wasn't doing any harm,' she said, trying to calm her nerves, stalking away across the garden. She had the presence of mind to walk past the *Ricinus* and break off a seed pod for comparison, but now her hands are shaking and sweaty as she turns left onto the sandy track, walking quickly towards the lake, her heart beating fast, shocked both at what she's found and at being discovered. She's walked twenty metres or so before she realises that her car, with her phone inside, is parked in the other direction, at the top of the path, back the way she's come. She dithers for a moment. She doesn't want to walk back past the cabin, invite more aggressive attention from someone who, she suspects, could well be a double murderer. She starts walking towards the water again, realising belatedly the danger she might have put herself in.

Her heart is thumping, the silence loud in her ears, and now she's wishing fervently that she weren't alone out here. Wishes there were other people in their gardens, kids playing on the empty swings or jumping and swimming in the water. She fights the urge to run, forces some steel into her spine. She can walk along the lake, turn left and go back to the car via the next lane. Yes, she decides, walking alongside the water is her best bet. With luck, there might be someone else there, having a swim or a post-work beer.

She's walking faster now, stumbling a little, her steps hurried and uneven. The water, shimmering in the sunshine, is clearly visible through the trees that ring the edge of the lake. The colony is still silent. No sound, no voices, no people. She shouldn't have come out here. What was she thinking, what madness made her do this? She wanted to be the one to make the connections others missed. Wanted to congratulate herself on being smarter than the rest. She won't do this again – she'll leave the detective work to the police.

Sweating and breathless, she can hear her heart thump-thump-thump in her ears. Then, out of nowhere, she thinks she hears someone behind her. She gives a cry and turns. 'Who's there?' Her voice is wobbly. But the sandy track is empty. Her fear is making her overly anxious. She walks on but a moment later she hears a definite crack and rustle behind her. This time when she spins round they're standing there, much closer than she expected. She sees the arm raised, the gleam of a blade as it catches the light. 'No,' she cries out. 'No!'

She tries to run. Pure instinct turns her body around, takes her feet forward, her terror so great that everything is happening in slow motion. Her feet take steps of their own volition, her mouth is open, she can hear herself screaming, and then she's falling, her body hitting the ground with a thud. She's fighting for air, she can taste blood – she must have bitten her tongue, her mouth is full of blood. Then there's a ripping, a tear, an unbearable pain in her shoulder and another in her side. Her back, her chest, her neck, it's all agony, she is nothing but a body of pain.

• • •

The haze of killing, the rage and fear, take time to disappear. I don't know how long I stand there before the afternoon comes back into focus. The woman has finally stopped moving, her hands no longer scrabbling in the dirt. She's lying face down on the path, her right arm stretched out in front of her, evidence of her last desperate bid to crawl away. But once I've decided, once I've chosen someone, they can't get away from me.

Whoever she is, she knew. I watched her. The way she tensed and quivered like a dog scenting a bird when she saw the berries was a complete giveaway. How did she work it out?

She pretended to be a botanist but that seems unlikely. And with that headscarf she's not police either. Who knows. Whoever she is, she found the berries so she had to die. I dumped them in the compost, covered them well, so that evidence is gone. As for her, there was no time to plan, only time to act, and looking at the body now I can see it's messy, not well executed. The body has too many wounds. Attacking from behind might give the element of surprise but it's harder to know where to plunge the knife.

The adrenaline rush that has been building since I first saw her is slowing. Adrenaline is useful. It's important when you need to make rapid life-and-death decisions: it helped me plunge my knife deep into her back. But now, as it subsides, my hands are shaking and weak, the knife is hard to hold, my legs feel wobbly. I'm sweating and light-headed – I don't feel good at all.

But there's no time to stand here thinking. I need to move. The lake is only a few steps away. I take one step, then I pause: my hands and arms are covered in her blood. What if someone is walking along the track, what if someone sees my bloody clothes, the bloody knife, the woman's body? I'll just have to deal with that as it happens. There's no other option. I walk calmly across the track and down to the water. Don't look left or right, don't draw attention. Heart beating fast. Then I'm in the treeline, at the water's edge. Safe.

I take a final glance back and notice my footprints across the track. A giveaway. I look around and spot a small branch lying under the trees that line the bank. It's leafy and exactly the right size, a natural broom. An offer of help from the gods. I pick it up, walk back to the path and gently sweep my prints away. Look left, look right: still no one in sight.

I take the branch with me into the water and swim, slowly, calmly. I'm shivering a little bit – the water isn't cold but my body temperature must be falling from the adrenaline comedown.

When I'm far enough out, the water deep and dark beneath me, I break the branch into three pieces and let it float away. I hold on to the knife for a moment longer. I know I need to leave it here where no one can find it, but it's been so useful, such a good friend. 'Drop it!' I tell myself, and let it go, watching as the blade catches the sun, then disappears into the brown depths. I duck under, rub my hands and arms to remove her blood, wipe my face, scrub at my clothes. Clean myself of her stain.

I'm shivering now, teeth chattering. This afternoon has been tough – it's taken everything out of me. I swim, and it feels like a long time before I'm on the beach. The small sandy bay is empty, and I lie in the sun, trying to warm up and dry out before I walk home. My clothes are still a bit stained but not too badly. My skin is clean. I'm safe. For the moment, at least. But if this woman knew, if this woman worked it out, maybe others will too. Maybe she was just lucky. Maybe no one else will make the connection. But I need to plan just in case. I can't be caught out like this again.

Chapter 41

Berlin
7 p.m.

Lucas is carrying a plastic bag, the tops of two bottles of wine poking through the handles. He presents it to her a little sheepishly. 'Do your parents drink? I didn't know what to bring . . .'

'You didn't have to bring anything, but thank you – they love wine, especially my dad.'

Barbara has parked outside the apartment where Lucas is staying; they're driving to her parents' place for dinner. As he folds himself into the car, she's conscious once again of his physicality, his male presence, in the small space. His broad shoulders, the strong arms, the curve of his jaw, his smile. Where Seb is all muscle, a solidity like stone, Walker has a softer, more fluid strength.

'Do your parents speak English?' he asks as she gets the car underway in the stop-start Neukölln traffic.

'Not really. My dad speaks a little, but he's shy about it. We speak Spanish at home and they speak German, of course, but not English.

But don't worry, Rita and I will translate.'

'It's bloody impressive how everyone here speaks a couple of languages. I'm only just managing in English,' says Walker, laughing.

She glances across and smiles. He's handsome, she thinks. She feels relaxed and at ease with him, and they have a strong connection, the kind of connection she doesn't have with Seb, or with anyone else.

He smiles back. 'How was your day?' he asks.

'Well... Actually I don't know. I thought for sure we had him, that Leon Kaiser killed them both. But he denies it. He claims he saw the first victim dying, but thought he was just high on drugs so he didn't do anything. He says he doesn't know anything about Hartmann's death. The prosecutor thinks he's lying, but I'm not sure. He's a weird guy but the story has a ring of truth to it...'

'You're a good cop,' says Lucas. 'I reckon you should trust your gut.'

'Yes, but that would mean we still have a killer on the loose and no clues about who they might be.'

As she drives out of Berlin, negotiating the end-of-week traffic, they toss a few theories around – Willie Koch's name emerges top of the list – and Walker gives her an update on his case too. 'With a bit of luck I'll be meeting Markovich on Sunday. I spoke to the local team here and we're meeting tomorrow morning. I think they're going to work with me to pull him in. We might actually get him in custody.'

With Walker in the car, the drive passes more quickly than usual. When they arrive on the outskirts of Kummerfeld, she says: 'This is where I grew up. The buzzing metropolis of Kummerfeld.'

Walker looks from side to side, his eyes alive with interest, taking the measure of the place. She remembers the heat, the wide-open roads, the endless pale grasslands, the colourful parrots and mango trees in his grandmother's garden in Australia. A whole world away.

'Not much like Caloodie, is it?' she says.

'Well, it's much greener,' he says, 'but it has the same kind of peaceful small-town vibe.'

As she pulls up outside her parents' place, the front door opens. Her mother must have been waiting for them to arrive, thinks Barbara. Her jaw drops when she sees Schmidt and Rita, not her mother, emerge from inside.

'What the hell is he doing here?' she says. There's no reason for Schmidt to be here, unless there's been some kind of breakthrough in the case. But he's not in uniform – he's wearing jeans and a white t-shirt, his hair loose, long blond waves cascading down to his shoulders – so it doesn't look like an official call. 'This better not be a fucking social visit,' she says.

As the thought runs through her mind, Schmidt says something and Rita smiles. Barbara's heart catches at the sight, half of what it once was but, still, a smile. Her eyes stinging slightly, she steps out of the car and shuts the door with a bang. Schmidt turns towards her, and Rita disappears inside.

'What are you doing here?' she says.

He walks down the path towards the gate, looking a little sheepish, not entirely meeting her eyes. 'I bumped into your mother at Lidl. She invited me over for a coffee.'

Barbara needs to have words with her mother. Schmidt is a colleague, he's not going to become a family friend.

'Right, well . . .' She's lost for words. 'Don't make a habit of it!'

Schmidt notices Walker coming round to stand beside her. 'Hi, I'm Max Schmidt,' he says, extending his hand. 'I work with Barbara.'

'G'day. Lucas Walker. I'm visiting from Australia.'

'Yes, right, well, see you later, Schmidt,' says Barbara firmly. She wants him gone, doesn't want her mother to see them chatting and extend a dinner invitation, to include him in their life any more than she already has.

'Have a nice weekend,' Schmidt says. Before he walks off, he casts a final glance at the living room window and raises his hand in a wave goodbye. Barbara looks at the window, sees Rita's face, a raised hand in return.

She's processing this, staring after Schmidt, when Walker says: 'You don't like him?'

'Scheisse, was it that obvious? He's the local officer who is helping me with the case. I don't know why my mother is inviting him for coffee.'

They go up to the house, and what with introducing Walker to her parents and pouring and drinking the first glass of Sekt, and her mother hugging Walker and crying, her father shaking Walker's hand in both of his, also close to tears, and both of them saying thank you, thank you, thank you, thoughts of Schmidt and why he was at the house are put aside.

At first Rita is nowhere to be seen, but Maria goes upstairs and brings her down and she stays for a few minutes, at the edge, looking like a frightened fawn, one that could startle at anything and dart away. Walker gives her a half-smile and Barbara is about to introduce them properly but Rita slips out again. Her parents look chagrined, but Walker explains that he understands, he fully understands, and then there's more translation and more chat and it's close to an hour before she has a chance to talk with her mother alone, in the kitchen, as they make the final preparations for dinner.

'Mamá, what was Max Schmidt doing here?'

'He came for a coffee.'

'Well, don't invite him again, please. We work together, it's not appropriate.'

'I didn't invite him for you. He brought Rita flowers.'

'He what? Why?'

'Maybe because he's a nice man and your sister is a lovely young woman.'

'Mamá, that's weird. Why would he bring Rita flowers? Don't ask him here again, please!'

Maria puts down the bowl of salsa she's holding and folds her arms across her chest. Barbara recognises the stance: it means she's not going to like what's coming next.

'I *will* be asking him again. He brought Rita flowers a couple of days ago and Rita hasn't stopped talking about it since. And she's washed her hair and she put on a pair of jeans, not those horrible jogging bottoms. And when I asked her if she'd like to see him again, she didn't say no, so when I saw him at Lidl I invited him home. They talked to each other – your sister was talking to him!' Maria uses the back of her hand to wipe her eyes. 'And, yes, I have already invited him again so you will have to get used to it.'

Barbara drops the subject; tonight isn't the right time for a discussion like this. It's good news that Rita is talking to people, but Schmidt shouldn't have brought her flowers – she can't figure out what would have made him do something like that. He barely knows Rita. She'll have to talk to him to get to the bottom of this and make sure he backs off. Rita is too fragile to be the plaything of a guy like Schmidt. With looks like that, he's likely to move on to a new conquest without thought for what he's leaving behind.

Rita reappears – Lola in her arms – and this time she and Walker have a chat, Lola once again the glue that gives them something to bond over. Then the five of them eat the massive dinner Maria has prepared: empanadas de pino with minced beef, onions, black olives and egg wrapped in pastry and served with a spicy salsa, followed by prawns fried in garlic butter with a smoky chilli sauce, and, for main, her famous plateada, a slow-cooked beef in red wine and garlic, a family favourite that takes hours to cook and is reserved for special occasions.

'You're really getting the special treatment today,' Barbara says to Walker.

'Your mum is an amazing cook. Tell her thank you for making all of this – it's all so good.'

'He is the perfect guest,' says her mother when Barbara translates, nodding approvingly as Walker eats a generous plateful of every dish and doesn't say no to seconds.

They sit at the table for a long time. Rita, with Lola on her lap, doesn't dart off at the first opportunity; her parents and Walker work their way through a couple of bottles of wine. Even though Barbara's on water because she'll be driving them back to Berlin later and has to translate from Spanish to English and back again to keep the conversation going, she's having a good time. Having a visitor changes the dynamic. Walker is relaxing company, he doesn't stand on ceremony, compliments her mother's cooking, answers questions about his family and his job, talks with her father about wine and Chile and with Rita about Lola. Even Rita takes part in the conversation, her English rusty but improving as the meal goes on. Barbara's heart warms as she watches them. Walker fits in so well that it almost feels like he's part of the family. That he belongs.

Chapter 42

Mildersee
11 p.m.

The stark blue-and-white lights of an ambulance and a couple of police cruisers are cutting through the dark forest as Barbara pulls up in the Peugeot, Walker in the passenger seat beside her. They'd been on their way back to Berlin, sated and relaxed, planning a night out in one of the city's clubs, when the call came through.

'I can't let you visit Berlin without at least one night out,' Barbara had said. 'Monika will never let me hear the end of it. She's at some gallery opening tonight and there'll be an after-party – we can go to that if you'd like?'

Walker had acquiesced, more out of politeness than any great urge to go partying. He'd enjoyed this evening, getting to know Barbara's family, and what he'd really wanted to do next was find a nice bar and spend more time with Barbara. But they got no further with their plans, Barbara's phone interrupting their conversation. She pulled over, spoke in fast German. Walker couldn't work out what was being said but saw her face go grim.

'There's been another murder at the lake,' she said when she hung up, executing a tight turn on the small country lane. A minute later: 'Perhaps it's best if I drop you off at the train station – it's not much of a detour.'

'Whatever works for you,' he said. 'I don't mind waiting in the car for you. We can drive back to Berlin together afterwards.'

He saw her hesitate, but the urgency of the call won out and now he's here, the balmy night air wafting in through the open door of Barbara's car, a group of grim-faced uniform police standing off to the side. Barbara has disappeared. She was met by the long-haired cop who was at the house earlier and the two of them walked away in the direction of the scene, over to the right, out of Walker's sight. About ten minutes later a SOC team arrives and is led the same way.

He looks around, taking in what he can. There's a civilian vehicle, a dark-grey sedan of some sort, he can't see the make, parked just ahead, next to the ambulance, which has its back door open, the siren off but the light still turning. The ambulance crew are standing and chatting with the police, the older of the two smoking a cigarette. Nothing much happens for a while, then one of the cops leans into the cruiser and picks up his radio, has a short conversation. After this, the older ambo drops his ciggie, crushes it underfoot, and the two of them close the doors of the vehicle and the ambulance departs, emergency light off, bumping down the lane in the direction he and Barbara arrived from.

Walker gets out of the car to stretch his legs and one of the uniform police comes over. 'Australia?' he asks.

Barbara has obviously explained his presence. 'Ah yeah, that's right. Australian Federal Police.'

'Aussie kangaroo!' The cop seems happy to have an Aussie reference he can pull out.

Walker nods. 'What's happened down there?' he asks.

'A lady, dead, with a knife, many times...'

Stabbed, not poisoned like the previous victims, thinks Walker. If the crimes are linked this is a worrying change of pattern. The cop ambles back to his colleagues, and Walker gets back into the car, pushes the seat as far back as he can. He might as well get a bit of rest while he's waiting. He's half dozing, thinking about Markovich, how their meeting might play out, when something catches his peripheral vision. A young bloke is standing among the trees at the edge of the forest. He's wearing camouflage gear – trousers and a long-sleeved shirt – and his hair is shorn tight to his head. He's pressed against the trees, trying to keep out of sight, but staring with intensity at the police and in the direction of where Barbara went. Walker looks at him, noting as many details as he can, memorising the face. He's about to get out of the car, point him out to the cop he spoke with, when the bloke turns and disappears, vanishing into the dark of the forest.

Walker watches for a while to see if he reappears, but at some point he gives up and closes his eyes. He doesn't know how long he's been sleeping, wakes with a start when Barbara touches his shoulder.

'We're done for tonight,' she says. 'I can take you back to Berlin now.'

He glances at the digital clock on the dashboard: 1.15 a.m.

'You sure? I'm fine if you need to stay out here?'

'No. I would like to sleep at my place tonight.'

He lets her focus on driving the dark country lanes but when they're on the highway, well lit, not much traffic, he says: 'The uniforms told me it was a stabbing...'

She nods. 'Yes, very different to the last two cases. This was an attack from behind, lots of wounds. It looked angry, desperate. According to the SOCOs she was likely killed early evening sometime, so that rules out our suspect Leon Kaiser – he was still being interviewed.'

'Your instinct was right there, then,' says Walker. 'It seems unlikely there would be two murderers in a small community like this, don't you think? This must be connected to your poisonings.'

'Probably,' she says. 'The body was found very near to the first victim's cabin. But this victim, she's not from the colony. I know her. Her name is Amina Khan. She's a forensic botanist and she worked on Nina Hartmann's case. She called me this afternoon – she was upset about Nina Hartmann's death. I think maybe she was out here looking around, trying to find something to help us with the case.'

Walker thinks about it. 'So perhaps this murder wasn't planned,' he says. 'She found something and someone felt threatened and reacted. Reached for a knife, killed her. No time for poisons or anything like that.'

'Yes,' agrees Barbara. 'That could be it. Forensics will be able to tell us more. Hopefully we'll get some DNA traces from the scene. As it wasn't planned, perhaps the killer made other mistakes.' She's quiet for a moment. 'Amina shouldn't have been out here alone. When I spoke with her this afternoon, I told her I didn't have the budget to involve her ... I wish she'd called me, told me what she was doing. I feel responsible somehow.'

It's almost 2 a.m. before they arrive back in the city. Barbara finds a spot to park, switches off the ignition and turns to him.

'How tired are you?' she says. 'I could really use a drink.'

'Absolutely,' he says. 'I'm up for that.' They walk down a street lined with bars. He can hear music, smell the scent of cigarette smoke emanating from open doors. 'That's a blast from the past,' he says. 'You can't smoke in Aussie pubs anymore.'

'You're not really allowed to smoke in bars in Germany either, but Berlin – well, Berlin is Berlin, and it's not enforced.'

She leads them to a bar on a corner, still busy despite the late hour. It has high ceilings and walls of rough unpainted plaster, and mismatched furniture that shouldn't work together but somehow does. The colourful bottles of booze behind the bar are artfully lit and the crowd is uniformly fashionable. Not in the Sydney way of designer labels, high heels and glossy hair, but more like the furniture: a seemingly random mix of clothing, edgy haircuts and lots of tattoos combining to give the effect of cool.

They stand at the bar, the staff busy mixing drinks or chatting with each other, none of them making eye contact. 'I come here sometimes with Monika,' says Barbara. 'The service sucks but the drinks are good and it has a very Berlin vibe.'

Walker wonders if she's chosen it because she likes it or to give him a flavour of the city. He smiles at one of the women behind the bar. She doesn't return his smile but walks over, empty glass in hand. 'Sorry, it's table service only tonight,' she says. They look around. The tables are all taken; no one looks as if they're making to leave. He turns back to the bar, and before he can say anything the bartender shrugs. 'You'll have to wait,' she says. 'It could be half an hour, maybe more.'

'Let's go somewhere else,' he suggests to Barbara. 'I think we need a drink more than we need the vibe, right?'

Barbara runs her hand through her hair. He can tell she's frustrated. 'I really want to show you some of the cool places in Berlin,' she says. 'It's a great city and it's Friday night and all you've seen is my parents' place and a crime scene.'

'It was nice to meet your parents and I'm a cop – crime scenes are my thing. All I want is a beer. I don't care about cool bars. Really. I'm happy anywhere we can get a beer and have a chat.'

They walk away from the busy street, down a quieter residential one. She stops at what looks like a shopfront, glances in and nods. 'Not busy,' she says.

They walk into a small room with a bar tucked in one corner. The crowd – well, that's an exaggeration: the handful of other patrons – are late thirties or older and far less self-consciously cool, jeans and black t-shirts seeming to be almost uniform. Posters of gigs and exhibitions long past are tacked to the wall and although the furniture is mismatched, here it looks like it's for cost reasons rather than style – the table they sit at is wobbly and the chairs are hard. But there are candles on the tables, the soft light welcoming, there's music playing but not so loud that it overtakes the gentle hum of conversation, and the bartender is at their table in less than a minute. The beers he brings are big and cold, and before he departs he leans down, jams a folded cardboard coaster under the dodgy leg, making sure the table is steady. They look at each other and clink glasses. Walker takes a drink, Barbara an even longer one.

'Great choice,' he says. 'This is my kind of place.'

'Yeah, I like it too. Monika thinks it's boring and Seb thinks it's grubby but I come here quite often. It's peaceful.'

Walker looks at his phone: 2.04. 'What time does it close?' he asks.

'Whenever the barman's had enough. There aren't closing hours, really.'

That's a surprise to Walker, but what's more surprising is that this laxity doesn't seem to have created a big drinking energy. The raucous, binge-drinking, fighting and vomiting crowd seem to be conspicuously absent. 'People don't seem to get as drunk here as they do at home,' he says.

'They do,' says Barbara. 'You have to choose the right place, that's all.'

They order more beers. She doesn't bring up her case and they talk about other things, unwinding, letting the day slip off their shoulders. There's an ease to being with Barbara, thinks Walker, he can say anything or nothing at all. He's conscious of how beautiful she is too, with her dark hair, big eyes, generous mouth and sensuous lips. She's wearing a short-sleeved red blouse. The colour suits her and the cut, nipped at the waist, accentuates her curves. It's almost 4 a.m. before they call it a night and, despite her assurances that she doesn't need him to, he walks her back to her place. Most of the apartment buildings are dark, and the cobbled streets are empty and quiet.

At her door, she asks, 'Do you want to come up for a coffee or a tea or something?'

He looks at her, sees the tiredness on her face and in her eyes. 'Nah, you're right,' he says. 'We'd both better get some sleep. But if you have time tomorrow, let me know. I'm meeting the LKA detectives in the morning, but I won't be busy in the afternoon.' He's not sure how the op with Markovich will pan out but it won't happen until at least Sunday. He'd like to spend more time with her before he leaves but he knows she'll be busy with this case tomorrow.

'Of course,' she says. 'I'll call you, OK?'

'Perfect,' he says, a smile coming to his face.

They look at each other for a second. 'OK, so see you tomorrow,' she says, stepping forward and giving him a hug.

He has his arms around her waist, the top of her head against his cheek. He can smell the scent of her shampoo, something fresh and citrussy, feel the warmth of her body against his chest. They stand there, close, for what feels like a long time, then she steps slowly back. He looks down at her, reminds himself she has a man in her life, that she's a friend, nothing more, and doesn't do what he most wants to do, which is to kiss her.

Chapter 43

Hewett
Saturday, 10 a.m.

'We're not moving,' says Shell, her mouth set, her arms crossed. 'We've talked about it and we've agreed. We're not moving and that's that.'

The senior officer of the protection squad turns to Nick. 'Nick, please, talk some sense into her. You can't stay in one place too long. You're not safe—'

'I don't believe that,' says Shell, interrupting. 'You want us to move because we don't want you here no more, because we want to get our lives back to normal. You're just trying to scare us, get us back under your control. I'm not living that way. I can't have you wannabe heroes here day and night messing with our nerves. Megan's got school, she's made friends. We've decided. We're not moving, and we don't want you here no more.'

'Mrs Mitchell, your lives are in danger if you stay here. I can't put it more plainly than that.'

'Bullshit. Stefan's gone – he's not even in Australia, you told us that. And Aaron and the rest of them are banged up for the foreseeable. No one knows where we are and if someone sees me at the shopping centre what's he gonna do, come and gun us down?'

'They could very well do that,' says the officer. 'Nick, please, tell her...'

Nick thinks back to his Vandals days, to Stefan's implacable desire for vengeance when he thinks he's been betrayed. He knows that if you let Stefan down, let alone rat him out, your life isn't worth living. You're history. Maybe not today, maybe not tomorrow, but one day, for sure, someone, somewhere, will find him and put a bullet in his head. He's made his peace with it. He's just hoping they'll leave Shell and the girls out of it, that's his real worry. But Nat's already in Melbourne, doing her own thing; only a few more months and Megan will be out of school and safe too; and him and Shell will duck and dive, they'll survive. And he's got the gun now. He can keep them safe. He reckons Shell has it right. They're not in danger anytime soon. Not while Stefan and the others are in the bin or out of the country. The business is fucked, the Vandals are leaderless, they'll have all sorts of other priorities before him. And Shell's right, as always, about the protection officers too. Having them in the house is a nightmare. Living with pigs doesn't work for anyone. They make Megan anxious with their guns and their attitude, and they get up his and Shell's noses as well.

'Shell is right,' he says, moving over to stand beside her. 'We're OK. We'll keep our heads down. Adelaide is a big place and we're a long way from town. They won't find us. We don't need you around no more – we'll take care of ourselves.'

'We're not willing to sit outside in the car all day. That's not tenable. If you can't let us in, you'll have to do without.'

'All the fucken better,' says Shell. 'That's what we want.'

The officer doesn't like it, hangs around arguing with them for another half-hour, but him and Shell aren't budging and eventually Shell's had enough. She asks the pig to leave, and he goes, taking the officer on duty with him.

Afterwards, him and Shell sit at the kitchen table drinking a couple of beers, Megan in her room on her iPad.

'It's the first time I've felt like we've got our lives back,' says Shell. 'The first time since all this shit went down that things feel normal.' He reaches for her hand and squeezes it. She looks at him for a long minute. 'We've made the right decision, haven't we? They won't find us?'

He's not sure what to say. He doesn't reckon Stefan will ever let this go – they'll never be totally safe. But with Stefan out of the country, well, it's the closest to safe they'll ever get. They might as well make the most of it.

'We did the right thing, love,' he tells her. 'We'll be alright.'

• • •

Dan Rutherford can't believe what he's hearing. 'Mitchell won't move his family and he doesn't want protection? Does he have a fucking death wish?'

'Sir, I tried very hard to convince them otherwise. They seem to think that Markovich won't make a move on them while he's out of the country.'

'I wish I was as certain of that as they seem to be. They're playing with their lives here. Did you tell them we won't be able to guarantee their safety?'

'I spent an hour and a half with them, begging, pleading, insisting, demanding, you name it. Nothing doing. They're not budging.'

'For fuck's sake.' Rutherford exhales. 'Righto, leave it with me.'

He calls Sophie. 'How much more does Nick Mitchell have to give us?' he asks her. 'Are we relying on him for any further prosecutions? Do we need him as a witness? Do you think he has significantly more information for us?'

'He's been a very useful witness, but we don't have any outstanding prosecutions going forward. Except for Markovich, of course, depending on how that goes with Lucas in Berlin. I think Mitchell has probably given us most of the information he's got. He was very deeply debriefed when they admitted him to the witness protection programme. And things have changed a lot on the ground since we brought him in. I don't think his intel would be all that up to date anymore.'

'We might lose him,' says Rutherford. 'He's declined protection.'

'What? Why would he do that?'

'Don't ask me. I just want to make sure it won't stuff up anything we've got going on.'

'No, sir. He'd be very useful for Markovich if we get him, but we probably have enough to get a conviction without him.'

Rutherford ends the call and sits for a moment thinking. He's not sure he agrees with Sophie. Mitchell's testimony would make sure beyond any doubt that Markovich goes down. He could bring Mitchell back into custody, ensure that he's alive to testify. But if Mitchell's in custody he'll be an unwilling witness at best. He might change his mind and stop talking completely. And there's no reason to think the Vandals couldn't get to him in jail anyway. There's nothing for it. Walker has to get things moving fast in Germany. Meantime, they'll have to keep an eye on Mitchell from a distance and hope for the best.

He pulls out the burner and sends a message to Wayne. *Your bike is due for its next service, let me know when you can bring it in.* Wayne will call when he gets a chance. With luck, Wayne will get intel from Markovich on what he's planning for Mitchell well in advance of any action, and give them a heads-up before anything serious goes down.

Rutherford calls the protection officer. 'Leave them to it,' he says. 'See if you can get the local cops to drive by the house on their shifts.

It might just put the Vandals off if there's a visible police presence.'

There's a short pause. 'We could keep a team outside, sir,' says the officer. 'Keep an eye on them at least?'

'No. If Mitchell and his wife are going to be running around doing their own thing, we'll just be putting your lives in danger. There's nothing we can do if he won't cooperate. It's his fucking decision. Let him sign his own death warrant, for all I care.'

Chapter 44

Berlin
Saturday, 7.30 a.m.

Barbara's alarm wakes her from a sleep that was too short but better than she'd expected. No visions of Amina Khan's bloodied damaged body, no dreams haunted by Amina's unseeing eyes. She lies there for a moment, still only half awake, her thoughts going to Lucas, the easy intimacy she has with him, the hug she'd instigated and the feeling of his arms around her, the urge she'd had but not acted on, to invite him to spend the night. She feels the same electric fizz of desire that she had last night, standing in his arms. She sighs. Yes, he's handsome, yes, he makes her feel good, yes, they have a lot in common, yes, they can talk about everything from work to their feelings, but he also lives on the other side of the world and his life is there, his work is there, his family is there. They're friends and she doesn't want to make this friendship awkward. It's too important to her for that.

She forces her mind away from Lucas and back to the job at

hand: Amina's death and the other murders at Mildersee. Fischer has promised to give her more resources, so that means she should have a bigger team as of today. And, first thing, she wants to revisit the scene at Mildersee in daylight.

She makes good time, the roads empty early on a Saturday morning. She made a thermos of coffee before she set off and drinks it as she drives; it wakes her up, revives her, and she reconstructs the crime in her head. They'd found Amina Khan's vehicle parked at Mildersee, her bag lying on the passenger seat, with her phone, wallet and a half-empty water bottle inside, along with some wilted leaves that could have been foraged in the forest. It seems that Amina had come to Mildersee, parked her car and gone into the forest to look for plants, thinks Barbara. But then she comes back to the car, drops off her bag, and for some reason walks or runs through the colony, where she is attacked from behind, stabbed violently multiple times in the back. Why would Amina leave the safety of her car if she was being chased, and why did she leave her bag and phone in her car? The more Barbara thinks about it, the less sense it makes.

The key suspect she has in mind is Willie Koch. The description of the man Lucas saw lurking at the edge of the forest last night matches Willie, and she remembers him stalking her down these same quiet lanes earlier in the week. She knows how quiet on his feet he can be; he could easily have crept up behind Amina. And he's a hunter – he has the strength and, she suspects, the rage to stab someone multiple times.

She parks her car beside a police cruiser, a sleepy-looking officer keeping bystanders and locals away from the scene, and walks down the track towards the white forensics tent. Last night, the SOC team had been working under the powerful glare of lights they'd brought with them, powered by a noisy portable generator. The harsh bright light, the forest casting long quavering shadows, the suited technicians ghostlike against the dark night, had lent the setting a nightmarish quality. But this morning, under a grey sky, it looks more forlorn than anything else.

She's expecting to be the only person here but as she walks towards the scene she can see the stocky shape of Marilyn Mather by the lake edge, cigarette in hand, staring across the water, still wearing her SOC suit. She turns as Barbara approaches and Barbara can see her face is pale, with dark rings of exhaustion under her eyes.

'Stop!' Mather barks. 'Don't step on the track.'

Good morning to you too, thinks Barbara, coming to a halt. 'Morning,' she says. 'Have you been here all night?'

Mather nods. 'Step very carefully, please. I'm still working here. Actually, let me show you, this might be useful for you.' Mather throws her cigarette in the water, where it expires with a hiss, then walks in a wide half-circle before stepping back onto the track some ten metres further along. She gestures at Barbara to do the same. 'Stay on the grass. Don't step onto the track until you reach me.'

Barbara walks carefully along the verge and joins Mather.

'Look, there – can you see?' says Mather, pointing. 'Someone has swept this area to remove their tracks.'

At first, Barbara's untrained eye struggles to pick out what Mather is pointing towards, but after a moment she sees it: a patch of sand has been smoothed, brushed with something, leaving visible horizontal lines.

'I think the killer came down the path towards the lake, crossed over here and then used something, a branch perhaps, to remove their footprints,' says Mather.

'That shows some foresight.'

'Yes. Someone who is calm enough in this situation to remove their traces. We think the killer walked down the grassy verge on the right of the victim's body to avoid leaving footprints, but they were forced to cross here. We found a few drops of blood on the verge; perhaps we'll get a DNA sample from that.'

That would be great news, thinks Barbara, something to give her a way into this. She looks back up the lane, reconstructing the crime. The killer approaches Amina from behind, stabs her and then runs down the grassy verge, across the path, sweeping their footprints away, and then . . . 'Do you think they went into the water afterwards? To clean off, to get away?'

Mather nods. 'I'm almost certain. It's the only way they could have gone without leaving some kind of print and I've had a very detailed look around the wider area. When my team arrive I'll have them do a proper fingertip search, but I'm ninety-nine per cent sure the perp must have swum away.'

'If the killer went into the water, there are jetties and small beaches all around the lake where they could have come out. It will be tricky to track them,' says Barbara. 'Have you found anything further up the lane? Presumably the killer approached her from behind . . .'

'We still have work to do but there's nothing obvious so far. But we did find one other thing. Follow me and step where I'm stepping, please.' She leads Barbara back towards where Amina's body was found. When they get to the spot where Amina died – the sand, leaves and grass dark with her blood – Mather points again. 'I think this was left here by the victim. It's exactly in the place where her hand was – maybe she was holding it when she died.'

Barbara recognises it instantly. Lying on the track is the same type of chestnut-sized spiky red seed head that Amina Khan had found by Nina Hartmann's body.

• • •

When Barbara gets back to the car park, Schmidt is standing by her vehicle. 'Good morning,' he says, his high-beam smile directed at her. She looks at him, thinks of Rita, thinks of telling him that his presence at the house, his possible friendship with her sister, is not welcome, but decides against it. When this case is over, she'll make sure she's clear with him that he's not welcome in their lives.

'Morning,' she says, and brings him quickly up to date with what Mather has told her. 'We're going to start by talking to Willie Koch.'

'What makes you think he might know anything?' Schmidt asks. 'We'll need good reason. Herr Koch is already threatening to sue us for harassment.'

'We have an eyewitness account that Willie was here at the colony, watching the police proceedings, last night. He's not above the law and it's not harassment when someone has been murdered in your back yard.'

She can see Schmidt doesn't like it, but she doesn't care. They walk in silence along the path through the woods towards the Koch property. The grey day and brutal murder cast a pall over her mood, and the forest, quiet, gloomy, alien, adds to her sense of dislocation. Give me a busy Berlin street any day, she thinks.

The trees and brush are dense and close around them. She leads the way this time and it's only because she's looking ahead, trying to negotiate the way forward, that she notices Willie Koch dart across the track some hundred metres or so in front of them. Wearing khaki trousers and a green t-shirt, he's there and gone in an instant. The moment he steps off the path, he blends in with the foliage and trees and disappears. She can't be certain, but she thinks he was carrying something, a small backpack perhaps. She raises her hand to stop Schmidt and puts her finger to her lips. He looks a question at her.

'Willie Koch,' she says in a low voice, 'just crossed the path ahead. I want to see where he's going, what he was carrying.'

'It's not a crime to walk in the woods,' says Schmidt, but he keeps his voice low too.

Barbara walks as quickly as she can towards the point where Willie crossed, keeping her eye on the trees where he disappeared. But when she gets there, she's doubtful. It all looks the same, dense and green. She's looking around, trying to see a way forward, when

Schmidt beckons to her – he's found a small path, used by deer probably, that weaves among the low branches and trees. Koch is probably hunting something, she thinks, but her instinct is telling her to follow him.

She and Schmidt step onto the path and she quickly realises she's no woodsman. The path is virtually invisible, fading away in a tangle of branches and shrubs that grab at her, catch on her blouse, scratch her face and whip around her jeans, tripping and slowing her. She has to push her way through, slowly, noisily. Most of the time she can't see the way forward, and she's not sure she'll find her way back to the main path either. She tries to be as quiet as she can but she's certain they're making enough noise to disturb everything that belongs here, and she finds a tinge of respect for the hunters who are at home in this alien world.

They've been walking a few minutes, no more, when she smells smoke and shortly afterwards hears the rustle and crackle of fire. She stops, her heart leaping and beating wildly. A fire, here – they'll struggle to get away. But the forest is damp and green, the summer has been wetter than usual; a fire shouldn't catch. She pushes forward and a moment later stops dead in her tracks again, Schmidt almost bumping into her at the suddenness of her halt.

Directly ahead in a small clearing, Willie Koch has built a fire, the flames leaping high, orange, red and gold in the grey morning light. It must be a place he comes to regularly: there's a log pulled up as a makeshift bench, and big stones in a circle, keeping the fire contained. As she watches, Willie pulls something from his backpack, shakes it out and holds it for a second. Barbara's eyes widen in shock: he's holding a pair of trousers covered in dried blood. As her mind processes what she's seeing, Willie douses the trousers in liquid before throwing them in the fire, where they smoulder for the barest second before dancing into flame.

Chapter 45

Berlin

9 a.m.

Walker, Hammer and Günther Schneider, the pain-in-the-arse detective director Walker met on his first day, are sitting in a bland meeting room at a budget hotel not far from Walker's apartment. Walker doesn't think he was followed from the Sofija yesterday but to be on the safe side he's taken a few evasive moves to get here, jumping on a bus going in the wrong direction, then into a cab. Only when he was certain that no one was on his tail did he make his way to the hotel. Hammer showed him to the room and offered him a coffee. Schneider, impatient at the small talk and hospitality, started by requesting a detailed summary of Walker's progress. Now that a witness has identified Markovich as possibly culpable for the drive-by shooting, it seems Schneider is on board to discuss an operation to pick him up, but there's disagreement about how best to proceed.

'If Markovich calls me tomorrow, I'm assuming he won't give me a lot of notice,' says Walker. 'He'll want to meet more or less immediately. He doesn't know me, he needs to be careful – he won't want to give me time to plan anything.'

'Are you sure he'll show up?' asks Hammer. 'Maybe he'll send some junior operative to check you out.'

Walker nods. 'Maybe. That's why I need to go to meet him on my own. Whatever the plan is, we can't have your team rushing in before I know for sure he's there. We're not going to get two chances to bring him in.'

'It's unfortunate that we don't know where the meeting is taking place. It means we can't keep watch on the area in advance,' says Schneider.

'I reckon he'll meet me at the Sofija,' says Walker. 'As you say, he'll want his people to check me out. Most likely he'll keep me waiting until they're confident it's not a set-up. We could act on the assumption that he'll use that bar and base our surveillance around that.'

'I disagree. We're far from certain about that,' says Schneider. 'And I don't have the resources to watch every bar and café linked to Ulić. We need more intel.'

'I can watch the Sofija,' says Hammer. 'It would be a good place to start.'

'I can't have you there on your own. This man is too dangerous.'

'He wouldn't shoot a cop . . .' says Walker.

'He might,' says Schneider. 'You say he's been on the run for more than two years. He's killed three people in a drive-by shooting. He has nothing to lose.'

'Fair point,' says Walker. Markovich has always been trouble, and no doubt he'll be even harder, angrier and more desperate after two years working with the international cartels. As he thinks this, some part of his animal brain registers a strong desire to be far away from Markovich, a man who has tried to have him killed before. But this time it's different. Markovich doesn't know who he's meeting.

This time Walker has the upper hand.

Hammer and Schneider have a discussion in German, the tone urgent and on the edge of being angry. Walker raises an eyebrow in question, and Schneider waves his hand as if to say it's not important.

'I want to watch the bar,' says Hammer. 'This chance is too good to miss.'

'And I've told him we're not doing this without planning, back-up and proper resources,' says Schneider, in a tone that brooks no argument.

Walker says nothing but he agrees with Hammer that this is a golden opportunity. Now they know where Markovich hangs out, there's a chance they can pick him up when he's not expecting trouble. Too much waiting and planning and they might miss the window.

Schneider is still talking: 'We need to include the Hamburg LKA, they've been tracking Ulić for years, and maybe the Feds too. We could get the SEK involved . . .'

'How soon would all of that happen?' asks Walker. He's remembering challenges he's experienced as part of multi-force operations back home. Lots of red tape, bickering over who has authority, who manages what, how it will all pan out. He's sure it'll be the same over here. It will take a few days at least and it sure as hell won't happen over a Saturday afternoon and Sunday morning.

'It will take some time,' agrees Schneider. 'But you could meet him tomorrow and make a plan for a future meeting. You say you are posing as a forger? You can require some time to make his documents, then we can pick him up at the collection point—'

'I think we need to take the chance while we have it.' Walker doesn't want to kick this can down the road, lose this chance. Markovich is suspicious, cautious and experienced. He's just as likely to send a junior grunt to pick up his forged papers. Not to mention that he has a history with the bloke and there's a better than reasonable chance Markovich will recognise him. A face-to-face will only succeed if they're bringing him in. 'Waiting isn't going to work,' he says firmly. 'Markovich will go underground again, that's my bet. He'll leave Berlin, leave Germany. If we lose him it'll take months to track him down and you won't get him for this drive-by shooting.'

'We can't do this without back-up. It's too dangerous,' says Schneider, mouth set. At an impasse, they sit there, saying nothing for a long moment.

'Look,' says Walker eventually. 'Whatever happens, I'm going to meet him tomorrow. If I contact you when he calls, can you at least send a team to the venue? He'll probably give me a bit of notice – I reckon you'll have an hour from when he calls.'

'An hour . . .' Schneider rolls his eyes. 'What can I do with that?'

Hammer interjects in German again, a long stream of words, his voice heavy with frustration.

'Ja, ja, OK, OK,' says Schneider. He looks at Walker. 'It's true this man has killed three people. We need to get him in custody. It will be a political coup for our team if we can bring him in.' There's a long pause. Then Schneider nods and says, 'OK. I will pull together a small team. They will be on standby tomorrow.'

Hammer gives Walker that same there-and-gone-in-an-instant smile. 'You meet him tomorrow, we'll arrest him.'

'Nice one,' says Walker. 'What do you need from me?'

'I need all the information you can give us on the man and the location,' says Schneider.

They sit for the next hour, planning and talking. Walker pulls up all the images of Markovich that the team in Canberra sent through to him, and Hammer prints off a handful of copies. Schneider brings up a map of the area, 3D and lifelike in detail. Walker points to the street out front. 'There are tables outside. They're likely to have some security types sitting here, keeping an eye out.' He draws the layout of the bar from memory, the handful of tables, the counter, the slot machine, the door to the back room. 'There could be more people out back – likely there's a back exit,' he says.

Schneider nods. 'I will have my team check it out . . .'

Hammer starts talking in German, pointing at the map, planning. Walker feels his heart beating fast. They're doing this. In less than thirty-six hours, Markovich could be off the streets and under lock and key.

Chapter 46

Mildersee

9.30 a.m.

Barbara reacts without thinking. She pulls her pistol from her holster and steps into the clearing, shouting, 'Police! Hands up. Step away from the fire.'

Willie Koch starts and turns.

'Hands up and step away from the fire!' Barbara is advancing towards him, her gun in firing position.

She's aware of Schmidt behind her, calling, 'Put your hands up, Willie.'

He does as he's asked, his hands raised to shoulder height, taking two steps away from the fire, which is blazing bright and strong.

'What the fuck have I done now?' he asks, as anger replaces his initial shock. 'It's not fucking illegal to start a fire at this time of the year.'

She ignores him, gun still trained on him, looking towards the fire. The trousers are already blackened, barely recognisable, but they might still get some DNA from them.

'Try to get the trousers out,' she says to Schmidt. The flames are high and scorching with heat. Schmidt looks around, runs to the side of the clearing, grabs a branch that's lying there and uses it to pull the trousers from the fire, stamping on them, putting them out. The material is blackened and burnt, but it's better than nothing.

'Check the backpack – see if there's anything else in there,' she says.

'What the fuck, you can't do this!' Willie turns towards Schmidt. 'Leave my fucking backpack alone.'

'Don't move, Willie,' says Barbara. 'We are investigating you in connection with a murder that took place last night and we are justified in checking that you are not disposing of evidence.'

Schmidt looks inside the backpack and pulls out a t-shirt, the hem of which is also covered in blood.

'This isn't evidence of anything,' says Willie. 'These are my old hunting clothes. They can't be cleaned, so I'm burning them.'

'Right – you're burning old clothes at a site hidden in the middle of the forest, the day after a murder?' Barbara lowers her gun and Willie Koch drops his hands.

'Look, it's what I do. I come here sometimes. I make a fire. I chill out. I burn stuff. I butchered a deer last week and these trousers won't clean. I don't know anything about no murder last night. It's deer blood, that's all.'

'Where were you yesterday afternoon?' asks Barbara.

'At home.'

'With your parents?'

'I was alone. They're at some political thing.'

'Well, we have a witness who saw you at the colony last night not long after the murder. Now you're burning bloodstained clothes. You have a lot of questions to answer.'

'Alright, it's true: I saw the lights in the colony last night, so I went for a look.' He sounds defeated, his anger subsiding. 'I have a friend in the police department, he told me what happened, but it's nothing to do with me.'

Barbara shakes her head. 'Not good enough, Willie. We're confiscating these items as evidence and taking you in for questioning.'

• • •

Back in Kummerfeld, Barbara grabs a cheese-and-ham roll from the local bakery and eats it at her desk while she waits for Willie Koch's lawyer to arrive. She's sent Koch's clothes for forensic analysis. If it is deer blood, as he claims, they'll get clarification on that, but probably not until Monday or Tuesday. She's had a message from DSS Fischer too. He's chasing extra manpower, but it's unlikely to materialise much before this afternoon or tomorrow. He's asked her to put together a detailed plan of the assistance she thinks she needs to help him argue the case for overtime. What a waste of my time, she's thinking, just as her phone rings on the desk beside her. *Seb.* She hasn't spoken to him for a couple of days, not since the dinner with Walker.

'Hello, hello,' she says.

'Hey babe, how did it go last night?' he asks without preamble.

'Last night?' She's confused.

'You know, the family dinner with your friend from Australia.' He sounds irritated.

'Oh, it was good. Yes, very nice. My parents were happy to meet him.'

'Well, I'm sure they'd be happy to meet me too.'

She's not certain that Seb, with his no-nonsense German-cop aura, would fit as naturally as Walker did with her parents, but she doesn't say so. 'I'm sure they would,' she says neutrally.

'What are you doing now?' he asks. 'Let's meet for lunch, hang out this afternoon?'

'Oh no, I can't – I'm at work. There's been another murder at Mildersee. It's linked to the case I'm working on, a woman stabbed this time—'

'When will you be done?' he interrupts, not interested in the details.

'I don't know but it'll be late.'

'A group of us are going to the sports bar this afternoon. We're going to watch the Hertha match and then there's a pool tournament. You should come. We'll be there till late.'

Football and pool are not Barbara's favourite ways to spend a Saturday, so she's not all that sorry to miss it. 'I don't think I'll make it. This case is at a critical point. If it's the same murderer, we have potentially three victims—'

'There's more to life than working all the time, Barbara. You need to make time for the people in your life too.'

'Come on, you're police, you know how it is.'

'Exactly. I know how it is. You don't have to work twenty-four-seven. Taking tonight off won't change anything.'

He's probably right but that's not how she operates. And anyway, she wants to see Lucas this evening. Now that the operation he came for is set up, and with his conference next week, he won't be in Berlin for much longer. She wants to spend time with him while she can. But telling Seb that will only cause an argument she's not in the mood to have.

'I'll try,' she says.

'Yeah, alright, see you maybe,' he says, and hangs up.

She sighs. She hasn't seen this side of Seb before. It feels like he wants to take the relationship to another level, beyond the occasional hook-up, but she's not sure that's what she wants. Despite being a cop, he can't seem to understand that, for her, sometimes the job takes precedence. This kind of conversation, when she's in the middle of a murder investigation, shows how little he gets her. She thinks of Walker and knows he'd understand, decides to call him, tell him she might not be able to meet him later. She dials his number.

'Hey Barbara.' Hearing his voice, the Aussie accent, sends a fizz of pleasure to her stomach.

'Listen, I don't think I'll be in Berlin until late tonight,' she says. 'This case is pretty intense and I'm not sure what time I'll make it back.'

'Of course, no worries,' he says. 'Where are you at with it?'

She updates him on this morning's events. 'Let's see what Willie Koch says when we interview him. What are you up to?' she asks.

'I'm at a bit of a loose end,' he says. 'The hope is that I'll be meeting Markovich tomorrow. The local guys have told me to keep a low profile until he calls – they want me involved as little as possible.'

'You could come out here if you like,' she says, surprising herself as the words come out. 'It might be a bit boring, I'll be working, but you could have a swim and we can head back to Berlin together later.'

'You're sure I won't be in the way?'

'No, it would be nice.' It's true. He's an ally, a friend. She likes being with him, trusts his opinions; maybe he can offer some insights on the case.

'Righto, I'll see you a bit later, then.'

After the call, taking a big bite of her roll, the crumbs littering the tabletop, she feels a renewed focus. Amina Khan died a horrible, violent death. She's going to find out who is responsible.

Chapter 47

Kummerfeld

12 p.m.

Koch's lawyer is in his early forties, wearing a shiny, expensive-looking suit, and is immediately on the attack. 'What offence is my client charged with?'

'At this stage he is not charged with anything. We are questioning him regarding the murder of Amina Khan, which took place at Mildersee last night. We are questioning him as a suspect because he was found disposing of bloodied clothing, close to the murder site, early this morning.'

'Why are you handling this questioning? Do you have a summons from the public prosecutor's office? Who is the prosecutor?'

Barbara shows him the summons. She completed the paperwork while they were waiting. 'The prosecutor agrees with me that the bloodied clothing warrants preliminary questioning. We're handling this on his behalf and your client will be free to leave after we've spoken. We've sent the clothing in question for DNA testing and, depending on the outcome of that testing, your client can then be further summoned, interviewed and possibly charged.'

'My client will be exercising his right to remain silent,' says the lawyer, and Willie Koch, who has his arms crossed over his chest and is looking cocky again, lets the beginnings of a grin appear on his face.

Barbara resists the urge to ask how Willie might incriminate himself by answering her questions, resists the urge to point out that it conveys guilt, and starts instead by running through the formalities. Then she asks: 'Where were you yesterday afternoon, Herr Koch?'

'No comment,' says Willie.

'You already told me that you went to see what was happening at the colony last night. Were you at the colony earlier in the afternoon too?'

'No comment.'

She puts a photograph of Amina Khan on the table in front of him. Her shocked family supplied it to officers last night after they'd been informed of her death. In the photo, a portrait of Amina holding her university degree, she's smiling, her brown eyes bright with enthusiasm and intelligence. Looking at it, Barbara has to fight to suppress her anger at the young thug sitting in front of her. Amina's death is a tragedy – she had so much potential, a bright future – and Willie, who quite likely snuffed out that future in a violent and terrible way, sits here, smug and very much alive, treating it all as a joke.

'Do you recognise this woman?' she asks.

He doesn't look at the photograph. 'No comment,' he says.

'Take a look, please,' she says. 'This woman was violently murdered at Mildersee yesterday; you at least owe her the courtesy of looking at her face.'

'I don't owe her or you anything,' says Willie. 'It's nothing to do with me.'

He stares at Barbara, she stares back, and after a long moment he looks down at the photograph. There's a pause – she thinks maybe he's taken aback at seeing the face of his victim, the reality of what he's done – but then he pushes the photo back towards her and gives a contemptuous sneer.

'I don't know any Kanakes,' he says. 'What was she doing at Mildersee anyway, bringing her fucked-up religion to our country? It will have been some other towelhead that killed her. Honour killing or some bullshit.'

Koch's lawyer winces slightly at the string of slurs, but Barbara presses on. 'I think you saw Amina at Mildersee yesterday...'

'No comment.'

'Where did you see her?'

'No comment.'

'What time did you see her?'

'No comment.'

'If you didn't kill her but you saw her yesterday afternoon, you can help put yourself in the clear. Tell us what time you saw her and where she was.'

Willie pauses as if he's considering this, but his lawyer interjects. 'My client has already said he didn't see the victim.'

She wants to reach over and slap the lawyer. A woman is dead and he's protecting a possible killer. Instead, she pushes another photograph across the desk, a close-up of the little spiky seed case they found by Amira Khan's body. 'Do you recognise this plant?' she asks.

Willie Koch glances at the photo, then pulls it towards him and looks at it more carefully. He shakes his head. 'Nah,' he says.

For the first time in the interview, she thinks he's telling the truth. If Willie has killed Amina Khan, it wasn't because of the seed case in her hand.

Barbara has one last question, a little left-field. 'Do you enjoy swimming, Willie? When was the last time you had a swim in the lake?'

His face flushes red, his hand bunches into a fist and slams hard on the table. 'Fuck you, Bullenschwein,' he shouts.

His lawyer places a restraining hand on his arm and Willie leans back, his face still red, his fist only slowly unfurling. 'I apologise on my client's behalf for his language,' says the lawyer.

The insult washed over her but Willie's reaction is a surprise. She's hit a nerve but she's not sure which one.

Barbara closes her notebook. It hasn't been a total waste of time but she's far from clarifying Koch's involvement either way. If the forensics results show Willie's clothes have samples of Amina Khan's blood on them, they'll arrest him, and the prosecutor will question him again.

'That's all we need today. We'll be back in touch when we have the results from your clothing,' she says.

• • •

Back in the office, she turns to Schmidt. 'What was all that about? He went ballistic when I asked him about swimming.'

Schmidt shakes his head. 'I don't know but we can ask Klein – he's good friends with Willie.'

Klein isn't on duty, so Schmidt calls him, puts his mobile phone on speaker. 'Moin, Rudy,' he says when Klein answers. 'I'm at the station with Detective Guerra from the Kriminalpolizei. We've interviewed Willie Koch and when we asked him a question he lost it. Almost put a fucking hole in the interview table and we don't know why.'

'What did you ask him?'

'I asked him if he liked swimming,' says Barbara. 'We're looking for a suspect who went into the lake.'

Klein laughs. 'No wonder he went ballistic – he thought you were taking the piss. He can't swim. Not a stroke. He hates the water; terrified of it. He fell out of a boat and almost drowned when he was a little kid. By the time they pulled him out he was unconscious, and they had to resuscitate him with mouth-to-mouth. It was really touch-and-go. Now he won't go near the lake or a pool or anything like that. We give him a lot of shit about it, and he's touchy as fuck on the subject.'

Chapter 48

Kummerfeld

2 p.m.

'I feel like I take one step forward and three steps back with this case,' says Barbara. She is sitting with Walker in a quiet corner of a local café. She's picked him up from the train and they've ordered coffee and a slice of cake each. Hers, a cheesecake, is sitting untouched at her elbow, Walker's Black Forest torte almost all gone.

'When I showed Willie Koch a picture of the victim, I think he recognised her. I think he saw her yesterday. But if he can't swim, is very scared of water, it's less likely that he killed her, because the SOCO team have strong reason to believe that the perp went into the water after the murder. And when I asked him about the plant we found by her body, he said he didn't recognise it. I believed him. It was the first time it seemed as if he wasn't trying to hide something. And I think that plant is the key to her death. It's the same one we found by Nina Hartmann's body. If Amina found someone growing the plant in the colony, they could well be Nina's murderer – and perhaps she confronted them, I don't know. We'll get forensics back on the blood on Willie's clothes tomorrow. Let's see what that shows.'

'The three murders are definitely linked, are they?' asks Walker.

'They must be. I mean, Mildersee is tiny. Amina was killed very near to Mattias Ritter's cabin and I'm certain she was out there looking into the plant she found at Nina Hartmann's murder. There must be a connection.'

Walker thinks it through. 'Why did the killer go into the water? If they have a connection with Mildersee, wouldn't it make more sense to go back to a cabin?'

'They would have been covered in blood and there's no running water at the colony, they only have hand pumps, so it might have been difficult to clean up properly, at least without being seen.'

'Who was out at the colony yesterday? Are there any witnesses?'

'So far, no. I asked Schmidt to call all the homeowners and all of them claim they weren't at the lake yesterday evening. Quite a few of the Berliners haven't been back since Mattias Ritter was killed last week. There are locals who visit more often, like Ralf Wagner. He said he was at his cabin until two p.m., when he went to meet Manfred Krause for a beer. Krause confirmed his alibi, said they were together until six. Wagner said he didn't see anyone else while he was out there. The murders are keeping people away.'

'Does Wagner's alibi fit with the time of death?'

'Not all of it. They've given us a window of between three and eight p.m. yesterday.' She pauses for a moment. 'Ralf Wagner was at the colony the day Mattias Ritter died and the day Nina Hartmann died too. We saw him that day, the older guy. Of all the residents, he's the most regular visitor. Always working on his cabin, or in his garden. And he's ex-Stasi, so he might have knowledge of poisons. It's possible he went back out there after he met Krause yesterday. Maybe he merits a closer look. I'm going to ask Schmidt to dig into his background again. And into the Krause couple and Renate Bauer. I let him talk me out of it the other day but there might be a connection from the past here that we're missing.'

Walker finishes off the last of his cake as she makes a call to Schmidt. Schmidt isn't totally happy with his assignment – he reiterates his belief that the victims are young Berliners, unlikely to be linked to the old-timers, as he calls them. But when she insists they need to cover all bases in their search for this killer, he listens to her instructions as assiduously as ever and she's sure he'll do a decent job. She ends the call full of renewed resolve.

'Right, let's go to Mildersee,' she says. 'I promised you a swim and I'm going to try to see if I can find the castor oil plant out there somewhere. I'm sure that's the key. I can start with Wagner's garden.'

'Should we take some back-up?' asks Walker. 'What if this killer is still out there?'

Barbara hesitates. It's a fair point but she doesn't want to ask Fischer – he'll be after that personnel request he's asked her for and he might even tell her not to go back to Mildersee until she has back-up. And she wants Schmidt to stay focused on his task of digging into the backgrounds of the colony residents. No. She can do this.

'We'll be fine,' she says. 'I don't think there's much chance the killer will be back today, not with all the cops and SOCOs around.'

'OK,' he says. 'Are you eating your cake? You should eat, you need energy . . .'

She rolls her eyes, smiling. 'I always forget what you're like with food. It's like being at work with my mother.'

• • •

When they get to the lake, Barbara notes that the police cordon has gone. She ponders again whether to call Schmidt for back-up but there are no cars in the car park and she doubts the killer would be hanging around, making themselves obvious. They'll be keeping a low profile, staying away from the colony until the police interest dies down. She thinks about where best to take Lucas for a swim. The beach she showed him last time is a twenty-minute walk or more. 'You can swim from one of the jetties,' she decides, leading him along the top of the colony, past the lane where Amina Khan was killed. Police tape is fluttering in the breeze, the lane closed off to visitors, but the SOCOs have gone, the white tent too.

When they reach the lake, the water looks uninviting to Barbara, reflecting the dark grey of the leaden sky above. She picks a jetty with a wooden bench on the swimming platform and a bright-yellow ladder leading down into the water. They walk out to the edge of the jetty. Looking across the water, she can see the gardens of the houses on the opposite shore, green lawns running down to the lake, some with jetties of their own, sailing boats moored against them. The lake is empty, no paddlers, swimmers or sailors today.

'You'd have to be a good swimmer to go all the way across, right?' she asks Lucas.

'Pretty good. Distances are deceptive across water – it's probably not as far as you think ... Maybe a kilometre.'

'How long do you think it would take to swim across?'

'I reckon it would take me about fifteen to twenty minutes.'

'There's no reason to assume the killer swam all the way over anyway,' she says. 'There are so many jetties to climb back out of the water.'

Lucas points to their left. 'Or they could have swum to that beach we were at the other day. Plenty of options, unfortunately.'

They stand there in silence for a moment. 'Do you still want to get into the water?' Barbara asks, looking up at the sky. Tall clouds in shades of grey are rising in high, bulbous shapes, the sun moving in and out, the temperature cool.

'Yeah, absolutely,' says Lucas. 'I'll swim over to the other side and see how long it takes.'

'OK. I'm going to try to trace Amina's path through the colony, have a look in the gardens, see if I can find this plant,' she says. 'I'll meet you at the car. Half an hour?'

'Maybe a bit longer,' he says.

She looks at her phone. 'How about four p.m.? That's an hour.'

• • •

Walker watches Barbara head back up the path they came down, then changes into his boardies and puts his towel beside his clothes on the bench. Despite the grey day, he's happy at the thought of a swim. He's still battling with bouts of tiredness and the prospect of a meeting with Markovich tomorrow is taking a mental toll too. He's more nervous than he wants to admit. Stretching out, swimming off his tiredness and anxiety, just being in the water, will help.

When he picks up his phone to start the timer to check how long the swim takes, he sees that the battery is low: 5 per cent. Shit, he's forgotten to charge it. Hopefully the timer won't use too much battery. He starts it, drops the phone on his towel and walks to the edge of the jetty. The water is an uninviting brown, but deep enough for a dive, the lakebed barely visible below. He dives in and starts swimming with long strokes, powering along until his heart is pumping and he's out of breath and warm from exertion. He lifts his head, checks his bearings – at least halfway across. He keeps swimming, pushing hard, until he reaches the other side. The water is clearer here, a sandy bed visible beneath him. He lets his feet touch the bottom, his heart thumping, the blood coursing around his body, his mind clear. He feels better than he's done all day.

He stands there for a minute, the water chest-deep, letting his heart rate slow, then turns and heads back. He's pushing himself, swimming at a good pace. He hasn't had done anything like this for a while: open water, a decent distance, a swim that really tests your fitness, quite different from lapping in a pool, where the black line marks your way and you can almost lose yourself in meditative thinking. Out here, constantly checking and adjusting his position, no breaks, he can feel the exertion in his chest, his arms, his lungs. His mind empties, nothing matters but the motion of his arms pulling him along, the water soft against his bare skin, the slight tilt of the head for air, legs kicking, helping to power him forward.

When he's almost back at the jetty, the bright-yellow ladder acting as a homing beacon, the sun comes out. He flips onto his back, takes a few slow backstrokes, then floats. The sky momentarily blue above, the sun warm on his face, his chest rising and falling. He feels good, exercise endorphins running through his system. His arms are heavy from the exertion but there's no pain in his leg, no pain anywhere. His recovery is complete. He stretches, turns, dives under, comes up, grinning like an idiot. He loves the water. Nothing beats a good swim.

Back on the jetty, he checks the timer on his phone: thirty-nine minutes. He took a break at the other side, a few more minutes at this end, so perhaps thirty-five minutes' total swimming. That makes his guess about right – it's probably just over a kilometre each way.

He stands with his towel around his shoulders, bare-chested, barefoot, looking out at the lake, enjoying the sensation of being damp and cool, retaining the feeling of water, of swimming, for as long as he can. His thoughts turn away from murder, away from Markovich and back to Barbara. He thinks about last night, holding her, coming so close to kissing her. When he saw her today, he felt a lift in his heart. He has to face it, Grace is right: he has feelings for Barbara that go beyond friendship.

He looks across the lake, at the foreign-looking houses that line its banks, at the church spire behind them, remembers the neatly demarcated wheat fields, the patches of forest. No vast paddocks, no red earth, no endless grasslands, no grey-green gums, no washed-out sky. The trees are green and leafy and the summer sky, a cool royal blue dotted with clouds, the soft touch of the sun, so different from the harsh light, the burning strength of it at home. He knows that Barbara isn't likely to want to come back to Australia. Her experience there is still deeply traumatising. If he wants to have some kind of relationship with her, something that goes beyond texts and calls, he'd have to find a way to spend more time over here. And that's complicated. Not to mention that she has a man, he reminds himself, and has never given any indication that she's interested in him as anything other than a friend.

He exhales a long sigh. No easy answers, mate, he tells himself. He looks at his phone: almost 4 p.m., the battery down to 2 per cent now. The sun goes behind a cloud and the wind picks up, goosebumps prickling across his chest. There might be rain coming. He dries off, pulls on his jeans and t-shirt. Around him the colony is silent. He sets off, in the direction he saw Barbara go. The colony is small – it shouldn't take him long to get back to the car.

Chapter 49

Mildersee
3.35 p.m.

Barbara is standing at the bottom of the lane where Amina Khan's body was found. This lane seems to be the epicentre of the murders. Mattias Ritter had a cabin here, Nina Hartmann was last seen alive here. The jetty where Kaiser and Hartmann pushed Ritter off in his boat, sent him to his death, is over to her left. And now Amina Khan has died here too.

There are so many questions she doesn't have the answers to, not least why Amina put her things in her car and then came this way. Did someone invite her, entice her, promise to show her the plant she was clutching when she died? All Barbara knows is that the castor oil seed found by Amina's body, the same type of seed they found near Nina Hartmann, is the best clue she has. She thinks of the Kochs' cabin, the shed with the lock on it. Perhaps there's a clue there. But she'll need a warrant to open it and she's unlikely to get that until they have more conclusive forensic evidence from the trousers. While she's here, she might as well start by searching the gardens on this lane.

There are fourteen cabins, seven on each side, between here and the main path. She starts at the lake end, by Ritter's cabin, and works up from there. She makes a quick search through Ritter's garden and it confirms what she already knows – there's no castor oil plant here. The place opposite looks half-abandoned. The dry grass is knee-high, herbs have broken out of the pots that contained them, a shrub, the leaves yellow and withered, almost as tall as she is, acting as a fence. She walks around the garden – no sign of the spiky pink-seeded plant she's looking for – then up to the cabin, which doesn't seem to have been opened in a while. Shutters over the windows, cracks in the concrete of the little porch, spiderwebs around the doorframe and the windows. The breeze is picking up, the pine trees quivering in the wind; the sound of a squirrel scuttling across the roof of the cabin makes her start.

She goes out the gate, which doesn't close properly, and stands on the sandy lane. The silence of the empty colony, the spate of murders, sends a shiver of apprehension down her back. Maybe she should walk back to the jetty, wait for Walker to get back from his swim – the two of them can do this walk through the gardens together. She turns towards the lake, hesitates, then tells herself to get a grip. This kind of fear, this kind of nervousness, is exactly why Fischer is pushing her away from the big cases. If she's going to be police, she needs to find some backbone. Anyway – she pats the shoulder of her jacket for comfort – she's carrying her service pistol, she's armed and prepared. She crosses the lane and into the next garden, which is neat enough, though the grass is brown, desperate for water. There's a lilac bush in the centre, its petals covering the ground beneath it. A big fragrant rosemary bush is growing in a bed near the cabin, lavender beside it, the hum of bees in the purple flowers. No castor oil plant.

The next cabin is Kaiser's. They went over his garden with a fine-tooth comb during the search so she skips it; she's certain the plant she's looking for didn't come from his place. The cabin next to Kaiser's has a gate that squeaks loudly as she pushes it open. There's an old trampoline in the centre of the yard, its black bounce mat sagging and torn, a swing hanging lopsided from the tree, one rope frayed so much by use that it has snapped. Again, it seems no one has been here for a while. There are no plants to speak of, only a patch of dry grass fading to moss, and pine needles under the shade of two tall trees, and an oak with a wooden climbing ladder, some of the planks missing, attached to its wide trunk. A climbing rose is pushing its way through a trellis alongside the porch, its yellow blooms blousy and faded, petals dusting the concrete. No pink-seeded castor oil plant.

The garden across the path is neat as a pin – the Krause cabin. She pushes the gate open and walks up the concrete path – feeling, for the first time, as if she's trespassing. The lawn that edges the path is a vivid Kodachrome green – there's obviously a watering system in place – and tightly mowed. The beds are weed-free, the flowers have been rigorously deadheaded, the bushes that line the fence are neatly trimmed into shape. There isn't a leaf, a twig, a petal out of place. It is alive but somehow lacking life at the same time. Nothing as wild and out of place as a castor oil plant.

Directly beside the Krause cabin is Ralf Wagner's place. Ralf Wagner, who has been at the colony every time someone has died. She goes through Wagner's gate; the door to his cabin is shut and, for once, there's no sign of him. She takes her time looking around. The garden is neat, the grass is mown, the bushes against the fence pruned, but it's not a gardener's garden. There are no plants being cultivated, no flowers, no herbs, only the lawn, the ever-present pine trees and the same evergreen bushes that everyone here seems to use to demarcate one cabin from another. Wagner has covered the concrete slab of the porch with terracotta tiles. A white plastic table with two chairs sits on the patio. She looks in through the window of his cabin. Inside is neat but old-fashioned. An armchair upholstered in a faded green is positioned to look out the window. The cushions are thin and bear the permanent imprint of Wagner's body. A small Formica-topped table, pushed up against the window on the left, has one low stool beside it. She can see an ancient-looking gas stove in the kitchen, alongside seventies-style kitchen units in dark brown. It's neat and clean but there's something lonely about the place. For all the hours Wagner spends out here, it isn't homely.

She walks around the back of the cabin and tries the door of the shed. Locked. Maybe she could get a warrant to search it, but there's no real cause. There's no sign of the pink spikes of the castor oil plant and Wagner has an alibi for yesterday. She walks around again, looking for something, anything, that might give her a clue, but the garden, like Wagner, is tight-lipped.

Back on the sandy path, she exhales and looks at her watch. Almost 4 p.m. She'll check one more cabin and then she'll walk back to the car and meet Lucas. She crosses the path to the cabin opposite Wagner's, which is virtually hidden by a hedge that's almost head height. She thinks for a moment, running through her mental map of the colony – of course, it's Renate Bauer's place. Curious, she steps forward, pushes open the gate and, more out of courtesy than expectation, calls 'Hallo?' as she steps through.

The garden that opens up is different from all the others she's seen. To her left are neat rows of vegetables running towards a small greenhouse. At the side of the cabin is a herb garden, she can catch the scent of rosemary and mint, and ivy winds its way up the exterior walls. A stone statue of an angel stands beneath an apple tree, heavy with small green fruit, in the centre of the garden. A vine, grape perhaps, grows in profusion across a trellis and makes a verdant ceiling for the porch. There's no sign of the pink-seeded ricin plant she's looking for but an alarm is chiming at the back of her mind, a small alert about something she's seeing, but she can't pick up what. She's looking around, trying to get a hold of what is setting her off, when the door to the cabin opens and Renate Bauer steps out, looking more casual than usual. Her hair is piled in a loose bun, strands falling around her face. She's wearing a white short-sleeved blouse with her grey trousers, and is holding a large glass of red liquid in her hand.

'Detective,' she says. 'Did you bring that handsome young officer with you?'

Chapter 50

Mildersee
4 p.m.

It's taking Walker a while to get his bearings. He walked confidently up the lane towards the forest and turned at the track that he thought led to the car park. Instead, it's taken him deeper into the colony, little cabins on each side, most of them empty and forlorn-looking. It comes to an end at an abandoned double-sized plot with a rusting kids' playground – a frame for swings, blocks that might once have held see-saws, a wooden climbing frame, rotten and falling apart – in front of a building that's bigger than the rest of the cabins. He's intrigued enough to walk over and have a look inside. Standing on tiptoe, he can see in through the side windows. A large room, the lino curling and torn, a pile of leaves and mould on the far side where one of the windows has been smashed. There's a small stage at one end and what might have been a bar at the other. Some kind of clubhouse, he hazards a guess, long since abandoned. Graffiti covers the walls, and it looks like someone has started a fire inside at some point, the walls to the right of the bar blackened with soot.

As he tramps back to the path through thigh-high grass – happy that there are no snakes in Germany, this would be a perfect home for them – he tries to imagine what the colony was like in its heyday, when all the cabins were in use, when families came out here regularly, when the bar was open, and kids were playing on the swings. He can imagine neighbours barbecuing, kids running free, boozy afternoons on the jetty, canoeing, sunbathing and sociable evenings with friends in the garden. The colony, which seemed so unappealing to him on his first visit, comes to life in this vision and he feels a twinge of sadness for its bereft state. Many of the cabins seem to be almost abandoned, and now that three people have been killed here it might be the death knell for the whole place.

He retraces his steps to the lane he first came up and looks back down to the lake. The yellow ladder on the jetty he used is a useful marker. He turns away from the water and walks on, coming at length to a wider path. This must be the one that leads to the car park. He turns onto it and tries to find a familiar landmark, but he hadn't been paying enough attention on the way down, happy to let Barbara lead the way. The colony is silent and empty. 'Desolate' is the word that comes to mind. No sound, barely a bird call on the air. He glances down all the lanes, hoping to see Barbara walking on one of them, but no joy. Then he sees a gleam of light on metal ahead. A vehicle. He's heading in the right direction. He walks faster, striding out now. When he reaches the car park, there's another vehicle parked beside Barbara's little Peugeot but no sign of Barbara.

The thought crosses his mind that perhaps she'd meant for him to wait at the jetty, and he hesitates, wondering if he should head back there. But he's certain she said to meet at the car. He stands for a moment in the sun, debating with himself, then pulls out his phone: *4.08*. It's not late – she's probably caught up in her search.

The battery still says 2 per cent, but when he dials her number and presses the Call button he only hears the ringtone for a brief second before the screen goes black and the phone dies.

• • •

Schmidt is peeved. He's stuck at the station, digging through ancient paperwork while the Berlin detective is out doing the proper investigating. She called him to say that she was going to the colony to search for some kind of plant and left him with instructions to look into the histories of the long-term residents at the colony, a task that he's convinced is futile and will lead to nothing but trouble if the chief finds out. The chief is sure to take it as more evidence that the Berlin detective has it in for the Ossis.

He sighs. Whatever it is she's doing, he'd rather be with her. He's certain it has more relevance to the case than the job she's given him, which feels more like something to keep him pointlessly busy rather than an integral part of the investigation. He's already run a search of police records and, as expected, found nothing for Ralf Wagner, Renate Bauer, Manfred Krause and his wife or any of the other long-term residents. Unsurprising, he thinks; they're all middle-class old people. He thinks back to her instructions: 'See if there's a police record. If not, see if there's any history of suspicious or sudden deaths in their families, any history of violence, anything that links them to toxic substances. Maybe they've worked in fields like pharmacy or medicine. You can try the Stasi records – there might be something in there.'

He walks down and looks into the archive room. There are ancient cases down here, the pre-unification stuff, but the room is cluttered and dusty and he's not sure where he would start. The rows of boxes, ordered by date rather than name, seem an impossible task. He goes back to his computer and decides he'll try a news search. If there were any suspicious or sudden deaths, it's likely they'd have been reported, at least since 1991, in the local newspaper. If only these oldsters had had Instagram or X or something like that, it would make things so much easier, he thinks.

Wagner's name only comes up once: he won a half-marathon in Honigsdorf, a nearby village, almost twenty years ago. The Krause couple are mentioned a few times. Manfred Krause once owned a small local manufacturing firm that won a few prizes for employer of the year in the early 2000s, and his wife is in a bridge pair that regularly wins the local league. What nonsense, Schmidt thinks to himself, a total waste of his policing time.

He gets up and makes himself a coffee, wondering if he should call the detective, see if she needs him at Mildersee. He'll drink his coffee first, he decides, then give her a call. Or maybe he'll just turn up out there. She's less likely to send him away if he's standing in front of her. He types in the next name on the list, Renate Bauer, and picks up his coffee.

A surprisingly long list of articles comes up under the search tab. The headline of the first story, dated six years ago – *Local man dies in mushroom poisoning incident* – brings him up short. He puts the coffee down, clicks on the link.

> Local man Hans Bauer, 64, died yesterday, five days after eating a meal containing foraged mushrooms. Coroner Herr Doktor Johann Canus said Bauer died from multi-organ failure after poisoning from the toxins found in lethal 'death cap' mushrooms (*Amanita phalloides*). Herr Bauer had been in hospital since the weekend. His wife, Renate Bauer, who also ate the mushrooms, was briefly hospitalised but survived. She was released from hospital earlier this week.

Chapter 51

Mildersee
4.15 p.m.

'Do you know a lot about plants?' asks Barbara. She's inside Renate Bauer's cabin. The space is gloomy and a little cold. There's a single bed in an alcove to her right – covered with a brown chenille bedspread and so tightly made you could bounce a coin on it – with a small crucifix affixed to the wall beside it. As neat and spartan as a nun's cell, thinks Barbara. In the main space, a table by the window is covered with an embroidered white tablecloth and has a jug of cherry juice sitting on top. The dark wooden kitchen counters are tidy except for a neat line of empty glass jars, perhaps for jam-making. Above them, herbs are hanging from a rack, drying. The only incongruous element is a bottle of vodka, almost empty, standing beside the glass jars on the counter.

They're in the cabin because of the cherry juice. Renate insisted that Barbara try it. She'd held up her glass. 'Would you like a cherry juice?' she offered. 'I made it myself, this morning, the last fruits from a friend's tree.'

Barbara declined, but only half-heartedly, and when Renate pressed, she gave in. Her mother had given them cherry spritzers as kids, a mix of cherry juice and sparkling water, and she always loved the drink. She hasn't had it in years, had almost forgotten how much she likes it. She's thirsty from her walk around the gardens in the warm afternoon too, and the cherry juice will be refreshing.

Barbara shrugs off her jacket, feels her service revolver bulky in its holster. She makes sure, as she hangs the jacket on the back of the chair, that the weapon isn't visible. Renate finds a glass in one of the kitchen units and half fills it with juice.

'Vodka?' she asks, directing her head towards the table.

'No thanks,' says Barbara. 'Just water. I'm working.'

'Of course you are,' says Renate. 'I won't put too much in.'

'No, really, juice and water is fine.'

Renate tops the glass up with sparkling water and hands it to Barbara, then picks up her own drink and says 'Prost!' touching glasses with her.

Barbara takes a sip, then a bigger mouthful. It's sweet, refreshing, but tastes slightly different from how she remembers. Childhood flavours are never the same as an adult.

'What did you ask me?' says Renate, taking a seat across from her at the table.

'Do you know a lot about plants? You have a nice garden...'

'I grew up on a farm and my mother was very knowledgeable. She could find wild mushrooms and other plants and fruits in the forest. I wasn't that interested, I was more into clothes and pretty things, but since my husband died, well, the garden has been a real balm.'

'Let me show you something,' says Barbara, pulling out her phone. She notices a missed call from Lucas, and another from Schmidt. She wonders what Schmidt wants; perhaps he's found something. She needs to get going, meet Lucas, call Schmidt.

Distracted, she pulls up a picture of the castor oil plant. 'Do you know this plant?'

Renate Bauer glances at the phone, then nods. 'Yes, the castor oil plant,' she says. 'It's a decorative plant – Frau Krause has one.'

'Really?' says Barbara, excitement building. 'Here at the colony?'

'No. On her balcony in Kummerfeld. She grows it in a pot because it wouldn't survive the winter outside. I don't think it's tolerant of cold, so I doubt you'd find it growing out here.'

Barbara hides her surprise and delight. Frau Krause! Frau Krause who was so specific in her witness statements. Who told them she'd heard Mattias Ritter arguing with someone. Perhaps it was all a massive misdirection. She needs to get back to Kummerfeld, talk with the Krause couple. She picks up her glass, finishes the juice and decides she definitely doesn't like it anymore. Perhaps it's nicer with vodka, she thinks wryly.

'Thank you for the juice,' she says. 'I need to go.' As she stands, her eye is drawn to the window, which neatly frames the little greenhouse at the side of Renate Bauer's garden. The greenhouse . . . The alarm that was chiming in her brain earlier gives a loud clang. The only person she's met at the colony who has any real gardening knowledge is Renate Bauer. And she was here when both Marcus Ritter and Nina Hartmann died. She's also here today, the day after Amina Khan died, the only person Barbara has seen all day. Out of nowhere, a shiver of fear runs through her. Perhaps Renate Bauer is lying to her. She recognised the seed head. Perhaps it's not Frau Krause who has the plant.

'Thank you for your help, Frau Bauer,' she says, picking up her bag, draping her jacket over her arm, comforted by the reassuring weight of her service weapon. She moves towards the door. The need to get out of the chilly cabin is rising in her – it's everything she can do not to run.

'Let me give you something before you go,' says Renate, rising to her feet.

Barbara pauses, hand on the door. Her heart is thumping hard in her chest; she can feel a rivulet of sweat run from under her arm down the side of her body.

Renate walks over and gestures to the door. 'It's outside,' she says. 'Follow me.'

Barbara steps out onto the porch, happy to be out of the gloomy cabin and back in the garden. The sun is out, the clouds parted for the moment, blue sky above the colony. She can hear a pigeon cooing in a tree nearby, the breeze rustling the high pines, and her fears start to feel fanciful. Renate Bauer was friends with Mattias Ritter. Just because she likes plants, doesn't mean she's a killer. She needs to find Walker, call Schmidt, talk to Frau Krause.

'This way,' says Renate, walking down the path, away from the gate, around the corner of the cabin. As she follows the older woman, her grey hair falling from the bun, a faint scent of booze emanating from her skin, Barbara relaxes. In the bright afternoon light, the thought that this woman could be the cold-hearted killer of three people seems unlikely. Renate Bauer leads her towards a wooden shed in the corner of the garden, surrounded on two sides by high hedges. She fiddles with a lock on the door, gets it open and holds the door wide.

'What is it?' asks Barbara.

'I have some spare cherry juice,' says Renate, smiling at her. 'Choose a bottle, you can take it with you for your sister – you said she always drank it too.'

Barbara's not sure Rita will like the juice any more than she did but it seems rude to refuse. She'll grab a bottle quickly, then she needs to go and find Lucas. He'll be waiting for her at the car. She can call Schmidt on the way and ask him to bring the Krause couple in for questioning.

The way the shed is situated against the shrubs means the door only opens wide enough for one person. Barbara drops her bag on the path and lies her jacket on top, then squeezes past Renate Bauer. The interior of the shed is shadowy. As she stands in the doorway, her eyes adjusting to the gloom, she can make out a high wooden table in front of her and a pile of firewood in the far corner.

'The juice is in the crate at the back,' says Renate.

Barbara steps inside, almost kicking over an empty terracotta planter that is sitting on the floor just beside the door. She still can't see the crate of juice but lying on top of the table is a large plant, its roots wrapped in a cream-coloured cloth. Barbara goes closer to get a better look. In the same moment that she recognises the spiky pink and red flowers of the castor oil plant she's been looking for, the door behind her shuts with a slam, plunging the shed into darkness. Barbara spins around, reaches towards the door and hears the sound of a bolt being pushed shut, followed by the harsh click of a lock.

Chapter 52

Mildersee

4.30 p.m.

Walker is starting to worry. He can see by the clock in Barbara's car that it's 4.30 p.m. and there's still no sign of her. He jogs back to the jetty with the yellow ladder. He must have got it wrong; she'll be sitting on the bench waiting for him. But when he gets there, the jetty is empty, the water is still, there's no one about. He runs back to the car, taking the lakeshore track, in case she's walked a different way. Checks the lanes again as he jogs by: no one, no one, no one. The car is still there but no Barbara. He stops, breathing a little heavily from the exertion.

He's panicking over nothing, he tells himself. Barbara is a bit late, but so what. She's looking for a plant, the plant that the victim had been holding in her hand. That means she'll be checking all the gardens. Checking fifty or more gardens is slow work. Perhaps she's lost track of time or wants to get it finished before she meets him. Most likely she's sent him a message, not realising his battery is flat. He'll find her and help her with the search. He thinks it through and reckons his best bet is to be methodical about it. Up and down each lane, looking in every garden, one by one.

He walks along the main path and takes the first left, goes slowly down the lane, looking into each garden, calling 'Barbara?' once in a while. His voice hangs on the quiet air. Sometimes, when he can't see the yard completely, he goes through the gate and into the garden to double-check, but they're all empty. No one around. He reaches the lake, walks along the waterfront, checking the little gardens as he goes, then turns right into the next lane, repeats his check of each yard. Nothing. At the top, he turns left and left again, walking and checking, walking and calling, garden by garden. Nothing and no one. Where the hell is she? He gets to the last of the cabins and stops. What now? he thinks.

The only lane he hasn't checked is the one with the crime scene tape; he didn't want to disturb the scene and, if he'd been the one searching the gardens, that would have been the first lane he checked. He figures Barbara would do the same and that means she should have long been finished there. He reckons his search has taken him the best part of half an hour. So it must be at least 5 p.m., maybe 5.15, which means it's over two hours since he last saw her and an hour past the time they were due to meet. Something has clearly gone wrong – she should have checked more than one lane in that time. But maybe not, maybe this is a more labour-intensive job than he thinks. He starts at the top of the lane, crime scene tape fluttering at the far end. Two gardens along, he finally sees someone. It's not Barbara. An older bloke in work clothes – navy-blue trousers and a matching shirt, both spotted with white paint, the hem of the trouser legs green with grass stains – is sitting in the sun on a white plastic chair on his lawn. The cabin behind him looks freshly painted, the grass freshly mowed, so he's probably run out of work to do. He's sitting the way old blokes sit. Quiet, still, eyes closed. Floating on memories of days past, perhaps, or making lists of jobs still to do. Walker glances down, sees the number 11 painted on the gate, realises with a jolt that this is the same bloke who was mowing his lawn the last time he was out here and that Barbara is suspicious of this man, a former Stasi operative. His anxiety for Barbara's well-being rises.

He calls out 'G'day' and the bloke opens his eyes and turns his head. 'Do you speak English?' Walker asks, hopeful. The old bloke turns his lips down and shakes his head.

He stands there, frustrated as hell at his lack of German. 'Polizei,' he says eventually, pointing at himself. The word close enough to the English that he's remembered it. 'Polizei.'

The bloke stares at him, assessing him, his eyebrows raised. Walker glances down at his jeans, his t-shirt, knows his hair will be a little wild from the swim. When he looks back up, the bloke has closed his eyes again. He curses his lack of German, racks his brain. 'Hey,' he calls again. The old bloke turns back, face uninterested. He's not making this easy, thinks Walker. 'Polizei Frau?' he asks, pointing around, at the garden, at the lane. 'Polizei Frau here?'

The bloke stands, walks over. His face is lined and bitter but he's not as old as Walker had thought; his body is wiry and strong, he moves easily. He says something to Walker in German, but Walker doesn't understand a word. Confusion must be written on his face for the old bloke raises his voice and says loud and slowly, 'Keine Polizei', shaking his head as he speaks. Walker gets the message. The bloke hasn't seen any police. Or, if he has, he's not admitting to it.

Chapter 53

Mildersee

4.30 p.m.

'Frau Bauer?' Barbara edges over to the door, hand out to feel the way. The shed is almost pitch black, no light coming in at all. Being locked in the dark is bringing back all the trauma of Australia, of Rita's terrible experience. She can feel herself sweating, her breathing shallow, her fear mounting. She needs to get out. 'Frau Bauer,' she says. 'Please, what are you doing? Open the door.'

'You're the second person who came looking for the castor oil plant,' says Renate Bauer from outside. 'The lady who came yesterday, she had no manners. She came into my garden uninvited, went through my shed, pretended she was a botanist. She didn't leave me any choice either.'

Barbara feels as if she's carrying a stone in her stomach. The fear she had a few minutes ago comes rushing back. And to hear Renate Bauer state the fact of Amina Khan's murder so blandly, so calmly, is somehow more frightening than if she were in a violent rage. Barbara pats the ground around her, looking for her phone, her weapon, then remembers with a sinking feeling that she's left her bag and jacket on the path outside.

'Let me out, Frau Bauer,' she says, 'and we can talk about yesterday, about whatever you want.'

'No,' says Frau Bauer. 'You're staying in there. It won't take long, a couple of hours at most. That's how long it took for Nina Hartmann, the little whore. You're smaller than she was, and you drank the same amount.'

Barbara's stomach cramps up. 'What do you mean . . . ?'

'The cherry juice. Devil's cherries, not sour cherries. *Atropa belladonna*, deadly nightshade. You've drunk it. Now the devil will come to take his due.'

Barbara goes quiet, forces herself to think, to take in what Renate Bauer is saying. The cherry juice had tasted wrong. Why did she drink it – what was she thinking? The darkness of the shed is pressing in on her. She can't breathe, can't concentrate, feels claustrophobia rising, drops of sweat running down under her arms, between her breasts. She wants to beat on the wooden door, scream at Renate Bauer, but forces herself to stay calm. She needs to keep Renate talking, needs to convince her to open the door.

'Tell me about Nina Hartmann,' she says. 'What happened?'

There's silence on the other side; perhaps Renate has already gone, left her here alone. Her heart starts beating double time. She's about to raise her hands, pummel on the door, when Renate Bauer says, 'She was nothing but a whore', her voice cold, angry, ugly. 'She was sleeping around, she flirted with all the men, led them on. Even Willie Koch. He was besotted, following her around, bringing her gifts, but she just told him he was pathetic. And she killed Mattias. It's because of her that Mattias died.'

'Mattias was your friend, wasn't he?'

'Yes, we had a very special friendship. He was such a kind man, and he deserved much better than that woman. Nina was always spending time with Kaiser, kissing him in public, sleeping in his cabin. Shameless whore. She killed Mattias. It's her fault he died.'

'Did she make the yew tea that killed Mattias?' asks Barbara. 'Was it deliberate or an accident?'

'She wouldn't have known about yew. She didn't know about anything.'

There's a silence.

'You made the tea,' says Barbara, shocked realisation dawning. 'It was meant for Nina, but Mattias drank it.'

'She was betraying Mattias, belittling him. His heart was breaking. I know how that feels. My husband . . . Thirty-eight years we were married. I spent thirty-eight years taking care of him, being there for him, running around after him, and then out of nowhere he told me he was leaving, that he didn't love me anymore, that he was in love with his secretary. Such a pathetic cliché. He didn't leave, of course. He died before he could go through with it. But it isn't mushroom season now, so I had to be a bit more original this time. Nina was always drinking tea from that thermos, like a baby sucking at a teat. She always had it with her. When I spotted her that day going to visit Kaiser without it, I knew it was a sign. I went to Mattias's cabin, I added the yew to her tea. But then . . .' She's quiet for a moment and when she speaks again it sounds as though she's fighting back tears. 'I don't know how she made Mattias drink it. I never saw him drinking tea before. But that day, he did. She must have forced him. She was the devil's work through and through.'

'But you paid her back,' says Barbara. She remembers the yellow thermos sitting on the table when she and Walker were waiting for Nina Hartmann. Nina had visited Kaiser, left her thermos at home once more. She feels a rush of guilt. If she'd told Nina how Mattias Ritter had been poisoned, she might be alive today.

'I watched her,' says Renate Bauer. 'I waited for my chance. She went back to Kaiser, he was the one she wanted – she didn't care about Mattias. She got what she deserved.'

There's a longer silence this time. Barbara can feel her temperature rising. The little shed is hot and stifling. She remembers Nina Hartmann, naked under the bushes, and feels a quake of fear. Perhaps the symptoms of the poison are already starting.

'Look, I can see you were trying to help Mattias, you didn't mean to hurt him. And I understand what you mean about Nina. Let me out and we can explain together how it happened—'

'No,' says Frau Bauer. 'You need to wait for the devil. You ate his fruit. He'll bring you visions, warm you up, ready you for hell. I'll leave you to enjoy it. Goodbye.'

'Frau Bauer, wait . . .' Barbara can hear her phone ringing in her bag outside. 'That's my phone, that's my colleague looking for me. He'll come here to find me any moment. Let me out – it will be better this way. We can work something out.'

'He won't find you and he won't find me,' says Renate Bauer. 'I drank the juice too. My son, my Max, has left me. I don't have anyone else. There's nothing here for me. I'm going.' Barbara can hear the ringtone of her phone receding. Renate Bauer has picked up her bag, is walking away.

'Frau Bauer, let me out, let me out!' She's shouting, hammering on the door. There's no reply.

'Help,' she shouts. 'Help!' Lucas is out there. He'll be looking for her. He might hear her. She shouts and shouts again and again until her voice is hoarse and she's sweating and flushed. She stops for a moment, feeling light-headed. The shed is still dark but maybe her eyes are starting to adjust; the shadows seem to be dancing and she can see a light, see the way to the door. She steps forward, stumbles in the dark, tripping over her feet, falling hard onto her knees, banging her head against the wall on her way down. The shock of the crash, the sharp pain in her knees and her head, sobers her. The poison she's drunk is taking effect. Before she does anything else, before she tries to get out of here, she needs to get this poison out of her body.

Chapter 54

Mildersee
5.20 p.m.

Walker and the old bloke are at an impasse, standing there staring at each other. Walker, increasingly concerned for Barbara and at a loss as to what to do next, is wondering if he should just barge in, search this garden and cabin to make sure Barbara isn't here, while the old bloke is seemingly struck by politeness, unable to walk away. They both start with relief at the sound of footsteps and a gate opening and then clanging shut. Walker turns, thinking it's Barbara, at last, but there's a different woman standing in front of him. In her mid-to-late sixties, her long grey hair wild and loose, her cheeks flushed, her pupils dilated. When she steps forward, eyes unfocused, saying something in German, the scent of alcohol pulses from her. On the crazy side of drunk, thinks Walker.

    The man behind him speaks. Walker steps to the side so that he can make eye contact with him while still keeping the woman in sight, in case she falls over; she doesn't look at all steady on her feet. The old bloke speaks again, his eyes on the woman, something between confusion and contempt on his face. She throws her head back, lifts her hands to the sky, moving in a kind of silent dance. Then she brings her arms down in a rapid movement and her face changes. There's rage, hatred even, in her eyes, and with swift, surprisingly steady steps, she moves towards the gate, pointing both her index fingers at the bloke, shouting something that, even with Walker's lack of comprehension, sounds like a stream of curses. The old bloke looks shocked, and Walker notices he takes a step back. The woman laughs, an edge of hysteria in it. She's definitely drunk – wasted too, maybe. She tries to twirl in a circle, loses her balance, falls in a pile on the sandy lane, landing on her knees, Walker too far away to catch her.

He goes over to her. 'Are you alright?' he asks. 'Here, let me help you up.' He bends down to offer his hand and, as he does, she turns, still on her hands and knees, and looks at him. Her face transforms into a grimace of fear and she screams, a sound filled with pure terror, the loudest scream he's ever heard. Instinctively, he takes a step back, his own heart beating fast with the shock of it, looking over his shoulder at what might have scared her. There's nothing there.

The old bloke says something, his tone filled with contempt. He looks at Walker and shakes his head and makes a dismissive gesture with his hand in the direction of the woman, then turns and walks away, back to his chair. The message is clear: he's washed his hands of the situation.

Walker looks back towards the woman. She's on her feet now, unsteady as hell, weaving from side to side, heading in the direction of the lake. He hesitates, unsure as to what he should do. He doesn't want to frighten her further but she's in no condition to be wandering around the empty colony. He wishes Barbara were here. She can speak German, and she wouldn't be perceived as a threat by this woman either. The scream, the sound of it, must have reverberated throughout the colony. Surely Barbara, wherever she is, will have heard it, will be coming to see what's happened.

He's lost in his thoughts, half an eye on the woman's slow meandering progress down the lane, when she stops, makes an incoherent sound, drops to her knees, then projectile-vomits across the lane and into the shrubs of the neighbouring garden.

Fucksake, thinks Walker. He doesn't have water, doesn't have anything to give her. He's walking back towards the old bloke's garden – he'll have water – when he hears a strangled sound. He turns. The woman is on the ground, having some kind of fit, spasms racking her body.

'Help me,' he shouts to the old bloke. 'We need help, call a doctor!' Then he runs across to the woman. Her shuddering has stopped and as Walker gets nearer he can see that her face is blue, her eyes are rolled back in her head and bile and vomit are leaking from her lips. Overdose. Or, the thought comes to him in a rush, poison. The murders here have mostly been with poison. This woman could be a fourth victim. Where the hell is Barbara?

He places the woman in the recovery position, checks her airways are clear. She's breathing, ragged but breathing. Her pulse is irregular, first way too fast, then slowing again, then fast. Her skin is warm, feverish almost. He looks up. The old bloke is standing at his gate, watching.

'Call an ambulance,' shouts Walker. Fuck, the bloke doesn't understand English. Walker gets to his feet, runs over to him. 'Phone,' he says, miming a phone call to his ear. 'Phone.'

The bloke pulls out a mobile phone from his trouser pocket, hands it over. The screen is locked. Walker presses the Emergency Call button, hands the phone back. 'Doctor,' he says, pointing at the woman, who is shuddering and twitching on the lane. The bloke nods, puts the phone to his ear, starts talking a moment later. Walker waits. He doesn't understand what's being said but he wants to communicate his anxiety and urgency. When the old bloke ends the call, he looks at Walker and says, 'Fünfzehn Minuten', then shows Walker ten fingers, folds them down and brings five up again. 'Fünfzehn,' he says, repeating the action.

Walker gets it. 'Fifteen minutes,' he says, copying the motion of the fingers. As he runs back to where the woman is lying, he only hopes it will be soon enough.

Chapter 55

Mildersee
5.30 p.m.

The old bloke has followed Walker and is watching as he checks the woman's vital signs once more. Her face is still the same unhealthy colour and there's foamy mucus coming out of her mouth. Walker remembers what Barbara told him about the poisonings out here – the vomiting, the blue-tinged skin. She's still breathing, but it doesn't look good; her skin is hot and her pulse way too fast.

'We need water,' he says, not looking up. 'We can give her a drink, if she can keep it down, and use it to cool her.'

The bloke says something in German and Walker exhales in frustration. Not being able to communicate could cost this woman her life. He needs to find water, maybe see if he can discover what she's taken too – that will help the ambos when they get here. The bloke crouches down beside him, hands him a cloth, a tea towel by the look. Walker uses it to wipe her mouth, clean the foul-smelling liquid from her face.

He picks up her hand and gives it to the bloke, forces him to hold it. Then he gives him the tea towel, and stands. The bloke looks at him, shock in his eyes, speaks in rapid German, jerks his hand away. He doesn't want to be left alone with her.

Walker puts his hand on the bloke's shoulder and looks directly at him. 'I'm only going for water. Water,' he says in his calmest, most reassuring voice, miming a drinking action. 'I'll be back in two minutes. Two minutes.' He raises two fingers as he says it, repeats it twice. The bloke's panicked look subsides. Walker presses the woman's hand into his once more, then runs to the cabin she came from. There might be water there and hopefully he can find out what she's been taking.

The cabin door is unlocked and opens into a weird, dark little room, a kitchen with a dining table and three chairs. Two glasses, both empty, are sitting at one end of the table. An empty bottle of vodka is lying on its side on the kitchen counter beside a jug with the last dregs of a red liquid inside. He sniffs it, a sweetish smell, perhaps a fruit juice. The vodka explains her drunkenness; perhaps the juice explains the rest. He thinks back to what Barbara told him about the poisonings: the victims had drunk tea, not juice. Maybe this is a coincidence, he tells himself, unconvinced.

He picks up the jug and the empty vodka bottle – they'll be useful props if the ambos don't speak English – and looks around for water. Can't find a sink or a tap and remembers belatedly that Barbara said there was no running water out here. He heads out the door, doesn't want to leave the old bloke on his own for too long, and spots a blue crate on the patio filled with bottled water. Most of the bottles are empty and he goes through half a dozen before he gets a full one, then he's running across the garden and back down the lane towards the woman. He puts the vodka and the jug on the side of the track and takes the water over to her. They work together, the old bloke wetting the tea towel and wiping her face while Walker tries to drip some liquid into her mouth. She isn't drinking, seems to be unconscious, the water dribbling out of her mouth. He feels her pulse, the same irregular beat, her skin feverish.

As he tends to her, his mind is working. There's something that he's missed, something important. He gives the water to the bloke, gets to his feet, thinking. When the reason for his concern comes to him – like a bolt of lightning, an electric charge that runs through his body – he turns and runs back towards the cabin. There were two glasses on the table. Two people have drunk this poison.

He pushes open the gate, charges into the cabin, over to the two glasses on the table, both with shallow puddles of red liquid in the bottom. He picks them up, sniffs them. One has the scent of vodka, the other doesn't. He looks around again, forcing himself to stay calm, to read the scene. The place is austere: a single bed, dark wooden cabinets, a crucifix on the walls. No colour or warmth. He searches quickly, peering under the bed, opening the kitchen units, not sure what he's looking for until he finds it. Under the table, almost invisible in the gloom, is a bag. He pulls it out and recognises it immediately: it's Barbara's. He opens it: her notebook, her purse, her phone are all in there. His stomach churns in fear. Barbara was here. Barbara drank this poison. Barbara is sick, maybe unconscious like the woman in the lane, but all alone somewhere.

He goes out onto the porch, shouting, 'Barbara? Barbara!' listening for an answer. Nothing. She has to be here somewhere – he's been through the rest of the colony, he's checked all the gardens. He notices a greenhouse at the end of a vegetable bed, runs down, wrenches open the door and steps into a warm, moist space reeking of vegetation and fungi. There are two shelves on each side, stacked with plant pots and gardening tools, and two watering cans are standing at the far end. No sign of Barbara. He backs out, looks around. Behind the cabin, wedged into a corner, is a shed.

He runs over. It's locked. A shiny metal padlock around a bolt.

The lock looks new. He bangs on the door. 'Barbara? Barbara?'

He hears a scrabbling, a scratching, something. A rodent, perhaps. 'Barbara, are you in there?' he tries once more, standing right by the door.

'Lucas. Help me, Lucas.' Her voice is low and raspy. 'She poisoned me. She poisoned them all.'

'You're OK, don't worry. I'm here. I'll get you out.'

His heart is beating fast with shock. He doesn't have much time. He needs to get Barbara out, get her medical attention. He looks more closely at the lock. Not expensive, it's pickable, but he doesn't have his kit with him. He needs an angle grinder or a bolt cutter. He looks at the bolt on the door. It could be unscrewed, perhaps, but it's ancient, the screws probably tighter than the flimsy lock.

'I'm going for tools, Barbara. I'll only be one minute. I'm going to get you out, I promise.'

He runs to the lane, shouts 'Help!' at the old bloke, who is still crouched beside the woman. He gestures at him, shouts 'I need help' one more time, then runs into the old bloke's garden. The pristine cabin, the neat garden, all of it suggests the bloke will have tools, that he'll have something that might help him get Barbara out. Sure enough, there's a shed in the yard, also behind the cabin. The door is open, a mower standing just inside. Rows of tools hanging on the wall above a workbench, the shed as organised and tidy as the rest of the property. Walker runs his eyes across the selection – no angle grinder. There's a bolt cutter but it's a small one, too small. There are a couple of wrenches that might do the job, and he grabs those and a hammer. Sometimes brute force can work as a last resort with cheaper locks. He's on his way back across the garden when the old bloke appears at the gate. 'Help me,' says Walker, pushing past him and running back to where Barbara is locked up.

'I'm here, Barbara, I'm back, I'll have you out in a minute,' he says, keeping his voice calm. 'Talk to me.'

Silence. No answer. Shit.

'Hold on, Barbara, hold on. I'll have you out in a minute.'

He tries the wrenches first, putting the open lip of one inside the shackle as leverage, using the lip of the other to try to lever the shackle out. The old bloke arrives at his side, takes a look at what Walker is doing, says something in German and disappears again. Walker keeps working at the lock but the shackle is too high – he can't get enough purchase. He needs bigger wrenches. He tries once more, angling the wrench, trying to get leverage, but it won't work. Cursing silently, he drops the wrenches, picks up the hammer.

'Not long now, Barbara,' he says. 'I'm on it.'

He looks at the way the lock hangs, dangling free. A hammer won't do it. He needs another hammer, something to brace the lock against. He's halfway across the garden when the old bloke reappears, carrying a small black leather pouch, which he holds out towards Walker. 'Besser,' he says.

Walker grabs it, pulls the flap up and finds a dated but professional-looking set of lock picks. No idea why this bloke has lock picks but thank god he does. He gives a quick thumbs-up, races back to Barbara.

The lock is a simple one, it gives him no problems; within seconds he feels it click. He pulls it off and wrenches the door open. Barbara is lying, curled up, on the floor of the shed, her head by the door. Her face is flushed and sweaty and she's been violently sick, the floor around her covered in vomit.

'Barbara.' He can hear the quiver of fear in his voice as he says her name, as he bends down towards her. Please let her be OK. She has to be OK. He strokes her cheek; her skin is hot and sweaty but doesn't have the awful blue tinge. She opens her eyes, tries to speak.

'Shh, it's OK, I'm here, you're safe, I've got you,' he says. He can hear the sound of a vehicle on the lane outside, voices in German. The ambos. He leans forward, puts one arm gently under her shoulders, the other under her knees, and picks her up. Cradling her close, feeling the heat of her skin, her heart beating fast against his chest, he carries her across the garden and into the lane, towards the open doors of the ambulance.

Chapter 56

Berlin

Sunday, 9.30 a.m.

It's the church bells that wake Walker. A pleasant sound, coming from a distance, infiltrating his consciousness. He rolls onto his back, his mind fuzzy and tired, experiences a moment of calm before memories of yesterday come flooding back in.

His first thoughts are of Barbara. Her young colleague Schmidt arrived hot on the heels of the ambulance and Walker was relieved to be in the company of an English speaker and a fellow cop. When Walker told him what Barbara had said about the poisonings and shown him the empty bottles he'd found in the cabin, he saw fear for Barbara in Schmidt's eyes.

'I think this lady, Renate Bauer, might have poisoned her husband with mushrooms a few years ago,' Schmidt said. 'It was treated as an accidental death at the time, but now . . . Well, perhaps she killed him and she's killed again, more than once.'

Schmidt spoke in urgent German to the paramedics, who acted

immediately, the ambulance departing at speed. Walker, sick to his stomach with fear for Barbara, followed the ambulance to the hospital in Schmidt's car. Young and green as Schmidt no doubt is, Walker thinks he made good decisions, calling for back-up to secure the colony and an SOC team to go through the cabin where Barbara had been poisoned. He also asked for manpower at the hospital to guard and question the older woman. 'Should I call the detective's family?' he asked out loud before answering his own question: 'Maybe it's better to see what they say at the hospital, so I have proper information to give them.'

Once at the hospital, Barbara was rushed into an operating theatre, Schmidt into a huddle with a couple of senior officers who'd arrived shortly after them, and Walker had nothing to do but wait. He was given very little information, his lack of German not helping his case, his Aussie police badge of limited use. He was left pacing in frustration in the waiting area, regularly hassling various nurses and receptionists for updates, until an English-speaking nurse relented and led him to Barbara's ward.

'She is very lucky,' she told him. 'She was clever, she made herself vomit so most of the poison did not get into her system. But for the safe side we performed a Magenspülung – I do not know the English word. We emptied her stomach? She is resting now but she will be OK.'

The doctors had given Barbara a sedative of some kind and she was asleep when the nurse showed him into her ward. Her face pale, her mouth a little swollen and bruised from the procedure but her breathing regular, her pulse and heartbeat too. The fear he'd been tamping down for hours, that Barbara might not survive this, that she might be left with life-changing injuries, subsided, relief rising in such a wave that it threatened to overwhelm him. He sat with her for a few minutes, holding her hand, until the same nurse came to collect him. Visiting hours long over, he had to leave. On his way back to the waiting room, he saw Barbara's parents being shepherded along the corridor by Schmidt, but they didn't recognise him, didn't see him perhaps, in their anxiety for their daughter.

The young cop, Schmidt, came to find him quite a lot later. He confirmed that Barbara was OK, still sedated but fine. The older woman was in worse shape. Her stomach had also been pumped and she was expected to survive, though perhaps with some long-term side-effects. She'd be questioned when fully recovered, which wouldn't be until at least the next day or Monday. 'I'm sure Barbara found our murderer,' Schmidt said. 'We have many questions to ask her.'

Schmidt disappeared back to work and Walker waited around a while longer until the English-speaking nurse found him and firmly sent him home. 'Your friend is sleeping – you won't be allowed to speak with her until tomorrow. The police are here, her family too. You'll be better able to support her tomorrow if you've had some rest tonight.'

He was loath to leave but in the end reason prevailed. Barbara was in safe hands, nothing more he could do. He caught a taxi then a train then another taxi, arrived home just before midnight. He showered and then, pumped with adrenaline and far from sleepy, took a beer from the fridge onto the balcony, sitting there long into the dark night, replaying the day just gone, trying to deal with the aftermath of the fear he'd felt at the thought of losing Barbara. The knowledge of what Barbara means to him, how important she is to him, growing with every moment. He needs to talk to her before he goes, see if she feels the same way. Perhaps they can find a way to spend more time together.

Now, the church bells come to a crescendo and then stop, the echo of their sound hanging in the still morning air. Through the sheer curtains he can see it's bright and sunny but the street outside is quieter than usual. No voices, no vehicles, only a pigeon or dove cooing in the tree outside. He looks at his phone: *9.38*. He's only had a few hours' sleep, and bad sleep at that, fear and worry for Barbara mixed with dread in anticipation of today's meeting with Markovich. He sends a message to Barbara: How are you feeling this morning? Do you need anything? I can come to visit if you want.

He notices that there's only one tick beside it after he presses Send. Her phone's not in receiving mode. Perhaps she doesn't have it on. Perhaps it's not allowed in the hospital. Or perhaps she's still sleeping, recovering.

He can feel the beginnings of a headache thumping in his skull, his eyes scratchy with lack of sleep. He needs to pick himself up. His meeting with Markovich is looming. The thought gives him a jolt of nervous anxiety. He gets up and goes to the kitchen to make a coffee and, as has become his habit, drinks it on the balcony, standing, looking over the trees at the water. Afterwards, his hands jittery, his stomach acidic, he thinks he should have skipped the coffee this morning. Last night's drama, today's operation – he's wired enough already and doesn't need the caffeine coursing through his veins. But his headache has eased at least. He pulls on his jeans and a t-shirt, wonders what he should do next. He doubts Markovich is an early riser, doubts that he'll be calling – if he calls at all – anytime before late evening. He could go and see Barbara, make sure she's OK. But maybe she'd rather be with her family. Better to wait. She'll text him when she feels well enough.

He decides he'll spend the day in the area around the Sofija, try to get ahead of Markovich. He remembers the last meeting he had with the Vandals, where his misplaced confidence almost got him killed. He'll be better prepared this time, so long as Markovich decides to meet him at the Sofija. If Markovich chooses a different location, the bikie will have the upper hand again.

He calls Schneider, to touch base. 'We have a team standing by,' says the German cop. 'When you receive the call, you let us know and I will decide if we proceed. If the venue is not the Sofija bar, I can't promise that we will go ahead. At short notice, if the venue is too dangerous, if we do not have time to scope it out and make it secure, if there is too much risk to the team, then we will cancel the operation. If this is our decision, I would advise that you also cancel your meeting.'

Walker understands. Rutherford would take the same approach in the circumstances. He'll decide later, trust his instinct in the moment. But he's not sure he can cancel. If he doesn't meet Markovich today, he might not get another chance, and this whole trip will have been a wasted effort.

He makes his way to the Sofija and finds a bakery down the road, within sightline of the bar, and orders two pretzels – soft, salty and chewy, they've become his favourite snack here. He chooses a stool at a high bench running along the window to eat them. The city's distinctive TV tower is clearly visible, looming above the buildings opposite him, sunlight reflecting off its bulb-like top, giving it the appearance of a huge mirror ball. The shutters of the Sofija are still down, so he takes his time. He's used to waiting. Used to being on surveillance, used to passing mindless hours. But this morning is different. He can't seem to settle, an undercurrent of anxiety making him restless. Barbara still hasn't replied to his message. Perhaps she's not as well as the nurse led him to believe yesterday. He forces himself to focus on the task at hand. Sometime later this evening he will walk into a meeting with his old enemy. He'll be unarmed and largely unofficial. The big bikie is clever and wily, and Walker feels far from certain that the cards will finally fall in his favour.

Chapter 57

Berlin
12 p.m.

Walker has almost finished his snack, the church bells chiming midday, when he spots the young bloke with the mean eyes and spooky tattoos walking down the other side of the road. Lithe and lean, he moves smoothly, his relaxed body language at odds with the way his eyes scan the street around him. He reminds Walker of a street cat on the prowl, nothing in particular catching his interest but ready to pounce should the situation change. Walker drops his eyes to his phone, glancing up as unobtrusively as possible to watch the bloke's progress. As he does so, he clocks a man sitting in the driver's side of an old black VW Polo, parked further down from the bakery. He has earbuds in, is seemingly having a conversation with someone, but is also sliding down a little in his seat. He could be getting comfortable but something about the movement speaks of a desire to be unseen. Walker makes a quick calculation: although the vehicle is hidden from the Sofija by the cars and trees in the middle of the road, the driver likely has visibility of the entrance to the bar.

Walker watches him for a second, then turns his attention back to the Sofija, where the menacing young barman is bending down, unlocking the metal grille that covers the entrance and pushing it up. He unlocks the door, flips the *Closed* sign to *Open* and props the door ajar before disappearing from view. A moment later the exterior blinds across the big window that faces the street roll up, and shortly afterwards the bloke emerges carrying a stack of tables, which he distributes along the footpath before making two trips to do the same with chairs. Walker watches him, occasionally flicking his eyes to the bloke in the black Polo. He's definitely watching the bar too.

The tattooed barman finishes with the second load of chairs and, unexpectedly, looks across the road. Walker stops breathing for a second, hoping he hasn't been spotted and recognised. But the barman raises a hand in greeting and calls something across the street, and Walker realises he's not looking at the bakery but at the kebab place a few stores up. After a couple of shouted to-and-fros, the young bloke raises his hand again and turns away, vanishing inside. The bar is open for business. Now it's a waiting game to see if Markovich shows.

Walker shifts his attention back to the Polo and, as he watches, the driver sits up again and picks up his phone. As he catches a clear sight of his face, Walker recognises him. It's Hammer.

Walker crumples the paper bag his pretzels came in and drops it into the bin as he walks towards the Polo. Hammer, engrossed in his phone, his eyes flicking once in a while to the bar across the road, doesn't see him coming. When Walker bends down and knocks on the passenger-side window, Hammer starts in surprise. It takes him a second to work out who Walker is; when he does, the fleeting smile makes an appearance. Hammer presses a button to unlock the doors and reaches over to clear a space on the passenger seat.

'G'day,' says Walker as he gets in. 'I wasn't expecting to see you here.'

Hammer nods. Up close, Walker can see he looks exhausted, his eyes bleary and dark-circled. The car too has the messy, whiffy energy of a vehicle that's been used for a long surveillance: food wrappers, empty bottles of energy drink, disposable coffee cups scattered in the footwell. 'You've been here a while,' says Walker.

'Yes. I watched the bar until late last night,' says Hammer. 'Didn't see your man.'

Walker is surprised. 'You watched the bar on your own? Was Schneider OK with that?'

Hammer shrugs. 'He doesn't know. It's my own business where I park my car,' he says, and laughs. Then his face gets more serious. 'There are many known criminals here. It's not a good meeting spot for you.'

Walker nods. Hammer is right. The men who own and run this place are dangerous, no doubt about it. Even the youth behind the bar emanates violence. It's not the place he'd choose if he had more control.

• • •

The afternoon passes slowly, Walker and Hammer sitting in companionable silence in Hammer's car, which is old enough and far enough from the bar to be inconspicuous. The street is quiet. Occasional light traffic and a few pedestrians, mostly family groups, coming to eat at the kebab restaurant. On the other side of the road there's a short queue outside an ice cream place a few doors down from the bar. There's been virtually no action at the Sofija. Walker is happy to see how quiet it is. If it stays this way it should be an easy job for Schneider's team to pick up Markovich.

At one point a big bloke, almost as big as Markovich, bald and muscled in a tight t-shirt and jeans, arrives in a fancy-looking Merc and goes into the bar, the vehicle idling outside, waiting for him. He's in and out in a few minutes but Hammer takes the chance to snap a few shots of both the man and the vehicle, zooming in to note the rego and sending it to his team. 'It's good to get a list of cars connected to this group,' he says after it's pulled away. 'We might even find the one that was used in the drive-by.'

Hammer is reading a football magazine. Walker is thinking about Barbara, reminding himself of Seb, of the fact that she's in a relationship, and coming to the conclusion that whatever feelings he might have are unlikely to be reciprocated, when the sound of his phone ringing pulls him out of his reverie. Hammer looks over, both of them on high alert until Walker sees it's not Markovich but Rutherford. 'My boss in Australia,' he says to Hammer, and picks up.

'G'day, sir. No news yet. We're still waiting to hear from him.'

'I think we might have a problem,' is Rutherford's reply. 'Markovich has sent Wayne some pictures of you.'

'What?' Walker's confused.

'Surveillance shots by the looks. Markovich was asking Wayne to confirm you're the bloke he knows,' says Rutherford. 'The photos aren't great, your face isn't clear, and you look very different to the picture on your old police ID so it's possible Markovich hasn't recognised you...'

'And he's only met me once, briefly, a couple of years ago when I was out in Caloodie. I doubt he'd remember me from that either.'

'Yeah, well, that's not the only problem. They might know where you're staying. There's one of you at the door to an apartment block.'

Walker is furious with himself. How has he let this happen? 'Shit. They're more professional than I thought. I only got the sense I was being followed once and took evasive steps.'

'What's done is done,' says Rutherford. 'I'll send you the pictures. Talk with the team over there but you know this means you can't go into the meeting with Markovich. You're likely being set up again.'

There's a long pause as Walker digests this news.

'You hear me, DS?' says Rutherford, a warning tone in his voice.

'Yes, sir,' says Walker. 'I'll talk to the team over here. We'll come up with a new plan.'

'I'll send those pictures now,' says Rutherford, and the phone goes dead.

'Fuck,' says Walker, low and angry. They're so close to Markovich and he's messed it up, got himself followed, got himself identified. His phone pings as the pictures come through. He pulls them up – as Rutherford said, they're poor quality, the first one, on the train, could be anyone, ditto for the second taken from behind. In the third, his face is in profile but, with his hair shorter at the sides and slicked back, Rutherford is right: he looks nothing like his ID shot and completely different from the one time he met the bikie in person, almost three years ago now, too. He'd bet good money Markovich doesn't know who he is.

The momentary relief he feels is shattered when he looks at the last picture more closely and realises with a jolt that the apartment block he's standing in front of is Barbara's place. He thinks back, remembers the bloke who'd followed him in and gone through to the garden. If they know which apartment he was visiting, Barbara could be in danger. She can't come back to Berlin today. She needs to stay with her parents until they sort this out. He grabs his phone, dials her number. Her phone rings and rings and then switches to voicemail. Probably she's still in the hospital and can't answer. Good. That's the safest place for her. He calls Schneider, explains the situation.

Schneider is furious. 'This means the whole operation has been compromised,' he says.

'No,' says Walker. 'I don't think they know who I am. The pictures are far from clear. But my friend, she's a cop, she could be in danger. I don't speak German, otherwise I'd call the hospital. We need to warn her, tell her not to come back to Berlin. She needs to stay in the hospital or with her parents.'

'I'll deal with it,' says Schneider, taking down the details. 'I'll call you back.'

There's a long wait, Walker drumming the dashboard with impatience, until Schneider calls back. 'Your friend checked herself out, about an hour ago.'

Walker's heart sinks. 'Maybe she went to her parents' place,' he says.

'No,' says Schneider. 'I spoke with them too.'

'We need to get hold of her,' says Walker. 'She can't go back to the Berlin apartment.'

'I've got someone on it,' says Schneider, 'but I don't think we can go ahead with the operation now.'

'I think it'll be fine,' says Walker. He doesn't want to lose his chance to finally get Markovich into custody. 'I'll send you the images – they're very unclear. Markovich has only met me once and I very much doubt he'd recognise me from these shots. And if he did, I don't think he'd try to meet me – he wouldn't take the risk.' Walker's not sure this is entirely true; Markovich might take the risk of meeting him if only to exact revenge.

There's a long pause. 'If the meeting is somewhere other than the Sofija, we will cancel,' says Schneider. 'We won't know who we'll be meeting. But if he turns up at the Sofija, if you set eyes on him, you call me.'

'Deal,' says Walker.

As soon as Schneider hangs up, Walker dials Barbara's number again. Her phone rings and rings, then goes to voicemail again. He leaves a message. 'Barbara, it's me. Look, you can't go back to your Berlin place. We've found out it's being watched by the gangsters linked to my case. Can you give me a quick call, let me know you've got this and that you're OK . . . ?'

Chapter 58

Berlin

1 p.m.

Stefan Markovich is nursing a beer and another foul mood. He needs a couple of shots of bourbon to wake him up and get him going after the Hamburg job, a dull and boring event, nothing but disrespect and hanging around. First a three-hour drive to Hamburg, taking Popo to some meeting. Popo hadn't said a word to him the whole time, spent the entire drive talking on his phone, which meant he couldn't even put any music on. When he'd given the car a bit of grunt, taken it up to 150 kilometres and then 180 – the only good thing about this country is that you can drive as fast as you like on the highway – Popo had said, 'Slow the fuck down, we don't need any attention', and that had been the end of that. They'd arrived in Hamburg and he'd had to stand around, acting as muscle outside the meeting, then drop Popo off at a hotel, hand over some cash and pick up some gear, drop this off, pick that up. Running around like a fucken junior courier. Popo probably doing it on purpose, trying to show him who's boss, where his place is. He'll enjoy putting a bullet in Popo's head all the more for the disrespect he's been shown this weekend.

Finally done, he found a bar, had a few drinks, but didn't like the crowd – Arabs and Moroccans, mostly – and slept a couple of hours in the car before collecting Popo and some cheap hooker he'd spent the night with, dropping the bitch off somewhere, then driving Popo back to Berlin. He felt like a fucken dogsbody – the whole bloody point of the exercise, no doubt. He'd had half a mind to do the deed and get rid of Popo then and there, only thoughts of Vaso's displeasure staying his hand.

Instead, he used the time to take a few other matters in hand. Brains called him to say he'd found Nick and his family. 'Easy as,' he said. 'They went shopping together at the fucken supermarket. Woulda thought Nick had more smarts than that. You want me to finish the business?'

Markovich thought about it for a long moment. Then he said: 'Do it.' He'd wanted the pleasure of taking Nick and his missus out himself, but it didn't make sense to wait. Nick needed to be dead.

'All of them?' Brains asked.

'Yep. Him last, if you can. Let him see what ratting us out has cost him.'

Brains named a price, Markovich agreed, and that is that with respect to Nick fucken Mitchell. Brains always gets the job done.

Then he sent the pictures that Popo's bloke had taken of Donnie Young to Wayne, double-checking the bloke was legit. Wayne gave the bloke the nod and said again that he's the best forger he knows. So fuck Popo, fuck all this bullshit. He's gonna get a new ID, get himself home. Vaso and the Banker will have to suck it up. He'll be back in charge of the Vandals, back on the bike, back making money, back having fun, and fuck this whole Germany thing. He's fed up to the back teeth with this place.

Lastly, he called Mateo, one of the few blokes in Berlin he likes and trusts. They've worked together a few times, got into a couple of fights together, and the bloke is solid. He can hold his booze and pack a punch and doesn't take any shit. As a final precaution, he's asked Mateo to check out the address of the bird this mate of Wayne's is staying with. Never hurts to cover all the bases. 'Leave a mess,' he told him. 'Make sure they know we were there.' Giving the bloke a bit of a fright makes sense – let him know who he's dealing with, who's in charge. Once Mateo gives the all-clear, he'll call this Donnie Young character and meet him, tonight. He's getting the fuck out of here.

The thought of finally going home is making him restless. He downs the rest of the beer and decides to go to the bar for a bourbon. The short walk along the quiet streets does nothing to improve his mood. It reminds him of Sundays when he was a kid. That feeling that nothing was ever going to happen, the tedium and the restlessness. There might be something happening somewhere but it's sure as fuck not here. Thinks again of the Gold Coast. Sunday afternoon, he'd be at the casino, at the blackjack table, the noise of the pokies in the background, a cold JD and Coke in his hand, clinking the ice cubes as he waits for the dealer. Not long and he'll be back there.

He's disappointed to find the bar empty when he arrives, only the TV in the corner playing a soccer match as usual. Fucken soccer never stops. There's no proper football here, no rugby or AFL, just soccer all the bloody time, day and night, a load of poofs kicking a ball around. Christ, he hates this place. He calls out, 'Oi, Vuk?' When there's no answer he walks behind the bar and takes a bottle of beer out of the fridge.

Sits at a table, keeps half an eye on the door. Good habit. No point letting a quiet Sunday lull you into stupidity. He cracks the bottle open on the table edge, takes a long drink. The sooner he can meet this forger, the sooner he can get the fuck out of this place.

• • •

Walker is anxious to hear back from Barbara, feeling shit about the fact that his carelessness has compromised her home. His eyes are on the street but his mind is a million miles away when Hammer comes out of his slouch, sits up straight, eyes on the rear-view mirror. Walker snaps into alertness and looks in the wing mirror. His heart clenches. Stefan Markovich, bigger than ever, carrying some extra weight, not all of it muscle, is walking down the footpath towards them. He's wearing black jeans and a black t-shirt that is tight across his chest. The same meaty biceps and huge hands. Markovich's hair is shorter, neatly cut, and he has a short beard too, manicured and tidy, following the shape of his jaw. He looks both different and exactly the same.

'That's him,' says Walker, his throat dry. 'That's Stefan Markovich.' He slides lower in his seat, keeping his eyes on the wing mirror, watching Markovich as he strides down towards them. Markovich gets close enough that Walker can see his features, the heavy eyebrows, the full lips, a new scar running across his left cheek. He feels a frisson of anxiety mixed with excitement run through him. Finally, after all these years, he has Markovich in his sights. The bikie is only a couple of cars behind them when he turns and walks across the street, over the tree-lined centre meridian and crosses the other lane, towards the bar. They watch him go into the Sofija and then exhale, in unison.

Walker picks up his phone and calls Schneider.

'He's here,' he says when Schneider answers. 'He hasn't called me yet, so I don't know what the plan is as regards my meeting. But he's gone into the Sofija. Do you want to wait for him to call me or do you want to bring the team down now?'

Walker favours action now. There's every chance Markovich will be more relaxed when he's not expecting anyone. But as Walker won't be in there, sussing out the situation, Schneider's team would have to go into the bar cold, unsure of exactly who, other than

Markovich, is inside.

'Phone, please,' says Hammer, holding his hand out. 'I want to update.'

Walker passes the phone over. There's a quick exchange in German between Hammer and Schneider, then Hammer hands the phone back.

'OK, we will come now,' says Schneider. 'Hammer has been watching the bar all morning and he says it's empty. Markovich and the man who works at the bar are the only two he thinks are inside.'

'Yeah, that's right, we haven't seen anyone else go in, at least not through the front door – but there might be a back entrance.' Walker pauses, remembering the young bloke behind the bar, the hard eyes, the violence in him. 'The bloke behind the bar won't be a pushover and there's every chance Markovich'll resist arrest. There's a possibility at least one of them will be armed,' he says. 'Even if it's just the two of them, it won't be straightforward.'

'I know,' says Schneider. Despite his earlier reluctance and hesitation, his voice is calm. 'But we have our service weapons, we will be five against two, and we have the advantage of surprise.'

Despite the unknowns, Walker is happy with the decision. Acting fast, not giving Markovich time to scent danger, to disappear again, works for him. He only hopes Schneider is right and that five cops will be enough.

Chapter 59

Berlin
2 p.m.

Barbara manoeuvres the Peugeot into the parking space, turns off the engine and exhales in relief. The drive back to Berlin has taken more out of her than she'd expected. She rests her head against the side window for a moment. Her stomach hurts and her throat is raw from the tube they'd inserted before pumping her stomach. She's still dealing with the shock of yesterday's events, and her hands are shaky with exhaustion. She probably should have stayed in hospital for the extra night as the doctors had advised, but she wanted to get home, back to a sense of normality. She hasn't told her parents that she's checked herself out early. She doesn't want their cloying attention right now; doesn't want to hear their worries about the dangers inherent in the job.

She allows herself a moment's satisfaction at a case resolved. She's given the details of the story Renate told her to DSS Fischer and the prosecutor, who will move the case forward once Bauer is out of hospital. They'll need to interview her formally, try to get a confession on record. There's also a full search of her cabin underway this morning – Barbara saw Schmidt and the rest of his team in action when she picked up her car from the Mildersee car park. She's certain they'll find enough evidence to charge Renate. Her actions have the tinge of madness, Barbara thinks, but whether she's of sound mind and capable of being tried is a question for others to answer.

She grabs her bag, locks the car and walks slowly home. The streets are quiet, the bars not yet open, the shops closed for Sunday. Clouds are gathering in the sky, grey, ominous. She forces herself to quicken her pace – the last thing she needs now is to be soaked by a rainstorm. She can hear her phone ringing inside her bag, puts her hand in, searching for it as she walks. By the time she finds it, the caller has hung up. She looks at the screen – missed call from Lucas. Her heart lifts. The nurses teased her about her handsome English boyfriend who'd paced the waiting room for hours, had sat with her, holding her hand while she was unconscious. She was confused and it took a while to register that they meant Lucas. Australian not English, she told them, though she didn't correct their mistake about him being her boyfriend. She liked the thought of it, let the fantasy of it run through her mind as she lay half sleeping, half dreaming, in the bed this morning. She hasn't heard from Seb; she's not sure if he knows she's been in hospital. Lucas texted her earlier, offering to visit, but she knows he's working, hoping to pull in the gangster he's come here to find. She won't disturb him today, she tells herself as she drops the phone back into her bag, unanswered. They can talk tomorrow.

A few steps later she feels her phone vibrating in her bag. A message, then another. Seb, maybe, or her mother. She ignores it for the moment. Her mother will only panic and she knows she has to have a proper conversation with Seb about what they're both looking for, what they want. The way she feels about Lucas has shown her what she doesn't feel for Seb. She sighs. Another call to push to tomorrow, when she's feeling less exhausted.

She's at the front door of the block when the phone starts ringing again. She has her keys in her right hand, lets it ring out. Whoever it is, most likely her mother has heard that she's left the hospital, can wait. She'll call her back once she's upstairs, once she's had a shower, a coffee, something to eat.

The walk up the four flights of stairs takes her longer than usual. She's exhausted. The hospital gave her a light breakfast but she only picked at it, and everything she ate yesterday was violently ejected. She's wondering what she has in the house that she might want when her phone starts ringing again. Not Lucas, she thinks. He wouldn't chase her like this. Her mother, for sure, upset that she's checked out and hasn't come home. She sighs; she doesn't have the strength to argue right now. She rounds the last corner, the final ten stairs ahead of her, and comes to a stop. The door to her apartment is visible from here and it's swinging open.

She stares at it. She definitely locked it – she always locks it. It can't be open. No one else has a key. No one else would be inside. The thought dawns slowly, creeping through her exhausted brain, that someone has broken into her apartment and might even still be inside. She hesitates a moment, then climbs the stairs as quietly as she can. Her mind is clear now, all thoughts of Lucas, of her mother, of the exhaustion coursing through her body, forgotten. At the landing outside her door, she stops, listens. There's no sound. Whoever was here has gone. She takes a step towards the door, then freezes again as she hears a drawer being pulled open, objects clattering heavily to the floor.

The noise jolts her into action. Someone is still in her apartment, rifling through her things, stealing from her. She doesn't have a weapon. Walker brought her bag to the hospital yesterday, but not her jacket with the weapon inside. She hopes Schmidt's team has found it at Renate Bauer's place, and kicks herself for not stopping by to check this morning. She pulls out her badge, all she has to bolster her sense of authority, puts her bag down and pushes the front door with her foot. As it swings open, she can see into the living room on her right. The space is an unbelievable mess, books strewn across the floor, a plant fallen from the shelf, the pot cracked, dirt and leaves spread across the room. Two pictures in frames, the glass smashed, lie on the rug beside it. Anger rises in her.

She steps inside, away from the cover of the door, and looks to her left into the kitchen. She can see the back of the intruder, a man wearing black jeans and a dark jacket. 'Police!' she shouts as loudly as she can. 'Turn around, put your hands up . . .'

He freezes mid-motion. 'Police,' she shouts again. 'You're under arrest for breaking and entering. Turn around, put your hands up . . .'

He turns, slowly raising his hands in front of him. He's in his thirties, dark hair, dark eyes, solidly built, strong and muscular. She'd assumed the intruder would be a junkie – increasingly prevalent in the neighbourhood – looking for something to sell to fund the next hit. But this man's no addict – he doesn't have the nervous tics, the thinness, the ravaged skin. He's clean, his clothes are clean, only the dark fuzz of twenty-four hours without shaving on his cheeks. His eyes narrow as he looks at her, noting her lack of weapon, perhaps, or maybe he's identified her as the owner of the apartment from the photos he's smashed in the living room.

She holds her badge out like a shield. 'Police. What are you doing in this apartment?'

He doesn't answer her, his eyes darting left and right. She wishes she had a weapon. If he comes at her, he's easily strong enough to overpower her. She steps back towards the open door, an escape route if need be. At the same moment, he moves too, leaning down and picking up one of her kitchen knives in a smooth, efficient movement. He's no hapless intruder, she thinks; he has the stealth of a professional. Silently – he hasn't said a word since she's come in – he steps towards her, the blade of the knife catching the light as he points it in her direction.

Chapter 60

Berlin

2.20 p.m.

Barbara forces herself to look away from the blade and watch, instead, the eyes of the man advancing slowly towards her.

'I'm a police officer. Drop the blade now. You don't want to face charges of aggravated assault along with breaking and entering.' She keeps her voice calm and reasonable, standing her ground as he takes another step towards her.

He doesn't acknowledge her words. Perhaps he doesn't speak German, she thinks. He's only four or five strides away from her now. She doesn't break eye contact - she wants him to keep looking at her, hoping his eyes will telegraph his intentions, but she moves backwards slightly until she feels the edge of the front door against her left shoulder and hip. An idea takes hold. All she needs to do is move backwards, out into the shared hallway, shut the door on him. That will give her at least a momentary advantage. Maybe she can even lock him in. She's watching him, waiting for the right moment, when his phone starts ringing, the tone loud and jarring in the silence, the sound echoing around the apartment. He pauses, distracted, and Barbara takes her chance, turns to her left, takes two rapid steps out of the apartment, grabs the door handle, slams it shut behind her. But he's faster than she anticipates and stronger too – the door jerks back as he pulls against it. She won't win this battle of strength so she lets go. The door jumps back, slightly wrong-footing her assailant. But she's barely made any progress across the landing at the top of the stairs before he's out of the door, moving fast now, coming towards her, the knife close to his body, ready to slash.

As he comes at her, she feints to her left and kicks her right foot hard at his ankles. She feels the knife graze her right arm as he loses his footing and misjudges the distance of his thrust. Then she's behind him, his momentum taking him past her. She steps towards his back, pushes him as hard as she can, using both hands, towards the stairs. He stumbles, loses his footing again and falls with a crash, tumbling down the stairs. He's a professional, he's learnt to fall: he lands hard on his shoulder but rolls with it, takes the flight of stairs in a couple of tumbles and is up on his feet again at the next landing. Winded perhaps, bruised certainly, but on his feet. He doesn't turn to look back at her but runs down the stairs, taking them two at a time, disappearing from view.

Barbara listens to him go. She's breathing fast, clasping her right arm with her left hand, blood seeping through her fingers from where the knife has cut her skin, her heart beating loud in her ears. The noise of his footsteps recedes, then she hears the faint sound of the door to the apartment block slamming shut. He's gone. She's shaking all over with fear, pain and fatigue. Her legs are wobbly and she has to hold on to the banister for support. She should call for back-up, she should go into her apartment, sit down, but all she can do is stand there, reeling from the shock of what's just happened.

She's not sure how long she's been standing there – minutes, seconds – when the bell to her apartment buzzes loudly behind her. She starts, the noise loud and sudden. The bell buzzes again and she walks slowly into her apartment, picks up the intercom phone. 'Hello?' she says.

'Hello, this is Officer Schäfer from the Berlin Schutzpolizei. We've been asked to check on your well-being . . .'

• • •

Stefan Markovich is on his second beer, his mood not improving exactly but the grog delivering a more contemplative edge to his anger. The reason he's stuck here, the reason it's all gone so wrong in his life, is down to two blokes. Nick, the traitorous bastard, is number one. But equally, that Fed who kept sniffing around, getting in the way of the big money-earner he'd set up. They'd been making their own gear, flooding rural and coastal Queensland with meth, taking all the profits, cutting out the middleman and the need for shipping. By not trafficking the gear across the border, no customs checks, no Border Force involved, it had saved a lot of hassle from the pigs. Make it, deliver it, cash in. It had been good as gold, before that curly-haired pig turned up and broke it all. Markovich has chewed over the events that have forced him on the run for years now. In his darkest moments, he's cursed himself for asking Aaron and Nick to kill the cop. It should have been easy, straightforward – two against one, knife him, dump the body. But they cocked it up. He should have handled it himself – the pig would have been shark food and the Vandals would be rolling in dough.

But the pig survived, Aaron and Nick were arrested, and he only managed to get away by the skin of his teeth. He left the country, figuring he'd be away a few months, come back when the heat died down a bit. But then Nick started squealing, spilling all their secrets, giving up all their names. After all their years of friendship, Nick – the one bloke he'd fully trusted, the one he'd considered his real mate – Nick ratted him out. Nick's a dead man but the curly-haired Fed is untouchable, according to the Banker. For now, at least. They'll watch him, keep an eye on his career. He'll fuck up, or he'll retire, he'll lose the protection of his badge, and then he's history too. The Banker has a long memory and a lot of patience.

Markovich downs the beer. 'Oi, Vuk,' he calls to the barman, who turned up a few minutes after he'd arrived, carrying a box of beer from the loading bay out back, giving him the usual hard-eyed, suspicious look. 'Get us a JD and Coke,' he says.

The JD comes without ice. He downs it in one, orders another. 'Give us some ice this time, for fuck's sake,' he says. 'And another beer too.'

Markovich doesn't have the same patience as the Banker. He likes to see vengeance swiftly enacted. Nick's already a dead man walking. And when he gets home he's gonna find the pig and deal with him, properly this time. No one who fucks his life up gets away with it. That pig is the reason he's sitting in this shitty city, driving people from pillar to post, acting as a fucken dogsbody. The reason he's not leading the Vandals, not sitting pretty at the coast, not riding his bike, pulling in the cash, having a laugh. That pig's gonna pay. Sooner than fucken later.

His phone buzzes across the table – incoming call. Probably fucken Popo, wanting another ride somewhere. He pulls it towards him, sees Mateo's name, picks it up.

'She's a pig,' says Mateo, his voice slightly breathless. Markovich can hear that he's on a street, the sound of traffic, of Mateo taking fast steps, not running but walking quickly. 'She came home while I was looking around the place, tried to fucking arrest me. Bitch. I had a knife, but . . .' His voice trails off. 'She's alive. And there's other pigs there now, a couple of uniforms, walked right past me as I was leaving. I saw them ringing at the door. She got a good look at me too. I'll need to keep my head down for a bit.'

Markovich hears the beep of a car lock, the door slamming, the street sounds receding. 'Good job, mate,' he says. 'Go to Hamburg – I'll set it up with the boss. There's plenty of jobs need doing there. I'll be in touch.'

'OK,' says Mateo, and cuts the call.

Markovich pulls out his SIM card, crushes it and drops it in the ashtray on the table in front of him. Mateo is likely doing the same thing but you can never be too certain, and if this pig bitch puts a KLO4 on Mateo, Hamburg might not be far enough. Fucksake. Donnie Young must be a pig too. Another set-up. And they know about the Sofija, so this isn't a safe place to be. He needs to move on, move out, get himself back to Rotterdam or somewhere.

But Wayne knows this bloke. Does that mean Wayne is another fucken rat? Or did they con Wayne too, put a pig in the cell with him? They do that undercover shit sometimes. He parks Wayne for another day, pulls up the pictures of Donnie Young again. Looks at the bloke more closely. The pictures are shit. Still, he memorises as many details as he can: the earring, the slicked-back hair. The bloke looks like a twat but not much like a cop. Goes to show. The rage that's been simmering inside him reaches a boil. Whoever this fucker is, he's history.

Chapter 61

Berlin

2.45 p.m.

Walker and Hammer are in the car, silent, alert, all their attention on the bar across the road. Schneider and the team should be here soon. Walker checks his phone – less than ten minutes away, he reckons. He's buzzing with adrenaline. Markovich is across the road and will be under arrest within the hour. He'd give anything to be able to go in and cuff the bloke himself. Enjoy the shocked moment of recognition on the big bikie's face.

Eyes on the bar, Walker catches a movement inside, and a moment later Markovich comes out, his face dark and furious. Whatever happened in there, it wasn't good news for the biker, or their operation.

'Shit,' says Walker, watching Markovich taking long strides down the other side of the street, back the way he arrived, away from them. 'He's on the move . . .'

'Maybe he is going to another bar,' says Hammer.

To Walker, Markovich's urgency suggests something more than a bar crawl. 'Nah,' he says, 'I don't reckon so. I'll follow him – you talk to Schneider and the team. If he gets in a car, are you OK to follow? He might lead us to the meeting point.'

Walker is halfway out the door when the radio in Hammer's vehicle crackles and staccato rapid-fire German, loud and distorted, bursts into the quiet of the car. Hammer grabs the receiver, says something in reply. There's a quick to-and-fro, then Hammer turns to Walker. 'That was Schneider. He'll be here in five minutes. He's calling back-up. He says to stay here, not to leave the car.'

'No, we need a man on the street tailing him,' says Walker. 'You stay here, I'll go after him.'

The quick smile darts across Hammer's face. 'I told the boss you were already gone . . .'

Walker is out of the vehicle and moving fast. He's thirty yards or more behind Markovich, who is moving with speed and purpose, striding out, barrelling past a couple of other pedestrians, pushing his way through the small queue at the ice cream store. Everyone makes room, no one complains. The threat of violence emanating from the big man is tangible.

Somewhere in the distance, Walker hears a police siren start up, pulsing and insistent. Markovich pauses mid-stride, looks back over his shoulder, then speeds up. Walker curses whatever vehicle has turned on its siren, most likely a coincidence and not related to their operation. Surely Schneider wouldn't give that kind of notice to Markovich, unless perhaps the back-up vehicles haven't been fully briefed.

There's a break in the traffic and Walker takes the chance to dart across to the centre island. Cars are parked haphazardly along it, giving him some cover. He's running now, trying to catch Markovich. The sound of the siren has disappeared. Markovich slows, looks back over his shoulder; Walker drops down beside a car. When he looks up again, Markovich is walking away. Walker decides against running – it's too obvious. If Markovich looks back again and sees him, it'll give the game away. He crosses to the footpath on Markovich's side of the street and for a moment he thinks he's lost him, a huddle of teenage girls looking at a phone blocking his view. He takes a few quick steps past the group in time to see Markovich disappear off to the right. He marks the spot, a pale-yellow apartment block, and starts running properly. He can't lose him, won't lose him. He won't get this close and let him get away again.

The police sirens start up again, closer now. Walker curses out loud. Fear of being caught will make the bikie more unpredictable, more likely to respond with violence. He slows down as he approaches the pale-yellow block. There's an alleyway running alongside it. That's where Markovich turned. If he has spotted the tail, he could be waiting, ready to attack, and Walker doesn't fancy his chances one on one with a bloke who has half a foot and at least twenty-five kilograms on him. He's standing as close to the wall as he can, edging slowly forward, when he hears voices behind him. A mother and two young boys are coming down the footpath, the kids running, kicking a soccer ball, the mother calling to them, words he doesn't understand. He has to act now; he doesn't want the kids caught up in something violent.

His heart in his mouth, he steps forward and around the corner. The alley is empty. He feels his shoulders slump. He's lost him, Markovich has disappeared. The alley ends in a line of garages. He can see three, their roll-top doors painted in the same pale yellow as the building. Perhaps Markovich has hidden himself in one of those. He takes a few steps into the lane and notices a wooden gate set into a high wall on his left. It looks like it leads into the back yard of the apartment block. He tries it. Locked. Maybe Markovich has a key, maybe he has a place here. This is Schneider's territory, he decides. Schneider and his team will have to conduct a formal search.

As he pulls his phone out of his pocket to send Hammer his location, he hears an engine revving around the corner of the alley, out of his line of sight. It's a throaty roar, a big vehicle. Markovich. Walker would put money on it. He hesitates. He can't stop a car single-handedly and he wouldn't put it past Markovich to mow him down if he stands in his way. The nose of a black Mercedes comes into view at the far end of the alley at exactly the same time as a red-and-black soccer ball bounces off the fence beside him, the two boys he saw on the street following it in.

More of the Mercedes comes into view. The turn is tight, forcing the driver to go slowly. Walker acts on instinct, running towards the boys, picking the youngest one up under one arm, grabbing the older boy's hand and pulling him as fast as he can towards the street. The boys are crying, the one under his arm wriggling and squirming, Walker struggling to hold him, the other stumbling along beside him, held fast in Walker's grip. He hears the car behind him clear the bend, hears it accelerate, the engine revving. Time turns to slow motion. The vehicle behind him is a dozen metres away, no more, the roar and power of the engine approaching fast.

The kids' mother comes into view, her eyes wide with shock. Walker reaches her, mows straight into her, pushing her hard to his left, out of the mouth of the alley, out of the path of the Mercedes. He surges left too, bringing the kids in front of him and dropping towards the ground, covering their small bodies with his. The Mercedes roars past, no hint of deceleration; the driver must be doing thirty kilometres or more already. The car is so close he can feel the warm air of its passing on the back of his arms and his neck.

It takes a millisecond in the aftermath for life to return to normal speed, for Walker's heart to slow, for the roaring in his ears to diminish. He hears the screech of tyres as the Mercedes turns onto the street, the sound of another car braking and an angry horn, the police siren coming closer, fast. Underneath him, the kids are bawling and wriggling and he moves back, gives them space. Their mother, scrambling to her feet, hijab askew, reaches for them, pulls them close, looking at Walker, unsure of whether he is friend or foe.

As Walker gets to his feet, a convoy of two unmarked police cars, both with sirens blaring, come roaring down the street, gaining on the Merc, which is slowing slightly as it approaches a red light. Hearing the sirens, seeing the vehicles in his rear-view mirror, perhaps, the driver of the Merc slams on the accelerator and, ignoring the red light, drives into the intersection and throws a U-ey at speed, back tyres sliding to the right. Walker hears the screech of brakes as drivers on the green light try to avoid impact, then the heavy bang of a collision as two vehicles slam into each other. The Merc, unscathed, makes a sharp turn back down the other side of the street. The two unmarked cop cars, driving more safely, approach the tangle of traffic and accidents at the red light, losing the advantage.

Walker runs across the road, onto the centre island, the Merc screaming back towards him. He sees Markovich in the driving seat as the car passes, going at an ungodly speed. Markovich is getting away – they're so close but he's getting away. Driven by sheer frustration, Walker starts running, pointlessly, after the speeding vehicle. The Merc is pulling rapidly away when a small black car swings out of a parking spot and blocks the road. It takes a split second for Walker to register that it's Hammer's vehicle, the same car he's been sitting in all afternoon. The Mercedes doesn't slow, the driver running on fear or adrenaline or rage or some combination of the three. Walker sees it pull to the left, mount the centre island but not quite far enough. The right side of the vehicle ploughs at full speed into the bonnet of Hammer's car.

The explosion of sound from the impact of the two vehicles ricochets up the buildings that line the street and reaches Walker with an almost physical blow. Hammer's car absorbs most of the impact, flying to the right and smashing with another sickening thud into the vehicles parked on the kerb, metal crumpling, glass shattering. The Merc spins 180 degrees, rear-ending a parked car on the centre island on its way through, flipping over onto its roof, wheels spinning in the air, metal screeching as it slides along the street. It comes to a halt and there's a moment of silence after the storm of noise. No movement and no sound – nothing. A shocked vacuum of emptiness as the entire street registers the carnage. Then Walker starts running. He's thinking of Hammer, sitting at the wheel of his car as a 2.5-ton vehicle ploughs into its side at 100 clicks. Walker is hoping he's survived the impact, is still alive. He speeds up, sprinting now towards the accident scene.

He's aware, subliminally, that the Mercedes's engine is still running. The front right of the vehicle, pointing towards him, is smashed and mangled, but the engine is still audible. He wonders if Markovich is alive inside. As he draws nearer, his attention moves to Hammer's car, a terrible mess of crushed metal, crumpled into an almost unrecognisable shape. He slows. He's calling Hammer's name, but his voice is drowned out in the bawl of police sirens coming up behind him.

Chapter 62

Berlin
4.30 p.m.

Barbara thinks this might be one of the crappiest days she's ever had. She sent the uniforms to look for the intruder, and they must have missed him by minutes. While they were away, she listened to Lucas's message and realisation dawned. The intruder was a professional, linked to Lucas's operation – she'd been lucky to get away relatively unharmed. She sent Lucas a text, reassuring him that she's fine.

The uniforms came back ten minutes later, empty-handed, having found no one who matched her description. All they had were the plates of a car seen speeding along Weserstrasse and running a red light. It might turn up something, it might not. She doubts a professional would have been driving in a way to draw attention to himself and around here there are plenty of motorheads who drive like lunatics.

Then a SOCO arrived, called by the uniforms. She waited, shocked and dazed, while he did his job, dusting for prints, taking some evidence. After he left, she made a half-hearted attempt to tidy up the mess but couldn't face it. She's too exhausted, too shaken. Instead, she makes herself a tea, adding honey to the brew to give her energy, and pulls the blanket from her bed. Soft mohair in pink and red, a Christmas gift from Monika. She wraps it around her shoulders and goes to sit on the sofa, curls up, holding the warm tea for comfort. She checks her messages on her phone, wishing for a reply from Lucas, but there's nothing. Her message not yet seen or read.

She debates whether to call him. She'd like nothing more than to be with Lucas right now. But he already feels guilty that she's been dragged into his operation, she could hear it in his voice, and she doesn't want to stress him further. It might impact his stakeout, the whole reason he's come to Berlin hanging in the balance, a chance to finally arrest the bikie who tried to kill him. Her small shock doesn't warrant upsetting that. She briefly toys with calling Seb but decides against it almost immediately. He's not who she wants to see, not who she needs.

To pass the time and distract herself, she scrolls through Instagram. A story from Seb is at the top of her feed. She clicks on it, finds a series of pictures from yesterday evening. Seb and some friends, playing pool, drinking beers; Seb holding a pool cue, looking good in a white t-shirt and jeans, his blue eyes shining, big smile on his face. Seb standing beside a blonde woman, younger, mid-twenties perhaps, wearing a fitted dress that highlights her figure, clinking shot glasses and laughing. Another of Seb standing with the same woman, his arm around her waist. He's tagged the woman as @elenaq2000. Despite herself, Barbara clicks onto the account. *A beauty technician who loves good times*, says the profile. Barbara scrolls through. Lots of selfies; she's glamorous, gorgeous. Barbara clicks on the girl's Stories, sees another picture of Seb from yesterday and then one of the two of them in bed together, the sheet exposing Seb's bare chest, the girl wearing his t-shirt, both smiling. *Perfect Sunday morning*, reads the caption. Barbara feels a fleeting rush of heat, shock and jealousy, but it's there and gone in a moment. Seb has moved on but so has she. Being with Lucas has highlighted the paucity of her feelings for him, showed her all that Seb can't give her. She sighs. If only, she thinks, Lucas didn't live a whole wide world away.

She opens WhatsApp, starts writing a message to Monika. Halfway through, she changes her mind and calls instead.

'Babs!' says Monika.

Barbara can hear the sound of cutlery chinking, music and conversation in the background. 'Am I interrupting? Is this a bad time?'

'Nah, not at all. I'm leaving a lunch,' says Monika. 'Hang on one second...' There's a muffled conversation, goodbyes, see-you-laters, then the background noise subsides and Monika returns. 'You picked a good time,' she says, 'gave me the perfect excuse to get out of there. How are you? How is your hot Aussie?'

Barbara opens her mouth to answer and finds, to her surprise, that she can't speak for crying.

• • •

The floor of the hospital corridor is scuffed grey-green lino, the walls painted a matching colour, and the harsh fluorescent light reflecting from both gives everyone's skin a sickly hue. For the second evening in a row, Walker is sitting on an uncomfortable plastic chair in a hospital waiting room, this time with Schneider pacing the corridor in front of him.

Schneider's unmarked police vehicles arrived at the scene of the crash seconds after Walker, heading directly for the Mercedes. Markovich – groggy and semiconscious – was largely uninjured by the collision. A broken collarbone, minor neck strain, fractured ankle, nothing serious or life-threatening. He was taken under armed guard to a different hospital.

But it took almost an hour to pull Hammer from the wreck of his vehicle, the fire service and a host of police working with the jaws of life to cut him free. He was unresponsive, unconscious, made no sound during the long procedure to extract him. Walker and Schneider followed Hammer's ambulance, not speaking, Walker's relief at having Markovich in custody lost in his anxiety for Hammer, who has been in an operating theatre for over two hours now.

Walker pulls out his phone to message Rutherford. It's the middle of the night, 1.30 a.m., in Canberra, so he doesn't expect a reply, but he knows Rutherford likes to be in the loop. He types Markovich in German police custody then hesitates, wondering how much more information to give. Decides the details can wait until a verbal debrief, and presses Send.

He received Barbara's message earlier – I'm safe, uniforms outside keeping watch – and felt relief mixed with guilt. It's his fault that her apartment is no longer safe, that she needs uniform police outside. He wants to see her, to reassure himself that she's fine, but he needs to wait until he has news of Hammer. When he speaks with Barbara, he'll see if he can encourage her to move back with her parents for a while, or in with Seb, until the heat around Markovich's arrest dies down. The arrest could inspire some revenge attacks, though whether they'd be arrogant enough to target a cop, he can't say. His thoughts of Barbara are interrupted when the doors to the operating area open and a medic comes out, his face grim. Schneider walks to meet him; Walker stands. He doesn't understand the words the medic says but he recognises the tone, reads the sympathy in his eyes, sees Schneider visibly deflate. His heart sinks. This isn't good news.

Schneider turns, looks at Walker. 'He's still in intensive care. They tried to repair a spinal injury, but they won't know until he recovers consciousness if he's still got movement or the degree of his brain injury. They've done what they can, but there are no guarantees.'

Chapter 63

Hewett

Monday, 7 p.m.

Brains is in his car, a nondescript grey Toyota Camry that he stole from a car park in Adelaide earlier this morning. He watched a woman park it and get out, dressed in office clothes, skirt and jacket and heels, and carrying a laptop bag. Most likely she won't notice it's gone until about now. But if she did report it earlier, it doesn't matter. He's changed the plates and he reckons there isn't a cop in the country that would pay it the slightest bit of attention. Just another boring sedan, parked in a normal residential suburb.

He's sitting as far from the street lights as he can get on a side street in Hewett that gives him a view of the cul-de-sac where Nick and his family live. Hewett's not a bad little spot, he thinks to himself, especially if you've got kids. He's spent a bit of time here the last couple of days, first looking for Nick, then getting the lay of the land. There's lots of families around and it must be safe. He's seen plenty of kids unsupervised, riding their bikes, messing around with a football in the park, the kind of freedom you don't see so much in a big city or on the Gold Coast these days. Everyone scared of the worst that might happen. Come tomorrow they probably won't be out there, he thinks to himself, a rare grin coming to his face. Won't feel so fucken safe tomorrow morning.

He pulled up about thirty minutes ago, just as the street lights were coming on. It's a lot earlier than he'd like but as he's been watching the place he's noticed that the cops come past regularly during the night. From about 8 p.m. onwards they're liable to drive by upwards of once an hour. Before that, though, they're nowhere to be seen. He'll wait a bit longer, just until it's properly dark and all the neighbours are inside, eating dinner, watching telly. He's got a silencer – it won't take him longer than a couple of minutes to do the three of them, the wife, the teenage daughter and Nick. Stefan wants Nick shot last but that's not happening. Nick's the only one who might offer any threat so he'll be the first to go. He waits until 7.35 p.m. It's dark and the wind is biting when he gets out of the car. Good. Fewer people walking their dogs or jogging or any of that shit, and no one would think it strange that he's wearing gloves, a cap pulled low and a big jacket, pistol concealed inside.

In the end, Stefan gets his wish, but only because the wife and daughter answer the door. He keeps his cap low, stands to the side, avoiding the bell as much as he can in case it has a camera in it. He wasn't certain anyone would come to the door, had planned some convoluted story about a gas leak, but he doesn't need it. He can hear the two of them arguing, Nick's wife saying, 'No, you're not to answer it, not even for the pizza delivery' as the door opens. Then she says, 'That was quick' as she turns towards him. There's a fleeting second of fear in her eyes before he shoots her point blank in the forehead and pushes the door fully open with his shoulder. The daughter stands there frozen, doesn't even open her mouth to scream, and he puts a bullet between her eyes too. Less than twenty seconds gone and he's in the house, closing the door behind him, the only noise the phhtt-phhtt of the two shots and the thuds of their bodies hitting the floor.

He stands with his back against the door, ready for Nick, gun in firing position. Nick doesn't appear. The TV is going in the other room, so he steps carefully over the bodies and walks towards the sound. He moves quickly into the open doorway but the living room is empty. He's kicking himself for not checking they were all at home. Thinking: fucksake, if Nick's not here, Stefan won't be happy. He might even not get paid. Then he hears the hot-water system clicking behind him somewhere. Someone's using the water. He walks quickly and quietly down the hallway. There's a kitchen and dining room on the left – empty. The table set for three, plates and cutlery, a couple of glasses of red wine and a can of Diet Coke. Mitchell must be in a bathroom. He goes past a bedroom, bed unmade, lots of pink, posters on the wall. The next room along, the door's closed. He puts his ear to it and listens. He can hear water running. Sounds like Nick's having a shower. He wishes he knew the layout of the bathroom, wonders briefly if it's a shower over the bath or if it's one of those with glass screens. Whatever, he'll sort it.

Quietly, slowly, he pushes the door open. Instinctively, without really thinking about it, he surveys the space, noting a sink to the right, a toilet directly ahead on the far wall. The shower is over a bath to his left, Mitchell humming some tune, screened by a shower curtain decorated with lime-green palm trees. The shower curtain moves slightly with the breeze from the open door.

'Shut the door, Shell,' says Mitchell from behind the curtain, 'you're letting all the cold air in.'

Brains steps towards the bath, pulls the shower curtain aside. Mitchell's facing the far wall, the water running over his head and back, but he turns at the sound of the curtain, making it easier. Brains fires two shots in quick succession: head and then chest.

There's a crash as Mitchell hits the wall, then falls into the tub. He puts two more in Mitchell's head just to be sure, the shower still running, the water turning the blood pink.

Back in the hallway, the two bodies are blocking the front door and the pizza delivery bloke might be pulling up any minute. He goes into the kitchen, holsters the weapon inside his jacket, pulls his cap low and slides open the side door. As he steps out, a blaze of light illuminates the back garden. He stays close to the wall, turns down the side return, then out onto the street. No neighbours come out for a look, no one's seen or heard anything. A minute later he's back in the car. Checks the time: *7.41.*

It's barely a ten-minute drive to the A20 from here but he goes the long way round. There might be cameras on the exit and the cops will likely check CCTV all around. He drives towards Adelaide. He's left his own car in a service station car park about fifteen kilometres out of the city. It's not a twenty-four-hour servo and he's chosen a dark far corner, no cameras. He leaves the stolen vehicle there, wipes the inside down, changes the plates back, climbs into his car and starts the long drive back to Queensland.

Chapter 64

Kummerfeld
Monday, 10 a.m.

It might be Monday morning, but Schmidt has a spring in his step. The Mildersee case is over, Renate Bauer under arrest for the murders, and he'll surely get some credit for his role in resolving it. But that's not the cause of the smile on his face. He can't stop thinking about Rita, with her beautiful eyes, the way her face lights up on the rare occasions he manages to inspire a smile, the protectiveness he feels whenever he looks at her. From the first time he met her, he wanted to make good whatever it was that had hurt her so badly. Barbara is a little intimidating, frosty even. She doesn't like him, but Rita's mother has shown him only generosity from the first day he turned up at their warm and welcoming home. He admires the love she so evidently has for both her daughters, and he wants to get to know Rita and her family much better. It's Chilean hospitality, he thinks, warmer, more easy-going and open than his family would be. He stopped at the pet store on the way to work today and bought Lola a new toy, and he's planning to visit Rita later. He's hoping that Rita is starting to look forward to seeing him as much as he looks forward to seeing her.

The office is quiet when he gets in, Rudy Klein sitting at his desk, his eyes puffy. 'You look like shit,' says Schmidt, smiling to take the sting from his words.

'Yeah, party at the Kochs' last night,' says Rudy. 'Herr Koch won again yesterday. He's the mayor for another four years.'

Schmidt nods. The news is neither here nor there to him, though it means they'll be cleaning up after Willie for a few more years. He's barely sat down when Barsch sticks his head out of the office and says, 'Schmidt, get in here . . .'

The chief doesn't look much better than Rudy – he's obviously been partying with the Kochs too. Schmidt has been half hoping for a commendation on a job well done but Barsch just says, 'How are you doing with that detective?' as soon as Schmidt has closed the door. 'You slept with her yet? I know this case is resolved but it won't hurt to have some dirt on her. You never know when it might come in handy.'

Schmidt thinks of Barbara, who has never paid him the slightest attention beyond the professional. He admires the way she works, even if she is a bit cool with him. The focused diligence, the by-the-book approach, her commitment to ferreting out the truth, no matter who is involved. It would be good to work with her, instead of the likes of Barsch and Rudy.

'Nothing, sir,' he says. 'She's back in Berlin. I don't have any reason to stay in touch.'

'For fuck's sake, you'll never make a decent police officer, Schmidt, if you can't even use your looks, the only god-given talent you've got, to get a woman into bed telling you her secrets.'

Schmidt is about to mention Rita, then remembers the way she lights up his heart and decides against it. Sharing Rita with Barsch, sitting on the other side of the desk like a fat toad with his plans and machinations, would taint and diminish something special.

'Yes, sir,' he says.

'Get out, get out . . .' Barsch waves his hand, dismissing him.

Back at his desk, Schmidt thinks maybe Barsch has a point. If this is what policing means, arse-kissing bigwigs, minor corruption, dishonesty, brushing things under the carpet, seducing women to get them to tell you their secrets, then he won't make a good police officer. He feels momentarily depressed, then pushes the thought to the side. There will be another way. Maybe he can take a sideways step into a different unit. And he's seeing Rita this evening – that's enough to get him through another day.

• • •

'I don't understand why you don't tell him that you've broken up with Seb, that you want to see him, that you've spent all night crying because he's leaving and that you will miss him.' Monika is facing Barbara, her arms crossed on her chest, a stern look on her face.

'I wasn't crying over him,' says Barbara crossly. 'It was the release of stress – you know, the case, and the attack and the burglar. It was all too much.'

'OK, even if I believe that, which for the record I don't, you're also sad because he's leaving. You're sad that he doesn't live nearby. You're sad because you think you're in love with him and you can't be together. You said so yourself, about a hundred times last night.'

'It wasn't a hundred times. I might have said it once.'

'Whatever. You need to tell him the truth. I think he feels the same way. The message he left last night . . . He's so sweet. I could tell he really wanted to see you . . .'

Barbara sighs. Monika is right but she's not sure she's ready to have that conversation. Lucas sees her, he understands her, and while that makes their friendship special it also brings complications. Being police means sometimes bottling things up, building a wall around yourself to stay strong, to hold it all together. Lucas might dismantle that wall and she's not ready for the consequences of that.

'I can't see him, Monika,' she says, firm in her resolution. 'I can't. I'll end up crying, and then he'll feel bad. He has a new job to go to – he needs to focus on that, not worry about me.'

'He's a grown man. He can cope if you're crying. Maybe he'll say that he feels the same way. Maybe he'll even come back, spend more time here.'

'No,' says Barbara. 'That's exactly what I don't want to do. I don't want to guilt him into something. No. I'm not seeing him. I'll call him to say goodbye and that's it.'

Normally Monika has a way of getting Barbara to do exactly what she wants. They've been friends for so long that Monika knows how to cajole her and what buttons to press to move her into action. But this time Barbara is standing firm. She knows Monika is right. If she talked with Lucas, if she told him how she felt, if she asked him to come back, to spend more time here, he might even do that. There is something between them, that's undeniable.

But she also knows, without question, that Berlin and Germany wouldn't make Lucas happy. She remembers him in Caloodie, swimming at the waterhole, eating bacon-and-egg sandwiches at the bakery, sitting in the garden at his grandmother's place. Relaxed, fully himself, fully at home. He fits there, belongs there. He'd find Berlin's streets, and the villages of Brandenburg, claustrophobic in no time. The language, the food, the culture, the buildings, the weather: all foreign, all wrong. That's how she felt in Australia. It was like being on another planet, a place where nothing and no one was familiar, where everything from the climate and the natural world to the people and the way they spoke, the way they thought, the way they lived, all felt alien. It would be the same for Walker here. He's a man of the outback and that's where he belongs.

• • •

Walker is showered, shaved, back in his respectable cop outfit – ironed shirt, moleskins, R. M. Williams boots – at Berlin Airport. He'd even squeezed in a quick trip to a local barber this morning. His curls gone, his head shorn. Markovich has associates in The Netherlands and while it's unlikely they'll be tracking him, anything that makes him less identifiable is only a good thing. And it probably won't hurt to turn up at the conference with a neat haircut anyway. He's taking a flight to Amsterdam shortly, followed by a train to The Hague. The conference starts on Wednesday, but alongside the talks he has a full agenda of meetings that his new boss, Assistant Commissioner Hanson, has set up. Meetings with police officers and other specialists from the US and Europe, all dealing with the growing threat of domestic extremists: white supremacists, violent nationalists, and others. He has a huge wad of reading to do too, to get himself up to speed. Rutherford is satisfied with the outcome of the operation, the rest of the team delighted, his phone lighting up with messages all night long. His own pleasure at the result diminished first by Hammer's injuries, and then by the knowledge that the success of the operation also means his imminent departure from Berlin.

He called Barbara last night as he left the hospital, but she didn't answer. He left a voice message updating her on the afternoon's events, asking how she was, asking if she felt well enough to meet. He told her he'd be leaving and wanted to see her, say goodbye in person. She texted back to say she was feeling very shaken and weak from the poisoning, and she was staying with friends, already in bed, under doctor's orders to rest. Understandable, totally understandable, but he hadn't been able to repress a wash of disappointment. He'd badly wanted to see her, to make sure she was OK, to spend another evening with her, perhaps even tell her how much he wants to see her again and maybe plan to come back sometime.

He's walking across the cavernous Berlin Airport departure zone when his phone buzzes. *Barbara.* He stops walking, finds somewhere quiet to stand. 'Hey Barbara. How are you? Are you OK?'

'Yes, thank you, yes, I'm OK.' She sounds different. Her voice hoarse, a bit nasal, as if she has a cold.

'Are you still feeling some after-effects from Saturday?'

'Not really. A little bit sore in the throat and stomach, but I'm fine. Thank you for everything you did, Lucas. You saved me again.'

'I'm just glad you're OK. Are you back at your apartment? I'm so sorry about that. It was my fault. They followed me—'

'Don't worry. It's OK. I'm staying with a friend now and I don't think they will threaten me. You are happy with how it went yesterday?'

For once Walker doesn't want to talk about work. He wants to tell her how much he's liked being here, spending time with her, about how he'll miss her, not this chit-chat about their cases. 'Yeah,' he says, keeping it brief. 'I'm very happy to have Markovich in custody, of course, but it's down to one of your cops that we caught him. What he did was really brave. I hope he's going to be OK . . .'

'I'm happy it worked out,' she says.

Walker hesitates, slightly at a loss. Their conversation feels stilted somehow, which has never happened in the past. As he pauses, a security announcement reverberates around the hall, making speech impossible.

'You're at the airport?' says Barbara when the noise subsides.

'Yeah, my flight leaves in just over an hour . . .' This is the moment to tell her he's sorry he's leaving; that he really wants to see her again. 'So—' he begins.

'Yes,' she interrupts, 'I'll let you go. We will stay in touch, right? You'll let me know how your new job goes?'

'Ah yeah, of course,' he says. 'Of course I will.'

'OK,' she says. 'Well . . . I hope the conference goes well.'

'Yeah,' he says. 'Listen, it was beaut to see you and hang out this week. Take care of yourself. I'll miss you . . .'

'Yes, I'll miss you too,' she says. 'We'll talk soon, yes?'
'Ah yeah, sure . . .'
'OK! Have a good flight. Bye for now.'
'Yeah, yeah, bye . . .'

Afterwards he stands for a moment, looking at his phone. What was that about? he thinks. He'd been expecting more, but obviously he's read the situation all wrong. He pockets his phone, passes through security and makes his way to the gate, stopping along the way to pick up a coffee and a pretzel. His heart is heavy. He's never understood that phrase before but now he can physically feel a rock-sized weight in his left chest. He and Barbara haven't fallen out, they're friends like they always have been, so why does he feel like he's lost something, that something has ended?

He stands in the queue to board the flight, finds his seat, grabs the papers he needs to read, then puts his bag in the overhead locker. He's in the middle seat, between two other travellers, his long legs uncomfortable in the tight space. At least it's a short flight. He pulls his phone out to switch it to airplane mode, sees there's a message from Barbara. A smile comes to his face as he reads it.

> Monika says it's a disgrace that I only showed you crime scenes and none of the fun side of Berlin but I told her that crime scenes are our idea of a good time! Have a great trip, talk soon. Besitos xx

The plane taxis then takes off. Looking over his neighbour's shoulder, he catches a glimpse of the city below, quickly replaced by fields and lakes, then clouds and sky, and that's it: Berlin and Barbara disappear into the distance. The heavy feeling in his heart is back. He chastises himself for it. He and Barbara are still good friends who can count on each other. That was enough before and that hasn't changed. He moves the documents from his lap onto the little tray table and turns the first page, forcing his mind away from Barbara, away from what might have been. He has a new job to do, and the work starts here.

Notes and Acknowledgements

This is the first book in the DS Walker series that doesn't take place in Queensland, Australia. Because so many readers got in touch to ask me about Barbara and how she was getting on, I decided to bring Barbara and Walker back together in person. That also gave me the chance to set the book in Berlin, the city I currently call home. It was interesting to bring Lucas across to the other side of the world, where he is a bit of a fish out of water. I think he missed some aspects of being in Australia and I know I did – not one Cherry Ripe was eaten in the writing of this book! It was also a new challenge for me to write about a country and a city that I'm still getting to know, and this book has been a great way for me to grow closer to the vibrant, multicultural city of Berlin and the lake-filled Brandenburg countryside that surrounds it. I hope you enjoyed the new location and seeing how Barbara and Walker's relationship progresses.

As a former journalist I always try to cleave as closely to reality as I can in my books, but the lovely thing about writing fiction is that you can make things up as you go along to serve the interests of the story! The Australian Federal Police does work overseas on cases that have Australian relevance, collaborating with the National Crime Agency in the UK, Europol and Interpol, among others. Overseas AFP cases are fully coordinated with local law enforcement agencies, to protect both prosecutions and extraditions. But as this is a work of fiction, and in the interests of telling a faster-moving story, I've given

Walker more freedom in Berlin than might be true to life.

I've also taken small liberties with German policing. In Germany, uniform and CID policing are handled by two separate agencies. The Schutzpolizei, or Schupo for short, are the uniform police, and the agency that handles criminal investigations is called the Kriminalpolizei (or Kripo). Each German state also has a state police force - the Landespolizei (LKA) - and then there's the German Federal Police, who handle border protection and homeland security, among other things. In this book, Barbara works for the Kripo division but collaborates with the uniform police, while two of her other colleagues are collaborating with the LKA. This kind of collaboration does sometimes happen but, again, perhaps not in the informal way that I've set it up here.

This book is set partly in Berlin and partly at Mildersee lake colony and the town of Kummerfeld, two fictional places in the (real) state of Brandenburg. Although Mildersee is fictional, the type of colony I describe is very real. Called Schrebergärten, these small, rented plots of land (around 200-400 square metres) are usually found on the outskirts of towns and cities, but some, like Mildersee, also line waterways and lakes. Schrebergärten are a bit like British allotment gardens but with the addition of a small shack or cabin where you can sleep and cook. Germans use their Schrebergärten for growing fruit and vegetables or simply for relaxation. By some counts, there are more than one million Schrebergärten across Germany today.

I owe a big thank you to my good friend Tatiana Reimann for the many weekends I've enjoyed at her beautiful and peaceful Schrebergärten, by a lake near Ludwigsfelde on the outskirts of Berlin. Long summer days spent swinging in the hammock, drinking wine on the jetty, floating in the lake and meeting the many and diverse families and couples who have gardens out there inspired me to set the book in a similar (though far more murderous!) colony.

I've lived in Berlin on and off since 2009 and have many friends in the city who encouraged me, advised me and supported me during the writing of this book. Big thanks to you all and my gratitude especially to Daniel and Diogo, my Berlin family and suppliers of motivation and insight over countless dinners and bottles of wine. Daniel's take on the forest as a source of both medicinal and poisonous plants helped inspire several characters in the book. Diogo's support and confidence in me as a writer keeps me going on those days when I'm struggling to move forward. Thank you both – this book wouldn't be here without you!

Thanks also to Simka Senyak of The Wild Path. Simka's professional advice helped me identify some of the plants that were used in the book. We walked together through forest and fields and her obvious love of foraging and using wild plants has changed the way I look at our forests, meadows and lanes – they've become as much a larder as a green space to simply enjoy.

As ever, I owe huge thanks to my agent, Stephanie Glencross, who always offers invaluable insights and support. The same goes for my editor, Jane Snelgrove, whose magic touch refines the manuscript, and copy editor Silvia Crompton for her unmatchable attention to detail and forensic analysis of the words I choose. This book and the others in the series would be far less readable without them. Thanks also to all the team at Embla, my publishers in the UK. There are too many people to mention across marketing, design, distribution, editing and more, but they all play a massive part in turning a rough manuscript into the book you're holding in your hands.

It is a real source of pride to me that the DS Walker series is published and successful at home in Australia, and Echo, my Australian publishers, do an amazing job in getting the book to readers all over the country. Thanks to all the team at Echo, especially Juliet Rogers and Cherie Baird, for their support for the series, and Emily Banyard for her tireless promotional efforts. I'd also like to say a massive thank-you to all the libraries and bookshops that hosted me for talks and conversations on my recent visit to Australia and to all of the readers who came to say hello and asked me probing questions about Walker, Ginger and Barbara. It was a lot of fun meeting you all!

And of course, as always, thank you for reading! I'm super grateful to all of you for taking Walker and Barbara to heart and I hope you enjoyed this latest instalment!

Two backpackers disappear
without a trace

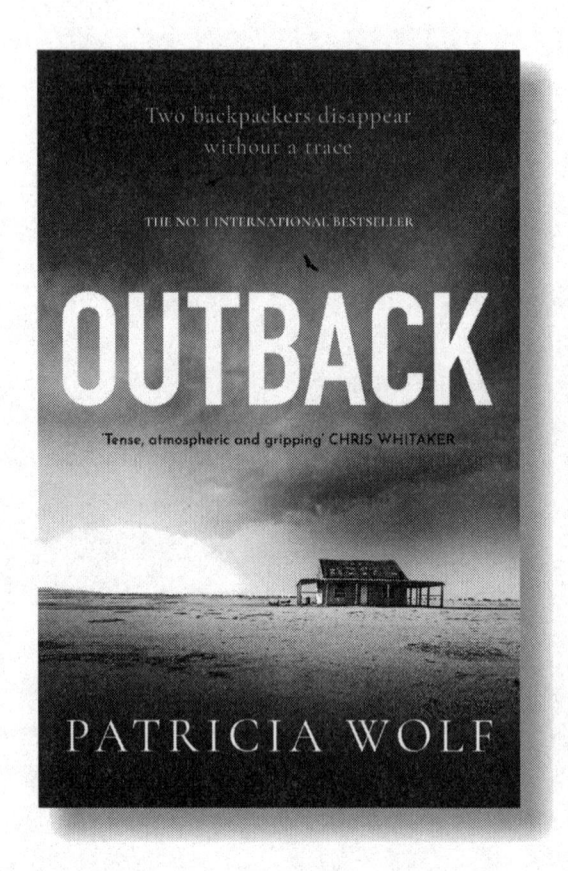

THE NO. 1 INTERNATIONAL BESTSELLER

OUTBACK

'Tense, atmospheric and gripping' CHRIS WHITAKER

PATRICIA WOLF

Two missing backpackers. One vast outback.

DS Lucas Walker is on leave in his hometown, Caloodie, taking care of his dying grandmother. When two young German backpackers, Berndt and Rita, vanish from the area, he finds himself unofficially on the case.

But why all the interest from the Federal Police when they have probably just ditched the heat and dust of the outback for the coast? Working in the organised crime unit has opened Walker's eyes to the growing drug trade in Australia's remote interior – and he becomes convinced there is more at play.

As the number of days since the couple's disappearance climbs, Walker is joined by Rita's older sister. A detective herself with Berlin CID, she has flown to Australia – desperate to find her sister.

Their search becomes ever more urgent as temperatures soar. Even if Walker does find the young couple, will it be too late?

This deeply atmospheric thriller is the gripping opening of a new crime series for fans of Jane Harper, Cara Hunter and Chris Whitaker.

A young family. A shocking attack.
A dark case on the Gold Coast.

PARADISE

A DS WALKER THRILLER

PATRICIA WOLF

On a stunningly beautiful stretch of coastline, a young mother is brutally murdered. The only witness to the crime, her daughter Gabby, is left in a coma, fighting for her life ...

DS Lucas Walker has just arrived in Surfers Paradise for some much-needed recovery after injuries sustained in his last investigation. But he is soon pulled into the dark twists and turns of this home invasion gone wrong, vowing to find the men responsible.

As Walker digs deeper into the dark underbelly of this shimmering city by the ocean, a case from his own past resurfaces, with deadly consequences.

And as eight-year-old Gabby wakes in her hospital bed, Walker is in a race against time to stop those responsible for her mother's murder before they return to silence her forever ...

Mining, money and murder from the
bestselling author of *Outback* and *Paradise*

OPAL

A DS WALKER THRILLER

PATRICIA WOLF

**A small mining community. A murderer at large.
And a flood that has trapped them all.**

DS Lucas Walker is off duty. His young half-sister Grace is visiting from Boston, and he's supposed to be spending time with her at his home in Caloodie in outback Queensland. But instead they've driven 400 kilometres west to the tiny mining town of Kanpara to pick up Walker's cousin Blair, who's been digging for boulder opals and is suddenly very keen to get out. It's not like Blair to quit so easily. Walker has the definite sense that something is off.

On their arrival, the atmosphere is already tense with rumours of a life-changing opal discovery. The following day, they awake to find that Kanpara has been completely cut off by a flood and the roads will be closed for days. As they take in their predicament, Blair receives a shocking phone call.

A man and a woman have been found brutally murdered.

The murdered woman's husband is an immediate suspect, but Walker isn't convinced. Could the killings be connected to the rumoured opal find? When the police take Blair in for questioning, the stakes couldn't be higher for Walker. He must now work with his fellow officers to uncover the killer in the community's midst before the waters recede and make escape possible. Can he unravel the mystery quickly enough to save his cousin and keep Grace safe?